Sign up for our newsletter to hear
about new and upcoming releases.

www.ylva-publishing.com

Other Books from G Benson

All the Little Moments

All Wrapped Up

FLINGING IT

by G Benson

Ylva

Acknowledgements

To my Beta Reading Wonder Team: Erin, Katie, Katja, and Alex. Katie, you kept me motivated and talked over any idea I needed to. Katja, you kept my plot on track and helped shape Jack. Alex, you made sure Jack rang true. Erin, your feedback was as invaluable as ever and you helped me keep the character's voices strong and distinct. You guys should be given half the credit and this story wouldn't be half of what it is without your input. Thank you!

To Concha, because she had to deal with me disappearing into this book, yet supplied me with endless coffees and reminded me that sometimes I need to take a break.

To the YLVA team, as always. Michelle, editor extraordinaire, who sometimes thinks I'm funny and who catches my terrible grammar mistakes. To think I teach English as a second language... Astrid, the best publisher, project manager and friend. And for you, Steffi, because you have endless patience when it comes to formatting. I owe you at least one thousand Mythos beers. *Genau.*

CHAPTER ONE

Frazer was awake before sunrise on a Monday. A combination that was already exhausting. Yet screaming was echoing down the hallway, bouncing off walls to reverberate in her ears, making that combination even more painful.

The sound was enough to make a grown man cower. Sure enough, she spotted one doing just that before a closed door through which emerged the bloodcurdling screams. Frazer approached him and stifled a yawn. The man pressed his hands harder against his ears, his eyes screwed shut as if that could shut out the sound. The corridor was dim, the lights not yet on for the day.

Frazer waited to see if he'd look up. He didn't, but a loud grunt from the other room made him wince. She tried to smother any amusement that may have appeared on her face.

"Sean?"

Nothing.

"Sean?" She raised her voice slightly. Still nothing. Frazer brushed his arm and he startled. Red eyes opened to stare at her. His mouth partly dropped open.

"Hey." She grinned at him.

His shoulders sagged. "Frazer! I'm so glad you're here. We knew we couldn't guarantee we'd get you, even if you'd been with us from the beginning."

"Lucky for you, I'm covering an on call tonight."

Which was super unlucky for Frazer since her Monday was going to be as normal, meaning a meeting in five hours and then her usual work day. Thankfully, the night had been uneventful thus far, and she'd slept in the on call room on the top bunk above a snoring resident she'd never met.

"What are you doing out here, Sean?"

Even in the dull light, Frazer could see the red that swept up his neck and into his cheeks.

"She kicked me out."

Frazer was unable to bite back her amusement. "She throw something at you?"

After a pause, he nodded. "A tissue box."

Frazer snorted and Sean smiled weakly as he rubbed the back of his neck. "Let's go see how Tanya is doing."

For a minute, Frazer thought he'd refuse, but then he straightened his shoulders and gave a nod. It was as if he was about to go into battle. Frazer almost felt bad for him.

Almost.

Even as tired as she was, the usual excitement overtook her. She missed on calls sometimes. But she supposed she was lucky that being the head of Midwifery still left her a few days a week on the ward. She'd go crazy if all she ever did was deal with budgets and rostering and staffing issues. Besides, it was kind of nice to go back to her roots.

Inside the room, Frazer was hit by fluorescent lights and a woman on the bed who looked ready to cry. Or scream. Or all of the above. Her large, pregnant belly was straining and Frazer remembered that the nurse who had woken her had told her that Tanya was at nine centimetres and almost ready to go.

"Frazer." The woman on the bed grunted, veins popping in her neck. "Thank God it's you. Sean is being fucking *useless.*"

Already next to the bed, Sean flinched, arms hanging at his side.

Frazer choked down a laugh. Tanya had never sworn in Frazer's presence before. Always soft spoken, gentle—she'd seemed on the timid side.

"Well," Frazer said as she washed her hands and looked over her shoulder so she could keep her patient's eyes on her, "it's your lucky night."

Tanya's already flushed cheeks were growing redder, and the sheen of sweat on her forehead shone in the light. With a flick of

2

her wrist, Frazer threw the paper towel in the bin and snapped on a pair of gloves. As Tanya huffed on the bed, her eyes screwed shut, Frazer dropped onto the wheeled stool by the sink and pushed herself to the edge of the bed. Tanya had already scooted down it.

"Do you want me to ask Sean to go?" She winked at him as he jolted up, staring at her wide-eyed as if she'd just betrayed him.

"No! No." Tanya's eyes snapped open, and she gripped Sean's arm, yanking him half onto the bed, her knuckles white. "No. I want him here."

Just as Frazer had known she would.

Sean gave Frazer a look that verged on grateful and let Tanya grip his hand, his face only twitching a little at what must have been a very hard grip.

"Great! Now that that's settled, you want to tell me why you waited so long to come in?"

It was still Monday morning.

Eight o'clock.

At least the sun was up now.

Another work meeting at the hospital. The only sounds Frazer could hear were the ticking clock and yawning.

Apparently this was the only hospital in Perth that had these meetings. Robin didn't have to suffer through them. Maybe Frazer could transfer and work with a friend and get to sleep in past eight on a Monday like a civilised person.

It was like some kind of hell. Looking around the half-asleep employees, Frazer hugged her coffee tighter against her chest and wondered what she'd done to deserve this. The seat wasn't even comfortable. She shifted, the hard plastic biting into her tailbone. Surely Alec could hold these meetings another day. Or at least another time. Eight in the morning on a Monday? Why?

Across the room, Frazer caught Tia's eye. Alec's secretary was plump and deceivingly pleasant looking, with an acidic tongue that shocked most employees and Frazer found utterly delightful. She paid out Frazer on an almost daily basis. Now, in the shifting, sighing silence of the room, Tia rolled her eyes and gave a pleading look towards the coffee in Frazer's hand. It only made Frazer clutch it tighter. There was no way she was giving up this liquid gold. Once Tanya had delivered a perfectly healthy baby, Frazer had run to her favourite coffee place so she could get through the meeting without murdering anyone.

In response to Frazer's small but unmistakable headshake, Tia's eyes narrowed. Frazer shot her an evil grin.

The door at the back of the room opened. Everybody straightened, then slipped back into their seats when they saw it was just a group of fellow employees. One of the women, the head of Social Work, slid into the seat next to Frazer, who gave her a lukewarm smile.

Alec's wife, Cora. For reasons that made no sense, Frazer blamed her by extension for the early hour. It was doubtful that Cora had anything to do with planning her husband's horrible morning meeting, but when Frazer was this tired, logic didn't play much of a role.

Did she have to sit next to Frazer? The two of them always clashed a little, and Frazer did *not* have the energy for that right now. Also, sitting next to someone who looked so damn put together so early in the morning was really not good for Frazer's self-esteem. How did she manage to look so flawless while Frazer looked like she'd scraped herself out of bed with a spatula? How did her hair look like *that* while Frazer's resembled a bird's nest?

Just because she was married to the guy that controlled all their budgets, she somehow got all the better deals on the money side of things. A fact that drove Frazer crazy.

Cora's returned smile was on the cold side, and Frazer was grateful for the heat of her takeaway cup.

"Morning, Cora."

Cora gave a nod, her amber eyes somehow bright when everyone else's were barely open. "Good morning."

"Excited for another meeting?"

The sarcasm in her voice was clear, and Cora's chin jutted out just slightly. "I wouldn't say excited, but aware that it's a necessary one."

Necessary? Frazer just barely bit her tongue. Every Monday they rehashed the same information and went over certain cases. As head of Midwifery and coordinator of her team, Frazer was required to attend. But after being on call all night, Frazer was even less inclined than usual to put up with it.

Still, she didn't go there. Clearly, this was not an argument she would win.

"Alec coming? He's late."

Again, there was a hard edge to Cora's eye. "He'll be on his way."

Strange—indirect information. Shouldn't she come in with her husband? Maybe even Alec was bored by her.

Guilt flared in Frazer's stomach as she sipped her coffee. That was an unfair thought. Granted, Frazer had trouble thinking fairly so early. Maybe Cora secretly hated the meetings too, and if she and Alec were in the same car together, she would request a divorce then and there out of spite. That thought made Frazer smirk against the lid of her coffee.

Finally, the door opened, everyone straightening again as Alec swept in, shoulders back and spine straightened with the sense of authority his higher position as a suit provided him. Even though he was on the lower end of the blurry hierarchy that ran the hospital, his power over budgets and staff cuts and the privilege of never dealing with anyone but the heads of departments seemed to have left him quite inflated. However, Frazer's thoughts about her boss were generally quite neutral. Right now, though, she was about to suffer through this meeting, seated next to his boring wife with legs to die for, and she blamed him for all of that.

Brown legs that were a welcome distraction, especially in the pencil skirt Cora was wearing.

Alec stood in front of them, one hand in his pocket and his laser pointer in the other. He looked as put together as his wife, though different in that he was clearly European descent as he was much paler. Maybe he was a vampire. Frazer hid her glee at the thought with another sip of her coffee. To be fair, he wasn't *that* pasty. There was a sharpness to his face, though, with his high cheekbones. His blonde hair, still slightly damp after a morning shower, was shorn close to his head.

The first projector slide was already up. It took everything within Frazer to stifle a yawn.

They spent a long time going over some recent cases, updates provided by other departments. After a long report from someone in Renal, Frazer almost fell asleep in her chair. When she caught Tia's raised eyebrows, Frazer sat up straighter and tried to ignore the fact that the look made her feel like a teenager rather than a grown woman in her thirties.

A slide covered in figures popped up, and Frazer wanted to scream. Next to her, Cora sat straight, legs crossed and eyes focussed on the screen, taking in everything Alec said.

God, maybe they discussed this stuff over dinner. How romantic.

Since the figures were up, department heads started raising questions about their budgets and grant distribution. Frazer felt a twist in her stomach. This was when she should speak up, but she really didn't want to. It would be much better to speak to Alec one-on-one.

"Obstetrics?"

Across the room, Lee spoke up, her glasses glinting in the fluorescent light. "Nothing from me, and no one's reported anything. But I know that Midwifery had something."

Inwardly, Frazer groaned as every eye in the room turned to her.

Alec raised his eyebrows, a placating smile on his face. "Okay. Ms Jindal?"

Straightening at her name, Frazer was ready to dump her coffee on Lee's head, chief of Obstetrics or not. Next time Lee wanted Frazer to adjust the Midwifery roster so she didn't have to work with someone that rubbed her the wrong way, she was going to be met with a glare. Even if Lee did always show up on the ward with coffee and muffins for everyone. "Uh. As brought up at the last meeting, I'm through the final stages of planning the outreach programme for hard-to-reach pregnancies, especially teenage parents. It's going to include topics on natural births versus caesareans, formula and breast feeding, drugs and alcohol—the usual topics, but with easier access and with incentives to come. The focus, however, will be support, rather than pushing information down their throats. The key to this being the mentors, of course."

Alec nodded. Frazer was just happy he'd apparently read her grant requests. All five of them she'd had to send through.

"Remind me of the projected start-up date?" he asked.

"Three months, all going to plan."

As she'd stated in all five of those requests.

"Great. I saw your report costs—you need to halve that."

Frazer's eyebrows shot up. Halve it? She'd already cut all the costs she could. A not so neutral feeling swelled in her chest. "Alec, that was the third revision of costs. If we cut any more, we may as well just sit in a box on the side of the road and throw condoms at people, for all the good it will do."

On the other side of the room, Tia snorted and Alec glared at her. Frazer winced internally. Professionalism, she reminded herself.

Alec turned his look back to her, and Frazer resisted the urge to poke her tongue out at him. "Revise the budget, have it on my desk." He turned his head, already moving on. "Then we can talk."

Clenching her jaw, Frazer nodded and Lee winced at her.

Traitor.

Smoothly, Alec moved on. Ten minutes later, he informed them of an increased budget for Social Work for the geriatric side, and Frazer turned her head so fast she almost got whiplash in order to glare at Cora. The woman kept her eyes on Alec.

Well. Wasn't *that* interesting.

When the meeting ended, Frazer stood up, jaw clenched, and practically ran for her office.

"Need some ice for that burn?"

Looking up from her desk, Frazer gave Tia, who stood outside her office door, a dirty look. "Funny."

Arms crossed, Tia stepped forward out of the way as someone ran past with a transport bed. She leant against the door frame.

"Oh, I thought so. If we were on Tumblr, I'd attach that photo with the burnt arm and the water."

"*You* have Tumblr?"

"I'll have you know, sweet summer child, I tumble with the best of 'em."

Frazer chuckled, leaning back against her chair. "I don't think thirty-five counts as a sweet summer child, Tia."

"Pish posh." Her hand waved in the air. "When you're in your sixties like me, you're definitely that. Though for you, we can forget the sweet."

"Did you need something, evil woman?"

The playful tone dropped out of Tia's voice and she rolled her eyes. "Alec wants the revised proposal."

"My God, it was six hours ago. I'm drowning in rosters, and I had two deliveries. Does he think I'm magic?"

Tia glanced behind her before she spoke, bit her lip, and walked in to stand in front of Frazer's desk. "I think he's hoping you'll give it up."

Of course he was. There was never enough money to go around in health. It was maddening.

They both paused as a code blue was announced over the PA system from the corridor, Frazer's muscles tensing automatically.

She sank back into her chair when the ward announced was orthopaedics.

"Well," Frazer resumed easily, "that's not going to happen any day soon."

The smile on Tia's face looked softer than her usual teasing one. "Good. That programme's going to do great things. My girl had a baby when she was sixteen, to a real messed-up guy. I wish something like your programme had been around then."

"Really?" Frazer was always amazed at the things you could learn about people you saw almost every day. People walked around, bumping into each other, and never knew what was going on. "What happened?"

Sighing, Tia shrugged. "She gave him up for adoption after six weeks. Even if the result would've been the same, having something like this openly available would have helped her a lot."

It took a moment for Frazer to catch her breath. Finally, she said, "Thanks, Tia."

Tia straightened. "Don't let the big fish get you down. And I may have sent you some links on some other government grants I heard mentioned through the office door just now."

She sauntered for the door and Frazer suppressed a laugh.

"You know," she called after Tia, "you're not awesome at all."

Without turning around, Tia held her hand up and wiggled her fingers in a wave.

Time to delve into her e-mail inbox. She opened up all the links and bookmarked them before opening one. She skimmed through the information as quickly as she could.

"Oh, and Frazer." Tia's head had poked around the doorway. "Instead of sulking that the others always get the grants they need, why not get those others on board?"

Frazer stared at the door once Tia had disappeared again. Maybe she was right?

Who was she kidding? Tia was always right.

Though maybe not about this. Working *with* Cora on Frazer's baby? There wasn't a worse idea in the world.

CHAPTER TWO

"A home?"

Mrs Stein trained her bright blue eyes on Cora and stared her down. Cora resisted the urge to turn tail and flee. This job was exhausting. There were times she returned home so emotionally drained that she fell into bed embarrassingly early.

"Yes, Mrs Stein. A home." When she said it, Cora didn't bother lacing her tone with enthusiasm. She wouldn't add insult to injury.

Wrinkles layered around her mouth as Mrs Stein pursed her lips. "I... I don't want to go to a home."

If it weren't for Mrs Stein's three despicable, ungrateful children, Cora's job would be solely researching the least terrible, government-funded aged-care facility to send a referral. But those charming children, who were selling their mother's house, refused to spend the money on a private facility so that they could ensure a greater inheritance when she passed away. Even more charming. On top of that, they didn't want to be the ones to tell her she'd be going into a public facility because they were greedy little worms.

If only this was something that rarely happened, rather than a common occurrence. A headache was starting behind Cora's eyes, and all she wanted to do was go home. Unfortunately, she still had hours to go. The day was dragging, not helped by those stupid early meetings Alec insisted on. Sometimes she wondered if he actually hated his staff since he put them all through that each Monday. At times, she found herself missing the days she wasn't head of the department simply because that had meant she didn't have to go.

Those sorrowful eyes stared at her unblinkingly and Cora gave in, sitting next to her patient and putting her hand over hers. "I'm sorry, Mrs Stein. You're unable to look after yourself anymore independently." Cora squeezed gently. "This is your third hospital admission in as many months."

The papery skin under Cora's hands was remarkably soft; translucent enough to show blue veins tracing their way up the wrist under her fingers. This skin was a map of a history of a woman that was now culminating in a loss of dignity she couldn't fight. Beneath Cora's thumb whispered a slow, thready pulse.

"Can't someone help me out at home?" Mrs Stein asked.

"The hours you could be supplied with by government funding were all used up last time." This was the point at which Cora could dump this woman's children in the blame pile, but really, who would that hurt in the end? Only Mrs Stein. "Your risk assessment score shows you need to be placed in a care facility, and with your hip broken again…"

Mrs Stein sagged against her pillows, her breath leaving her in a slow exhale. "I see." She stared out her window, lucky enough to have a view of the ocean, just visible from this height.

Cora wondered if she was thinking about the last time she'd actually dipped her toes in the salty water, the wind whipping her hair around her face in a dance. The times she'd taken her three small children to the beach to watch them kick up sand and create castles they could destroy with one quick motion, then rebuild as easily as a dream.

Or how she wouldn't do that again.

Wet eyes stayed focussed on that window. "Thank you, love."

Cora knew a dismissal when she heard one. Grateful, Cora left the poor woman contemplating the way her next years of life would play out under the constant, repetitive routine of overworked and understaffed carers.

Nurses bustled down the hallway, and Cora slipped past unnoticed, leaving her discharge notes on the desk for whoever found them. Tracing the maze of hallways she could now walk through blindfolded, Cora looked at her watch and, of course, slammed into someone very solid and very warm.

"Christ!"

That voice. God she didn't need that right now. Did it have to be Frazer? That woman stared daggers at her all day, and all Cora could do back was return them in the hopes that she looked half as threatening. Which she was fairly certain she didn't, because that wasn't something Cora had ever really mastered.

Sparking green eyes focussed on her. "You do know you're in a hospital and should probably watch where you're going?"

Yeah, Cora really didn't need this. She'd already started at stupid o'clock for the meetings her husband insisted they attend and insisted she support if her department wanted any funding. There'd been telephone calls with angry family members and from various wards whose resources were stretched too thin, asking if Cora could somehow work their patients into a suicide prevention programme that was already full or asking to change a denied request that was completely out of her hands. Her favourite coffee bar was closed, and instead, she'd drunk dregs from the coffeehouse where good coffee went to die. The stuff in her cup tasted faintly of burnt metal.

Finally, Cora said, "Yeah, I'm sorry."

Some of that spark cooled. Frazer crossed her arms and leant against the wall. "I should have been paying attention too, I suppose."

Cora's eyebrows shot up. The arrogance; it was up there with Alec's. At that thought, a retort slipped out before she could stop it. "You suppose?"

A toothy grin answered her and Cora wanted to roll her eyes.

"Well," Frazer said, "remove the suppose."

When Frazer wasn't glaring at her, she looked less like an angry viper and more like a snake lain out in the sun. Mildly less terrifying, but arrogant in her safety due to the fangs that lashed out so easily.

Frazer barely ever said anything to her, but it was clear enough she hated the way Alec never helped Midwifery and Obstetrics. Which wasn't completely true. He helped it as much as he helped most. His funding wasn't endless.

"If I remove the 'suppose' it's almost an apology." Cora said. Frazer winked. "Almost."

Frazer was being almost...playful. Definitely verging on nice. She was never rude to Cora, but was never overly friendly either. What was this?

Whatever it was, Cora didn't feel like playing games. The fact that she had to go and refer several more patients in Mrs Stein's position sat heavily on her shoulders. With a tight nod, she started to take a step around Frazer. "Okay. So. I'll just be going."

"Do you ever smile?"

Cora whipped her head around, eyebrows furrowed. "What?"

"Do you smile?" Frazer did so just then, easily. "You know, it's associated with happiness, though humans do it pretty automatically for a lot of other things."

"I have to go, Frazer."

And with those words, Cora's pager beeped, thankfully pulling her to the other end of the hospital.

"Yeah, okay." Frazer gave a wave. "I'll see you around."

Seriously, what had that been about? Again, Frazer had barely ever said more than three sentences in a row to her. Cora wasn't so sure she wanted her to again, even if it sounded genuine; or maybe because it did. Where would she see Frazer? Next Monday at the meeting?

That was far too bizarre.

"You know, bumping in to her isn't the same as asking for her help."

Frazer jumped, turning around. Why was Tia everywhere? Thankfully Cora was already turning the corner to go solve some social problem. "To be fair, she did most of the bumping. I even took some of the blame."

Tia narrowed her eyes, something like the fifth time that day and it was barely three o'clock. "You're terrible at socialising."

Mouth open to object, Frazer snapped it shut. "Just at work."

The nod Tia gave her was compassionate, but the glint in her eye did not match. "Still burnt from that surgeon that broke up with you?" she asked.

"Oh my God, even *you* know about that?"

"Honey, I'm pretty sure the morgue attendants know about that."

Frazer turned to walk away. She made sure that Tia heard her groan. "And now I'm going to go eat a kilo of chocolate and pretend you didn't say any of that."

Tia called after her, completely unrepentant. "If you want that project to work, you have to do more than that."

Frazer stopped. She closed her eyes. Drew in a breath. In the end, she turned back around. "I can't just ask her for her help the first time I see her. That would prove that—"

"That you need help?" Tia asked, eyebrows raised.

"No." Well, yes. "It would show I was just talking to her for a favour."

"You are."

The fact that she had two teenage sons she interrogated regularly at home, in addition to another two grown daughters, was incredibly obvious at that moment.

"Yes, but—"

"Look, don't beat around the bush with this thing. She's in Social Work. She has Alec's ear—if he listens to anyone, that is." They shared a look. "She's someone who can help."

"What if she doesn't want to help?"

"She will. And if not, then you know. But don't butter her up. It looks cheap."

Seriously, Frazer needed to work on her game if it was that obvious. Her cheeks warmed. "We never, you know, chat. I barely see her, and when I do, it's just in those stupid meetings. It felt rude to just ask for a favour."

Tia rolled her eyes. "You're not on different sides you know. You can help each other."

"What can I offer her?"

"Something down the road, I'm sure. What makes you think she wouldn't want to help this programme? It shoots right to the bleeding heart of a social worker."

"It's not like she ever spoke in support." Frazer jutted out her chin. One point to her, finally.

"It's not like she ever speaks in general."

Her shoulders sagged. Minus one point to her. "True."

Really true. Cora usually slipped into those meetings, then slipped out. Eyes downcast, off to save the world or whatever social workers did. Frazer had always assumed she was a bit... boring. But maybe she was just shy.

"Fine." Frazer scowled, feeling fifteen as she did so. "I'll speak to her like a grown-up."

"Good girl. Now off you go. Oh, and enjoy passing Lauren on your way through to her office."

Frazer groaned again. Loudly.

Tia tittered and walked off.

Frazer pursed her lips.

Really, Frazer had no idea why she liked that woman.

After a dramatic breech birth that had left even Frazer flinching, she finally managed to find the time to heed Tia's advice. She left the new parents lying on the lumpy hospital bed, their tiny bundle of new life nestled between them. Snapping off her gloves, Frazer rolled her shoulders and cracked her neck. Normally she would be buried in paperwork on a Monday, but this had called for someone with more experience, and Frazer had jumped at the opportunity. Warm water washed over her hands, the soap lathered between her fingers as she scrubbed at them.

A birth like that was far better than paperwork.

She left the first-year observing midwife to fill out the documentation Frazer would quickly check later and started up the stairs. Paperwork, the bane of any nurse or midwife's existence. Frazer was doing the new girl a favour, creating the opportunity to practice her documentation, just like people had once done for her.

She smirked to herself. No one would believe that excuse. She'd just been happy to handball the work to someone else.

The social services floor was empty, and that was bad. How could Frazer hide behind people and dash through to Cora's office when there was no one there?

"Frazer!"

There it was. Trying to look friendly and forcing her lips up in a way that probably wasn't normal, she walked over to the desk. "Hi, Lauren."

"How are you?"

Lauren was all teeth and lipstick right now, and she really was very nice. But so interested. And they worked together. And no.

"I'm good. Just looking for Cora, actually. Have you seen her?"

"She's in her office, but…" Lauren lowered her voice. "Alec's in there."

Of course he was. Frazer was really in no mood to speak with her boss. At all, actually. It was his fault she was even here. But she also didn't want to speak to Lauren. Rock, hard place, Frazer.

Choosing hard place, Frazer turned her attention to the woman who was still looking up at her with a soft look in her eye. "How long ago did he arrive?"

"About ten minutes."

Maybe they were canoodling. A smirk played at her lips at that thought. Cora didn't seem the type. Alec also didn't seem like a rule breaker.

"I'd take that look off your face. They won't be doing that." Lauren's voice lowered again. "They were yelling before."

Interesting.

It was one of those situations in which Cora didn't feel like she was in her own life.

How was it that she was sitting on the 'power' side of the desk, yet Alec was standing across from her, and it felt as if he was towering over her? No one wins in these situations.

"For God's sakes, Cora, if you just thought sometimes!"

The anger glinting in his eyes still took her by surprise every time she saw it. Which was all too often lately. Cora really didn't want to be doing this at work, but when Alec wanted to talk about something, it couldn't wait.

With an internal wince, she really wished he would lower his voice.

"It would be easier, if I knew everything that was actually *involved*, Alec." She hated the tone of her voice. Placating. Soothing. Yet raised a touch too high.

"Don't you try to turn this around on me." And with those words, he spun on his heel and left the room.

He closed the door too loudly for a work environment, and Cora had to resist the urge to throw something after him. She took a long, deep breath. Cora wasn't five. She didn't throw things.

How had that even started? Something about some words Cora had said wrong to Alec's parents? Or had it been about the tone of an e-mail Cora had sent?

If they had been at home, it would have escalated, but at least only the neighbours and not a building full of their colleagues would have overheard. How did they both become people she really didn't like the minute they were left alone together? How did two mature adults fight like such children? How was it that it was always her soothing Alec's hot temper, apologising when most of the time she didn't really know what for?

It was becoming exhausting.

Her cheeks hot, Cora clicked open her e-mail and promptly closed it again when she saw her inbox. When had her mother figured out e-mail? She glared at the screen, huffing. Had someone given her Cora's address? It must have been Alec. Damn. Just another way her mother could be constantly involved in her life, leaving Cora with no way left to dodge her. There was a time Cora had thought mobiles were a fantastic invention. Now everybody expected everyone else to be constantly contactable. Half of the time, her mobile was dead, left in the bottom of her bag. Usually with five missed calls from her mum.

A knock at the door jerked her head upwards. It couldn't be Alec. He never knocked. Knocking at an office door seemed absurd when you'd peed in the toilet while the other person showered.

"Come in."

When the door opened, she suppressed a groan. Frazer? Why? Just why?

"Hey! Sorry, am I interrupting?"

Cora leant back against her chair and gestured to the one across from her that Alec hadn't bothered to sit down in. "No, take a seat."

If there was anything Cora hoped for, it was that Frazer hadn't heard the tail end of Alec's exit. Like something toxic, she and Alec couldn't bury it down until they were in the safety of their own home anymore, smaller things echoing repeatedly in the shadow of themselves, building to a cacophony. It made her... sad. And tired. And mostly frustrated that while it seeped into Cora's consciousness, it was often Alec instigating it.

"Thanks." Frazer slid into the chair like she'd done it every day of her life. How was she so comfortable in an environment she'd never been in? "So, I have a favour to ask."

Startled, Cora laughed out loud.

Over the desk, Frazer simply smiled at her. "Shocking, I know."

If Frazer wasn't so arrogant, she could almost be charming. So that was why she'd been conversational in the hall.

Frazer shifted in her seat. "It was made apparent to me that, for some reason, if you need a favour, it's more polite to simply ask with a please, rather than beat around the bush."

"You're attempt to talk to me this morning was um..."

"Obvious?" Frazer asked.

"With hindsight, yeah, that's a good word for it."

"I need help." The words were said rapidly, as if Frazer had to force them out.

Well, that was unexpected. Cora blinked rapidly. "Wait, did you say you need help?"

"Yep." That grin Frazer so easily gave popped a dimple in her left cheek again. It was a little crooked, quirked higher on that side. It *was* almost endearing. "I really do. I need this project to get off the ground, Cora."

"And Alec is trying to cut down your funding to—what was it you said? Leave you throwing condoms at people?"

Something like a sheepish look flashed over Frazer's face at that comment. "I need the funding. If you could meet some of the people this could help..."

"People? I thought it was focussed on women?"

"It's focussed on all pregnant *people*." The emphasis threw Cora off for a moment, yet Frazer continued as if she hadn't noticed. "To begin, I'll focus on teens, though we'll broaden it to focus on a larger population when we find our feet. We already have a waiting list. We want them to have somewhere they can go and not feel judged, with a mentor they have access to throughout the pregnancy and into postnatal. The focus, in the long run, will be after birth, the support for the parent."

Frazer crossed her legs, her fingers locking together over her knee. Clearly, she'd been in the delivery room today. She was no longer in her clothes from that morning but in baby blue scrubs. Sometimes Cora eyed those scrubs with jealousy—she'd love to dress so comfortably. They were like pyjamas. Instead, she was stuck with staff polo shirts or smart casual clothes.

The reports and proposals Frazer had clearly spent months on sat in Cora's inbox, open for all employees to see. She'd read them. The work Frazer wanted to do was so necessary, exciting even. But really, what was it she expected from Cora? "The idea is a good one, Frazer."

"I know." Again with her arrogance. "But I think I was ambitious when I focussed it on my team." For a half a second, Frazer paused and looked away, then caught Cora's gaze again. "I want to combine forces."

Cora stared at her. "Frazer..." She took a second to order her thoughts. "I'm already involved in a lot of programmes, with more down the road that I want to get started. I'm constantly fighting for more time, for more money, for things that can help the elderly patients that keep getting pushed into understaffed care facilities." For a second, Cora could almost feel Mrs Stein's papery skin under her fingertips, and she clenched her hands together in her lap. "And you want to add another programme to my ever-growing list?"

"Look, I know your department is busy. I know your focus is on the geris. I know. But you're head of Social Work. You have employees who are involved in the cases that I see too. Wouldn't it be great if we could get intervention happening, support for these parents before your department had to step in? Providing a mentor that is always with the parent as support? Prevention, rather than waiting to have to intervene later?"

Frazer was on a roll, her green eyes bright as she talked about something she was obviously passionate about. A soft flush clouded her cheeks. The darkness of her skin against the redness that was there now made her look almost delicate. "Long term, we'd be freeing up funds and people and resources," she said. "With earlier intervention, we'd no longer be demonising these parents but helping them, getting them whatever help they need—ongoing care for parents and babies, support long after the baby is born, even long after the baby is given up or aborted."

The fathers were going to be involved too? Both parents meant more time, more funding, more of the services needed. Frazer might be biting off more than she could chew. No wonder Alec was trying to crush it before it started.

But it was a programme that could change things. One that deserved a chance.

Finally, Cora asked, "You want to team up for this, pool funding from both our departments?"

Slowly, Frazer smiled. "Exactly."

"And maybe use my connection with Alec."

When Frazer's smile grew, Cora nodded. She'd thought as much. Frazer thought that Cora would get some special treatment from Alec. If only she knew how Cora had to fight tooth and nail for what resources she was given.

But maybe with two of them behind this programme, Alec wouldn't be able to ignore it.

"Cora, if we get this up and running over the next few months, I have parents whose lives I can change. We can be a go-between for them and shelters, ongoing health care, adoption agencies, abortion clinics. We can offer them counselling and support. All free. They can make informed decisions and, most importantly, have ongoing care *after* the baby is born, not support that just disappears after they leave the hospital or relies on them having transport or free time. Not care focussed on the baby, but on *them*. The key to this is the mentor programme." The expression on Frazer's face was all serious now. Her eyes were intent on Cora's. "If we got some of your team on board, and mine, this could really make a difference. I just need the funding, and I need Alec to see the programme's worth."

Cora licked her lips. Her pager buzzed at her hip, but she ignored it.

"Okay. I'm in."

CHAPTER THREE

Hump day drinks had been a habit for far too long.

It was a habit they should have probably broken after university, yet somehow, almost every Wednesday, there they were. Drinks and gossip in hand. They should've grown out of it by now.

Clearly, Frazer's friends didn't agree.

The bar they were in was clearly trying to be edgy. Everything was black and chrome, with dim lighting that was a welcome contrast to the bright lights of the hospital environment. It was new, the smell of fresh paint still lingering, yet full of people, the surfaces scattered with half-drunk drinks.

"To Frazer! Too stubborn to let the bosses bring her down." Andy raised her gin and tonic to Frazer.

"That I'll toast to." Frazer said and clinked her glass against Andy's, unable to wipe the beam off her face. Her cheeks were starting to hurt. She tried to toast Rob's glass, but he was scrolling through his phone with one hand, glass in the other, hovering only vaguely in the general space before him.

"Rob." Andy rolled her eyes at Frazer when he didn't even look up. "Rob!"

He finally dropped his phone to his lap. "Sorry! Sorry. The new deal is closing, and I want to know the second it's gone through."

"Yeah." Frazer furrowed her brow seriously and nodded. "You've really got to make sure those deals close. They won't uh... close themselves."

Rob raised his perfect eyebrows. But at least he'd stopped looking at his phone. "What's my job title, Frazer?"

Frazer sought out Andy for help, but all she did was smirk. With a grimace and her hand waving vaguely in the air, Frazer said, "Deal...closing...market-share selling, uh, wonderfully dressed best friend?"

"Yeah. That. Exactly that." He shook his head at her. "It may have taken Daniel two years, but at least he learnt."

"He's your boyfriend. He's required to know."

Andy snorted. "Nice try, Frazer."

"What?" he asked. "And an over-a-decade-long friend shouldn't?"

"Rob." Frazer had definitely reached her drink limit for the night. She could hear herself whining. "You know I'm useless."

"Lucky you're pretty."

Andy was still smirking at them both. "Speaking of useless, when are you going on a date, Frazer?"

"Oh God!" This conversation was one Frazer could happily do without. "Never, if you keep going on about it."

Andy's eyes shone as she leant forward, her teeth glinting white in the gloom. "What if I said I ran into your sister, who said you've been at home with your fish every night you're not with us and that if you don't get your arse into gear, she's going to help us set up a dating profile for you?"

Frazer's face fell. "Shit, you're conspiring now?" When Andy did nothing but jut out her chin, Frazer sighed. "I liked it better when Jemma was my twerp of a sister who used to annoy you." As she paused to sulk further, Andy's words really sunk in. "An *online dating site*? Seriously?"

The snort Rob gave her and the way his eyes lit up doubled the anxiety. All three of them? An online dating site? The idea made her shudder.

She looked from one to the other, finding no sympathy on either face. "Why do you both hate me?"

Andy patted her leg. "It's because we love you. And if you buy any more fish, I'm going to wonder if you've replaced sex with fish, and that's just strange."

"I like my fish."

Rob laughed. "Lesbian."

Both Andy and Frazer turned their looks on him, and he quietened down. "Sorry. But come on. That was funny." They didn't take their glares off him. His eyes widened as his gaze darted from one to the other. "So. Frazer," he tried. "Hasn't been on a date in, like, forever…"

With a sniff, Andy turned back to Frazer. "So, come out with us this weekend, or online profile it is."

Frazer couldn't think of anything worse. She loved a night at the bar, but not one in which her friends tried to pimp her out. "I have a date already."

She did?

"You do?"

The surprise in Andy's voice hurt more than it should have.

"Yeah. With, uh…" Frazer's own eyes widened at the name that came out, "Lauren. From work."

Rob's hand froze on the way to take a sip of his drink. "You're going to date someone from *work*?"

"Well." Frazer gathered all the fake bravado she could. "It went so well last time."

Andy snorted again.

"She's obnoxious."

"I know."

Her sigh was heavy enough to ensure her best friend heard it over the line. Cora gripped the phone more tightly as she walked down a corridor crowded with patients and nurses.

"But Lisa, she's *really* obnoxious."

"I get it. But the programme sounds like a great one, and you can keep her head to a reasonable size."

With a side-step, she danced past an orderly with a cleaning cart. "Fat chance," she said.

"Do you like her proposal?"

Shoulders drooping, Cora nodded. "Yes."

"Do you think it will benefit lots of people?"

Another sigh. "Yes."

"So go help."

Frazer's office door loomed ahead of her, and Cora stopped in front of it. "Fine, oh reasonable one. I've got to go. Give my love to your mum."

"Will do. Enjoy the next hour."

"Har har." Cora pressed the *end call* button with more force than necessary, straightened, and knocked on the door. Her best friend was really not helpful sometimes.

At the muffled "come in," Cora took a breath and did just that.

It was for a good cause.

Frazer greeted her from her desk. "Hey, Cora. Thanks for meeting me here. I've got everything all set up on my computer and anything that's on paper here, so it seemed easier."

"No problem." Cora slid into a chair. "It was easy enough. No birthing mothers?"

Frazer nodded to the pager next to her keyboard. "There are always babies coming. It's almost as if they don't follow a schedule."

"Do many of the mothers understand that?"

"Oh my God, Cora." Frazer leant back in her chair heavily, throwing her hands up. "You've no idea. You should read some of the birthing plans the parents give me. One wanted to reserve three rooms in case one had bad energy."

"Like the hospital is a hotel?"

"Exactly." Frazer shook her head. "I'm all for trying to have a birth plan, especially because it helps a lot of parents feel less anxious. But to ask to be 'stimulated' during contractions by the midwife?"

Cora blinked. "*Stimulated?*"

"Stimulated."

"As in..."

"As in exactly what you're thinking." Frazer chuckled. "Can't make that up."

"Wow."

"Yup. So!" She clapped her hands together and sat up. "Did you have a chance to read through what I e-mailed you?"

"I did. It's solid."

For a moment, the carefree look on Frazer's face darkened. "Apparently not solid enough. But it will be. Any fresh ideas? I'll take anything—it's been pretty much me, solo, from the beginning."

Cora nodded in relief. Sometimes people were precious about their projects. "Well, to start, the mentor programme? This is where your idea shines. It's what makes it unique. Parents are always sent home with really minimal support afterwards. And that support doesn't take into account the at-risk parents—the ones who don't have their own support network, transport to their community nurse, all of that."

"Exactly!" Frazer's eyes lit up. She was nodding enthusiastically to everything Cora said.

"Well, let's pool our resources, like we already planned. Why just use midwives who volunteer as mentors? Let's source social workers, and even Accident and Emergency nurses—I chatted to some of the girls in A&E and my department and already have a preliminary list of those that are interested."

"Great! More people power."

"And..." Cora wasn't sure Frazer would go for this.

"And?"

Cora took a breath and surged ahead. "What if we used other parents as mentors? People already with kids, who are interested in doing it? Many won't be, I'm sure, they're so busy. But we could do a training week, go over expectations. Use them for the lower-risk people, have them involved from the beginning?"

Frazer's brow furrowed. She leant back against her chair again and stared at Cora.

Twisting her fingers in her lap, Cora shook her head. "It's probably a bad idea."

"No, it's good."

Cora's hands stilled. "Really?"

"Yeah. We need the people. If we advertise for people to have the correct checks, even source people with certain degrees, why not? And a training programme...I mean, that will cost money, but if I run it, that decreases the cost a lot." A slow smile had worked its way onto Frazer's face. "Like an AA supporter—someone who's been there."

"Yeah."

"To start with, each mentor can have one or two clients." Frazer was running with Cora's idea, almost vibrating with energy across the desk. "That way, people with full-time jobs won't get overwhelmed, and we can see more clearly what's working and what's not."

Warmth blossomed in Cora's chest. Maybe this wouldn't be so terrible.

Arms on the desk in front of her, Frazer asked, "What other ideas do you have in there? We can get this new proposal off to Alec in the next hour."

CHAPTER FOUR

The bar was warm and bustling, inviting, with its worn, leather seats smothered by the low buzz of conversation. The taste of opportunity was on Frazer's tongue as she led the way, her date pressed close behind. Her date. Not something she was incredibly thrilled about, but her stupid friends had left her no choice. Worse, when Frazer had asked Lauren out, she'd only been available that night, rather than the Friday Frazer had proposed.

A quick nod at the bartender was returned with a wink when he caught sight of Lauren next to her. Without a word, two white wines were put down in front of them.

Apparently, his memory went back years.

Glass aloft, Frazer held Lauren's gaze as she mimicked the gesture, the clink lost in the overall hum of the room.

"I'm so glad we're finally doing this."

"Me too, Lauren." The lie rolled off her tongue easily.

Damn her friends.

"I thought you were never going to ask me."

In place of any substantive answer, Frazer merely offered a shrug and a grin.

Here was what had become of her promise to never date at work again. After the last incident that had led to her hiding in a supply closet on and off for weeks to avoid her ex, she'd promised herself not to use the hospital's staff as her personal dating pool. And now Frazer was kicking herself because not only had she failed at her own resolution, she just wanted to go home and watch Netflix and chill—alone.

But then the image of an *Internet Loves* profile sliced into her mind, the photo most likely the scariest one Jemma and Andy could find. Maybe the one in which Frazer was wearing all denim.

A disaster. *"Lesbian too attached to fish tank in need of loving"* or some other hideous caption. Frazer swallowed heavily.

Lauren's eyes were intent on her, keen. She was talking about something that involved a lot of hand gestures.

Nodding, not really hearing a word, Frazer pressed her lips together and tried to appear interested. Poor Lauren. If only she knew Frazer was here because her name was the first one she could offer up to save herself.

So, maybe, since Frazer was only here after being threatened, this was more like bending the rules, not breaking them.

That didn't help.

She'd still rather be elsewhere.

They pushed past bodies and managed to find a booth in the corner. This part had always been awkward. The part where you'd moved from openly flirting to seeing where it could take you. Between them, the silence soon filled with meaningless chatter. Even as she managed to nod agreeably at the woman she'd been dancing around for months, Frazer's mind wandered.

There was a time she'd been really good at this.

Instead, she wanted to be ironing out the kinks in the redone report. Brainstorming with Cora.

Cora, who wanted to help.

Lauren laughed and brushed her fingers over Frazer's hands. The touch was light, relaxed and filled with meaning. This could be very, very easy.

Turning her attention to the woman in front of her, Frazer made herself forget everything else.

On the steps out the front of her best friend's house, Cora tried to remember to breathe. Her heart was thrumming against her ribs, her hands clammy. She hated arguments. She hated how words twisted in on themselves, became ugly and harsh. In the past, she'd been cowed by confrontations like that, but Alec had always pushed them, and these days, she found herself hurling back at him almost as she good as she got, regret thick on her tongue as soon as the words tumbled out. Things she didn't even know went through her head spewed past her lips, falling heavily over the kitchen tile like stones Alec could later sift through at his leisure and throw at her another day.

And he always did.

With her fingers gripping her knees, she bounced on her toes, agitated. Why did Lisa have to be out today? Cora had to remind herself to not be selfish—there could have been another emergency with Lisa's mother's health. Cora didn't know how Lisa supported her mother as well as her younger siblings, frankly.

So she was selfish. But Cora really, really needed a glass of wine with her best friend right at that moment. If this was any other day, she'd lean back on Lisa's couch, the wine washing over her tongue like a balm, and it would eventually get better, or at least not-so-awful. Lisa, the master of Cora's complicated thoughts, would artfully pull the story from her and nod sympathetically, filling up her glass until Cora grew sick of her own voice. And then Cora would be calm enough to face home again.

Not tonight, though. And Lisa *had* to be out on the night she had stormed dramatically from the house, her cheeks flaming in the cool night air. The night she'd watched Alec throw a glass that shattered against the wall over her head, dangerously close. The air between them had grown palpable, pulsing with harsh emotion—his anger and the flames of her own that had licked up in response. It worked well to cover the resentment that had been settling low in her stomach the last few years, bubbling yet never surfacing.

His wide, pale eyes had stared at her, strangely illuminated in the fluorescent light. She turned on her heel and fled.

Naturally, she went to Lisa's.

Naturally, Lisa wasn't home.

In front of Lisa's doorway, she made the decision: she wasn't going back home. There was no way she was getting back in that bed, to lie with metres of space between her and the husband that had once clung to her. To the ominous silence that hung around the house like something putrid.

To tiptoeing around somewhere she should stride through confidently, wondering how she got here and wishing she was anywhere else.

If Lisa wasn't around to drink wine with her, Cora would just drink wine alone. She could do that.

Cora could be alone.

Even if that wasn't something she'd done, well, ever.

Lauren was exceptionally pretty. She had a body to die for.

She was also, sadly, incredibly dull.

Taking a sip of her drink, Frazer tried to stop her eyes from drifting around the bar. Normally, she tried to avoid a bar filled with workmates, but Lauren had suggested it and Frazer had figured why not? If she was going to make her bed, she might as well lie in it. Roll around in it. Sleep in it, even.

Nights out with co-workers fed the rumour mills during the day, and looking around the bar now, Frazer was sure it would be spinning tomorrow. The gossip of who went home with whom and who had cheated on their spouse ran rampant in various departments, and she was sure she'd seen a clinical nurse from her ward disappear out the door with one of the obstetricians. Juicy.

With a nod at something Lauren said, Frazer tried to stop staring around the room. Really, she wasn't one to partake in gossip. But she just couldn't concentrate on the woman in front of her. It had been so long since she'd been out with work people, though. It had been easy to forget that in bars, coated in alcohol, things were said that should have stayed in bedrooms, the words flying around and people grasping at them to piece together stories so sensational, others couldn't help but mention them.

No wonder Frazer usually avoided them.

As Lauren talked about a trip she'd been on ("The beaches were even better than here, if you'd believe it"), Frazer saw Tia with another secretary, one Frazer was sure she recognised from a private hospital.

Apparently, Lauren realised Frazer wasn't paying attention anymore, because she turned to look at what had caught her eye. She chuckled. "Is that Sam and Tia?"

Sam! That was indeed who it was. With a nod, Frazer sipped her bourbon, amused.

"Don't their husbands hate each other?" Lauren's interest was back on Frazer as she waited for an answer everyone knew the answer to.

"They do—and apparently they hate their wives being together. Clearly, their wives don't care."

"Sam's husband screwed over Alec in some kind of deal years ago, didn't he?"

They both watched the two women laugh loudly over their martinis. Heads close together, they looked like conspirators. Tia's eyes were lit up, and Frazer wondered what titbit she'd learnt.

"Yeah, that was him." Frazer said.

Lauren stared at them a second longer.

"I wonder if they're lesbians..."

Curiosity laced Lauren's tone and Frazer almost choked, unable to completely restrain herself. Tia was one of the only people at the hospital Frazer really liked. "Doubt it. I accidentally walked in on Tia and her husband in the kitchen at the New Year's party the year before last—definitely seemed to be enjoying what he was doing."

"Doesn't mean much..."

"Does your gaydar go off?" Frazer raised an eyebrow at Lauren.

"Fine." Lauren collapsed against her chair. "No. It's just a pity. It's fun when there's more of us." She watched the two women for a moment. "Bummer."

The bell over the door rang, incredibly faint under all the noise. Lauren's head turned, and a smirk grew on her lips. "Kind of like her—also a bummer."

Drink in hand, Frazer turned to see who had caused such a reaction. Who could resist checking out potential talent? Standing in the entrance, hovering as if unsure of whether to enter or not, was Cora. A quick sip of her drink covered Frazer's wince. So much for not thinking about the programme—and therefore Cora.

Biting her lip, Cora pushed her hair behind her ear and entered the room. She skirted around her husband's receptionist, gaze glued to the floor, and sat at the opposite end of the bar to Tia. A flush covered her cheeks. Her eyes were downcast as she placed an order with the bartender. Earlier in the day, her eyes had been bright while she gripped Frazer's arm, the laugh trickling out of her easily as she talked about a project she was excited about.

"Never see her here."

Frazer took in a deep breath, suddenly desperate to be anywhere else. "Want to get out of here?" She didn't know what she wanted, but she knew she didn't want to be in this bar anymore.

Lauren's eyes lit up. "Sure."

Regret already lingered like a bad aftertaste as she knocked back the last of her drink and scooted out of the booth after Lauren. The two of them easily wove through the crowd, Frazer following close behind Lauren. Somehow, the bar was even fuller now, with people pressed together in tight groups. The scent of beer and spirits was almost overpowering, and voices and laughter raised higher, drowning out the music. It was just the kind of scene Frazer could usually enjoy herself in, but not tonight. For some reason, it felt hot and oppressive.

Outside, the air was cool and fresh, hinting at the autumn that was starting. The door swung closed, sealing off the ruckus inside. With her hands buried in her pockets, Lauren turned to smile at her, bathed in the light of a streetlight.

"Your place or mine?"

Meaning to say goodnight, Frazer found herself saying, "Yours?"

The delight on Lauren's face grew, and she turned on her heel. Without another word, Frazer fell in step next to her.

Sitting alone in a bar was quite depressing.

Cora watched Alec's receptionist talk loudly with her friend, a woman Cora knew for a fact was the wife of a man Tia's husband, and Cora's own, hated. Alec had told her more about it years ago, but Cora couldn't quite remember. Gossip had never interested her.

Maybe it should have more.

Maybe she would have listened to the rumours at university, the whispers of Alec's temper with his previous girlfriend.

But she'd been so swept off her feet by him. He was charming, funny. He could have had plenty of other girls on campus, but he'd turned his grin on her. And then, way too soon, the day came when the stick had turned blue, and it wasn't about being flattered by his attention anymore. Only a few months after they'd started dating, there she was, standing in a bathroom, thinking her life was going to end. In her mother's eyes, it would have. The Good Girl and the Good Guy pregnant? Unmarried? How could such a thing happen?

Hot sex, Mother.

Over another sip of wine, Cora looked around the bar. She'd been there for four hours. People-watching was one of her favourite things. If you sat quietly enough, people forgot you were there. In dribs and drabs, people from work and people she had never seen before floated in and out. People she knew were married left with others who weren't their spouse. An argument had erupted in the corner, and an involuntary flinch at the sound shifted her in her seat.

Frazer had disappeared out the door just after Cora had taken a seat at the bar. A flash of longing as she'd done so made Cora realise how lonely she felt—Frazer was the only person Cora really *knew* in there. Everyone else was an acquaintance or a stranger, people she somehow never got around to knowing. So was Frazer, really. But at least they'd spoken more than a few words together. Definitely more than a few, really, after their meeting about the programme.

Cora took a large sip of her drink.

If she was wishing to speak to *Frazer,* she must be lonely.

But if Frazer had stayed, they could have shared a drink and talked about the project that was finally coming together. The pitch might actually be enough to get everything moving sooner rather than later.

Lisa still hadn't replied and Alec hadn't tried to call. She didn't know if she was happy about the latter one or not. Alec often sulked after their arguments, coming back with puppy-dog eyes and a gift soaked in words, ones which soon turned to ash. The past year, he'd come back to her only with the words that quickly flared back to anger again.

The glass he'd thrown had been her great-grandmother's, one she had brought from Thailand with her; one of the only things she had managed to bring.

Maybe Cora could glue it back together.

Probably as well as she could glue her marriage back together.

That thought made Cora give a half-hearted snort.

Cora's mother would be devastated. Her father would be ropeable. Anything that had come from his grandparents' homelands was a treasure to him.

Of course, neither of them would find out.

The third wine of the evening was warming under her hands. How long could she sit here until she had to go home? Hopefully, Alec was on the couch.

Usually he was after this kind of night.

The bar smelt like stale beer—probably what regret would smell like if it had a scent.

An involuntary shiver accompanied the thought of the silence in the house. Of the coolness that would creep over her skin.

There were nights she woke up with her breath caught in her throat and the feeling that something was constricting her chest. With her heart pounding, Cora would lie in bed, staring at the ceiling as the extreme body heat of the man next to her rolled over her. It felt as if a band were around her chest, tightening more and more.

The sigh that heaved through her body was heavy, and a flush warmed her cheeks. No one could hear her in the bar. Really, she could be here or nowhere and no one would really know.

Morose was not normally something she allowed herself to feel, but tonight she was happy to wallow in her pitifulness.

The door opened. The bell over it was really quite annoying. No one else in the bar seemed to notice it, though. With a start, Cora caught sight of Frazer walking in. Why would she come back here of all places? Deciding not to care, Cora looked back to her drink. The glass was sweating, and the wine was far too dry for her liking. It was a bit sad to sit on her own and watch it warm up—usually that kind of thing was done with company. Almost desperately, she looked up, caught Frazer's eye and waved.

If she sat alone with her thoughts much longer, she'd go insane.

When Frazer slid into the chair next to her, Cora couldn't help but throw her a grateful look. "Thanks."

"Why?"

"For answering my obviously desperate plea." A glass of bourbon appeared very quickly in front of Frazer after a simple catch of the bartender's eye. Cora raised an eyebrow. "Come here often?"

The warm, rich chuckle sunk into Cora's chest. "I used to."

They lapsed into silence. Their conversations had been restricted to work and one drunken conversation at a Christmas party. Really, their work conversations had only started that week. Cora was realising she knew absolutely nothing about Frazer except that she was good at her job; but even that was spoilt by arrogance.

Yet, for once, Cora didn't feel the need to fill the silence. It wasn't oppressive. It wasn't angry. There was nothing teaming at the seams, nothing itching to tear it all apart the second someone opened their mouth.

"Do you think the on call is any good?"

Cora glanced up in surprise at the question. She blinked heavily. Frazer must mean the on call obstetrician. "Dave?"

"Yeah."

"How do I put this delicately?" Cora's brow pressed together, and she took a sip of her wine. "No."

Frazer slumped in obvious relief against the bar. "Thank God. I thought it was only me that saw it. I was genuinely scared when I was handing over. He looked at me so blankly."

"When Alec interviewed him, he came out singing his praises. And then I met him and honestly thought he was the strangest guy I'd ever met. It's like, he's *there* but he's not *there*. Ya know?"

"Lights are on, but—"

"No one's home."

They both chuckled.

This was nice. They were actually maintaining a conversation. Interesting.

"Exactly."

Silence fell over them, different than any that had ever swallowed them at work, easy and not remotely awkward. The warmth of the bar was comfortable, and the alcohol had left a pleasant buzz. Maybe she didn't dislike Frazer as much as she had thought. She thought back on the last week—maybe it was less arrogance that she had, and more a healthy heaping of self-confidence.

"Frazer, what in the hell brought you back to a bar at eleven o'clock? Didn't I see you leave hours ago?"

The shrug in response screamed nonchalance; as did the slow sip of bourbon that followed. "I didn't really feel like going home. Do you ever feel like that?"

Cocking her head, Cora stared at her a touch more intently than she had intended. "I get that. But I like being home normally. Alec's out this evening, though."

Lies were a thing Cora had never been comfortable with. They got you in trouble, buried you in deep. The past few years, though, she had been telling many lies. They came easily, slid off her tongue so often they didn't even taste bitter anymore.

No, Mum, I'm fine.

It's okay.

I know you love me.

Alec's just not coming because he's working...

"Do you guys have a white picket fence?" Frazer asked. Her lips curled up just slightly.

"Um, yeah?" Cora blinked at her. What did that have to do with anything?

"A dog?"

"We used to have a cat." The grin on Frazer's lips was catching, and Cora found herself mirroring it. "What?"

"You have the 1950s dream."

Cora snorted and drank her wine, her gaze inside her glass. "Sure."

They lapsed back into silence.

Her cheeks warm, Cora felt Frazer's gaze back on her. "You okay?" Frazer asked.

"I'm good." Cora's gaze stayed on her wine.

"Okay."

Frazer looked away. Cora was just glad Frazer didn't want to push it. With the mood she was in, instead of spilling lies, she might have accidentally dropped truth all over the bar top. There was no sweeping that up.

"Are you the kind of 'good' that wants to drink a lot?" Mischief laced the words.

Instead of the no that she meant to say, Cora found herself saying, "Yes."

"Excellent. Me too." She turned to the bartender. "Two tequilas?"

At the horrified look Cora was directing at her, Frazer shrugged. "What? It is before midnight, and we *are* adults."

She hadn't had tequila since university.

Why not?

"The thing about potatoes, Frazer, is that you can do *so* much with them."

Frazer was starting to think she had accidentally gotten her boss' wife drunk. The woman she was relying on to save her project was quite plastered. That had not been the plan. When Frazer spun on her chair to raise a question, the room lurched, and the thought that maybe she had gotten herself drunk too struck her. A shrug almost made her unbalance again. She was allowed to be drunk. Tomorrow was a day of paperwork, no patients.

Really, Frazer felt fairly entitled to be drunk. She'd just panicked at a potential easy, no-strings-attached date's house and had gone and walked around for hours before ending up in the same bar she'd started in.

Cora was still talking. "Don't shrug like you don't agree! When I was at university, potatoes were the only reason I didn't die of starvation."

The snort that left Frazer's body was incredibly unattractive. "I was shrugging because I don't care that I'm drunk."

Cora nodded and said "oh" as if that segued perfectly from what she had been saying.

"And I completely agree. Potatoes are amazing. *But* I disagree on one point."

As if Frazer was about to unveil the secrets of the universe, Cora stared at her.

"The best food to live off at university was cheese on rice."

She had come all the way back to this place with one thought in the back of her brain—that maybe she could find her boring co-worker.

Cora blinked. "An entire nation lived off potatoes for years. You really think rice with cheese beats potatoes?"

"Totally. There's more protein."

"There is not."

"There so is! It's *cheese*, Cora."

Apparently that was an argument. Frazer really needed to work on that. Tomorrow.

They stared at each other for a minute before Cora whipped out her phone.

"What are you doing?" Frazer asked.

"If it weren't for Google, we'd all be lost," Cora said. Frazer watched her as she squinted at her phone before finally closing one eye to stare at it.

In reality, Cora was less boring and more entertaining.

"Can't focus without closing an eye?"

"Shut up, Frazer. Oh! Here it is. Wow, Google has its own little converter thing on the page to tell you how much protein there is. Okay, 100 grams of cheese—twenty-five grams of protein." Her eyes looked predatory, and Frazer felt something strange in the pit of her stomach. "Potatoes are so going to win. Twenty-five grams? How much is that, like the weight of a coin, right? It's nothing. Okay, in 100 grams of potatoes..." Her face fell.

Already smug, Frazer asked, "How much is there, Cora?"

Silence.

"Cora?" Frazer practically sing-songed her name.

"Two grams."

"Oh. Two... What's that? Like, the weight of a mosquito?"

"Potatoes are still better." She slipped her phone into her bag and reached for her wine.

"Admit you lost."

Lips pressed together, Cora shook her head. "Nope."

"Admit I was right."

"Never."

Frazer was more than glad she'd left Lauren's and increasingly glad she'd come here. The thought of sitting in her quiet house with just her aquarium for company had made her mildly depressed, even with the recent addition of a Nemo and a Dory, since they seemed to hate each other. Probably because they were actually two clownfish; maybe she should have called them Nemo and Marlin. Now she really didn't mind about all that. The air of sadness that always sat around Cora had eased. She seemed more relaxed, to be genuinely enjoying herself.

That was nice.

Look at them, getting along.

Poking Cora in the arm, Frazer asked, "You're stubborn, aren't you?"

"You're competitive, aren't you?" Cora met Frazer's smug look with raised eyebrows.

"Got me there."

"Well, I'm not *that* stubborn."

"Sure you're not."

Apparently choosing to ignore her, Cora glanced at their empty shot glasses. "Another?"

"Shouldn't you be getting home to your husband?"

Cora wrinkled her nose and looked exactly like Frazer's four-year-old niece when she was told to go to bed. "Shouldn't *you* be getting home to your, um, housemate?"

At Frazer's shake of her head, Cora pursed her lips. "Partner?"

Another shake. "Cat?"

Another shake. "Fish!"

Frazer nodded. Cora fist-pumped. "Yes! Shouldn't *you* be getting home to your fish?"

"My fish can cope without me."

"So can my husband."

"Okay."

Two more shots appeared, and they clinked the glasses, liquor spilling over and making their fingers sticky. They'd forgone the lemon a couple of hours ago. Everything was pleasantly foggy, and Frazer was at the point of no return, where she no longer cared about how bad work was going to be tomorrow.

That was never a good point.

"Do you think Alec will approve everything we sent through?" Frazer hadn't wanted to talk about work, but she needed to know.

Cora pursed her lips. "I really don't know. He should. But I don't know."

Silence. Again.

"Want to know a secret?"

Those words made Frazer desperately want to say no, she didn't want to know a secret. Secrets were bad and got people in to trouble. She'd never liked secrets.

"Um..."

"I told my husband I wanted to leave him tonight."

In her current state, there was no way Frazer could stop her mouth from dropping open. Or her eyes going wide. She just stared at Cora, who stared at her glass.

Sure, she'd heard them arguing the day before in Cora's office. But hell, Frazer argued with her fish sometimes. Everyone *argued*.

"Oh."

"He didn't take it well."

"Oh."

"I probably won't leave him."

"Oh." Frazer wanted to kick herself. She needed to give back something more than that. "Okay."

Something more than that too. What do you say to someone who says that? Especially someone you don't really know? Especially someone who was married to your boss and who you kind of thought was hot? Hot and uptight and not at all Frazer's type. Did she mention that the someone was her boss' wife?

"I won't, though. Leave him, I mean."

Advice wasn't always the best thing to give. Considering Frazer knew nothing of the situation or the people involved, it would be stupid to even try to give any. You could give what seemed like sound advice, but when the person chose to ignore it, that advice would come back and bite you in the ass. Marriage was a complicated subject involving two people completely committed, who went so far as to sign a document attesting to that fact.

And she'd heard the rumours of raised voices. Of how Cora had started out her job passionate and a little pushy—the only time people had said she was like that—and then slowly had disappeared into herself over the years.

No. Frazer had no idea about any of it and should therefore keep her mouth shut.

"Are you happy?"

Or just ignore her own advice and ask a deep and philosophical question.

Turning on her chair, Cora looked at her. Her elbow leaned heavily against the bar top. "What is that?"

The look in her eye had Frazer shifting in her seat. It was genuine, almost a challenge. "What?" Even though Frazer knew exactly what.

"Happy. What even is that?"

They looked at each other for a moment. "Good question."

Giving a nod, Cora turned back to her drink and Frazer reached for the bourbon she was using as a chaser. This was not the conversation she had expected to fall in to. Stupid big mouth.

"Are you going to leave?" She finally asked. Because since she had ignored her own advice the first time, Frazer might as well keep asking deeply private questions.

"One day."

"Okay."

"Want more tequila?"

"Okay."

The burn of tequila and the sound of drunken laughter were all Frazer could remember of the next hour. A lot of laughter about things that probably weren't very funny. Unlike at work, Cora had a sarcasm that bordered on delightful and was enjoyably odd.

Or maybe that was the tequila talking.

The night air was cool, and Cora had no real memory of leaving the bar. Yet here she was, leaning heavily against Frazer while the woman looked for a taxi. It was lucky Frazer was a head taller, because Cora fit nicely against her shoulder and didn't have to do a lot to hold herself up. Work was going to suck tomorrow.

She let out a groan. The human pillow under her head bounced a little, and a chuckle reached her ears.

"Why are you laughing at me?" Cora murmured.

"You groaned like a dying cow."

"Well, you will too when I tell you what of I thought... I mean, what I thought of."

"What's that?"

"We have work in five hours." The answering groan made Cora chortle. Her eyes were still closed. She crossed her arms over her chest. "See? That thought brings forth dying cow sounds." A yawn practically smothered the next sentence. "It will henceforth be called the 'dying cow noise.'"

"C'mon, you."

The warmth of the taxi just barely registered. Cora was half-asleep in seconds, leaning against the window. Numbness through alcohol wasn't the best way to deal with emotions. But that didn't mean it was the worst, and it was working beautifully right now. As they drew closer to her house, though, Cora felt most of that happiness fading. It would be quiet and oppressive in her house, and she didn't want to be there. Being somewhere easy sounded better, and right then, Frazer was easy. Frazer and her incredibly comfortable shoulder Cora had accidentally ended up leaning against.

Slightly stumbling steps took her out of the taxi, and she clung to the open door, sifting through her bag with one hand to find some cash. It didn't really surprise her when Frazer appeared on the other side of the door.

"I'll walk you up."

"That's really not necessary." Cora stood up straight and turned, her feet catching on the curb. She recovered nicely but looked up to see Frazer staring at her, one eyebrow raised. With a sigh, Cora gave in. "Fine. Walk with me if you must."

As close as a shadow, Frazer walked behind her, and Cora didn't entirely manage to hide her groan at the sight of her own porch steps. Crickets that were chirping loudly fell silent as she all but stomped up the stairs. Her intention had been to go quietly, not wanting to wake up Alec, but she found, with a touch of vindictiveness, that she hoped he did wake up. If she had to suffer a hangover at work the next day, he could be sleep deprived. Successfully, she scaled the stairs and turned in front of the door, hands on her hips like a triumphant superhero.

"See? I was fine."

"You tripped four times."

"But did I fall, Frazer?"

Teeth flashed white in the gloom as Frazer chuckled. "True." She held her hands up in peace, swaying a little. "You are victorious."

"I always am."

The chuckle washed over her ears again. It made warmth spread in her chest. The cool keys she'd gripped in her hand had become warm by now, and she slipped them into the lock on the second try, turning it and partially opening the door as she gave an awkward wave of her hand. "I'll see you at work, yeah?"

"See you tomorrow."

At the sight of Frazer's back, Cora called out, not yet willing to walk into her silent and hideous house. "Frazer."

"Yeah?" Frazer's light, questioning eyes were on her, and Cora swallowed, suddenly feeling like a child with a new friend. "I just wanted to say, uh, thanks. I needed the company tonight."

Cora crossed her arms over her stomach. Really, she did not want to go inside.

"Anytime."

With a nod, Cora hovered there, still unwilling to move.

Suddenly, warm fingers gripped her wrist and tugged her forward. Arms wrapped around her, and Cora was stiff for only a second before relaxing into the hug. It was warm and soft, and it felt so good to be able to sink into someone. It had been so long since Alec had hugged her with any real affection. Burying her face in Frazer's neck, Cora didn't even care if Frazer had simply meant to give her a quick goodbye squeeze. Everything felt raw. With a burning in her throat she would be ashamed of if more sober, Cora felt Frazer's cheek turn against her own. It was so soft. Hands ran up and down her back. If Cora had any say in it, she would stay there all night.

Through the fog in her brain, Cora realised she should probably let go. She should go inside. Pulling back slowly, her cheek brushed gently against Frazer's again as she started to extract herself from her arms.

Her skin really was so soft.

For a moment, they hovered, cheek to cheek, the corners of their lips almost but not quite brushing. Warm air fluttered against her skin. Fingertips stroked gently against Cora's neck once before suddenly, cool air was everywhere and that warmth had disappeared. With a heavy blink, Cora opened her eyes. Frazer looked at her, unreadable.

"Take care of yourself. I'll see you tomorrow, Cora."

When Cora nodded, Frazer turned and was swallowed by the evening.

Cora pushed the door shut behind her and leant against it.

That was new.

CHAPTER FIVE

Desperately, Frazer gripped her coffee and took a long, grateful sip. Waking up on her couch with a blurry recollection of the past evening was not uncommon, but it was never a fun experience. And it was one that got more painful with age. Bright sunlight was burning her eyes, even through dark sunglasses. She skulked down a back hallway, let herself into her office, and collapsed into her chair.

Why did people drink?

With eyes closed, her head fell back, and the throbbing behind her brow eased slightly. Maybe she could just stay in her office for the next three hours. Never mind all the paperwork that needed doing out on the wards. Was it a full moon? That meant lots of babies tonight and over the weekend, and Frazer could end up having to cover. For a short moment, she considered searching the internet for the answer, but the thought of an incredibly bright screen was not appealing.

God, why had she thought tequila was a good idea? If anyone asks, "Tequila?" the answer should always be no.

Though she was fairly certain she was the one who had suggested it.

A knock at the door had her yanking off her sunglasses, as if that would look better than the red-rimmed mess now on display. Mascara had smudged her cheeks when she woke up, and scrubbing had not really improved the overall look. As the door swung open, she straightened up and tried not to look like a drunken sixteen-year-old whose parents had just caught shushing a chair she'd walked into.

Which, of course, Frazer had never done. It had been a coffee table, thanks very much.

Tia poked around the corner. "Frazer—meeting in ten."

"Yeah, sure. I'll be there."

She looked Frazer over, her eyes dancing. "How you feeling?"

"Uh—fantastic. Great. I'm keen to update files, do rosters, and write reports."

Tia cackled. "Alec will be super excited to hear that. Shall I tell him to play loud rock music in the meeting?"

"Oh, please—and while you're at it, why not bring in some sugared-up two-year-olds with drums?"

Tia disappeared, her laughter fading as she walked down the hall.

It was going to be a really long day.

With clumsy fingers, Frazer jammed her sunglasses back on. She stared around her neat and ordered office before stopping to focus on the space under her desk. It looked cool and dark. Maybe she could sleep there—just for a little while.

Her head dropped back against the chair. Even the slight swivelling motion was starting to make her nauseated. One minute of closing her eyes wouldn't hurt. The darkness was soothing. Silence was addictive.

All at once, both her pager and her mobile trilled. With a groan, she took a glance. Both messages were from Tia, telling her not to fall asleep and to hurry up.

Frazer cursed. That woman had eyes everywhere.

Leaving her sunglasses behind with a stab of regret, Frazer pulled on a clean scrub shirt as if it could give her the air of credibility she was lacking. She squared her shoulders. No hangover would defeat her. She yanked her door open and stepped through it defiantly. Probably too defiantly. Her coffee and her body collided with someone who had been innocently walking by, the lid popping off and coffee sloshing everywhere. Mostly over—

Shit. It was Cora.

They stared at each other for a minute, coffee dripping on the floor, Cora's eyes as red as her own.

Her lips twitched. Cora's mimicked hers.

They cracked up.

"I'm so sorry."

"No—seriously Frazer, I'm barely awake. I'm sorry."

"I stormed out and spilt coffee all over you."

Glancing down at herself, Frazer grimaced. Somehow, her shirt was completely clean—how had that happened?

"That kinda day for me, I'm guessing." Cora cocked her head, looking her up and down. "You feeling as rough as me?"

"If you feel like you did the first time you pushed tequila too hard, then yes."

"I feel worse than that time—I was nineteen when I first did that. I had a far better constitution then."

A beeping came from her pocket. Frazer closed her eyes for a moment and took a deep breath. When she opened them, Cora was giving her a knowing look.

"Meeting?" Cora asked.

"Meeting." Frazer nodded. "I was considering wearing my sunglasses in there. Too unprofessional?"

"If you get to, so do I."

"Think the boss will allow it?"

A look too quick to discern flashed over Cora's face. "Probably not. I have to run and change my shirt—"

"Again, so sorry."

"Stop, it's fine. I love the smell of coffee, so I'll just embrace it as my perfume for the day."

"Still, sorry. Meet you in there?"

"I may miss it—I'll be late anyway. My clothes are in the car."

"Benefits of sleeping with your boss." Frazer winked, feeling cheap even as she did so.

"Yeah, something like that." Cora's face was unreadable. "See you around, Frazer."

With a final grimace in the direction of Cora's coffee-covered shirt, Frazer walked down the hallway. As she turned the corner, she remembered something through the haze of conversation last night.

Cora had mentioned wanting to leave her husband. Yet, there was Frazer making jokes about having special privileges because they were married.

Really, being hung-over should be an excuse not to face the world. It meant her foot lived permanently in her mouth.

And, oh God, the meeting was on statistics.

Today was going to be agonising.

At least Cora's shirt had been kind of see-through from the coffee.

"It just looks bad when even my own wife doesn't come to a meeting I call."

"Alec, I know—I'm sorry. I had to change my shirt and have a quick shower. By the time I was done, I figured I'd miss it."

Eyes flashing a hard blue, Alec leant back in his chair. "It's not my problem if you can't organise your personal routine like every other staff member. If you want to go out drinking all night, you still have to be an adult like everyone else."

Her head throbbed. Cora closed her eyes for a moment before opening them to stare him straight in the eye. His gaze didn't even waver. At the other side of his desk, she felt oddly like a teenager in front of a particularly bitchy principal.

"Someone ran into me in the corridor, and I was covered in coffee. I had to change."

"Or you were hung-over and clumsy and spilt it all over yourself."

On a good day, it was hard to get through a conversation like this. Today was not a good day. "I don't know what you want me to say. You call this many meetings, and people are bound to miss some."

Alec's entire body went still, and Cora knew instantly she shouldn't have said that.

But she did not have the energy to carefully pluck out words that would appease him. When she had woken up that morning,

Alec had already left, his blanket neatly folded at the end of the couch and the smell of his aftershave in the air like a reminder of something that started pleasantly but then began to burn.

Apparently, her lack of appearance in the meeting meant he didn't feel the need to hide away as he normally would after an argument like last night's.

"It's not important, Cora. Just don't do it again."

Cheeks burning, she nodded. "Is that all?"

He eyed her. She'd once found his gaze comforting, passionate, consuming. Now it still bordered on consuming, but the rest didn't linger. Dismissive: was that what he saw when she looked at him?

He shook his head. "No. I think we should continue the conversation we started last night."

Cora's gaze dropped to the floor, and her stomach turned over. There was no way she wanted to continue that conversation. It was one he had started to bring up again and again, and it left her panicked and unable to put sentences together. He quickly flared into anger anyway, leaving her trying to back-pedal out or else flare up alongside him, his flames fuelling her own. Then he would just walk away, taking away all her power to say what she wanted to.

Eggshells filled her house, and Cora was constantly walking over them. Sometimes, she tried to walk over them on tiptoes, other times on her heels. Big strides or ballerina steps—nothing helped. They still shattered under her feet.

"When we have kids—"

Here we go. "*If* we have kids," she said.

His glare was enough to make her wish she'd left it alone. "When we have kids, Cora, you have to quit your job."

She stared at him. The words still shocked her even though she'd heard them before.

He splayed his fingers over the top of his desk, the knuckles white. "It's not like I can quit mine."

At university, they'd read Plato together in bed, reciting their favourite parts and then tracing the words over each other's skin with their tongues.

51

Eyes still on his, she blinked. He didn't falter.

Turning on her heel, she walked out. She knew they would have to talk about it later. Knew they needed to speak about what she'd said to him last night, before that glass had shattered everywhere.

Sometimes, when she was near him, she felt as if all the air went out of the room and only he had the ability to put it back.

There was nothing more that Cora wanted right then than to be at her best friend's drinking wine, even with the hangover.

It was Friday. Alec had late meetings and didn't go home until late. Tonight she could do what she wanted. Outside her office, her phone in one hand, she almost shifted from foot to foot at her indecision.

Part of her wanted to ask Frazer out.

Yesterday she'd wanted to be anywhere else but walking into that meeting in Frazer's office. And now she was considering asking Frazer for another drink?

The woman would think her insane.

Last night had been almost fun. Distracting. For the first time in a long time, Cora had felt like herself. It was as if parts of her were buried, and then last night those parts of her had crawled their way back out, trampling over patterns Cora hadn't even known had been stomped onto her insides.

But then, Cora had already been too friendly. Hugs between new friends weren't supposed to go on so long. They didn't cling like that. Most likely, Frazer was creeped out and wouldn't want drinks anyway. While she'd been friendly in the hallway, Cora had gotten no indication that Frazer wanted to hang and chat.

It was probably safer to go to her friend's and overeat while watching bad television.

"And where were you last night?"

That voice had Frazer dropping her head against the table top. She'd just wanted sushi. Quiet, tasty, uncomplicated sushi. After the day she'd had, she was craving California rolls. Work had been insane, and a breech birth Frazer had been asked to advise on had taken too long, which meant there had been no lunch. In the state she was in, Frazer had simply given some advice to the midwife. But, there'd been screaming and yelling and then tearing—yeah, she just wanted a quiet, easy dinner. Of sushi.

"I can see you, Frazer."

That didn't mean she would look up. In fact, Frazer kept her head on the table and clutched her chopsticks, praying the voice would go away.

She heard the rustle of a chair next to her being pulled out.

There were days Frazer loved her sister.

And on other days, she really wished she'd go live in another country—on the other side of the world.

A finger poked her none too gently in the shoulder, digging in. "I am actually touching you now, Frazer."

Sitting up, Frazer beamed. "Jemma. Hi!"

Green eyes glared at her. "Funny."

"Don't know what you mean. Sushi?"

One final glower, and her sister grabbed a plate of sashimi from the sushi train. She yanked Frazer's chopsticks out of her hands and dropped a piece in her mouth. "Thash goosh."

"I assume that means it's good."

Jemma nodded. "I love this place. I'm always here. I think, big sister, you came here secretly hoping you'd run into me."

Next time, she'd have to remember to get takeaway. "Oh, nothing else crossed my mind, Jem."

"Why are you so bitchy today?"

Another piece popped into Jemma's mouth, and Frazer gave up on getting her chopsticks back. She signalled for another pair. "Not bitchy, just—"

"Hung-over?"

A beat.

"No."

Jemma smirked. "Hopefully your fumes didn't get any babies drunk today."

That earned her sister a poke in the leg with her new chopsticks before she snapped them apart. "Only the one, and I think she was grateful. She had a long trip—the umbilical cord was stuck, and she was breech." Frazer hadn't gone near the baby, but Jemma didn't need to know that.

It was all it took. Her sister turned slightly pale, a piece of sashimi hovering close to her lips. "No," she commanded. "No work talk."

And Frazer hadn't even mentioned the mucous plug. "You started it."

"Now I'm finishing it. Change of topic, please?"

"Fine." Frazer asked the first question that popped into her head, "How's uni?"

"Ugh. Bad choice. Why did I decide to go for a PhD?"

"Don't look at me. I was never the brains."

Her sister suddenly looked like the toddler Frazer remembered from over twenty years ago. "It's so *hard,* Frazer. Being an adult sucks."

"Yeah, it does."

"Why does Tony do it so well?"

Frazer had no idea how he'd ended up with genes that enabled him to open his own real estate company and live in some rich suburb with his two-point-five kids. Sometimes Frazer liked to think that their parents had put all their genius parenting skills into their eldest son and just faffed it with their younger daughters.

Actually, Frazer loved the kids; they could stay.

"Beats me." Frazer said. "He was alone with our parents for five years. Maybe they gave up when they realised he couldn't be perfect and so they had me."

"Yeah, then over ten years later, they had me, 'cause you were a failure too."

Damn. That had backfired.

"You were an accident." It was the best Frazer could muster in her condition.

"Keep telling yourself that. How's the new fish?"

She felt somehow better with her annoying sister there. Frazer leaned back as much as she could in her hard plastic chair. "Dory and Nemo hate each other."

"No! That's like...like blasphemy."

"Aren't you doing philosophy? You should know it's not that."

"I said *like*, oh, pedantic one."

"Oh!" With more enthusiasm than she thought she was capable of, Frazer leant forwards. The last vestiges of her hangover were starting to fade. "How's your lit lecturer?"

Redness coloured Jemma's face, and she looked around frantically. "Shh!"

"Little sis, you're sleeping with your lecturer. I will not shush."

"And where were *you* last night, since you weren't at Uncle Jay's birthday? Drunk? Sleeping with some poor receptionist? Wait, I forgot you're terminally single—were you knitting?" Studying her face, Jemma's eyes lit up. "Or were you actually, finally, on a *date*?"

Frazer's gaze dove back to her sushi, too late to hide the flinch. Jemma cackled.

"Knew it—who'd you sleep with?"

The strange thing was, she'd been thinking of her night with Cora, not about Lauren.

"I'm sorry."

Cora rolled her eyes for the fourth time now. "Stop."

"I really am sorry."

Engulfed in a bean bag was how everyone should live their life. Especially after having spent an entire work day hung-over and ill, avoiding your husband-slash-boss, and trying to pretend everything in life was fine and dandy.

The fact that there was a very large glass of wine in Cora's hand made it all a bit better.

"Lisa, I understand. It wasn't that important, and you have nothing to be sorry for. Is your mum better?"

On the couch, looking much more like a put-together adult than Cora did, smooshed into the bean bag, Lisa pushed her fringe back so that the black strands stood in spikes around her face.

"Not really. Dad's trying to get a visa in, but it's been denied again, and all she does is ask for him."

"It's still being denied? How?"

Lisa flopped her back against the couch. "Yeah, I've sent the paperwork from the doctors with the certificate; hopefully they're going to allow a compassionate visa. Sometimes I wish my parents had managed to get married before they'd left Vietnam. Then we all would have qualified as refugees together and this wouldn't even be an issue."

Cora was well familiar with Lisa's ongoing battle against the red tape layered over Australian immigration laws that had kept Lisa's father in Vietnam while the rest of his family was here. Her mum had come over as a refugee when Lisa had just been a toddler, but for some reason, her father hadn't qualified. "Could he at least visit?" Frazer asked. When money had finally become less of an issue, her father had been able to visit a few times.

"He's waiting to see if he can get the compassionate visa to stay first. For now, we can really only get enough money together for one more trip."

"I'm sorry."

Lisa gave her a shaky smile. "Don't be. It is what it is. Maybe Mum's Alzheimer's will disappear and Dad will get a visa. Then life can resume, and I can be their kid again."

She said it as if it had ever been that way.

"That or we'll develop teleportation and just zap him here."

"Honestly, that's probably more likely."

They shared a knowing look.

"Now," Lisa said, "my grim life is getting me down. What happened last night?"

Cora slid deeper into the beanbag, a loud groan escaping her lips. Last night, all she had wanted to do was fall into a heap with her best friend, and now she wanted to forget everything. Couldn't she just do that? That's what she and her husband normally did, just went on as normal. Cora and Alec—dream team at avoidance.

Why did he have to throw *that* glass?

"Cora? Hello?"

Maybe Cora could just keep her eyes closed and stay in the softness of the beanbag forever. Sink into it like it was a cloud and watch *Friends* reruns and eat ice-cream. Wine flavoured ice-cream.

"Cora, you're not a bloody ostrich. Keeping your eyes closed doesn't make me go away."

"We just had another argument." There. She spoke. Her eyes might still be closed, but it was something.

Lisa was silent. That couldn't be good.

The silence pressured Cora into speaking again. "It wasn't a big deal."

"Then why did you leave the house?"

Her friend knew her too well. There were *things*, though, things that went beyond this argument with Alec, things that Cora hadn't told her. For a moment, with Lisa's sincere, dark eyes staring at her, Cora considered coming clean: about all the other fights she didn't come crying to Lisa over, the anger, the way that she and Alec flared up at each other all the time, or more how Alec flared up at her and how lately, Cora had started responding in kind. The way Alec hated her having anything in her life that wasn't about him, and how he made it feel like Cora's fault. She couldn't remember the last time they'd sat together, at ease in their own company. She'd finally voiced that she wanted out, and he was ignoring it, and she was happily letting him because she didn't know what she really wanted.

A twist of nerves and embarrassment in her gut put her off such confessions. Lisa was so...together. To tell her what a mess her marriage was, to admit she was failing at something that should be easy—it was all too shameful. All the gory details felt private, drenched in something that stopped her from wanting to talk about it.

"Just another shouting match. I can't even remember what it was about anymore."

She really didn't. Not what started it. Not how they ended up on opposite sides of the room again, yelling absurd words that fell heavily onto each other.

And instead of retreating, or backing down, she'd looked him square in the eye and said she wanted a divorce. And even now, she didn't know if she'd meant it.

The glass had shattered right over her head before she'd even seen it coming.

No. Her cheeks burnt at the memory. There was no way she could tell Lisa. Not her best friend, who had known her since high school as this loud and goofy girl and had slowly watched her become…someone else.

The look in Lisa's eye made her turn away and pour another glass of wine. She had to rock forward to reach it and felt like a turtle stuck on her back. The thought made her giggle.

Lisa was watching her with delight. "Something funny?"

"My butt is stuck in the beanbag."

"Well, you look elegant."

"Oh, I feel it. It's a good way to cap off today's hangover shame."

"Should I be jealous? What fabulous new friend have you been going out with, Miss Antisocial?"

Cora's mouth fell open. "I'm not—"

"Oh, please." Sipping her wine, Lisa grinned. "How many Facebook friends do you have?"

"Not relevant. I don't have Facebook."

Holding her hands up, Lisa grimaced as wine sloshed in her glass. "I rest my case."

"Nope. Facebook means nothing."

"How many contacts on your phone?"

"About…" Cora stopped her fingers from ticking off names when Lisa's laugh rang out. Sometimes her friend was infuriating.

"What?"

"If you can count them on your fingers, you've proved me right again. Now, spill: who'd you go out with?"

Wriggling down into the beanbag again, Cora gave up her attempts to defend herself. It was common knowledge she kept to herself. Why bother fighting it? "No one. I went alone to a bar like a loser."

"Wow." Lisa's eyebrows raised. "I'm impressed."

"Why?"

"Alone?"

"Yeah."

"Like, alone? In a bar?"

"Yes."

"With no one? Just you and your wine and a dirty bar full of drunks? Alone?"

She clenched her jaw. "Yes, Lisa, alone. Though if you must know, a work colleague was there and we drank too much tequila and I don't really remember much after that. Except that I got a good hug. Which I needed."

"You hugged your colleague?" If Lisa's eyebrows raised any more, they'd leave her head altogether.

"I think. I don't really remember it. I was drunk and sad. She took pity on me."

Those eyebrows returned to their original location. "Oh. She. I was starting to think you had a spicy affair forming."

Cora barked a laugh. "An affair? Me?"

"Well, you never know. A rustic hug, his stubble rubbing along your neck...oh, or your cheek."

"Maybe *you* need to go on a date."

Lisa laughed and didn't deny it, but Cora was already thinking that maybe a smooth cheek, soft against her own would feel good. She blinked and turned her attention back to Lisa.

That was new.

Deja vu crept over her, and she had no idea why.

There had been no more flirting with Lauren for two weeks.

Not that there had really ever been flirting.

So really, what Frazer meant was that she'd avoided Lauren for two weeks, like a teenager after an embarrassing date.

For two weeks, Frazer ducked around corners and stayed away from communal areas. After a very brief run-in outside the hospital in which Frazer had flashed an apologetic look and said something about being super busy the next few months, evasion finally succeeded. She just tried to forget the slightly disappointed look that had flitted across Lauren's face.

Not only that but Frazer started avoiding the weekly after-work drinks with friends. Andy, Rob, and Daniel probably thought she was dead.

Yet that wasn't the issue.

The issue was that she *wanted* to go out. She felt like being in a bar—the buzz of conversation, the alcohol, and the random music.

But she wanted to go with Cora, where there was no pressure, no discussing Frazer's private life, her non-existent love life. It had been a strangely enjoyable evening. And it had been something Frazer hadn't had in a really long time.

So, Frazer felt like meeting Cora again. And she couldn't.

The struggle was real. And also quite ironic.

So Frazer turned to exercise. Always a fan of the odd swim in which she would usually float up and down with the seniors who, shamefully, often lapped her—Frazer had lately been at the gym every day swimming laps until she thought her lungs would burst. Most days, she made herself do tumble turns, twisting herself mercilessly underwater to kick off against the end of the pool and keep going, despite the burning in her chest and the strain in her legs.

The itch to see Cora didn't go away.

What she really felt like doing was going back to that night in the bar. To chat with Cora, to see that side of her that Frazer hadn't known existed.

Just to chat.

Not to admire the legs that Frazer was noticing more and more. Or to think about how warm Cora had been, wrapped in Frazer's arms in a hug that had surprised Frazer with its intensity. There was a fuzzy memory of soft breath against her neck.

But Frazer couldn't think of that.

Because, you know, married to the boss and all that.

The boss that they were still waiting to hear from about their project proposal.

Two terrible Monday morning meetings, and nothing so far.

For the last two weeks, the intention to organise a coffee date or a catch-up for drinks with Cora had been there, but somehow, it had never happened. It must have been a full moon or something two weeks ago, because suddenly women everywhere were going into labour that Frazer had to see and Cora was constantly pulled away to other parts of the hospital. Frazer had never really thought about it before, but social workers were busy.

Not that she cared. Because being attracted to this woman was a useless waste of time, and she had no reason to be around her; so Frazer would just avoid her.

Before, Frazer barely saw her anywhere. Now she noticed her in the strangest places.

Not that it mattered.

But it had happened a few times in the canteen, where they managed to say a quick hello before one was paged away. Then Frazer had turned the corner to see Cora standing and staring at the ground, a tinge to her cheeks as Alec hissed something at her. With flashing eyes, Cora had looked up at him and hissed something right back. With no reason to want to see an awkward couple argument, Frazer had slipped away, hoping Cora hadn't seen her.

The vague memory of Cora saying they were having problems hung heavily in her mind, tangled with the taste of tequila. From what she knew, married couples slipped in and out of good and bad. Her own parents had had patches in which Frazer had figured they'd separate. Especially when her mother had fallen pregnant, a miraculous ten years after her last child.

Who knew what went on in married couples' lives?

Nothing Frazer wanted to know about, that was for sure.

Then she saw Cora a final time, and Frazer almost had a panic attack. She'd just wanted get her lunch from the staff room.

Yet, no.

The door opened easily, and Frazer had stepped inside before she stopped dead. Standing in the middle of the room, without a shirt, was Cora.

A moment of silence passed.

Cora's mouth dropped open.

Frazer bit her lip.

Then spun as Cora quickly pulled a shirt down over her head and jerked the door closed so anyone in the hallway couldn't see in. Frazer rolled her eyes upwards at herself. *Good move.* She really should say something.

"Shit—I'm so, so sorry," Her heart was racing.

There had been a deep red bra. The tone of Cora's skin was set off by the colour. Not that Frazer had noticed all that in the one second. Nor had she noticed the way Cora's hips curved, or the soft roundness of her stomach.

Nope. None of that had been noticed.

"Frazer, it's fine. It's not like I have a gremlin in my shirt. You can turn back around."

Slowly, Frazer turned, hoping the heat in her cheeks was just a sensation and they weren't actually flaming red.

Cora shot her a shy smile. "Besides—I think you see more than that every day."

"True." Finally, Frazer managed a nonchalant grin. At least she hoped it was nonchalant. Now dressed in a black T-shirt, Cora picked up her bag, and Frazer tried to stop imagining her doing it in only that bra. She'd never looked at her before like this. God, how awkward. Clearly Frazer needed to go back out with her friends. Or go swimming. Something. "Uh...how are you?"

There was a reason she had come into this room, Frazer was sure. But now all she could think about was getting out of there. She stepped backwards, ready to flee, her hand nudging backwards blindly to pull the door open again.

"I'm good." Cora dug out a clean pair of socks from her bag and started slipping them on. "Better now that I'm not covered in the vomit a kid managed to get all over me."

That made Frazer pause. "Isn't that the joy of social work? You avoid bodily fluids?"

"Wrong place, wrong time." The face Cora made was priceless. "It's not something I want to repeat."

"You should try it with placenta."

Eyes comically round, Cora shook her head so hard, her hair whipped around her face. "No, thank you. I'm fine."

Even the thought of vomit and placenta wasn't getting the image of that bra out of her head. "Well, glad you're clean. I'm just, gonna...go."

Before her foot was even out the door, the single word stopped her. "Frazer!"

She closed her eyes for a minute. When she turned back around, she had schooled her face into something cool, calm, and collected. "Yeah?"

Why did Cora look so small on that couch? Was she nervous?

"Want to get a drink again sometime?"

A note of pleading made Frazer pause on her no. "O...okay. Sure."

"Great—soon, yeah?" The small smile Cora offered was definitely off. "I could use someone to talk to."

Already backing out, Frazer said, "Sure. Soon."

She leant back against the door she closed behind her. Clearly, Cora needed friends. If she was asking Frazer, that much was clear. Thinking back, there wasn't really a time Frazer could remember seeing Cora with friends. Just Alec.

Always with Alec.

The two weeks he'd avoided doing anything about their project were lucky, really.

It meant Frazer could easily avoid hanging out with Cora.

The image of that red bra against Cora's russet-coloured skin invaded Frazer's mind again, and her eyes snapped open. There was no way in hell that Frazer was going to be the leering lesbian, the one who drooled over friends. So she thought Cora was hot? Big deal. She could be friends.

But so much for just avoiding her.

First though, she needed a bit of time to get that attraction out of her head. Her fingers hovered over her phone's screen to invite Andy and Rob to drinks. But then, her jaw clenched, she dropped her phone back into her pocket.

She'd go swimming instead.

Thankfully, the restaurant was loud and bustling. Candles littered the tables, casting a soft glow, the clinking of cutlery on china their background music.

Before they'd left the house, Cora had suggested somewhere new to Alec, an Italian place on the other side of the city in Fremantle. It was an area she'd used to love, full of charm and old buildings, cottages next door to the ocean, peppermint trees lining the streets. On a Friday like today, the markets were open, full of things she didn't need and hadn't known she'd wanted until she cast eyes on them. The sniff Alec had given in answer had been sufficient to demonstrate his thoughts of the idea, and instead they were at the place ten minutes from their house, as usual. If he didn't have to, Alec didn't like to go south of the river that divided the city.

"I have a conference next week."

"Mm?" Cora sipped her wine. When she put the glass down, the ring it made on the white tablecloth bothered her. "Where?"

"Brisbane. I should be gone a week." He was barely looking at her as he cut into his steak, so rare that it looked ready to walk off his plate with an indignant 'moo'.

"Which dates?" How depressing. She really had no idea what to say to him beyond benign questions.

"Around the fifth."

She fished for something concrete that could actually start a discussion. "What's the conference on?"

Alec sighed. "Management on macro and micro scales."

With that, Cora had no idea what to say anymore. "Ah."

Back to silence. And slow eating. The waiter took their plates away in practised perfection and returned a few minutes later for their dessert orders. Alec checked his phone before dropping it back in his pocket. When he sipped his drink, his eyes were anywhere but on her.

"So…" Cora made one last ditch attempt. "Where will you stay?"

The thud of his hands dropping to the table made her blink in surprise as for the first time in ten minutes, he looked her in the eye. "Jesus, Cora, what's with the interrogation?"

Cora sucked in a surprised breath. It had only taken thirty minutes this time. She tried to ignore the burn that crept into her cheeks. "It was just a question."

"Well maybe I don't feel like explaining every detail of my life to you."

"Maybe I just wanted to have a conversation with you?" Cora picked up her glass, her fingers trembling slightly. "But apparently you don't know how to do that anymore."

A beat of silence.

Alec cleared his throat. "Apparently *we* don't know how to do that anymore."

They stared at each other for a moment. Finally, Cora broke the eye contact, the feeling that she wouldn't win this one crawling up her spine. She never won. How it would play out danced in front of her eyes: Alec's further anger, the guilt, the way he'd twist each word she said around and around. She went back to her drink.

They continued together in uncomfortable silence. Dessert didn't improve the situation. Prickly heat danced along Cora's arms and along her back, the urge to scratch her skin difficult to repress. That band was back, wrapped around her chest. Her breaths were strange and uneven. Her gaze jolted around the room, catching sight of relaxed, normal couples. Did any of them feel like this? Like they were stuck on pause, something significant missing that would actually make them move forward?

For their first date, Alec had taken Cora to the ballet. The dance was one she had never seen, and now she couldn't even remember its name. The information was buried under layers of other useless facts more important than the case at work she'd left behind that afternoon, yet completely unattainable. Afterwards, he'd touched her as if she were made of glass, as if she would shatter under his boiling passion—his fingers at her jaw and his thumb leaving an imprint she was sure would feel like love. His gaze, intense and blue, never left hers when he made her come undone, as easily as if he could read her.

"What ballet did you take me to, our first date?" she asked.

Again, Alec didn't look up from his cake, ordered before she could say she didn't want any. The richness of it made her feel ill.

"God, I don't remember, Cora." When he looked up and caught her expression, something around his eyes softened. Crinkles appeared in the corners, ever so slight ones, but enough to make that band in her loosen. "*Giselle*, I think."

Later, that night, Cora lay naked under her covers for the first time in months. Was it months? Her brow scrunched together, Alec's bare back to her a metre away. Yes, at least two. Maybe three. Like any married couple, they had sex less and less. Whenever his hands searched for her under the covers like tonight, it was nice, as always, even if it had lost that passion that used to feel all consuming. Nevertheless, Cora had found herself avoiding it. Tonight, like often happened, flashes of his eyes, the look in them that made her feel small and stupid, had entered her head, memories of all the times he had been cold to her or had told her off or had brought her down. She'd frozen. Every emotion associated with those memories settled over her, heavy and choking—the feeling in her stomach when she'd apologise to keep the peace, with no idea what she was apologising for, sure somehow that it should really be *him* saying it.

She often found herself turning her head away, even as his lips touched her cheek.

Overhead, shadows danced from the tree outside their window, and if she stared at them long enough, she could lose herself in picking out shapes.

Two weeks ago, she'd told him that she was leaving, and she'd thought she had meant it.

She still thought she had.

Yet, when the words built up in her lungs, worked their way up her throat, they always faltered on her tongue.

When had she lost her courage?

Her parents had once said there was a fire in her no one could ever put out. A fire that drove her curiosity, her determination. Her father had always laughed and said he hoped she'd never change.

But she had changed.

So slowly, she'd only just started to notice it.

CHAPTER SIX

"Push!"

"I can't."

The woman in front of Frazer was too exhausted to even sob. Her knees shook, and her hair, so perfectly done when she had arrived, was a limp mess around her face.

"One more, and the hard part's over." Frazer put a steadying hand on the woman's knee. "I promise."

That moment, that exact moment, was why she loved her job. Everything narrowed down to the exhausted patient and Frazer. Glazed eyes opened to stare at her and Frazer stared unblinkingly back. The woman's face was crimson. She bore down, and a new baby slithered out, wet, blue, and unmoving. This was the easy part. Tears streamed down the woman's face as she slumped back and Frazer placed the now-screaming baby on her stomach. Her partner ran trembling fingers gently over the dusting of hair on the newborn's tiny head. She dropped a blanket over the baby, soft and prc-warmed.

Frazer cleaned up, a few stitches almost gone unnoticed except for the quick glare from the mother that she met with a sympathetic wince. Fifteen minutes later, she left the room, hands scrubbed clean and the family curled up together on the bed.

She'd been with the family from the beginning, a part of their prenatal care, of their birthing plan—which, as Frazer had warned might happen, had gone completely out the window at the first plea for pain relief. She'd allowed herself an internal chuckle at that. Birthing plans were a great thing in theory, but rarely worked out. Part way through, the mother had thrown the ice chips to the floor that her partner was lovingly trying to feed her and hissed, "This is all your fault!"

A good sign that the birth was progressing nicely.

The rest of the day passed in much the same way, three births, one ending in a C-section, much to the mother's devastation. Frazer had gripped her hand. "I came from a C-section, and look how awesome I turned out."

The strangled chuckle was enough to feel as if she'd helped.

Exhausted, Frazer stumbled into her office to start some of the paperwork that needed doing so desperately. She had rosters to figure out, budgets to look at. A glance out of her window showed nothing but the car park. She slumped her head on the desk.

She needed a holiday.

The sudden knock on her door had her jerking up and self-consciously grabbing a pen, holding it over whatever random paper was on her desk.

"Come in!"

Tia popped her head around. "Hey, Frazer."

"Hi. Nice hair."

Tia toyed with the ends, newly red strands twirling around her fingers. "Thanks. My husband hates it."

"Great. Never change it."

They shared a wicked grin.

"Just wanted to let you know the on call midwife for tonight is sick," Tia said.

Frazer pouted at her. The shrug Tia gave back bordered on sympathetic.

"I know. Guess who's second on call?"

"Yes, I know. It's me. Great—can't wait." A thought occurred to Frazer, and she perked up. "Oh, drat," she said with heavy irony. "Now I have to cancel on dinner with my family."

"See—silver linings." Tia began to walk out, then popped her head around the door again. "Oh, and Frazer, you're writing all over the desk."

Frazer dropped her pen.

"That'll be all, Tia."

Tia snorted and disappeared.

"Wait!"

Her head appeared again. "I'm going to damage my neck soon." At Frazer's sheepish wince, Tia softened. "What?"

"Is Alec in his office?"

"Yeah. I'd get in quick, though."

And this time, she disappeared completely.

Great. Another on call. Who needed a life?

With a scowl at her in-tray, Frazer decided to go and bite the bullet. As she exited her office, she caught sight of Cora chatting at a nurse's desk. With an inward grimace, Frazer turned and disappeared down the other end of the hallway.

She'd be Cora's friend. Soon.

In front of Alec's door, she took in a deep breath and rapped her knuckles against the wood.

When Frazer entered, Alec's tight look of greeting made Frazer realise how truly terrible Alec was at hiding what he thought. It was obvious he didn't want to be talking to Frazer. The office, stark and grey, was as boring as her own.

"Hey, Alec!" If only she could appear that cheery to her own mother, life would be much easier.

Suspicion crinkled around his eyes. "Hi. Take a seat."

So she did. They stared at each other for a beat.

"So, how can I help you?"

Frazer smiled at him. Held his eye. Her chin jutted out slightly, and she thought she should rein it in, but wanted him to know she meant business. "Any news on the project approval? Surely you received my multiple e-mails asking if a decision was on the way?"

He gave a nod. "I received them."

Seriously? That's all he would say after making her send all of those revisions? This was why Frazer had always wanted to start this programme outside of the hospital system, to create her own clinic and avoid these games. But the idea of not having the safety net and resources from the hospital was a pretty scary thought. If she could just get Alec behind the project.

"Okay. Great." Frazer smiled again. Just keep playing the game. "You would have seen, then, that there were many changes put in place to make it less of a financial burden, to include more volunteers and to actually free up Social Work's budget."

Alec leaned back in his chair and nodded. "I saw."

God. Bosses did her head in. "Great. And what did you think?"

For a moment, she thought he wasn't going to answer since it would have required more than a three-word sentence. He proved her wrong, but only just. "It's gone to the board."

"And that means..." If she didn't know better, she could swear he was repressing enjoyment.

"I should have an answer by next week. I'm at a conference, but when I get back, I'll give you your answer in Monday's meeting."

Damn Mondays. At least this one had the potential to be good.

"Any hint?" She would have winked, but for some reason, he didn't strike her as the type who'd find it funny. She settled for a charming grin.

That hint of a smile must have been nothing, because he gave a curt shake of his head. "No."

"Okay." Standing to go, Frazer turned away. "Thanks for your time."

"Frazer?"

She paused in the doorway. Before she managed to get a look at him, his eyes were already back on the computer.

"Yeah?"

He let a beat pass. He still didn't look at her. "If it means anything," he said, "I hope they pass it. The revisions were good."

When she walked away, it was with a skip in her step.

If someone said yes to drinks, they should really have the courtesy to actually follow up on the invitation.

Instead, all Cora managed to do was see the back of Frazer's head in hallways or a glance of her at a nurse's station. She received a few e-mails saying that there'd been no news on the project and that they were waiting for Alec to come back from his conference. Somehow, there had been a hint in the e-mails that Alec was on board.

Cora and Alec didn't speak about it at home. It edged too close to a truth that had once bound them together, a pregnancy that had brought them together. It was as if he was completely ignoring her involvement, and that could keep that truth far away.

But stupid Frazer just avoided her; or at least that's what she seemed to be doing.

You would think that hospitals were huge, considering Cora could never seem to find Frazer. In reality, she had no idea why she was so determined to catch Frazer for a drink. Lisa was fantastic but so busy with her mother, and, really, besides her, Cora had no one. Frazer, whom she had once thought was kind of loud and obnoxious, was actually kind of funny. Maybe Cora just needed a good laugh and that was why she wanted to see Frazer more.

Also, now that Cora had gotten to know Frazer more, she found that the woman bordered less on the arrogant and more on the confident side of things. A certain cockiness coated her steps, and it could easily be misread, which, it seemed, was exactly what Cora had done.

Cora was trying with Alec. Her marriage was crumbling around her, and even as she desperately tried to gather it back up in her fingers and mesh it back together, she was left with the feeling that what she ended up with wouldn't be what she had started with.

What she had started with, she was beginning to believe, was gone.

However, the more she pulled away, the more Alec gripped tighter. It didn't feel like anything she did pleased him anymore. Sometimes all Alec had to do was breathe and she wanted to get up and walk out of the room. Once in sync, so long ago, they now grated. Cora had started to wonder if she'd imagined that synchronicity; now it felt like she couldn't rest easily until she and Alec were separated. Then she would float around, uncomfortable in her own home and her space, unsure where she belonged.

The gap between them when they slept was so wide that they could fit all of their issues in it and still have room to move. The urge to roll over and press herself against him never arose anymore, and he rarely sought her out deep in the night either like he used to, half-asleep but still wanting her close. There were days, years ago, when she'd slept pressed along his side, his arm hooked around her shoulders. Even their insecurities couldn't have slipped in between them. The scent of him had soothed her to sleep, etching him along her skin so she could carry him with her throughout the next day.

Now she found herself pushed aside until she was laying along the edge, leg hanging over as if poised to run at any moment.

What she needed was something else to occupy her mind, a friend to keep her distracted. Someone who knew nothing of her or her past or, well, anything.

Distraction. New friends. All of these were good things.

But why the avoidance? Maybe Frazer didn't want a new friend. She probably had a great, happening social life and didn't need the thirty-four-year-old married lady weighing her down. Or maybe the sight of her half-naked in the staff room had terrified Frazer and made her run away. It wasn't as if Cora didn't avoid her own image in the mirror too. Considering Frazer's job, though, surely she had seen worse.

But there had been that odd moment when Frazer had paused, biting her lip as she turned away, pink tinging her cheeks. It had struck Cora as a little strange.

Twisting her blue social worker's polo shirt to make it more comfortable, Cora stopped in her tracks. Frazer was by the canteen coffee cart, waiting for her order, leaning against a wall as she idly flicked through her phone.

"Hi." The word left Cora's lips even as she was still sucking up her courage. She tried to ignore feeling like the shy kid approaching a cooler one in the playground. She was an adult. An adult who would make decisions and take some control in her life. Being a grown up; that was what she was doing.

Frazer's warm smile lit up her features. It wasn't an angry smile, or an oh-God-leave-me-alone-already smile. That was good. Some of the tension fell from Cora's shoulders.

"Cora! Hey! So strange. I was going to find you today to see if you wanted to get that drink."

"You were? I mean...great. Cool." Seriously, there were days Cora hated her lack of social abilities. *Cool?* What was she, fourteen?

"Yeah, sorry it's been so long since I agreed to it. Work's been so hectic, you have no idea." Frazer's lips quirked up in a crooked grin, that prominent dimple on her left side showing. "Well, you work here, so, actually, you probably do."

The barista called Frazer's order.

As she leaned forward to take the coffee, Frazer's hair brushed along Cora's neck and shoulder. Goosebumps ran along Cora's skin, and the soft scent of citrus invaded her senses. Recognition itched at the back of her brain, and she remembered, vaguely, that hug on her porch.

Clearly, Cora was desperate for affection.

Frazer took a long sip of her coffee, her eyes closing in bliss.

"Needed a caffeine hit?" Cora asked.

That dimple appeared again. "I really did. I've had to cover so many on calls lately—I swear every woman in this city is having her baby at three a.m. just to get at me."

"Sure, blame the babies."

"Good idea. They can't defend themselves." Another sip of coffee, and Frazer's eyes took her in, making Cora feel slightly self-conscious. "You okay?"

Why did she ask that? "Yeah, I'm fine. Great. So—when are you free for that drink?"

"Tomorrow night?"

Tomorrow morning, Alec went on his week-long conference. It fit well with her plans for that evening. "Tomorrow sounds great. Any good bar ideas?"

"The Scraped Goat?"

Cora stared at her. "What?"

"The Scraped Goat."

"That's what I thought you said. That's a bar?"

"Yep, and a great one. You in?"

Cora nodded. "I'm in—as long as no goat is present."

When Frazer laughed, it was rich and warm, like toffee slowly melting on your tongue. "No goats. It's on the river, near the belltower. Good beer—do you like lager?"

"Of course. I lived in Fremantle in my uni days."

With a raise of her takeaway cup, as if to salute her, Frazer nodded. "Excellent. The Scraped Goat, tomorrow. Shall we say seven?"

"Seven it is."

"Great. I can tell you in more detail about how Alec gave me some hope for our programme."

Their programme? Inexplicable warmth spread over Cora.

The last thing Cora wanted to do was talk about Alec. But she offered a nod, one she hoped looked enthusiastic.

As Frazer walked off to deliver babies or direct others to do so, Cora wanted to pat herself on the back. Step one of turning her life around—making new friends—was coming along nicely. Now it could be time to start attempting those other steps.

Ones that had been clawing at her for so long, it felt like she'd become a professional at ignoring them.

"Where have you been?"

The accusatory glare that accompanied that statement could have made a child pee their pants. All it did to Frazer was incite an eye-roll.

"Hi, Jemma." Swinging her front door open, Frazer reminded herself she loved her sister even as Jemma swanned past, none-too-gently elbowing her in the side.

"Don't 'hi' me. You fell off the face of the earth for weeks. I think Mum was about to call the police."

By the time Frazer closed the door, Jemma was sprawled on her couch with her shoes kicked off.

"Please, make yourself at home."

"Oh, I will. Got any beers?"

Resigned to the next few hours, Frazer got two pale ales and shoved her sister's legs aside to sit down next to her, only to have those legs dumped back over her lap when she did. There were times a sister was more of a burden than a gift. The way her parents told the story, when Frazer was informed she was getting a sister, Frazer had stared at her parents until they had started to become concerned. Then she had simply turned on her heel and stalked off. All Frazer remembered was a heavy feeling of resentment.

"So, who's the girl?" Waggling her eyebrows, Jemma took a long sip.

"There's no girl, Jemma."

"Don't believe you."

"Okay."

Frazer counted down from five in her head, and right on cue, the silence got to Jemma, exactly as Frazer knew it would.

"Frazer! Why have you disappeared?"

When Jemma was young, she'd last three seconds. It was impressive, really, that at twenty-five, her sister now made it an entire two seconds longer. "You know Mum can't handle more than a day of no contact."

"She manages when I have a girlfriend she doesn't want to meet."

This time, Jemma responded with silence.

Sighing and dropping her head back on the couch, Frazer bit her lip. "Sorry. That was uncalled for."

Jemma squeezed her legs in a mock hug. "Not really. You know it's just, well, Mum. Traditionalists and all that. She still loves you. Dad does too."

They sat for a moment, drinking their beer. The ticking from the clock behind them was abnormally loud. The fizz in her beer was making her feel ill. Internally, Frazer kicked herself. This was one thing she really just had to keep her mouth shut about. Her mum tried, and her dad tried to make her mum try harder. It wasn't Jemma's fault that their mixed-descent southern Indian and Australian parents had had certain ideas so impressed upon them by their own parents and grandparents.

In the end, Jemma broke the slightly uneasy silence. "Anyway, stop detracting from my original question with your fake problems." The nudge from her foot took the sting from the words. "Where have you been?"

"Nowhere, I swear. I've just been, well, *busy*. I've been swimming again."

"Really? Like, not the one where you float by with the geriatrics but actually swimming? Like, with speed and purpose?"

In spite of wanting to strangle Jemma half of the time, at least she was amusing. There was no sulking with her little sister, even if it was mostly from bemusement. "That would be the one."

"Wow. I'm impressed. Now, the real question is—what drove you to that? I ran into Andy last week—you do remember her, right? Your best friend since university? You two were joined at the hip for years? About yay high?" Jemma held her hand up as high as she could from the couch. "Awesome dreadlocks and does wicked dot paintings and other traditional art with her cousin—her cousin Daniel, who's dating your other friend Rob? That Andy?" Jemma ignored the dirty look sent her way. "Well, *she* said she hasn't seen you in, like, three weeks. So that means you're not even going out."

"I've been busy." Frazer took a sip and tried to ignore the intense gaze on her.

With an abrupt movement, Jemma jerked up her legs and pushed herself onto her elbows, almost making Frazer chip her tooth on her beer bottle. "Oh my God. Did you get burnt?"

"What? No."

"You so did. Did someone break your icy heart, big sister?"

Frazer poked Jemma's leg and wished she hadn't answered the door. "Seriously, I've just been busy."

"Mhm. Well, the social butterfly sister *I* know sees her friends at least a few times a week. Oh my God." Jemma sat up completely, her heels pressing painfully into Frazer's thigh. "Did you re-enter the dating pool, and it went badly?"

"Jemma, I swear, you're not too old to wedgie."

Another glare, and Jemma looked five years old. "I swear to God if you ever do that again, I'll photocopy the journal you left at Mum's house and scan it to Facebook."

Grinning, Frazer shook her head. "No, you won't. I burnt it last year."

"Oh, please, I'll just write a fake one. I pretty much know it by heart anyway." Jemma cleared her throat as if about to give a world-changing speech, but when she spoke, it was with her best mimicking voice. *"Today I watched a movie with Drew Barrymore—I think I'm supposed to notice the guy, but all I could think about was her—"*

A pillow in the face cut Jemma off. She pulled it down against her stomach, looking smug, beer secure in her other hand.

"That wasn't at all how it went." The tone in Frazer's voice was too high-pitched, even to her.

"Sure, Sis."

"And besides, it was Jodie Foster, not Drew Barrymore."

"Same, same."

"It is *not* the same."

Jemma lay back down, her bottle resting on her stomach. "Whatever. Something's up with you."

"It's really not."

"Sure, Sis."

This was past irritating and rounding to kick-her-out-of-the-house zone.

"How's your lecturer?" Frazer asked.

Frazer ducked the pillow before it hit her in the face.

The words exploded, like a carbonated drink overshaken. For Cora, the morning had ticked by agonisingly slowly, the plan to say her piece when he couldn't argue, minutes before he left the house to make his plane.

If there was something Alec couldn't abide more than conversing with his wife, it was being late.

Afterwards, the words floated through the air like mist, impossible to pull back and ram down her throat. Alec stared at her, his face pale. The urge to make a retraction, to shake her head, to make the look leave his face reared, large and ugly.

"You what?" His voice was tight.

"I want to separate."

He blinked rapidly. His fist tightened around the handle of his carry-on suitcase. The suit he wore, ironed perfectly, sat so well on him that she felt a tug, low in her stomach. In that moment, he looked like he did the night they had graduated. When she'd straightened his tie and he'd kissed her, excitement strong on his tongue as his career lay out before him. Had it been happening even then? The suffocation, the feeling of being squeezed into a box?

"You don't mean it, Cora."

But she did. She meant every word.

The way her heart was beating made it difficult to hear herself think. She licked her lips. Next to her, on the mantelpiece, their wedding photos were lined up, a marching formation to nowhere.

"I do."

"You can't do this to me." The muscles in his jaw clenched.

But she had to. Before it got worse.

There was no knowing where they were going, but they'd beaten their marriage to death for too long. They'd tried. But over the years, she'd followed him, not noticing how he chipped away at her, how the steps demanded she left things behind so she could keep up. When had she started to do what he wanted, when he wanted, to pacify him? When she stumbled, when had he stopped helping her up instead of turning a frustrated glare at her, eventually not noticing at all? When had he stopped wanting to ask her about her day? And had he ever really asked?

When had she done everything, changed everything, to accommodate him?

She met his eye, took in a breath. "I can."

His face hardened, and he didn't look like that boy at graduation. "You won't."

The swallow almost hurt her throat. The urge to say she didn't mean it tightened her chest, begged to be said.

Maybe they could fix it.

A beep. He looked down at his watch. "I have to go. We'll talk when I get back."

And then he turned and walked out as if they were finished talking.

The door slammed, and she jumped.

The clock ticked behind her.

The thumping of her heart left her breathless, dizzy. She wrapped her arms around herself.

Really, Cora had no idea if she had managed to do what she had wanted or not.

Cora was Frazer's friend, and that was fine.

Great, even.

Because, clearly, this woman needed one.

"Marriage, Frazer, is stupid."

Clearly.

Though at least Cora was able to get married. Opening her mouth to say so, Frazer snapped it shut. It was an unhelpful comment, and her response would be unnecessary—Cora didn't mean anything by it. This wasn't about her. Being a good friend meant listening.

"*Really* stupid."

Also, Frazer was beginning to think she had gotten her boss's wife drunk.

Again.

Drinks had started easily. Being friends with Cora was not as difficult as Frazer had thought. It was clear that something was wrong. Cora was gnawing on her lip, her eyes darting around. However, after a pint of great lager Cora hadn't really taken the appropriate time to savour, she'd calmed down and left a slightly awkward pause in its wake.

Slowly conversation built, and after two more beers, it was almost flowing.

When they'd arrived, all the decent tables outside had been taken. Unable to sit near the water, they didn't bother facing the cooler weather without the great view, so they sat opposite each other in a booth. The bar was all smooth, with dark-red polished wood, cosy and warm. At some point, a flush had worked its way across Cora's cheek, faint but accentuating her cheek bones.

Yes, Cora was attractive, but she was funny and, when not being strange, easy to talk to. Frazer had never been on the search for a new friend—she had her few friends, and she found large groups exhausting. When she went out, she went with a tight-knit group, all who liked to drink and party but also to sit around talking each others' ears off.

But maybe a new friend wouldn't be so bad. Someone at work who she could unwind with over a drink and rant about work-type things. Andy and Rob both worked in economics, and so after one night of talking about Australia's apparently struggling economy, Frazer had started talking about a vaginal tear so bad that it had needed surgery. They had gotten the hint and didn't discuss work anymore.

If Cora wanted to rant about her marriage, she could go ahead. At work, Frazer would just pretend it wasn't Alec. She'd imagine Alec was some guy, her boss, and that was all. Like he had nothing to do with the man Cora was talking about.

"It *is* stupid." Frazer said.

Eyes lit up at Frazer's agreement, then Cora quickly narrowed them. "You're mocking me."

Maybe a little. But couples did this all the time. Hated their marriage, then loved it again. Had ups and downs. "Just the part that sounded like a teenager."

The door opened, and for some reason, Frazer looked up. Her mouth probably dropped open. Everything stopped for a moment.

"Frazer?"

She could feel Cora's eyes on her and the questioning tone in her voice. But Frazer still stared across the room at the group that had entered and wished she was anywhere but here. Her mouth now was strangely dry and Frazer licked her lips.

"Frazer!"

Tearing her gaze away, Frazer tried to give Cora a smile. She was fairly sure she just looked constipated.

"What's wrong?" As Cora looked around, her brow furrowed. But she seemed not to notice anything out of the ordinary.

"Can we go?" Frazer asked.

She didn't wait for an answer. The presence across the room was closing in on her. Cora was staring at her like she had no idea what was happening, which she probably didn't. Frazer grabbed Cora's hand and half dragged her up, her grip on Cora like a clamp as she wound around people.

"Frazer, we haven't even finished our drinks."

"They were overpriced anyway."

The door was so close. She could almost escape.

"Isn't that all the more reason to actually drink them?"

So close to the door. Hopefully, she'd get out before—

"Frazer, hi."

Face-to-face with the one person she was trying to escape. Frazer closed her eyes for a moment. Of course she couldn't just make a clean break out of here. And why was Naomi here, anyway? She'd transferred after leaving Frazer's life in ruins and destroying her trust in humanity.

Maybe Naomi made Frazer mildly dramatic. Maybe.

She opened her eyes. Made herself smile. It was harder than it should be. She wasn't a wreck anymore, but seeing her ex always brought up unwanted feelings of general grossness.

"Hi, Naomi."

They stared at each other for a moment. Frazer blinked. Why step in front of her if there was nothing to say?

"How are you?" Naomi asked.

Frazer could have sighed. Why did they have to do this? "Really well. And you?"

"I'm great." How nice for her. "I heard you're getting closer to getting that little project off the ground. That's fantastic."

Frazer felt like she was treading uneven ground. Was that "little" condescending or had it just been said innocently? Condescending wasn't something Naomi had ever seemed to do. But there had been a time Frazer hadn't thought she would just up and leave either.

Also, people were starting to hear about the programme, and that sparked some excitement in the back of Frazer's mind, excitement that was overshadowed by the panic that still had Frazer gripping Cora's hand.

Attempting friendly, Frazer nodded. "Yeah, hopefully."

Frazer could almost *feel* Cora behind her, watching the exchange.

"That's amazing. Good for you."

"Thanks." Was it too impolite to leave yet? "I heard you were, uh..." Frazer had heard nothing. Just as she preferred. "Are you still at the eastern suburbs hospital?"

Naomi nodded. "Yeah, I am, with Bee."

How nice. They were still together. "That's great."

They stood for a minute, in the type of awkward silence that always feels heavy. Naomi shifted from foot to foot. Maybe she had finally realised that this was a weird situation and that it would've been better to just pretend she hadn't seen Frazer.

"Great." Frazer said. "Well, it was *great* seeing you. Be well."

Be well?

And then, still dragging Cora, Frazer left the bar, only satisfied when the door swung shut behind them.

Once she was finally outside, Frazer dropped Cora's hand when it struck her that she hadn't yet done so. Her cheeks were hot with embarrassment. She'd been so anxious in that situation that she'd clung to a friend's hand. How adolescent.

The air was cool, the twilight a milky blue. Everything smelt crisp and clean, cyclists and joggers whirring their way along the river. Frazer's fingers felt clammy as a breeze played around them.

She grinned at Cora. The action hurt only a little. "So—different bar?"

Cora shook her head, one eyebrow raised. "Don't think you're getting away with not explaining whatever *that* was."

Shoulders sagging, Frazer dialled her grin down to normal. "Didn't think you'd let me."

"Old midwife rival? High school fight that you never got over?" Cora pursed her lips as she thought. "Ah, I know. She cursed you when you were a child, and that's why you're so sarcastic and brittle: you're hiding the fact that you're really nine hundred years old?"

Frazer could swear she heard crickets chirp as she stared at Cora. "What?"

With a shrug, Cora said, "I don't know. I'm really bad at guessing."

Now Frazer could say she was genuinely smiling. Unlike the one before, at least this one wouldn't scare small children. She really would have to say something about what just happened.

"That was the ex."

"Oh." An expression Frazer didn't recognise flitted across Cora's features. "Well, I was way off." A beat of silence. "She was so important she got a definite article before 'ex'?"

A chuckle bubbled out of Frazer's chest. "We all have one of those, don't we?"

"I don't."

"Seriously?" Frazer grimaced. "Way to make me feel inferior."

They started to walk, the river on their right, fingers buried in their pockets to ward off the chill.

"I wouldn't feel inferior. I think most of you mere mortals have 'the ex,'" Cora said, her voice low.

The breeze was brisk as it blew over the water, now deeply black in the fading light. Streetlights switched on, and the distant sound of traffic and the thudding of joggers' feet joined the lapping of the river against the bank.

Frazer pressed her hands deeper in her pockets. She nudged Cora with her shoulder. "Mere mortals?"

"Well, you can't all be perfect like me."

The sarcasm lacing her words was delicious.

"Yeah, we'll all bow down to your godliness."

"Good." Cora gave a nod.

Frazer sucked in a deep breath. "It wasn't even a terrible breakup, I was just left blindsided."

Frazer hated talking about it. Every time she did, even years later, the sting of it settled low in her stomach. She preferred it when she simply didn't see her ex-girlfriend.

"No warning?"

"I imagine most people feel like that, but there really hadn't been. Not that I'd noticed. I thought we were great. I was certainly happy."

"And then?"

"And then she told me she'd met someone." Frazer's voice sounded tight and she cleared her throat, wishing her body wouldn't betray her. "There hadn't been any cheating, just someone who made her realise she wanted more."

Inadequacy, sharp and cutting.

"Well, she was an idiot. Who wears shoes like that with those jeans? Clearly an idiot."

Frazer chuckled. "Clearly."

The unease in her stomach ebbed away.

"Have you seen dolphins here before?"

Blinking at the change of topic, but grateful for it, Frazer swept her gaze over the still river.

"Again, sadly, I'm a mere mortal and I've never had the luck."

Cora's teeth flashed white at her. "That's a pity—I saw a baby one with my friend Lisa the other week. They were swimming just a few metres from the embankment."

"Lucky."

They settled in silence, walking slowly. The buzz from the beer wore down to nothing. Finally, Frazer felt her balled fists relax, her nails no longer biting into her palm. Her ex was not someone she wanted to see. Ever. But it was hurting a lot less right then than it would normally. Maybe time had finally done its thing.

"So," Cora's voice broke into her thoughts, "when did you realise you were gay?"

Frazer laughed.

The third night after Alec left, he still hadn't messaged her. In return, neither had Cora. He liked to wait her out, for her to cave—to crawl back, at the times in which he could put all the blame on her. This time, she needed him to know she was serious.

She needed out.

"Cora, what's going on with you?"

Under the table, Lisa's foot nudged hers gently.

"Sorry." Cora raised her gaze, wincing at the softness in Lisa's. "I was thinking."

"That was obvious." As Lisa chewed slowly, her eyes never left Cora's. "Talk to me."

Cora waved her hand airily. "You have a lot on your plate."

Maybe she shouldn't have agreed to lunch. Her friend read her like a book.

Yet Cora had had drinks with Frazer. For some reason, that felt different. There was no history between them, it was easier to not talk if she didn't want to or not unleash the storm that was building in her head. Frazer had no real preconceived ideas about her. It was easier, sometimes, to be who you needed to be with someone new.

"Exactly. So distract me with your plate."

Her gaze roamed throughout the diner. Cora wondered why she hadn't chosen a different one. This was where she and Alec used to go on lunch breaks. The place was old with cracks on the linoleum floor. Water stains trudged along the tables, and the smell of somewhere people *used* to smoke hung in the air, damp and bordering on sickly sweet.

But the sandwiches were the best-kept secret in Perth, and the place gave a discount to hospital employees.

"Cora."

She forced herself to make eye contact. "Yeah?"

"Spill."

"I told Alec I wanted a divorce."

"Again?"

Cora answered with a nod. "Again. But seriously this time."

"Did he listen?"

"No. But I stuck to it. He said we'd speak when he got back, like it was negotiable."

For a moment, Lisa didn't say anything. When she answered, her words were measured. "I hope you meant it."

Cora's mouth fell slightly open as she stared at her. "You... you do?"

Lisa's words were a gift, wrapped warmly in Cora's chest, quelling the insecurity. "You haven't been yourself for a long time."

They went back to their sandwiches. The bite Cora took was big, the food tasting better than it had five minutes before.

"Don't let him get in your head, Cora."

Cora looked up sharply. "What do you mean?"

With a sigh, Lisa's fingers touched Cora's wrist, her fingertips just brushing the skin. "Each time you guys have an argument, it starts out with you angry, but then the next time I speak to you, you're suddenly feeling like it's your fault."

"That—that's not true." The tips of Cora's fingers felt like ice.

"Sometimes it is. Unless he's done something he knows he can't twist around. Then he comes back and makes you feel bad for him."

"I..." Cora didn't know what to say to that, how to confront the fact that Lisa's truth was as sharp as a splinter and was digging into Cora as if to make her gasp at the sudden shock of it.

"What are you going to do?" Lisa asked, fingers slipping off Cora's wrist.

At that, Cora floundered for a moment, covering her lack of planning by taking a long sip of water. "I don't know. I just—I need to stick to it. I need a distraction."

Her mind went to Frazer, to drinking too much, and to being hung-over at work.

Something almost cheeky flashed in Lisa's eye. "You need a toy boy."

Eyes wide, Cora felt a flush along her cheeks. "I'm sorry, what did you just say?"

"A toy boy. Someone younger, fresh. I mean, just to look at, clearly. Your marriage is up in the air. But just something to keep your eye on the prize?"

All Cora could do was stare.

"The prize being freedom," Lisa said as if that was the part Cora had been confused by.

"Got that, thanks, Lise." The wicked glint was still in her friend's eye. "What have you done with my best friend?"

"Oh, come on. You were always so *good*. Studied hard, married your university boy straight up—you don't want to go experience any of those things you didn't do back then?"

"What things are those, huh?" Cora leant forward. "What were you apparently doing while I was studying my butt off?"

"Not telling."

"Lisa." There was definitely a pleading note to Cora's voice. "Tell me."

"Just a few parties. Made some mistakes, but don't regret them."

"You," Cora said slowly, "are telling me nothing."

"True." The grin plastered on Lisa's face grew wider. "Oh, Cora. I just—I just didn't think sometimes. I went with things and learnt from them. Probably slept with a few too many boys. Tried cocaine."

Cora's mouth dropped open. "You *did*?"

At university, Cora hadn't been a nun. She'd gone out, she'd drunk some. But she hadn't pushed the edges. Hadn't thought she'd wanted to. Plus, she'd always had Alec pulling her to his side at parties and talking her into blowing off plans to stay with him.

"Yeah. And it was a stupid idea. But, you know, it was something to try."

There was something stronger playing at the edges of Lisa's eye.

"Lisa, what else?"

For some reason, Cora's heart was pounding.

"I slept with my housemate."

Sex was never something that made Cora blush—she may not have had as much fun as Lisa throughout university, but it wasn't something that caused her to feel shame. So why were her cheeks hot? "Your housemate was a girl."

That devilish grin was back. "Oh, I know."

"Was... Was it good?"

Why did Cora care?

The shrug Lisa gave did nothing to quench her curiosity. "It was an experience—it happened a few times, after parties."

"And?"

"Cora, go find out yourself!"

The urge to mention that her new friend was a lesbian rose up Cora's throat. She swallowed it down with a sip of water.

"I like men," Cora said instead.

"Yes, I know. Me too. So go find a toy boy instead. I'm telling you all this because you need to let yourself have some fun. Or join a yoga class—I really don't care, just do something for you."

Cora's mouth opened to say that she would, then snapped closed again. There was nothing in her mind to offer, nothing she knew she wanted to do. The hair on the back of her neck prickled as she realised she hadn't thought about things to do for herself in far too long. Her chest felt hollow. What had happened to that list she once had? Long and full of blossoming ideas, places to go, things to check off?

Lisa's eyes, deep and imploring, refused to look away, even as she watched Cora flounder for something to say.

Swallowing, Cora gave a nod. "Okay."

Lisa's lips curved up. "Good."

"Maybe I'll swim with sharks."

Lisa barked a laugh. "Or go cliff diving."

"Eat puffer fish."

"Try parkour."

"Go heli-skiing." Cora felt lighter, now.

"Or, you know, see your friends more." Lisa winked, reaching for the tomato sauce. "Whatever."

CHAPTER SEVEN

"Coffee?"

In the gap between the door and the frame, a coffee waggled, suspended by a hand with a fine silver watch on the wrist.

"God, yes." Frazer said.

As expected, Cora appeared from behind the door and sunk onto the chair opposite Frazer. A crease appeared between her eyebrows as she examined the room

"Frazer." She looked her dead in the eye. "Your office is boring."

Insulted, Frazer looked around. White walls. Simple desk. Phone. Computer. Filing cabinet she never used and dreaded finding out what old documents were buried there. She looked back to Cora.

"Is not." The raised eyebrows Cora gave her were too judgemental for Frazer's taste. "Did you come to insult my office or give me a coffee?"

Immediately, Cora held out the coffee, which Frazer snatched up. "Three sugars?"

Cora rolled her eyes. "Yes, five-year-old, three sugars."

"Thank you."

The pink of Cora's cheeks didn't fit Frazer's stock polite statement. Oddly, Cora dropped her eyes and took a sip of her own coffee. "No problem." She took a deep breath. "Got to keep your addiction level at functional."

"Me? Addicted? Says the queen of coffee."

Cora snorted, staring Frazer straight in the eye. Something in Frazer's stomach turned over. "This is my second," she told Frazer. "How many have you had?"

Cora had her there.

"Uh... This is my fourth."

Cora took a victory sip. "Case in point. That's one to me, and I think you're in the minus now."

"I'd argue, but they say it's best not to argue with a delusion."

Frazer took another sip and leaned back against her chair. Across from her, Cora's leg bounced as she stared at her coffee cup. For a second, the silence beat past them.

"Everything okay?"

Cora made eye contact and nodded enthusiastically. "Oh, yeah. Great. Busy today. A lot of discharges to get through. People needed extras set up for them. How about you? Lots of babies?"

"I've been on prenatal exams most of the morning." That leg was still bouncing, and Frazer watched it before asking, "Jokes aside, are you sure you really need more caffeine?"

"What?" Cora followed Frazer's gaze to her bouncing leg. "Oh. Probably not."

"When does Alec come back?"

The coffee in Cora's hand slipped slightly, and she sat straighter to avoid spilling it all over her shirt. Her breasts pressed against the polo shirt, and Frazer almost strained a muscle trying to keep her eyes on Cora's face, which was red again after almost dropping her cup.

"Ah...three days."

Considering the rants on marriage the other night, Frazer didn't really know if she should ask if she was looking forward to it. So she went for a cop out. "Three more days of freedom—what are you going to do with them?"

"Oh, you know"—for a second Cora hesitated, then straightened her shoulders, her lips twitching—"hire some bare-chested strippers with more abs than brains, withdraw our entire savings in five-dollar notes, and spend my time snapping them into their underwear." Cora wriggled her eyebrows up and down, cheeks pink again. "Want to join?"

"If by strippers you mean go for a drink, I'm in."

Dropping back in dramatic disappointment, Cora sighed heavily. "Fine. I'll settle for that. Tonight?"

"Great. We have a plan. Now go, I'm extremely busy."

Cora stared at her, unblinking.

"Well, then, I have to do a pelvic exam in, like, five minutes, if you want to join."

She stood up quickly. "Nope, I'm good, thanks. Shall we say six, bar around the corner?"

"Sounds good."

Lingering a moment, Cora gave her a look Frazer couldn't quite figure out before she turned around and left, leaving Frazer staring after her.

Friendship was going so well. Friendly-type friends. Yeah.

The house was quiet, and for once it was unsettling.

Usually, Cora liked to sit in the house alone to enjoy the solitude. A book in hand, she'd get lost in the pages and at the last minute, be rushing around to get dinner ready for Alec. The lounge room was her space, bookshelves lined with classics and romances and everything in between. The wood was dark, the couch a cream colour that Alec had once sniffed at and said it proved they didn't have kids.

Cora loved the couch. It enveloped her when she sat in it. When they'd first bought it, Alec had pushed her onto it and laughed when she'd pulled him down with her, their clothes scattered on the floor in a pattern slashed out of their carelessness.

These days, he stayed upstairs in his study, researching or planning or something. Those nights, she enjoyed the lack of interruption. Those nights meant they weren't arguing or, worse, sitting on opposite sides of the couch with a prickly gap between them, one impossible to cross without one of them compromising something. Usually Cora was the one coerced across.

Today, the lack of movement made her restless. She'd been restless for days, since Alec left, really. This huge step, one she'd built up to for so long, was only half-taken. It was as if she had built herself up to jump, the tension coiled in her muscles, and then, just as she'd let go, the power pumping her up and outwards, someone had grabbed her back. All that adrenaline, and nowhere for it to go.

There was still nothing from Alec. And she had said nothing in return.

She traced the backs of her books with her fingertips. Who would move out? Would they both move out?

Would they go through with it?

Would Cora mean it?

God. She'd have to tell her parents. Her traditionalist parents. Her mother, whose parents' South Korean tradition, culture, and expectations clung to her like lint despite her being born in Australia. Her dad's two-generation Australian lineage on his father's side made him the safer bet for this sort of news that required open-mindedness, but still...

Her chest heaved as she scanned the room almost desperately for something to fix her eyes on.

There was nothing here, nothing to distract her.

Lisa's words had been playing in her mind for days. However, the words that had stuck were probably not the ones that Lisa had intended.

Sex with a woman simply because why not?

Her friend had surprised her.

That idea had simply never crossed Cora's mind. She was eighteen when she met Alec. And he'd been everything she'd thought she wanted.

He *was* everything she had wanted. This version of him, who he was now, wasn't. Or had she just seen what she'd wanted in him and ignored the rest?

Cora was definitely straight. Apparently, so was Lisa even though she'd had that experience.

Shaking her head, Cora went upstairs to get ready. This train of thought was leading nowhere. What else had Lisa talked about? What had Cora been craving? Distraction.

So why not go out and get drunk that evening? Maybe Frazer could help her eye someone up.

She wasn't even part way to separated yet, but it didn't mean she couldn't *look*.

Over the next hour, Cora slowly got ready, trying to ignore the tie Alec had left curled on his bedside table, the familiarity of it prickling at her. The restless feeling still fluttered in her chest.

She needed to do *something*.

By accident or on purpose, she wasn't sure which, she arrived at the bar too early. It was the same one she'd come to after her last fight with Alec, and the familiarity was comforting. Suddenly grateful she was early, she ordered a white wine and slipped into a free booth. The worn leather sunk under her, crackling slightly. Around her, the bar slowly filled up, people trickling in. Again, she saw Alec's secretary, Tia, with the friend Tia's husband wouldn't want her seeing, the two women tucked away like giggling teens. Elbows on the bar top, they settled in, heads close as they cackled over something. In the corner, drums and a guitar sat, a clear sign that live music was on the agenda for the evening. Interns wandered in, desperate for an after-work beer as they blurrily congratulated each other on surviving another week.

Only a sip of her wine remained when Frazer slid opposite her, two fresh glasses in hand and a warm look of greeting on her face.

It was amusing now to think Cora had once found her obnoxious.

Already tingling inside from one glass, Cora took the new one, and their fingers brushed each other, the sensation flowing up Cora's arm in warm sparks.

"Hey! Sorry I'm a bit late. A woman decided to go into labour just as I was leaving, as they do. Had to get her settled before handing her over to the next midwife."

"No problem."

Frazer's eyes were incredibly green. She'd mentioned over one night of drinking that her parents both were of Indian descent. The darker tone of her skin from that heritage caused her eyes to stand out even more brightly.

Had Cora noticed that before?

What Cora noticed most was that the second Frazer sat down, open and friendly, Alec flew to the very back of her mind.

There was an intimacy to how far forward Cora leant, her attention stuck on Frazer as she regaled her with a story.

Her dress gaped slightly, and when Cora reached for her glass, Frazer couldn't stop her gaze from dropping down and running, quickly, over the smoothness of Cora's skin and up the slope of her neck. Under the table, Cora's foot had fallen against hers yet hadn't moved.

On their fourth glass of wine, Frazer had stopped keeping her words in check and instead relaxed. When she spoke, she held Cora's eye, a finger occasionally resting on her forearm while explaining something.

Slowly, Frazer began to realise that Cora's eyes were doing exactly what her own were. It was as if she could feel them tracing her skin and leaving it feeling uncomfortably warm.

Friends.

That word had disappeared after the third glass.

It was too easy to flirt, too easy to enjoy a tint of red that went down Cora's neck and spread over her chest.

Frazer hadn't done this in so long that it had taken her a while to realise what they were doing.

Which was probably a bad thing.

Consciously or not, Cora's eyes stared at an angle far below her mouth. Had Frazer missed something?

Her brain was fuzzy and she stopped thinking of it.

"You slept with the football captain in high school? Frazer, how cliché."

"She was really, really hot, if that helps at all."

"I just never pegged you as so...predictable." Her eyes were shining as she cocked her head. From here, Frazer could see how the outer iris was a rich, golden brown which deepened into almost black around her pupil. A kaleidoscope of colour. "Discovering you were gay your final year of high school with the captain of the girl's footy team?"

"Hey." Frazer smirked. "I knew I was gay *way* before that. Thanks to the goalie from the soccer team two years before."

The snort Cora gave should have verged on unattractive, but there was something endearing about her when she finally let herself go in mirth. "Did you just make your way through all the sports teams?"

Frazer drank, rather than answer, and Cora's eyes widened. "My God, you did. Did you turn any of them?"

Frazer dropped her gaze, chuckling. Cora was suddenly very interested in her sexual history. "Maybe—though you don't really *turn* people."

The look on Cora's face was open, curious.

Frazer was trying. But Cora was making it way, way too hard.

On her fifth glass of wine, Cora forgot everything.

A voice in the back of her head, one that sounded much like Lisa's, said something about how she had wanted to go find a toy boy to stare at. But instead, she just wanted to talk to Frazer.

That didn't have to mean anything.

Each time Frazer touched her arm, warmth was left behind, an imprint patterning her skin. Their foreheads were close together as they shared anecdotes and stories Cora wouldn't remember in the morning. When Frazer said something particularly funny, her lips quirked in a half smile, crooked almost. She had long lashes, black and thick without any evidence of make-up. There was something almost sensual about that mouth. Had Cora ever thought something like that before? The word sensual was not one she'd ever thought, she was sure. All her memories were taken up by Alec. Not that it had to matter. Things could be seen as simple distraction. Some fun. No harm, no foul.

Laughing, Cora leant backwards in her chair, Frazer mimicking the motion. As her mirth died down, the noise of the room invaded her senses.

In their corner booth, with their heads pressed in close as they talked, everything was muted. But their bubble broke as a musician strummed a guitar and people started shouting out across the room. The way to the bar was overcrowded with people shoved up against each other like prizes inside a claw machine game. It was fast becoming a night out that Cora had no interest in having. Clubs hadn't really been her thing even when she was the right age for them.

Somehow, her eyes were back on Frazer's lips even before they moved, the words lost in the room. "What?" Cora asked, leaning forwards.

Frazer raised her voice. "It's getting noisy!"

"Clearly!" A moment's hesitation, shortened by wine, had Cora shrugging internally. Why not? "Want to drink at my place instead?"

For a moment, Frazer didn't answer. Disappointment so strong welled up in Cora as her lips parted, ready to cover the comment in excuses.

Instead of the no she expected, though, Frazer nodded and grabbed her jacket, sliding out the booth and leading the way towards the door.

Shoulders brushed past, and the hot press of people was almost suffocating. Cold air washed over them as they exited, and Cora took a deep breath in. It filled her lungs like relief. The door closed behind them, the sound muting to a dull roar inside. Cora glanced at her watch, wincing at the late hour. At least it was the weekend. She was going to need a day in bed, judging by the way the earth was spinning. She chuckled. The earth was always spinning, that was just physics. Though she was certain you weren't supposed to be aware of it. Did that make her the best physicist ever?

"Want to share a ride?"

Cora stared at Frazer, whose eyes were a little fuzzy at the edges. Green and fuzzy. Or maybe that was Cora's vision. "Everything's spinning."

"Everything's blurry."

"How many glasses of wine did we have?" Cora was absolutely certain it wasn't too many.

"Three?"

"I remember five."

Frazer's face fell. "Ah, well. That's a discrepancy."

A taxi pulled up, its charges spilling out in a messier group than theirs. One guy tripped and fell, half pulling his female friend down with him. She shrieked with laughter as she teetered on heels too tall to be considered safe at any level of sobriety. The driver leant over and called through the window at Frazer and Cora. "You ladies need a taxi?"

Still giggling at the display of the drunken group, Cora nodded at him and slid inside. Frazer followed suit, staring out the window as they watched the group make their way inside. "That woman looks like a baby giraffe in those heels," she said.

Cora laughed, then snorted and slapped her hand over her mouth, cheeks already hot.

Frazer's head whipped around. The grin on her face was wicked. "Did you just snort? Again?"

"No?" The words were spoken through her fingers and were muffled with mortification.

"Drunk baby giraffe."

Another snort, amplified by tightly pressed fingers, was all it took for them to dissolve into laughter.

An annoyed voice came from the front. "Address, ladies? And no chundering in the car."

Suddenly, the taxi pulled up at the house. Surely that hadn't been a twenty-minute drive? As Cora was the only one with cash, she won the fight over who was going to pay. Frazer made a mental note to get the next one, as their fingers fumbled with seatbelts and door handles and they finally got out, the annoyed glare of the taxi driver easily left behind.

It didn't help the laughter.

On the front porch, they hovered as Cora hunted for her keys, then finally yanked them out in delighted victory. Eyebrows pressed tightly together, she closed one eye as she lined the right key up with the keyhole.

And missed.

Déjà vu crept up Frazer's spine. That foggy hug, always playing at her memory, was easier to remember when standing in the same place. The perfume Cora wore, subtle and sweet, was as close as it had been that night. The sensation of their cheeks brushing each other, feather light, the distant touch of the corners of their lips. If she stepped forward and pressed Cora to the door, ran her hands up her sides and buried them in her hair, would Cora push her away? Or invite her in? Crush their lips together in a frantic kiss, the energy sparking off their skin?

Why did Frazer have to think of that? Especially about the straight, married friend.

It was a gross cliché.

"Got it!" The door swung open, and Cora looked as proud as if she'd cured cancer.

Biting her lip, Frazer gave a weak "Yay."

Frazer needed to stop thinking like that. She'd said no to herself. Friends. Being a friendly-type friend for the friend who needed a best-friend-ever friend.

Instead, that thought was flooded out by wine and the sight of Cora's eyes tracing an imaginary line down her throat. Cora's fingers were soft along the inside of her wrist.

Frazer felt warm in places she shouldn't.

Those fingers wrapped around hers again and tugged Frazer through the doorway.

Obviously comfortable in a space that was hers, Cora led her down a hallway, flicking lights on as she went. Turning right at some point, they ended up in a kitchen. Not just a kitchen, but an open-plan kitchen, dining and lounge room. When Frazer was left standing alone, she looked around and let out a "Wow."

Already with her head half-buried in the fridge, Cora rummaged, then peered around the door, holding a bottle of wine. As Frazer looked all around, Cora rolled her eyes. "Oh, I know. It's excessive."

Excessive? It was gorgeous. The timber walls were something not many houses exhibited anymore. The kitchen was a huge space with an island in the middle, pots and pans hanging over it from a hook. Another bench ran around in an L shape, cutting it off slightly to make it more like one room. From there, you could walk through to the dining section, where a huge eight-seater jarrah wood table, shining and rustic and bare, took centre place. From there was a sunken lounge room. One step led down to the modular couch big enough for more friends than Frazer had.

"It's incredible."

Cora took a glance around. Her nose wrinkled slightly. "It's nice, yeah."

Maybe Cora hadn't contributed much to the design?

Grabbing glasses, she said, "Take a seat on the couch. It's to die for. I love it so much I almost branded my name on it."

With a chuckle, Frazer wandered through, her fingers running over the smoothness of the dining table. The carpet in the lounge room was soft and deep. Her sodden brain finally looked around the space properly, eyes wide. It was like a library.

"Do you like to read? Because—" She spun around to ask the question. As she did she, naturally, collided with Cora. One glass in Cora's hands fell to the ground while Frazer rescued the other.

Momentum carried Cora forward, and Frazer's arms instinctively wrapped around her to steady them both. "Sorry" built up behind her tongue, yet Cora was already laughing, clutching Frazer's shirt, pressing her forehead against her shoulder. Frazer was too drunk to care that she should probably let go. When Cora finally lifted her head, the laughter had faded to gentle curving lips. Suddenly, everything was them—the solidness of Cora in her arms, the flush in her cheeks, the warmth of her breath against Frazer's lips. Her eyes were dark, and, this close, Frazer couldn't help what slipped out as she took in each minute detail on Cora's face.

"You have freckles on your nose." Frazer didn't recognise her own voice.

Meanwhile, Cora's voice was husky and warm and laced with something Frazer hadn't heard before. "You have a freckle in your eye."

Swallowing, Frazer nodded.

Parts of her were becoming aware that Cora's chest was pressed to hers. Dark eyes looked from Frazer's lips back to her eyes, back to her lips, and then Cora's head moved forward just the inch or two it needed.

Everything in her body tensed. Panic flared in Frazer's stomach. She hadn't reacted like this since the first time someone in her life had stepped forward, an intention to their mouth.

Cora's eyes were almost closed, and warm breath mingled with Frazer's own. If she moved, she thought, everything would shatter and Cora would disappear, as impossible to keep as water in a cupped hand.

"Is this okay?"

The words Cora whispered were barely audible, and Frazer risked moving. She nodded, barely, and then the gap was no more.

It was a simple kiss, a pressing of mouths. And Frazer, terrified of scaring her off, again didn't move.

Though as Cora tentatively moved her lips, a soft sigh escaped her body, and Frazer realised she needn't have worried. Cora's lips parted, her tongue flicking Frazer's lip. That was all it took, and Frazer dropped the glass, with a thud, to bury her hands in Cora's hair.

It made no sense, the two of them doing this. There was no long history to tie them together, no buried love, no angst built over longing looks. But Frazer couldn't stop herself if she tried. When she finally allowed her tongue to brush against Cora's, the throaty groan she got in response made warmth pool in her belly.

Her confidence grew, and Frazer pressed forward, the kiss all tongue and teeth, messy and delicious as they stumbled up the step. They both jolted as Cora finally hit the table behind her, Frazer's hands now flat against the wood surface. And even as Cora responded to the kiss, Frazer felt the pause, the flash of hesitancy when Cora pushed up and sat on the table's edge. Slowly, Cora's lips moved from Frazer's, to her jaw, and down against her neck. Warmth spread across her skin as Cora flicked her tongue, warm and wet, against her pulse point.

Her knees weakened. "Cora?"

"Mm?" The humming against her neck wasn't making this any easier.

"We can stop?"

Cora pulled back, and Frazer nearly groaned. Her bruised lips shone, and when Cora bit on her bottom one, Frazer felt a tug low in her stomach. She could see where this was going as Cora dropped her gaze down. *That one time I kissed a woman.* Frazer had been that experiment before, but here, now, she didn't want to be; she didn't want it to end there.

Those eyes, dark and deep, finally caught her own again. "I don't want to stop," Cora said, but Frazer thought maybe she did. "I just, I don't know how—" Cora stopped as if frustrated with herself, biting her lip and looking up at the ceiling.

So that's what it was. Damn. How did she tell Cora that Frazer was almost there with merely five minutes of simple kisses? She felt like a seventeen-year-old.

Kissing seemed like Frazer's best move right now. She smiled at Cora, her voice low. "I'll show you."

Cora's pupils blew wide.

When Frazer kissed her again, Cora grabbed her shirt, hard, and pulled her closer. Frazer decided there and then: if Cora wanted this, even for just one night, then Frazer would make sure it was a night she would remember.

She tugged at the material of Cora's dress. Frazer pulled it up to sit around the hips, her fingers stroking the bare skin of Cora's thigh. Soft like silk, warm. Cora obliged and pulled Frazer even closer, now firmly between her legs. Slowly, gently, Frazer ran her fingers along soft skin, feeling Cora roll her hips, drawing a groan that could have been from either of them. The warmth in Frazer's stomach made her pull her lips down to Cora's neck, nipping at the skin. Slow. She would be slow. That moment of hesitancy earlier was enough to make Frazer wary of pushing.

But then Frazer bit at Cora's neck, her tongue immediately soothing the spot, and Cora groaned way in the back of her throat, the sound vibrating against Frazer's lips.

That was enough.

She crashed her lips to Cora's, and hands tangled in Frazer's hair. Fingers yanked that black dress up and over, and Frazer tossed it somewhere behind her. For one moment, she got to stare at Cora half-naked, a glimpse of a black bra and soft breasts, before Cora dragged her tighter against her.

Their teeth clashed, and Cora wrapped her legs around Frazer's waist, hips grinding against her. Frazer was already wet. Harder than she intended, Frazer dragged her nails over Cora's skin, up her sides and against her bra. Cora's moan encouraged her, and with the strap as her guide, Frazer undid it and pulled the bra away, cupping the softness of her breasts the second she could. Her thumbs rolled over already hard nipples.

With panting breaths in her ear, Frazer kissed Cora's neck, tongue running over the ridge of her collarbone. Everything was Cora—her movement. The rocking of her hips that were desperate for touch. As she grazed her lips back to kiss Cora again, her fingers ran down Cora's stomach, hands clutching at lace. Somehow, the buttons of Frazer's shirt were undone and she tugged at Cora's underwear in her hands, pulling them down and stepping back to remove them completely, her gaze never leaving Cora's.

Cora was leaning back against the table, skin flushed and wearing only a pair of heels. Frazer slowly ran her hands from

Cora's knees along her thighs, goose bumps rising under her palm. Slower than before, Frazer kissed her again, the back of her fingers running over soft curls and softer skin. With a sigh, Cora's head fell back as she sat completely on the table and Frazer ran her tongue down her neck, over her nipple, her fingers stroking, a whisper of a touch against sensitive flesh. The rhythm of her tongue against Cora's breast was faster than her fingers. Hips seemed to beg at her to do more, but Frazer resisted, enjoying the subtle warmth against her fingers and dragging out Cora's obvious enjoyment.

"Please." The sound was a whisper or a groan or something in between.

Frazer bit down gently, and this time, the response was definitely a groan.

Then fingers were in her hair, pushing her down. "Please!"

That had definitely been spoken.

Dropping to her knees, Frazer traced patterns against Cora's thigh, even as she did so. She pushed two fingers inside, curling them enough that Cora shouted, lying down on the table and reaching out blindly to grip at Frazer's shoulders. Heels dug deliciously into Frazer's back.

Those fingers gripped hard enough to bruise when Frazer pressed her tongue against Cora's centre, stroking to match the rhythm of her hand.

At that moment, nothing existed but the pace Cora set with her hips, the taste of her, and the overwhelming urge to make her come, yet to have this last forever.

"Fuck, Frazer."

Her name had never sounded like that before, a breathy invocation.

Fingers finally released her shoulders in order to return to her hair, nails digging into her scalp as Cora tensed, hips losing their rhythm. "Harder."

Frazer wrapped a hand around the hip, her fingers splaying over her stomach to hold Cora against her.

"Don't stop."

Stopping would be the problem. When Frazer curled a third finger, Cora came in a rush of words and fingers that gripped her like desperation. Frazer rode it out with her, only stopping when the fingers in her hair fell slack.

Frazer stood, her knees aching, and then crawled up Cora's body to straddle her hips. Gently, she pushed dishevelled hair off Cora's sweaty forehead. Breathing was the only sound in the room. As Cora opened her eyes, Frazer chuckled at the glazed look she found there.

"Hi," she murmured.

"Holy fuck."

Unable to hold it in, Frazer laughed and Cora smiled, sheepish.

"Frazer, that's a compliment."

"Oh, I know."

Apparently able to move again, Cora ran a finger over Frazer's bare thigh where her skirt had ridden up.

She shook her head as she watched her own fingers against bare skin. "That was—you—" She shook her head again. Frazer's hand was right next to Cora's ear, palm flat on the table so she could hold herself up, and Cora turned, her gaze on Frazer's as she kissed the skin at her wrist. The touch sent a throb straight to Frazer's centre. Cora's hands ran up Frazer's thighs, brushing the hem of her skirt and grabbing her open shirt that hung at her shoulders. She guided Frazer's face to hers, kissing her.

"You," Cora said, "have a shirt on. While I don't."

Even drunk and definitely interested, Frazer hesitated, unsure of just how far Cora wanted this to go. All she knew was that after the feeling of Cora coming undone, it wasn't going to take very long for Frazer to follow. She sat up, her thighs straddling Cora's hips. Her fingers ran between her own breasts and down to her stomach to toy with the hem of her shirt. "This shirt?"

Those usually amber eyes, now dark and searching, followed her hands, and Cora's tongue darted out against her lips. She nodded, and Frazer slowly peeled the shirt off.

Cora slipped her finger under Frazer's waistband and tugged. It sent Frazer falling forward. Her lips crashed into Cora's as she balanced herself with a hand alongside Cora's body. Shivers ran up her back as Cora's hands trailed along her thighs, her stomach, the edges of her breasts. When nails grazed her spine, Frazer instinctively ground down on Cora, who gasped into Frazer's mouth.

Achingly slowly, Cora's hands coaxed the material of Frazer's skirt up her thighs. Fingers played at the edge of her underwear, each time dangerously close to touching the skin there before drifting back down to stroke her thighs, only to come back up and play the game again. It was all Frazer could do to control her hips, to not seek the pressure she wanted. To not rush Cora into anything.

Just as Frazer thought that one more subtle movement of her hips against the brush of Cora's fingers would unravel her, she pulled her lips away, moving them to Cora's ear, almost desperate with need. Still, she said it.

"You don't have to."

Cora went still. Her face was in Frazer's hair. "I want to—but what if..."

Frazer pulled back to look her in the eye. "What?"

"I've never... I've never done this before." The embarrassed laugh Cora gave made Frazer wince internally for her. "I don't know what I'm doing. What if I can't make you feel as good as I did?"

That was the worry? Frazer rested her hand on Cora's, which was still on her thigh. She tugged at it. Cora relaxed and let Frazer lead both their fingers slowly over her underwear. Frazer bit her lip at the sensation and groaned softly, her lips against Cora's ear.

"Cora. You already *have*."

"Show me?"

Her voice was low and breathy, and Frazer thought Cora *had* to know what she was doing to her. This time, Frazer gently guided their hands into her underwear, running their fingers together over her wetness.

"Jesus, Cora."

When Cora pushed Frazer's hand away and pushed her own fingers up and inside, Frazer flew up onto her knees and threw her head back. She tried to keep her eyes on Cora, tried to reassure her, but the feeling of her fingers moving so slowly, hesitantly, but with gaining confidence, made her lose the ability to do anything but feel.

It was too slow, achingly so, but somehow that made it more intense, and her hips moved with Cora's small strokes. When another finger was pushed in, she gasped, and her gaze plummeted down to Cora. "That," she groaned as Cora watched her wide-eyed, "feels so good."

Cora's other hand grabbed Frazer's hip, moving with it. When she curled her fingers, Frazer thought she could die, just there, like that. She gripped Cora's hand against her hip, Frazer's nails biting her skin.

"You look—" Cora didn't finish, and Frazer barely heard her.

Cora's leg was bent behind her, biting into her back, and Frazer leant against it, her hips moving faster, as much as she tried to let Cora set the pace. Cora's hand shifted slightly, her thumb brushing in just the right place, and Frazer whimpered. That thumb pressed down, and everything in Frazer tightened, was thrumming. Warmth spread from her stomach until her eyes slammed shut and she finally came undone on Cora's hand, tumbling forward, pressing her forehead against Cora's chest. Her blood pounded in her ears for seemingly forever until dawning awareness told her that Cora's hand still hadn't moved, that the other was stroking her back. Frazer's breathing slowed, and she opened her eyes.

The smile Cora gave from below her was soft, almost shy. "Was that okay?"

Frazer laughed, dropping her full weight on top of her.

She was in trouble.

CHAPTER EIGHT

Waking up with a dry mouth was not a nice feeling.

Nor was the feeling that sandpaper had replaced your tongue.

Nor that one second that stretched forever, the one in which you had no idea where you were.

Slowly, her eyes opened, but only to slits, and the room Frazer was in settled around her. There was no way she dared open her eyes fully, the light slipping past her lids already too much to bear.

As much as she could, Frazer took stock.

So, she was naked. There were definitely no clothes on her body. None. Zilch. She could feel crisp sheets against her skin. Something warm and soft was pressed to her front. And in her hand? That was skin. Last night crept its way back into her hung-over brain.

Was Cora's boob in her hand?

Yes. And her naked back was pressed to Frazer's front. Frazer's arm was moving up and down in time to Cora's breathing.

She was naked and in bed with Cora. After a night of—she cast her mind back and felt colour swarm her face. A night of very, very good sex.

Heat flared in her stomach at the thought even as she scrunched her face up, resisting the urge to bury it in Cora's hair in the hopes the memory would go away.

Her stomach was heavy. She felt slightly ill. Frazer would love to blame it on a hangover, but sitting with that feeling for just a second was all it took to recognise it.

Hot, heavy shame sat there.

Cora was married. Problems or not, she had a husband.

Who was Frazer's boss.

And now, instead of being *the woman I kissed once*, Frazer had become *the woman I slept with once and cheated on my husband with.*

Frazer had promised herself she would be her friend.

God. Worst. Friend. Ever.

Or best friend ever.

She was too hung-over to know.

This time, she let herself groan, rolling onto her back and throwing her arm over her eyes.

Cora was married.

A muffled laugh came from Cora, then a groan.

Despite the angst, Frazer snorted. "Did you just laugh at my clearly hung-over groan and then hurt your head?"

A beat of silence.

"Maybe."

"Sucker." Frazer kept her eyes closed under her arm. Everything was bright. Why was it all so bright?

"You groaned first." Cora's voice was a rasp. Frazer felt her roll over, could feel her eyes on her. "Ouch, and I can see why."

"Hey! I may look like crap, but give me ten minutes and a coffee and I quickly become...mildly less hung-over."

They lapsed into an incredibly awkward silence.

This was hideous. How did they move past this? They needed to enter the stage where this wasn't hideous anymore. Where Frazer couldn't taste shame and a hangover thick on her tongue.

While bracing herself for the light to come, Frazer lifted her arm up and saw that Cora had managed to make it onto her back, her eyes closed and a hand over her own face. Clearly Frazer wasn't the only one. The sheet coated Cora's curves, only barely covering the swell of her breast. This couldn't go anywhere good.

Sitting up, the world spun savagely. Frazer clutched her head, turning to sit on the edge of the bed—Cora's marriage bed. A crime book sat on the bedside table, as did a tie, dark blue, pooled next to the lamp. Nausea bubbled in her. This had been a terrible, terrible idea.

What she needed were clothes. Clothes and coffee and paracetamol.

And eggs. And toast. Buttery, buttery toast.

There should be a skirt and a bra and her underwear somewhere. Vaguely, she remembered coming in here with those *on.*

Finally, Frazer spotted them half kicked under the bed. She slid her underwear up her legs and shimmied on her skirt. Once her bra was in place, she almost felt respectable. She took a deep breath, pain thumping at her temples. This was going to be a long, disgusting day. When she turned, Frazer finally made eye contact with Cora. Her eyes were peeking out from under her hand, a little red-rimmed.

Way back when, in this sort of situation, she would have said 'See ya' and sauntered out the door.

This was different. They were kind of friends. Cora was extremely married. Frazer worked with Cora.

God, she was meant to *not* be sleeping with co-workers.

She thought she had learnt that lesson.

Especially married co-workers.

The stipulation about marriage had never been a part of the rules, but Frazer had thought her morals were good enough without needing to say that.

Apparently not.

What a way to escalate an already bad idea.

"I, uh—I should go..."

One step towards the door, followed by another. Those eyes, shadowed by Cora's hand and difficult to read, followed her movements.

Another step.

Cora sat up, wrapping her arms around her knees and hugging them to her chest. "Okay."

If she'd had the energy, Frazer would've winced. It had just gone from hideous to hideously uncomfortable.

"You may need a shirt for that." Cora smirked.

With a look down at her bra-clad chest, Frazer smiled, the motion making everything else seem a little easier. "Probably."

Her eyes kept drifting to that bedside table. To her boss's tie. Cora's husband's tie.

When her gaze dragged back to Cora, Cora's eyes were staring at it too. Her hair was a mess, face drawn and tight. Her skin was ashen, an unnatural look on her.

Cora looked at her again. "I'll see you at work?" The question should've been easy.

"Of course." Frazer nodded, suddenly feeling like covering her stomach, her hands snaking over the skin. "So, I'll see you."

She almost made it to the door.

"Frazer."

Only hesitating for a second, Frazer turned back. On the bed, wrapped in a sheet, Cora looked so small.

"Yeah?"

Owlishly, Cora blinked at her, shadows under her eyes. She asked, "Be my friend?"

Without thinking, Frazer said, "Of course."

And she left.

The walls in the corridor were bare, no photos until the end as she turned into that incredible kitchen. A wedding photo Frazer refused to examine, her stomach twisting in knots.

Her white shirt was spilt like a stain on the floor by the dining table. She scooped it up and put it on, fingers shaky as she worked on the buttons. The table stared at her, a dent from Cora's high heels on the edge. It may as well have been a glaring sign. It stared at her. Blinking. There was no way to get rid of it.

Instead, she picked up the wine glasses and gingerly placed them in the sink, then got out of there as fast as she could.

Frazer didn't know herself anymore.

The door slammed, the sound bouncing off the walls, amplified and loud. The ache in Cora's head felt deserved; it throbbed like karma.

No longer high on alcohol, instead soaked in hangover and regret, Cora could no longer hide from her own understanding that her experiment, this distraction, was long past seeming like a good idea. Why she'd kissed Frazer befuddled her. The plan had been to look, to not touch. To find some muscled, bearded young thing and gaze at him, then go home *alone*.

Cora sunk low on the bed, pulling the covers up and over her head. A scent of citrus, of sweat and sex that wasn't her husband's, engulfed her until her eyes burned.

She wanted out of her marriage, not an affair. Or she thought she did. That's what she had told her husband.

But she wasn't out of it; not at all.

Yet that grey area was pooled around her, and her arms and legs felt stuck in it. If she moved a part of herself, it just landed in a part even greyer.

Essentially, she had just cheated on her husband. Even if she was planning on divorcing him. Even if it had been just for a distraction.

Or did that make it worse?

And why a woman?

Cora groaned, rolling over and burying her face in the pillow. The pain in her throat as she screamed, the ache in her head, were like a penance. She was straight. That wasn't the problem. Man or woman, she had cheated. She had taken that step, one she had seen people at the hospital take, one that had seemed dirty, deceiving, and far from her. Maybe if she hadn't let Lisa's words get in her head Cora would have just stared at men too young and only in the realm of her imagination, then gone home and not fallen into bed—or on the table—with a woman she'd barely become friends with.

But she needed that friendship.

It was only recently that she had been finally able to breathe. Was it selfish to want a friendship after that? Would Frazer *want* to be her friend?

Should they be friends?

113

Really, it was all too hard to think about. There was a churning in her stomach as everything around her pitched and rolled. Why was Alec's stupid tie there?

Cora only just made it to the bathroom in time to throw up everything in her stomach. An hour later, trembling, she was still retching on and off as she clung to the cool porcelain.

None of it tasted like last night's alcohol; it was guilt that burnt her throat.

"Come out, Frazer."

"No."

Frazer switched the phone to her other ear and shoved her bag into the gym locker. An old lady in the corner glared at her as half the stuff tumbled back out with a crash and Frazer swore loudly.

"God, no need for the f-bomb. Just trying to get you outta the house."

Pinching her nose between her fingers, Frazer took a moment. Her sister was just trying to be nice. Jemma liked to think she helped.

"Jem," Frazer said, "I'm out of the house."

A beat of silence over the phone. "Are you at the gym?"

For a moment, Frazer considered lying. But she didn't want her entire day to be one big regret. "Yes."

The groan over the phone sounded as if Jemma was in agonising pain. "See? The gym's your second home these days. Come out for a drink."

The contents of the bag finally crammed into the locker. Small victories. Frazer's stomach turned over at the idea of alcohol. "I can't. I'm—I'm busy."

Another silence that felt full of judgement. "With what?"

Damn it.

"Frazer—what ya doing tonight?"

This is why you don't lie. "I'm...um..."

"Great, I'll come over at six. See you then!"

And Jemma hung up.

Frazer missed the days of flip phones when she could sassily snap it shut to express her annoyance. She settled for dropping it on top of her gym bag. The locker door got slammed shut for good measure. As she slipped the key onto its plastic bracelet over her wrist, Frazer turned around to see the old woman still glaring at her. Frazer wiggled her fingers back at her. The glare intensified, and Frazer walked past, she hoped breezily.

Her head raged at her as she dove into the pool and stayed under as long as she could. She emerged only when the pressure in her lungs demanded it.

Nothing felt good that day.

After a steaming shower that didn't do a lot to make her feel better about herself and then sitting at home for a few hours, Frazer had given up. Of course she'd gone to the gym again. She needed meditation. Repetition. Stroke, stroke, breathe. Repeat.

The rhythm occurred naturally. By the time Frazer crawled out of the pool an hour and a half later, her arms were shaking, the muscles spasming. Everything burned, and this time, it wasn't with deep shame.

Exhaustion she could deal with.

Wrapped in a towel and still breathing hard, Frazer padded into the empty changing room. When she opened the locker and saw a message alert from Cora, everything ached for a different reason, and Frazer threw her phone back in the locker.

Thirty seconds later, cool water again surrounded her flushed skin. Her muscles screamed in protest.

Another hour would do her good.

"Did you have sex?"

Cora stared at Lisa through her screen door. How did she know? All Cora had done was knock on the door—probably a bit desperately, if she was honest with herself—but Lisa had swung the door open without a word from Cora and had just asked. How could Lisa know? Cora had showered for an hour, hoping the boiling water could erase what she had done.

"What?" Because that was smooth and didn't sound guilty at all.

In the murky front light, Lisa squinted at her. "Did you have sex?"

Cora's heart pounded. The fact that this was probably just a question seeped into her consciousness. "Uh—no. Alec is away."

"Well, I know that. I thought you were toyboying."

"S—still no. Sorry. You gonna let me in?"

Lisa pushed the door open. As Cora walked through, she tried to pretend she still held some dignity.

"Well, of course I knew you weren't gonna *do* anything." Lisa followed her into her lounge room. "I just thought you'd perve. Remind yourself what you were missing."

Cora raised her eyes to the half-filled-out *Cosmo* quiz left open on the coffee table.

"Keeping busy, Lisa?"

A flush crawled along Lisa's cheeks. "We all have things we do when we think no one's watching. Mine just happens to be embarrassing life quizzes."

Something must have cracked the *I'm fine* mask Cora had skilfully drawn on with the help of *Bitch Red* lipstick, because Lisa dropped her playful tone. "Hey. You okay?"

"Yeah. I'm good." Cora took in a deep breath, and tried to not look like she was about to shake apart. She tried hard. "Do you have wine?"

"Of course."

When Lisa came back with two glasses, filled nicely, Cora had the trembling in her hands under control. She'd come to escape the judgement of the dent in her table and the wine stains on her carpet, not to confess to her friend who had more important things to deal with than Cora destroying her marriage. Which may or may not have already been destroyed; but that had somehow stopped being relevant in her mind.

Cora sat on the couch and accepted a glass, happy when Lisa sat next to her.

"Can we watch a movie?"

Lisa eyed her but nodded anyway. "Sure. What one?"

"Anything."

It took only moments to find an old nineties movie on the regional channel. Feet next to each other on the coffee table, Cora slowly put her head on Lisa's shoulder, the wine glass clutched against her chest.

Lisa even pretended not to notice the unmistakable tears on her cheeks halfway through the film or the way her shoulders shook. All she did was wrap an arm around Cora, pulling her in tighter.

The message from Cora had only said "sorry."

And there was nothing Frazer could think to say back to that, so nothing was said.

Sorry could mean anything. Sorry it happened. Sorry for asking the impossible after it. Sorry for the situation you're in. Sorry I'm married. Sorry I fell on your face in more ways than one.

Sorry.

Now, though, Frazer would probably have to say sorry for not saying anything to Cora's sorry.

It was all a little ridiculous.

"So. Family lunch tomorrow. You're in, yes? Yes."

Not even trying for soft, Frazer dug her toe into Jemma's thigh from where she sat on the other end of the couch. "Why must I?"

Jemma pinched Frazer's foot with no less mercy. Ignoring the "ow!" she said, "You're in such a mood, seriously. You haven't been there in weeks, and I'm sick of hearing them talk about it. Come. Eat. Smile. Then we can go to a bar, and you can tell me who put the stick up your arse so we can go about getting it removed, because you're certainly not gonna open up tonight."

With a loud groan, Frazer dropped her head back. "Fine. But I'm not smiling."

"Yeah, you will. Gran's coming, and she's a riot once she has a wine."

Trying to hide the amusement that *that* thought induced, Frazer sat up straighter. "Gran's coming?"

"Yeah." Jemma's eyes sparkled.

"Well, you could've led with that."

"Dear sister, I was hoping my charm would be enough. Also, she's excited because Tony's coming with the kids."

Frazer groaned again. Louder than before.

"Yeah." Jemma patted Frazer's foot. "See?"

It wasn't the kids. Frazer liked her nephews and niece. They were funny and sweet and loud. Her golden brother and his golden wife were actually doing a good job raising them.

It was the comments that would come Frazer's way with their presence. Family ideals. Kids. Marriage.

A quiet comment about finding a husband that her mother would slip out when she thought Frazer's father wasn't listening.

"Don't worry. Maybe I'll tell them about my affair with a lecturer. Then the attention can fall to me." Jemma winked.

"You love me, but not that much."

"That's true. Maybe one of the kids will vomit on Mum's bed again. That should work."

Frazer chuckled. "Yeah. I'll feed Lyle lemonade then give him a piggyback ride again."

"*Lyle.*" Jemma said, her face wrinkled up. "And *Tabitha*. And *Laurent*."

"I *know*."

They caught each other's eyes and burst out laughing.

There was silence in the house, and Cora couldn't stop bouncing her leg. Everything was spotless. Yesterday, she'd possibly gone overboard with the cleaning—it had taken a full two hours to get the wine out of the carpet. Her arms ached from 'blotting' as the internet had informed her to do.

Nothing got the dent out of the table.

Her face flamed whenever she looked at it. Constantly, her eye was drawn there again and again until she'd thrown a table cloth over it.

Then promptly removed it an hour later.

It looked even more suspicious.

They never covered that table—it was too pretty to cover, the wood gleaming. It was ridiculously heavy and the one thing besides the couch Cora really liked in the house.

There was the sound of a key in the lock. Cora straightened. Her fingers gripped her knees. She stilled her bouncing leg.

Wheels pulled down the hallway. The sound of the handle retracting back down. Footsteps thudded, almost as loud as her heart in her ears.

Alec entered the kitchen and didn't even notice her. He pulled open the fridge door. A beer fizzed open, and finally he turned, beer pausing at his mouth when he saw her.

He lowered the bottle down onto the kitchen bench. "Hi."

Cora swallowed. Her mouth felt dry, and she ran her tongue over her bottom lip. "Hi."

They stared at each other, and Cora felt guilt creep across her chest. Alec looked rumpled, his clothes obviously pulled from his suitcase that morning and deemed plane appropriate. He hadn't shaved that morning, and his hair had an uncombed look.

He'd dressed expecting discussions at home. Not expecting to find out his wife had slept with someone else.

He looked like she loved him to look, and in the end, Cora blinked rapidly, hoping it would ease the burning in her eyes. The dent on the table seemed huge. Metres wide instead of an inch long.

Remembering she wasn't supposed to be staring at it, she gazed at a spot on Alec's face that wasn't his eyes but close enough that she wasn't *not* looking at him. "Hi," she said again.

Alec tugged at his tie and pulled it over his head. It looped around his hand and he dropped it next to his beer, rolled up just like the one upstairs. Beer in hand, he sat on the step that led to the sunken lounge room.

"How was your week?" he asked.

"Fine." *Fine?* "How was yours?"

"Stressful. I half expected divorce papers in my inbox all week."

"Oh."

He picked at the label of his beer. Took a sip. His foot rested right next to where the wine *had* stained the carpet.

Cora had cheated on her husband. For a moment, she thought she was going to vomit again. Everything between them had been messy. Uncomfortable. But they were still married. So what if she had mentioned she wanted it? The words had tumbled out right before he got on a plane, no discussion, no closure. They hadn't settled anything.

"Don't leave, Cora."

The words were quiet. Husky. As if he'd held them in for days and days and they only now had managed to creep out.

She looked up sharply. "Why?"

They weren't happy. Were they? Her eyes darted to the dent again. Back to his face. All she felt was guilt. Like a fog had settled and covered everything else that had been there.

"You can't do this to me. You can't. You'll destroy everything I've worked for." He was staring at the ground, shoulders slumped. His fingers continued to pick at the label.

Couldn't she? No she couldn't. She couldn't do that. Not that, too. Not after cheating on him.

"But what can we do?" How she managed to ask that, she would never know. She hadn't even realised she'd thought it.

"I made an appointment. With a therapist." He looked up now, his eyes oddly hard considering his tone of voice. The last few years, she could never figure him out. Cora had suggested a therapist, tentatively, a year ago. The reaction had been explosive, negative. "Come with me. Don't put me through this."

A headache built behind her eyes as she did everything she could to not look at the table again. She held his eye. "No" was on her tongue. No. It wasn't good for them. For her. For him. It was time to end it.

She remembered Frazer, sitting on her, shirt open and mouth parted. Her hips moving. The way Cora came undone on Frazer's tongue.

"Okay." She said.

He nodded. "Okay."

Hours later, in the bed with sheets different from the day before, Cora lay naked. Again.

Across that canyon that was always there, even when attempting to reconcile, her husband lay, radiating heat and breathing deeply. When he rolled, he pulled the sheets with him, the wall of his back cutting her off from him as she put her hand over her mouth and sobbed.

Monday morning.

Almost eight o'clock.

Again.

Today Frazer would find out the answer to her project. That she had to do with Cora. Who she had slept with three days ago.

And the answer would come from Alec, her husband.

How lovely.

Surly and a little tired, her muscles aching from too much swimming and a headache induced by a family meal, Frazer slammed her door shut. The sound bounced off the parking garage's walls. Maybe she'd done that too hard.

So. She would find out. Then she would be happy or sad. She would look at Cora as if they were workmates who were building a friendship. Not only that, she would smile or scowl at Alec, only depending on the answer he gave her. Nothing would be about her mixed-up emotions about his wife. She and Cora would discuss the outcome. Frazer would snark with Tia, and all would be normal. Frazer would be a friend, as Cora had asked her to be.

Completely normal.

As she exited the stairwell, Frazer somehow managed to turn the corner that led them through to the main hospital building and come face to face with Alec.

She blinked at him. "Hey, Alec."

I had sex with your wife.

Why the hell was he here early, for once?

On your table. And in your bed.

At least Cora never came in with him.

"Hi, Frazer."

His face was a little drawn, a little pale. Would she normally notice that?

"Hey, Frazer."

Oh, good God. Why was Cora with him?

Frazer stepped back, putting some space between them all. Yup. There was Cora, stepping out from behind Alec to stand next to him, looking as pale and drawn as he did. Was it just Frazer, or were her eyes red-rimmed? Not that it mattered. It wasn't any of Frazer's business.

"Hey, Cora!" Frazer pressed her lips together. She needed to dial back the enthusiasm. "So, Mondays. Nice and early. Who doesn't love that?"

Alec was looking at her like she'd just pulled her pants down in the hallway. *I had sex with your wife.*

"Yes, well, only time it's easy to get everyone together at once." He cleared his throat and pointedly looked at his watch.

They all stepped forward in one happy group and started walking.

His arm brushed hers, and she jerked away, looking into her bag to hide the motion.

I had sex with your wife.

"How was your conference, Alec?" If there was anything Frazer was good at, it was obnoxious conversation to cover her awkward feelings.

"It was good, thank you. How was your weekend?"

Heat crawled over Frazer's cheeks. She even felt her chest grow warm. She didn't dare look, but she could bet Cora was staring straight ahead with a face as red as Frazer's felt. "Um. Quiet. Family lunch."

I had sex with your wife.

At least that hideous thought made sense in this context.

"Very nice."

They finally came to a stop outside the conference room.

"Sorry, ladies." Alec gave them a smile that didn't quite reach his eyes. "I need some things from my office."

For the first time in her life, Frazer watched Alec's back longingly. When he turned the corner, she had to look back to Cora.

Frazer offered a wave. "Hey."

"Hi." Cora was looking anywhere but at her face, and Frazer couldn't blame her. "Alec was sure you'd ask him about the project the second you saw him."

"I was...distracted."

Cora's cheeks grew redder than they already were. "Well, I'll see you inside."

Cursing herself, Frazer followed and sat on the opposite side of the room. Which was a ridiculous idea as now she had to resist the urge to look over at her every three seconds.

Perfume invaded her senses, and then the warm body of Tia plopped into the chair next to her. The insane urge to wrap her arms around the woman and sob into her motherly neck nearly overtook her.

"Frazer. I didn't have time for coffee."

The sad face Tia made was so overdramatic Frazer almost laughed. "I had two."

The piercing look was even better. "You," Tia said, "are horrible. How was your weekend?"

"Same old. Swam. Saw some family."

"Oh. Exciting."

Frazer elbowed her. "What did you do, party until five a.m.?"

Fluffing her hair, Tia said, "You don't know. Maybe I did. Are you nervous?"

Frazer tore her attention from the back of Cora's head. "About what?"

"You find out today: yay or nay to the project."

"Ah, yeah. I'm trying not to think about it." Or it had been driven from her mind.

"Well, now that you've got Cora on your side, I don't see how it can't be a yes."

"Cora isn't on my side." The words left her mouth too quickly, too obviously.

"I meant you two are working on it together." Tia shook her head at Frazer. "I thought you two were getting along now?"

Adamantly staring at the front and ignoring the tick in her eye, Frazer said, "Yeah. Having her on my side hopefully makes a difference."

Thankfully, Alec entered, people straightening in their seats. Frazer sank into her own.

Tia practically vibrated next to her. "Oh! Here we go!"

He started with a slide on discharge numbers.

Tia snorted next to her. "Oh, he's not gonna make you wait through all this, is he?"

His next slide slid over to a comparison of the numbers from the same time last year.

"Oh, dear God. He is."

If it had been appropriate, Frazer would have groaned. For thirty minutes, they had statistics thrown at them, in more detail than anyone really cared about. Then a rundown on how each department could improve discharge numbers, patient turnover, and length of stay. Finally, the separate departments came up, and all of a sudden—

"Midwifery and Obstetrics project proposal has been accepted, they're now merging with Social Work on it. Cora is to be the liaison for that."

And then he was speaking about the new diabetes trial, and Frazer was grinning so hard, her cheeks hurt. Fingers wrapped around her bicep, and she nudged Tia, who made an "ee!" noise as quietly as she could.

Alec didn't even make eye contact. Across the room, Cora turned around with a beam to match Frazer's. For a moment, Frazer forgot everything and instead simply felt elated. If she wasn't half-asleep, she'd probably have floated out the room.

Her project was happening.

When her gaze fell back on Alec, he caught Frazer's eye. Her face froze.

I had sex with your wife.

"We did it!"

Frazer's entire face was lit up, looking at Cora as if she hadn't seen her naked, and that made Cora feel even worse. Maybe Frazer regretted it? Of course she did. Cora was married, and it had all been a ridiculous idea. Why had Cora had to kiss her?

"We did." Cora said.

The water cooler in the staff room made a weird bubble noise between them, and Cora actually jumped. Suddenly, the look Frazer gave her bordered on pitying. Why couldn't Cora just crawl into a hole? Why did she agree to therapy?

Why did she do most of the things she did?

"You okay?" Frazer asked.

Her eyes were soft. The look was strangely like the one she'd used on her right after Cora had kissed her, when she'd been pressed between Frazer and her glorious table and hesitated.

It was full of understanding.

"Yeah." Cora nodded in case that wasn't convincing enough. "Yeah, yeah. I'm great."

Except Frazer hadn't answered her message. Not that there was a lot to be said to a single word. Well, really, there was a lot that could be said to *that* single word. And she was worrying about Frazer not replying to her message, not the fact that Cora had cheated on her husband and her marriage was crumbling and she was on her way to *couples* therapy in a few days.

But yet, here she was, acting like a teenager and worrying about an unanswered message.

A silence settled over them, awkward like it hadn't been since they first started becoming more than workmates who mildly grated on each other. There were other staff members in the room, someone chewing loud enough to set Cora's nerves on edge. The sound of pages turning in a magazine sounded like a cannon going off over and over.

"So... I'll see you soon?" Frazer asked.

"You will?" Cora was anything but smooth, anything but able to hold it together. She needed to be staying away from Frazer.

"Yeah, we should have a meeting soon, once I've received the documentation and budget outline."

Oh, the project. "Yeah." Cora nodded again. She should probably stop that. "Great, just send me a message."

Or it would be really nice if Frazer answered the original one.

The jumper Frazer had on showed a smooth expanse of chest, and Cora made herself stare at her eyes instead. Cora didn't look down women's shirts, or men's. She was married. Very married. With a husband. A manly husband. Who she owed it to to at least *try*, at least a little.

"Okay. I'll see you, then. Less than I did on the weekend, though." Frazer winked.

And Frazer left.

She'd made a stupid joke and left.

Couldn't they still get a coffee?

Cora was used to their coffees. To actually thinking of Frazer as a friend.

Were they still friends?

Did friends make jokes about the time they'd had confusingly good sex on a dining table?

As long as Cora never had to repeat that morning, blinking between Frazer and Alec and feeling hot guilt sitting on her shoulders, she wanted to. It happened once; an accident, a distraction. Did that excuse it? No. She had cheated. But her marriage wasn't over.

She would fix this with Alec, because that's what he needed. And she could be friends with Frazer, because that's what she was meant to be.

Friends.

"Go dance with her."

Rob was staring at Frazer and all she wanted to do was dump her drink on his head. "No."

There had been enough dancing, figuratively or whatever, to last her a lifetime. Clustered around the bar, taking up all the free stools in their favourite pub, her friends had reached the point at which they started to annoy her to be more social than she wanted. The pub had also reached the point where people started dancing, the music turning up that one decibel too loud. All of this meant *Frazer* had reached the point when she normally skived off and went home. To her fish. And her comfy, quiet bed.

"Come on." Andy poked her in the ribs. "We know you cut your date with that receptionist short. Jemma told us." Leaning forward, Andy eyed her. "Which, by the way, we were very disappointed to hear about from *Jemma*." Andy turned her slightly glazed eyes to the man in question. "Rob, do you remember the days we actually spoke to *Frazer*? And *she* told us about her life, saw us more than every now and again?"

"Nope. Can't recall."

Now Frazer considered dumping her drink on Andy's head. "Guys. It's not been *that* bad. I've been busy. My project is finally getting somewhere."

Rob's eyes widened. "Wait. You've met a *girl*, haven't you?"

Looking from one of her friends to the other, Frazer furrowed her brow. "In which part of my sentence did I say that?"

"Oh, come on." He poked her with his straw, not noticing that he dripped rum and coke all down her white shirt. Now *she* looked like the messy drunk. "There has to be a girl. You never disappear from us."

"No girl."

"Mhm." Andy was looking at her with the same expression as Rob. "Sure there isn't."

"I'm telling you, there's no girl."

No girl. One night of a girl, not even really a whole girl since she belonged to someone else. Frazer wrinkled up her nose—ew, since when did she think marriage meant you *belonged* to someone else?

"Alright, shit. No need to look so disgusted with the notion." Andy shook her head woefully. "Some people *like* dating."

"Yes, well, to some people, it sounds like hell." Frazer sipped her soda water and smiled at her with the straw between her teeth.

"You know." Rob actually looked thoughtful, which was always a scary thing. "If you had just never gone out with Asshat from three years ago, we could have our old Casanova Frazer back."

Andy stared off into the distance and added, "I really liked her."

Scowling at them didn't feel sufficient, and Frazer had to resist the urge to add a swift kick to both of their shins. "I was not a Casanova!"

Turning to Rob, Andy said, "Remember when she slept with that nun?"

"There was no nun!"

Rob grabbed Andy's arm. "Or her old university lecturer."

"Which one?" Andy snickered. "The cougar, or the new one who resigned afterward because she felt like she'd broken some code of ethics?"

"Oh my God, you are both horrendous!" Or Frazer had been horrendous. Either one. Or both.

Leaning between them to slam her drink down on the bar top, Frazer glared at them.

"I'm going home. Where I'm appreciated." She grabbed her jacket with more than enough flair to show the depth of her irritation.

They both blinked at her. Like they were so confused. Like they didn't know how annoying they were.

"By who?" Rob cocked his head. "Your fish?"

Andy was still grinning like a shark. "That butt indent on your couch does miss you, I'm sure."

Pressing her lips together so as not to show her entertainment at their asshattery, Frazer pulled on her jacket. Her biggest mistake would be to show that she found them funny.

"Oh! I see a smile!" Rob tried to poke her in the stomach.

Damn.

Andy threw an arm around her shoulders. "You know we love you. Don't go." She batted her eyelashes. "We just miss you."

Frazer looked from one puppy dog face to the next and finally sighed. "Fine. But no more talk about dating."

"Deal." Rob held up two fingers. "Scout's honour."

"Or discussion of my dubious past."

"Whose dubious past?"

Frazer spun around to laugh delightedly at the sight of Daniel. Finally, someone who normally stuck up for her. She threw her arms around him. Even as Daniel leant forward to drop a kiss on Rob's lips, she clung to his arm.

"Daniel!" Andy grinned at him, her smile a twin of his. Sometimes Frazer thought they were more like siblings than cousins, but it could just be that they were so close. "We didn't know you were coming. And we were talking about Frazer's colourful and exciting past."

"I don't have a colourful and exciting past. The word we should be using is *dubious*."

All three turned raised eyebrows at Frazer. Even Daniel, the traitor.

"Andy." Frazer laced all the warning she could into her tone.

Andy made a face, then huffed when Frazer just stared at her. "Fine. No discussions of your awesome past."

"Dubious."

"*Dubious* past, then. Now!" Andy pulled her against the bar and signalled the bartender. "Let's get you a *real* drink."

Frazer was going to regret this.

Yup. Definitely regretted it.

The next morning, the all-too-familiar feeling of blurry eyes and a headache cheerfully greeted her upon waking.

Thankfully, she was in her bed. With no one next to her.

Once that was confirmed, she fell back against her pillow and groaned.

Alcohol and she should no longer be friends. She was too old for this. She'd been too old for it ten years ago. Or maybe forever ago.

At her left, a glass of water filled to the brim and a packet of paracetamol sat as if the divine hand of God had put it there. The world spun when she sat up too fast in her excitement, but she ignored it and swallowed the pills, drinking almost the entire glass. A note sat next to the now-open box.

Getting you to bed was like getting a two-year-old there. Or, at least, what I imagine it would be like—thanks for confirming my lack of desire to have kids. Enjoy work today, Sunshine! —Andy

Her friends were assholes. Once Frazer wasn't blinded by the brightness of her phone's screen, she sent a message to both Andy and Rob, saying exactly that. With the phone in her hand, Frazer started to get an odd feeling low in her gut. It wasn't alcohol induced.

She'd been staring at her phone in the crowded bathroom the night before. Why?

All at once, her mouth went dry again. She hadn't done that, had she? Surely she wasn't the person that did *that*.

Taking a deep breath, she opened her sent messages. There, at the top of the list staring at her like regret incarnate, was a message to Cora.

Because she felt like some self-flagellation, Frazer opened it.

I'm not sorry.

What? Yes she was!

Frazer threw her phone on the end of the bed and groaned loudly, pulling the blanket over her head.

Yep, she definitely regretted it.

CHAPTER NINE

Frazer wasn't sorry?

What the hell did that mean? For the last two days, Frazer had seemed to purposefully avoid Cora at work. From what Cora had gleaned, Frazer was definitely sorry. As she should be. Just like Cora was; it was all a big mistake.

Squinting at the message for the tenth time that morning, Cora finally noticed the timestamp.

03:14.

A smirk played at her lips that she should have tried harder to wipe away. Frazer had drunk-texted her. Breathing out slowly, Cora shoved her phone into her pocket. Frazer hadn't meant it; unless she had.

A nurse popped her head into the room. "Hey, Cora, you have a minute?"

Closing the patient's note that had been in front of her, Cora turned to face her. Anything to stop this back-and-forth in her head. "Sure, what's up, Jess?"

She was a younger nurse, one of the many new graduates. But as the ward was one Cora frequented, she made an effort to learn their names. The ward was mostly filled with older patients needing referrals and help with the government documents or paperwork before moving into an aged-care facility. Cora did everything from sign and witness last will and testaments to doing what she did all too frequently: holding someone's hand to tell them they wouldn't be going back to their own home again.

"Mr Sodhi's family is here. They want to know what their options are."

Cora must have shown her thoughts on her face because Jess chuckled. "Don't worry, they seem nice."

Just yesterday, Cora had made the recommendation for sending Mr Sodhi to a home. There was no way he could look after himself anymore. His wife had passed away ten years ago, and his weight had dropped from his last hospital admission by fifteen kilos. After an hour of discussion, he had admitted he didn't want to be a bother to his family and had been living off tinned tomatoes and hiding the bruises he gained from frequent falls.

Once again, Cora had found herself appalled at life.

Following Jess out, she spotted three middle-aged men at the end of the hall, watching Jess anxiously. Once introduced, she and Mr Sodhi's three sons settled into one of the rooms set aside for just this. It was barren and fairly depressing, with a dejected-looking painting of a seascape whose copies resided in about ten other rooms in the hospital.

"So," Cora smiled at them, gently and not too widely. The amount, she'd learnt, set people at ease but didn't make her seem flippant or too cheerful during a situation that was anything but. "How can I help you?"

Two of the men looked to the middle son, introduced as Raj. "We hear our father has had more problems than he let on?"

Cora nodded. "Yes, his weight has dropped dramatically. He keeps having falls. I'm afraid it's time he's moved into a home, where he can have the care he—"

"Absolutely not."

Cora shut her mouth with an almost audible snap. "Sorry?"

"Our father will not be cared for by strangers." Dark brown eyes stared at her from beneath a deep set brow. "Absolutely not."

"Well, there are other options." Cora looked between them.

The younger-looking brother spoke then. "Of course there are. He'll be at home with my wife and I."

Cora felt her smile slipping into something genuine.

The middle son leant forward. "Our father is stubborn. We didn't know how bad it was—but he will be at home with his family. We'll take care of him."

Sometimes, Cora loved her job. "Great. Let's go over the paperwork and some services I can make available to you."

When she walked out twenty minutes later, the feeling settling over Cora was very different than the usual one after these sorts of meetings.

A buzzing in her pocket distracted her. In the one second that it took for her to pull her phone out, that wonderful feeling dissipated and a heavy feeling settled in her stomach. She had to be in couples therapy in ten minutes.

The last few days, Alec had been glued to work, catching up on everything he had missed. It had been a relief to feign sleep when she felt the mattress dip late at night. His heavy breathing would fill the room, and she'd blink at the wall for hours, a mix of feelings swirling in her gut too complex to pull apart and examine.

He'd booked a therapist for them not far from the hospital, within walking distance. A woman Cora had thankfully never met nor would likely ever have to see outside of their sessions. Alec had insisted he wouldn't have time to make it to someone further from the hospital with his hours. This woman, who Cora had searched for on the internet, was apparently one of the best available.

She'd written three books. And too many journal articles to count. Surely, if anyone could help Cora piece something resembling a marriage back together, she could.

Maybe she would simply look at Cora and know what she'd done. This woman, Doctor Massey, had probably seen hundreds of cheaters.

The thought that she was going to vomit again overtook her, and she only just made it to the bathroom. Thankfully, the room was empty. The last thing she needed was pregnancy rumours.

Ten minutes later, Cora was walking down a street, marvelling at how the dark clouds from that morning had started to split apart with streaks of lightning. It was eerie with no thunder to accompany it. It only took a short walk to reach the psychologist's office, but she was grateful to slip inside away from the odd weather. In the waiting room, teeth clean thanks to the toothbrush pinched from one of the wards, Cora tried to ignore the way her stomach still roiled. The room was bland. There weren't even motivational posters on the wall. It seemed a little...trite. The paint was hospital-issue white. At three on the dot, the door opened, and Cora's heart rate, which had finally started to slow, sped up again. She tried to ignore it.

Her therapist—Cora didn't know why those words made her flinch—was smiling. Using the same kind of smile Cora wore sometimes with her patients. Her heart sped up more at the thought that, dear God, Cora was the patient. The patient of someone with perfect white teeth and perfectly neat hair. Her eyes searched the room, obviously expecting two people since this was couples therapy, yet her look didn't falter when she caught Cora's eye.

"Alec running late, then?"

It was at that moment that Cora remembered this woman would know Alec. Or at least of him. Probably the latter as Alec wouldn't meet someone he knew privately, and of course Doctor Massey wouldn't either. That would be seriously unethical.

"I imagine so." Cora smoothed her skirt over her legs. "Though he'll be here any minute, I'm sure."

"No problem. Do you want to come in?"

No.

"Sure." Cora smiled too, because she could offer a benign smile as well as a psychologist, and stood.

The only thing that could be worse than being stuck with Alec and a psychologist was being stuck alone with the same psychologist. Before Cora could take a step, though, Alec entered, neat and calm in his suit.

"Sorry I'm late."

Doctor Massey smiled again. It was so easy for her. Easier than for Cora, it seemed. Though she had to do this all day. Even more than a social worker. Just that thought exhausted Cora. "No problem, Alec. Follow me."

With Alec in the lead, they entered behind their therapist into a room that had probably seen more marriages break down than the bar down the road.

If they didn't fix their marriage, or at least try to, Cora would always wonder if it was the cheating that had done it.

So here Alec and Cora were, actually sitting on a couch and being stared at by a woman they didn't know from Adam but who could apparently help them repair everything.

That fog that had settled over her the last few days, suffocating her and leaving her feeling disconnected, became even more stifling.

The lights flickered strangely. The lightning storm outside was wreaking havoc.

Doctor Massey watched them, her face unreadable and passive.

She introduced herself, then had them introduce themselves. Too long was spent going over the confidentiality agreement that, of course, both Alec and Cora understood, but was a legal requirement. And then they were asked what they wanted to achieve in therapy.

The gap between Alec and Cora on the couch was so much like the one that lay between them when they slept. This one, though, wasn't filled with the things at home. That's what this room was for. To fill up that gap and see if the words could build a bridge for her to cross over and meet him.

Or if all those words were too light, too full of falseness and anger and bitterness, and fell apart if they even stepped a foot on them.

Why did she always feel as if she had to bridge that gap? Why didn't she feel that he could walk over it all to meet her? Or that they could meet in the middle?

Because you cheated. You slept with someone else.

136

That voice sounded shockingly like her mother's, and that made Cora feel even more uncomfortable than that room or the gap between them did.

"So. Why are you here?"

Cora looked to Alec. Who stared at Doctor Massey.

He cleared his throat like he did in a meeting. "We need to get back on track."

It was a good answer, solid—it was better than Cora could have provided. Cora looked back to Doctor Massey, who nodded. "Okay. Good. How are you off track?"

Which was a good question. How *weren't* they off track would be better, but she didn't know to ask that. Cora watched Alec again. In all honesty, Cora wanted to hear what he had to say. To hear if he changed his answer from the things he hissed at her in anger or typed passive aggressively in messages.

"We can't seem to have a conversation without being angry at each other anymore. If we do manage to start one without yelling, Cora always walks away instead of finishing."

Heat flushed her face. She looked down at the floor before taking a deep breath and looking up to see Doctor Massey now staring at her. That bothered her so much, because often it was Alec who would just walk away if what Cora said hit too close to home.

"Okay." Doctor Massey looked from one to the other. "Let's start here: where did you meet?"

"At university." Alec answered.

"Great. And Cora, how old were you?"

"Eighteen." Cora tried to sound confident.

"And what did you first notice about Alec?"

Alec turned to stare at her.

"His hair."

With a chuckle, Doctor Massey turned to Alec. "And you, Alec?"

"Her eyes."

"And what brought you two together?"

Memory lane was going to be exhausting.

They talked about things that Cora found almost painful. Doctor Massey explained that in the first session, she needed to get to know them, and that they would mostly speak with her. However, in the next sessions, she'd be facilitating discussions between the two of them. So they talked to her about the start of their relationship, about why they got married. It left Cora with a hollow feeling. The answer "because I was pregnant," considered so far after the fact, felt hollow, immature. How was that a reason to get married? Or better yet, to stay married?

"Was that the only reason?" Doctor Massey asked them, her expression impassive.

"We would have eventually anyway," Alec said.

Nodding her agreement, Cora wondered if she meant it.

"When did you first think about separating?"

The questions got harder, more direct. The answers sparked between them, setting fire to the shaky bridge they'd built with memories of times when they were happy together. They bit at each other, bit at each other's answers. Alec tore at things she said, and then Cora stopped answering entirely, just as she did at home. It was easier, less exhausting, than saying something that would just get twisted around.

But then, when he interrupted her, Doctor Massey held up a gentle hand, one that cut him off. "Cora was speaking."

Such a simple thing to say.

"Why do you walk away, Cora?"

Now she could feel the heat of Alec's gaze on her. The relaxed, open look of Doctor Massey was easier to look at. "I don't know."

"Yes, you do," she countered.

Cora took a deep breath, her teeth clenched. Should she be honest or did she say what Alec wanted her to say?

"I, uh," she refused to look at Alec, "I feel like whichever direction the conversation goes, it'll be my fault anyway. So, if I walk away, the same result happens without all the discussion. If I—"

"So walking away solves everything?" Alec interjected.

Cora still couldn't look at him. "Often, it's like he just interrupts me before I can say—"

"That's not true."

Cora kept her eyes on Doctor Massey and wondered if Alec saw the irony in what had just occurred.

He kept talking, so apparently not.

But then Doctor Massey stopped him again. Reminded him that in this room, they both had to listen to what the other person said.

"I feel Alec talks over me."

"What do you think about that, Alec?"

And Alec, the microphone in his hand, apparently thought a lot about that.

Cora's face felt so hot that she wondered if it looked as painted with shame as she felt. It was never-ending. Cora heard that she was too sensitive: if she only fought back harder, he'd respect her more. If he was too dominant, it was only because she was too submissive.

Then the doctor turned to her and asked, "What do you think is the number one problem in your relationship?"

I slept with someone else.

Cora had never been more aware of her breathing. Alec was staring at her. Doctor Massey was staring at her. "I don't know."

"Think."

Alec started to speak, and the doctor turned to him, that smile in place. "Alec, you had your turn, it's Cora's turn to speak."

Everything seemed too quiet and too loud all at once.

"I think we've lost the ability to communicate."

Doctor Massey nodded. Cora had no idea if that was the right answer or not. She also wasn't sure if they'd ever had the ability to communicate to start with. In the beginning, Cora mostly remembered listening to Alec with a sensation akin to awe. Slowly, as she'd started to speak more, she'd shaped her answers around him. Then, as she'd stopped doing that, he'd lashed out. Scorned her, made her feel stupid.

They talked more. Doctor Massey talked more.

She ended by saying, "These sessions aren't here to 'fix' your relationship. They're here to give you the tools to communicate with each other and to give you the space to do just that." She looked from one to the other. "Before the next session, I want you to work on one thing each: Alec, if Cora is telling you something, let her finish. Try to hear what she's saying. And Cora..."

Why did just the sound of her name make Cora feel nervous?

"I want you to come back with a list of the nice things Alec does for you between now and the next session, including times you felt he listened."

They both made noises of acquiescence.

She told them about the pamphlets outside they could feel free to take, then said she'd see them in two days' time.

A minute later, they were ejected into the fluorescent light of a hallway, Cora feeling slightly stunned.

"That went well," Alec said.

Cora felt like she had said about five sentences. But she nodded. "It did."

His words, *you can't do this to me*, ran around and around her head.

"I'll see you at home."

"Okay."

And he turned, disappearing down the hallway.

Someone walked past her. "Sorry."

They didn't even look up.

Everything in her felt out of sorts, like parts had been pulled forcefully out of her, then jammed back in all wrong. Breathing felt like something she had to think about doing and, somehow, she wasn't doing it right. The wall on her left was lined with pamphlets, glossy covers mixed in with cheaper paper ones. She plucked a few out, not really thinking, taking ones that hinted at topics about marriage and overcoming differences. Walking down the hallway, she flicked through the few she'd grabbed. The last one, solid in her hand but its weight nothing, made her blink. She hadn't even realised she'd taken it.

Emotional Abuse: Signs

Swallowing heavily, she shoved it in her bag, as deep down as it could go.

By two o'clock, Frazer's hangover was better, and she just wanted to sleep.

What business did her drunk brain have sending Cora a message at three a.m.?

The entire day, Tia had been catching her eye and smirking. When Frazer caught sight of herself in the bathroom mirror, it became pretty clear why: she looked ashen, and her eyes were a creepy shade of red with black smudges underneath.

Hangovers could die in the fiery pits of hell where they belonged for all she cared.

And the weird lightning outside needed to stop happening. Frazer loved storms, but the strange light show was off-putting, and she was not enjoying it. The clouds were a heavy purple colour, sitting low over the harbour. They were the same colour as the clouds last year when she'd gone to Japan for her first and only attempt at skiing. After falling face first down the baby slopes too many times to count, she'd settled for sitting in various bars and restaurants. She was more of an *après* skier anyway, and the view alone made it worthwhile: huge mountains, snow everywhere, and that incredible stillness that happened right before the heavens dumped a load of snow. Clouds never went that colour in Perth.

But now they were surprisingly close to the right colour, and the sky was lighting up spectacularly to go along with it. But they wouldn't be getting snow, just a huge storm.

Which meant driving home in the rain.

Which meant dealing with people who had suddenly forgotten how to drive. People would bounce between going way too fast on newly wet roads and dropping their speed ridiculously, endangering every person driving nearby.

Tearing her eyes from the view, Frazer checked her pager. New parents had arrived, waters broken en route.

At least they'd be able to boast that the baby had come out during what was probably going to be one of the biggest storms that year.

Which, for other cities, would be a minor storm, but they'd take what they could.

Hands buried in her pockets, Frazer rocked back and forth on her heels as she waited for the elevator to arrive. She was going to redeem herself and her terrible hangover by bringing new life into the world.

Or, rather, by observing their newest midwife bring new life into the world. Frazer may have gotten irresponsibly hung-over, but only because she was not supposed to be touching a patient that day.

When all that was done, she would then check her e-mails for the twentieth time that day to see if Alec had sent through the material to get started with the programme. Nervous energy played in her stomach as Frazer pressed the down button again.

Which she knew did nothing to help, but it made her feel better. Everything in this hospital was *slow* today. Or maybe it was just her.

If the e-mail was through, Frazer could start calling the parents she had on the waiting list she'd started. Which she shouldn't have really started without being sure the project would be given the green light. But she had figured it was good to send out positive vibes into the universe. Or something.

The elevator finally dinged, and the doors slid open. It was mercifully empty. With a contented sigh, Frazer pressed the button for ground floor and leant back against the wall. Silence.

There was about to be none of that.

The elevator stopped again too soon, doors sliding open at the next floor. But it wasn't a screaming birth that broke the silence.

Frazer wanted to tell whoever was waiting at the open doors to go away, but she looked up politely. Then she froze.

Cora blinked at her. She slid into the elevator car slowly, like she wanted to be anywhere else.

Frazer almost laughed.

Of course that's who it was.

"Hey." Frazer even managed to look friendly. Or a reasonable portrayal of friendly, she hoped. Maybe she looked terrifying.

Cora cocked her head. "Hi."

They didn't move.

Frazer indicated the control panel with her head. "You, uh, have to press a button, or the doors will take forever to close."

Hospital elevators always took so long to close, in case someone was hobbling in on crutches.

"Oh." Cora laughed, breathy and nervous. "Yeah."

She hit the button.

They moved.

Then stopped again.

"What the hell?" Cora asked, looking around as if she could find answers on the ceiling. "Have we stopped?"

"Considering we aren't moving, I'd say yes."

Cora gave Frazer the same look most people did when she was a sarcastic ass. "Thanks. Listen, though."

They both tilted their heads, focussed.

Frazer shrugged. "Nothing."

"Exactly." Cora leant back against the doors. "Nothing."

"Seriously?" Frazer slid down the wall to sit on the floor, staring up at Cora. "We're stuck?"

Listlessly, Cora pressed the "help" button. Nothing. "There is zero power. Zilch. Nada. Nothing—"

"Got it."

"Just making sure." Cora gave a grin that made Frazer chuckle.

"So why are there lights?"

Looking up as if she'd just noticed that, Cora said, "I don't know. Maybe separate fuses were blown?"

Frazer nodded like she had any idea what that meant.

After avoiding Cora skilfully for days on end, it was nice to chat with her again. And that was all. Chat.

Were they seriously stuck in an elevator together? How clichéd.

Frazer tried not to think about how Cora had looked naked.

Digging into her deep pockets, Frazer fished out her phone. "No signal. Why is there never any signal in an elevator?"

Cora had her own in hand, staring down at it with an accusatory look. "Seriously?"

"I have a patient arriving. Her water's broken already."

"Someone else will be on it."

Frazer stuck out her bottom lip. "I wanted to be a part of this one."

Mimicking Frazer, Cora slid down the doors and sat cross-legged. "This specific one was so important to you?"

"I wanted to end on a win since I started this day on an epic fail."

"Nice and hung-over, are we, Frazer?"

Cora was enjoying this far too much for Frazer's liking.

"Started with a headache?"

Frazer's text message hung between them, not replied to and not spoken of.

Okay, maybe not ignored.

"I may have drunk a tad too much last night." Frazer stuck her legs out, crossing them at the ankle. Her feet sat close to Cora's knee. An elevator was really small. How had she never noticed that before?

Cora had her hair up. The long line of her neck was open to Frazer's gaze, and she purposefully kept her eyes away from it.

Her lips had been just there.

Cora's lips had been on her neck. And her collarbone. Frazer shifted slightly, her thighs clinching together.

Don't think about it. She's married.

Still.

"Did you go out with anyone in particular?"

Was it just Frazer's imagination, or did Cora sound more curious than was normal?

Frazer flipped her phone in her hands. "Just some friends from university who still like to drink in the middle of the week."

"Yes." Cora smirked, a look that was delightful on her. "Because I've *never* seen you do that."

A bark of laughter from Frazer. Across from her, Cora looked satisfied at the sound. "Nope. I hate alcohol."

"Sure."

Silence settled around them.

Frazer stared at her phone. It was much easier than looking at the woman across from her. All the air felt sucked out of the room. The ease that had started to accompany them had already dissipated.

"Frazer."

She looked up sharply. "Yeah?"

The look on Cora's face was soft. Slight. "I just wanted to see if you would look at me."

"I was looking at you before."

"Not properly."

"Cora..." Frazer breathed her name out, felt it whisper across her lips.

This time, Cora looked down, and Frazer wondered if that name had felt as heavy to Cora as it had to her.

It filled the room.

"Truth or dare?"

Cora laughed. "What?"

Seriously, Frazer asked again. "Truth or dare?"

"Truth."

It was easier to meet each other's eyes when this was what they spoke about. "Um...crap. Should've thought of a question first. First kiss?"

"Sean Carbon. Year 9. Behind the bike shed. Yours?"

"Tom Peters. Year 8."

Cora's eyebrows raised, and Frazer spoke before she could. "Yes, I kissed boys. Not for long, though."

Cora chuckled. "Well, you can't blame me for expecting it to be a girl."

"No, the girls were six months later." Frazer winked and Cora snickered. "Your turn."

"Truth or dare."

"Truth." Frazer said with zero hesitation.

"Favourite book?"

"Like... Just one?" Frazer shook her head. "Impossible."

"Fine—one of your favourite books."

"What? List a few and miss some out? No way. They'll feel hurt."

"Really, Frazer?" Cora was looking at her like she was insane.

"Yes, really."

"Fine. Book you liked but *also* liked the movie."

"Seriously?"

"There has to be one."

That was not an easy question.

"Oh!" Frazer bounced a little as an answer entered her mind. "*Anne of Green Gables.*"

Cora made a face. "I didn't like that book."

Mouth dropped open, Frazer stared at her. "Are you talking smack about my first love?"

Hands held up, Cora shook her head. "No, no. I was joking. I love them. The books were great."

"That's better."

With her back settled against the wall, Frazer licked her lips and tried to think of another question. Any questions that wasn't, *did you enjoy that night? Do you kind of want to do it again? Why do you have to be married? Are you really sorry?*

"Truth or dare?"

Cora grinned. "Truth." When Frazer rolled her eyes, Cora poked her tongue out. "I'm boring."

Her hand fell on Frazer's ankle like it was the most natural thing in the word. Was it natural? Friends did that. Gave affection. Touched. Frazer and Andy probably looked like a couple after a few drinks. But she'd never slept with Andy.

Heat crept up Frazer's shin. Her foot tingled.

She should move her leg. Subtly. Away. Or Cora should move her hand.

Neither of them did.

"Biggest regret?"

It slipped out. Frazer had meant to ask about her most embarrassing moment.

That hand didn't move, but the grip tightened. Just a little.

Enough to notice.

Cora looked to the floor. Her chest was moving up and down noticeably.

"Different question." Cora's voice was tight.

"O-kay. Most embarrassing moment?"

Frazer let out a small breath she hadn't realised she'd been holding when she saw a smile play on Cora's features.

"Being dacked at the school camp when I was nine. Underwear and all."

Frazer bit her lip. Her jaw clenched.

"It's okay, Frazer, you can laugh."

A bark of laughter made it out, and Cora sighed theatrically. Frazer tried to tamp down on her amusement. "I'm so sorry. I know that would have been so embarrassing, but really?"

"Yeah. It was night, too. My butt practically glowed."

"Poor thing."

"Yeah, you clearly think that; you're still laughing."

Frazer managed to drop her eyes back to her phone, thumb scrolling over and over as she felt Cora's eyes on her.

"Truth or dare?" Cora asked.

"Dare."

Because why not? This was boring, and it wasn't like there was much she could do in there, anyway.

"Kiss me."

The words were nothing but a whisper, but they filled Frazer's ears as if they'd been shouted. Her neck cricked as she looked up too quickly. She stared at Cora, who was looking at her steadily. Too steadily. Frazer looked back at her phone again.

"What?"

Cora said it again, as if it were nothing this time. "Kiss me."

Neither of them moved. The space in the lift wasn't big enough to hold all of this. Cora's hand shifted up from her ankle. Her fingers wrapped around Frazer's shin, and Frazer felt pressure there as Cora pushed herself upwards. There was the sound of her body moving forward, and then Cora surrounded her senses. Her legs were straddling Frazer. The smell of sweet perfume, which reminded her of her own skin and the scent that had lingered on Saturday morning, played in the air between them. Cora's chest was level with Frazer's face, and if Frazer leant forward slightly, she would be able to bury her face in the softness of her—rest her forehead between Cora's breasts and breathe her in.

"Frazer."

Hands cupped her face. Tilted her head up.

Heat trailed all over her skin, and Frazer shut her eyes.

"Kiss me."

The words whispered against her lips. And Cora didn't move. She waited. For Frazer.

The thought that she shouldn't do this barely existed in Frazer's mind anymore. She shouldn't, sure, but she couldn't not. Not with Cora this close, with her fingers biting into Frazer's skin, with their breath mingling between them.

Even though she shouldn't, even though it was wrong, Frazer closed the gap.

It was barely a movement. The gap barely existed.

Cora's lips parted and pressed against her own. She sighed.

Or Frazer did. One of them sighed—Frazer couldn't tell who.

Cora tasted of something forbidden, something unknown. Something that Frazer shouldn't have on her lips. Cora's tongue brushed hers, soft and sweet and everything. Cora's hand fell to Frazer's shoulders, and Frazer tangled her hands in Cora's hair, suddenly desperate to have her closer. Fingers ran over Frazer's chest, along her sides. They clutched at her shirt and pulled her closer.

A hum filled the air.

A slight jolt.

The elevator moved.

Cora pulled away. Cool air swirled in the space between them.

This time, Cora's eyes were closed, and when they opened, Cora stared at her.

Frazer couldn't read the expression. Wasn't aware of anything except that suddenly, Cora was standing and Frazer was following suit. When the doors opened, Cora disappeared past the woman in overalls staring at them with a toolbox in hand. Cora walked away without a backwards glance and left Frazer to make an excuse to the woman who had just freed them.

What did Cora regret most?

Frazer probably thought Cora would answer "that night." But what she really wanted to tell Frazer she regretted most? Her marriage.

But that was something too terrible to say. Those words should never be voiced. Instead, they should be locked away, put in a box, and ignored—never shown to the light.

Because Cora wasn't someone who cheated. She wasn't someone who had affairs. But ever so slowly, the facts were building up against her. They were stacking higher, and bit by bit, moment by moment, she was becoming that person.

That night, over cooling spaghetti and even cooler words, Alec looked at her and asked her if she liked the therapist.

"She seems nice."

Alec gave a nod, his fork twirling. "She's the best."

Only ever the best. "Good."

The pasta was like dust in her mouth. The dent on the table was covered by a table runner she'd found. It may as well have burnt a hole through it. She chewed. Sipped water. She swallowed. It sat heavily in her stomach, for something that had started so light.

"I was thinking." Cora said. "Maybe we should have our parents over for dinner again."

Chewing slowly, Alec set his fork down. Folded his hands together and rested his elbows on the table. "Okay. Just remember how dry the meat was last time. I mean, I don't really mind, but you know how it looks to people."

Heat warmed her cheeks. As he'd pointed out in front of everyone at the table. His eyes were back on his plate, fork in hand again.

"When were you thinking for dinner?" he asked.

"Friday night?"

"Saturday night is better. Then no one has to work the next day."

"Okay." She'd thought she could go out with Lisa that night. "Then Friday, I might see Lisa for dinner."

"Shouldn't you cook ahead that night?"

"I can cook in the afternoon on Saturday." Or he could cook. But he hated cooking. Not that he often liked what she cooked.

"Isn't it better that you be at home?"

Cora sipped her water. Licked her lips. When she didn't answer, he shook his head. "The therapist said we should make sure to spend time together. Complete our homework."

Yes, speak to her because someone told you to.

His tone made it a statement. A fact. No arguments.

"Okay."

In the back of her mind, she wished he was still at his conference. She wanted to see her friend. She was always making her plans around his. It seemed that following the therapist's advice meant doing what she had always done.

"Don't you work late on Fridays, though?" Really, she shouldn't have asked it.

"Yes, but it's work. It's important." He put his knife and fork down on his empty plate. "That was pretty spicy..."

He was looking at her. Waiting for something.

"Sorry," she said.

150

At that, he gave a nod like she'd offered him something he deserved.

When she was washing up, she decided to make spaghetti for Saturday night too.

With extra chili.

With Alec in his study, Cora let herself relax. She sank into the couch, a wine in hand, and stared at the television without really watching it. It was a relief to be in quiet, to not have Alec near her, or Frazer.

Frazer.

Cora really had no idea what she was doing with her life anymore.

Movement in the corner of her eye made Cora turn her head to see Alec standing in the kitchen. He was hovering, as if lost. Her heart clenched, beating too fast at the sight. Alec was always sure, always confident. Now he looked like he was caught between worlds with no idea what he should do.

When they caught each other's eye, he kept walking until he was sitting on the couch, the space between them slightly smaller than usual.

"What are you watching?" His eyes remained on the television.

She stared at him, unsure. "An old movie." He didn't really respond and Cora wasn't sure what to do next. "Do you want me to change it?" she asked him.

"The football is on..."

At that, she reached for the remote, but his fingers on hers, cool and sure, almost made her jump. He blinked at her when she looked up sharply. "Do you want to watch this movie?"

Not particularly, but curiosity won out.

She gave a nod. His fingers tugged at hers, pulling her hand to sit between them, fingers entwined. A halfway point.

"Leave it on," he said, his eyes back on the screen.

When they went to therapy again, Doctor Massey watched them as she had the first appointment. Cora had felt the pamphlet she'd squashed down in her bag but hadn't thrown away as if it held the weight of a secret. When her fingers had brushed it the night before, leaving a sensation like burning, she'd thought about making an appointment to see Doctor Massey alone. The thought had been quickly dismissed.

Doctor Massey asked if Alec had managed to interrupt less.

"Of course," Alec had said.

Doctor Massey asked Cora.

She swallowed and took a breath, trying to remember he'd been trying while Cora had been pressing her lips to someone else's in elevators. "He's been better. He's been trying to think of me. Though..." Both of the other people in the room stared at her, waiting for it. "On Saturday, it all felt like back to normal. Dinner with our parents... I felt..."

"How did you feel, Cora?"

"Like Alec would say things purposefully to embarrass me."

"I did no such thing, Cora."

The rest of the session went on like that—old arguments, Alec's blame.

Doctor Massey would steer him to listen to things Cora said. Cora didn't want to say much. Doctor Massey mentioned the tool of manipulation. Of dominant and submissive personalities.

When he heard that, Alec said, "If Cora weren't so submissive, we wouldn't have such a problem."

Maybe he was right. Something must have flashed across her face to hint at that thought, because Doctor Massey sat back, looked at them both, and talked about balance. Self-awareness.

It was exhausting.

All Cora wanted to do was stand up and ask, "What about cheating? What about tasting someone else's lips, going over the memory of their skin under your hands while you lie next to your husband in bed and try not to drown in the guilt of it all?

Why had she kissed Frazer again?

Why did she feel the need to bury herself in this other person?

Tears burnt her eyes, and when she and Alec finished, they walked out together. The street to the hospital was full of people. He spoke about how good it was to get everything in the open.

Cora didn't say a word, and he kept speaking.

In her office, alone and tired, Cora typed the words *manipulation in relationships* into Google. The results made her flinch. Made shame sink in her stomach. What had she become?

When had it become like this?

Maybe he would change. Maybe therapy would help. Or maybe she needed to stop repeating that refrain to herself.

Ignoring the shaking of her hands, Cora closed the browser. She took a steadying breath and opened her e-mails. There was one from Frazer, letting her know that she had the outlines they needed and that they should start implementing everything.

The thought of spending more time with Frazer sent a thrill through her. An excuse to spend time together. Did Cora really want that?

Shouldn't she stay away from her?

She was asking herself so many *shoulds,* she thought she might explode from not knowing the right answer.

They would talk about the project. That was all. They could start to make timetables and secure the after-hours rooms Frazer had already sourced. One by one, they could call in patients, set up protocols, and plan the training week.

Cora would not let herself think once more about that night or about the elevator. Their eyes wouldn't linger over files with words unsaid, and Cora would *not* think about falling into the oblivion that was Frazer's tongue. She would not use her as an excuse to forget her marriage. To forget her husband.

Not once.

Frazer felt like she was walking on sunshine. Her programme was actually happening.

It was all going to finally get off the ground and become something.

And now Cora was on her way to her office to start making it actually happen.

Frazer was not excited about that.

The kiss in the elevator yesterday had awakened all sorts of urges Frazer had managed to bury deep down for the last few years. Urges she'd been quite happy ignoring. Her aquarium and her job kept her busy enough. Her messy work breakup had damaged her more than she would like to admit.

So, no giving in to urges.

Especially urges she should not be having towards a married woman.

Especially one who was married to her boss.

A knock at the door had Frazer straightening up. She stopped herself from running a hand through her hair and resisted the urge to roll her eyes at herself. Doing that was not part of resisting all this.

They would be professional. Focus on the programme, which was easy for Frazer as she was just so damn excited.

"Come in."

The door opened slowly. Cora walked in, started to close the door behind her, and stopped part way. The door stayed half open behind her, and she gave a small smile as she sat down.

For a moment, they stared.

She would not let this get awkward. "Hi! How's your day?"

It was too loud and perky, even in Frazer's ears, but she was going to roll with it.

There was a split second of hesitation. Then Cora said, "Good. And yours?"

She was wearing her hair up. Strands framed her face and made her jaw look stronger, more stubborn. It suited her.

"Great. So glad we can get this going. I'll admit, I got excited and called the first few patients and rang the shelter contacts they gave me to get this set up."

Cora chuckled. Her elbows leant on the desk. "Don't we need to get the first few people trained?"

"Well…" Frazer held her hands up. "The first few are kind of—you and I? And there's another midwife on staff that has been really excited for this from the beginning."

With a flick of her wrist, Frazer turned the computer screen so Cora could see. She leant forward too, settling against the desk. Their heads were a foot apart, and Frazer tried to ignore it.

To ignore the perfume that wafted across the small space.

"Here's the spreadsheet I've just e-mailed through to you." Frazer clicked on a new tab. "You can click on all the tabs and open up a whole bunch of things on figures, donations, people who are supplying things with no charge—for example, we have two rooms available after-hours for nothing; they're usually used for the prenatal exams, which comes under day clinics. They can be used for consults for the midwives, for chats, for time with you and your team to sort out any government assistance you can help people with."

After another ten minutes, Frazer started to realise she was info-dumping on Cora pretty hard. When Frazer finally shut her mouth, Cora looked almost blurry eyed.

Frazer grimaced. "Sorry. I'm kind of excited." She was still staring at the computer screen.

"I can see that."

Cora's words breathed across her cheek. Down her back, goosebumps erupted.

What was it about Cora?

Frazer's heart was beating too hard in her chest. Her eyes were almost watering with the effort to not turn her head and meet Cora's eyes.

Because she could feel Cora looking at her.

Warmth spread across her cheeks, and Frazer wanted to be angry. What was this married woman doing?

But she couldn't.

"Yeah, well." Frazer swallowed. "It's something I've been trying for years now."

"I'm glad it's worked out."

Frazer caved. She turned her head. A foot of distance could feel like a mile or like nothing. At that moment, it felt like both. Cora didn't blink. Didn't move. Frazer ran her tongue over her lips, and only then did Cora's eyes flick down and then back up.

A tiny fraction. That was as far as Cora leant forward, but it was enough to make Frazer match it.

The door was still open. Only partly, halfway. Enough.

She looked at it and back to Cora.

"We can't." Frazer whispered it, as if that could stop it from being heard.

She hated herself that it was only the open door that stopped her.

Cora's brow furrowed. Slightly, but enough to show disappointment. "I know."

Did that disappointment have Cora hating herself just as much?

The door flew open, and they flew apart.

"Frazer! Alec needs to see you—" Tia stopped in her tracks. Looked from one of them to the other. "Hi, Cora."

Her heart thudding so hard she felt nauseated, Frazer turned her computer back around and slumped back into her chair.

"H-hey, Tia."

After a moment that felt too long, Tia tore her eyes from Cora's flushed face to speak to Frazer. "Can you?"

"Can I what?" Frazer tried to look relaxed and probably looked constipated.

"See Alec?" Tia raised her eyebrows at her.

"Yeah, yeah, sure. I just need fifteen minutes. I have to go over a schedule with Cora, and then I'm free."

"Okay." Tia stared at them for another moment that felt too long but could have been normal. Between them, Cora fumbled with her phone and flicked her thumb through her messages. "See you then."

When Tia walked out, the door was left wide open.

Breathing became possible again. Frazer reached for her mouse. "Well, uh—tomorrow night at six okay?"

"What?" Cora asked.

"Tomorrow at six? I can introduce you to one of the clients I thought would be a good fit. For many, we'll both get to know them, but there's one I thought you'd be great for as a mentor. The appointment's for six thirty, so if we meet at six, I can brief you?"

"Sure."

Cora stood. "I'll see you at six tomorrow." At the door, she paused. Turned back. "Maybe we could have a coffee at five?"

Frazer stared at her. "Really?"

"Friends do that?"

Why did she say it as a question, then? Frazer nodded. Tried to smile. "Okay. Five, then."

The door snicked closed. Frazer let her head drop heavily onto the desk in front of her.

A groan left her involuntarily.

Now to go face Alec.

Lunch with her sister was the perfect way to catch up. It always had a time limit. And it meant she could try the new Italian restaurant around the corner from work easily.

"Stop checking your watch, Frazer, or I'll pelt my olives at you."

Not even sheepish, Frazer picked up her fork. "I have an appointment at two. I can't miss it."

Jemma narrowed her eyes. "I'm completely aware that you agreed to lunch instead of dinner because you get to leave."

Damn. "That's not true!" If nothing else, Frazer didn't have to admit to that. "I couldn't do dinner tonight because I'm finally starting the program up."

"Seriously?" Jemma leant forward, eyes intent on Frazer.

"Seriously."

"Frazer! That's awesome. You've been trying to get this going for ages."

At times like this, Frazer remembered she actually enjoyed seeing her younger sister. "Yeah, we finally got funding."

"God, that took ages. What stick lives up your boss's ass? He doesn't think helping pregnant people is important?"

The use of *people* gave Frazer a flash of pride. Only one quick explanation, and her sister had adopted it. Maybe she should stop avoiding Jemma so much.

"I think some of it was red tape. Some of it is indeed the stick up his ass the size of a flag pole." There was a prick of guilt in her gut at the statement and Frazer took a large sip of water to try and drown it. It was normal to bag out your boss. It was something that generally came naturally. But that was before she'd slept with his wife and kept kissing her. Kept almost kissing her. Kept almost being kissed by her?

Whichever it was.

"Frazer? Hello?"

"Sorry." Frazer put her glass down. "The stick must have shrunk a little, because by the end, I think he was actually interested in what I'm doing."

"So he should be. It's a great idea, and there need to be more programmes like this out there."

Her little sister was awesome. "Thanks."

"Now you just need to find a girlfriend."

Never mind. Frazer hated her little sister. "Not you, too."

"Yes, me too. Go on a date." Jemma bit into her salad almost viciously, speaking while she chewed. Charming. "You need it."

"I don't need it! There's nothing wrong with being single. I have my friends. And my fish. And yes, sadly, you. Besides, I went on a date."

"Yeah, I remember. That receptionist." Jemma stabbed some more salad. "And what was wrong with her?"

"She was...boring."

"Boring?" Jemma eyed her. "Why?"

"I don't know. Because she was. Now, leave me alone. I went on a damn date." She also slept with her programme partner. Or friend. Or boss's wife.

"You don't give people a chance. Especially since your ex dumped you with zero warning and left you broken-hearted. And just broken."

Sometimes Jemma hit too close to home.

"Hey, I'm giving you a chance right now to shut up." Frazer grinned at her. "You going to take it?"

"When have I ever shut up when you asked me to?"

Frazer put her fork down and cocked her head as she stared at her sister. "How's your lecturer?"

"Stop deflecting."

"Stop avoiding."

Jemma nodded and thrust her water glass at Frazer like she was making a toast. "Truce?"

"You have to talk about it eventually."

"Do not. I like to ignore my problems." Jemma jutted her chin out. "I learned it from you."

"I don't have any problems."

"Sure, Sis."

When the painful lunch of all painful lunches was finally over, Frazer made it back in time to see her patient. She even passed Alec in the hall and gave him a stiff hello. She refused to think of him as Cora's husband, because when she did, sickly shame settled in her stomach.

The last time she'd spent even ten minutes with him had felt like an eternity. All her traitor brain had done the entire time was throw around images of Cora on that kitchen table.

The kitchen table Alec ate at.

Her boss didn't deserve what Frazer was doing—had done—to him.

By the end of the day. Frazer wanted to text and cancel the coffee with Cora. But apparently she was a masochist, because that message never got sent.

Coffee with Frazer was nice, like it had been from the beginning.

They were in a public place, and they chatted and laughed, and it was all very friendly. Which was what Cora had wanted to prove to herself could happen, that they could be friends.

In reality, Cora had no idea what she was doing. Why she kept chasing Frazer even as she tried to slot back into her marriage. It was a distraction. From the silences at home, from the way she felt there.

Cora felt...like herself with Frazer. She relaxed and said what she thought and didn't feel stupid for it.

So they would be friends. In public places like the café around the corner from the hospital.

At six, Frazer said, "We should go?"

The café was empty. A lone waiter wiped down tables on the other side of the room, soft-rock playing over the speakers.

"Why don't you fill me in here?"

Frazer looked around the room, apparently to make sure no one was in earshot. "Okay. So, the case I have in mind for you is kind of...complex. And close to my heart. Part of the reason I thought you should be the mentor for this kid."

"Kid?"

Elbows on the table, Frazer said, "Yeah. Kid. Seventeen. Living in a shelter. Needs a lot of work on the social services side. I'm already down to be the midwife. This case will be almost shared."

Seventeen, pregnant, and in a shelter wasn't so complex. Cora was already going over the ways she could help, thinking of the assistance schemes that so many people didn't know were available, thinking about housing programs. Just being an ear, someone who checked in helped these cases a lot. "Sounds okay."

"There's another thing. The reason Jack is in a shelter is his parents kicked him out: he's trans."

Everything stilled for a moment.

"Oh, shit."

For a moment, Cora stared at her. Trans? And pregnant?

"Was he raped?"

Something like relief, which didn't suit the question, swept over Frazer's features. "No. He's bisexual. Had a friend, who has now disappeared. Jack really only started transitioning in the last few months and found out he was pregnant two months ago. He's in a lot of distress."

Cora felt a little embarrassed that such a horrible situation occurred to her before the idea that Jack could have been gay or bisexual. That taught her to make assumptions.

"I bet. Hormones?" Cora asked.

"Hasn't started. Parents refused, and now he can't afford them."

Cora nodded slowly. "I can easily refer him to a child psychologist who's experienced in LGBT cases to help him through this. With the referral, he won't have to pay once we get him his own Medicare card." A thought occurred to her. "He didn't want an abortion?"

"It's too late."

"Shit." There didn't seem much else to say. Cora needed to do a lot of reading. "Frazer, why do you look relieved?"

Hesitation, only lasting a second, flickered across Frazer's face.

It wasn't something Cora was used to seeing.

"You used *he* straight away."

"I've had trans patients before, Frazer. He says he's he, then he's *he*."

"It's just refreshing."

"It shouldn't have to be."

Now Cora couldn't recognise Frazer's expression. "No, it shouldn't be."

"Have you spoken about adoption?"

"He's undecided. I think he just needs to talk. A psychologist will be good, if they're the right one. But he'll need you to be an ear, someone there for support."

"I have a friend who works in a centre. I'll get a psych recommendation from him. The changes with his body, not being on hormones—I imagine he'll need a lot of support regardless of the decision with the baby."

"Exactly."

For a moment, they stared at each other, smiling, revelling in the fact that a programme now existed that could help people in these situations.

"Well." Cora looked down at her watch. It was easier than looking at Frazer. Then she'd have to acknowledge what they'd done, what danced between their gaze like smoke. "We should go."

They walked shoulder to shoulder back to the hospital. Outside, the air was almost sweet. It had rained the entire day before, and now, somehow, everything felt clean. It was as if both of them were humming with the excitement of getting this project started. The circumstances some of the clients would be in were terrible, but the difference they could start to make was at the forefront of her mind.

"Who do you have coming tomorrow?" Cora asked as Frazer slid her key into the lock of one of the ground-floor rooms.

"Two more teens currently in shelters also. No support."

Once in the room, Cora sat on the couch in the corner. "Couches?"

"The consult room is next door. This room will be for checking in, talks. Going over paperwork you get going. That kind of thing."

"I like it."

There was a desk in the corner, the couch Cora was on, an armchair.

"Is this a psych room?" Cora asked.

"Yeah."

In the middle of the room, Frazer almost floated. She crossed her arms over her chest. There was no way Cora was going to ask her to sit next to her on the couch. They were friends.

"Are you going to sit?"

Why did Cora ask that? She'd just decided she wasn't going to. Her awkwardness just increased as Frazer stared at her.

The soft knock at the door that had them both turning around earned Cora's undying gratitude.

Standing half in the room, half out, as if he had nowhere to go, was a teen who looked much younger than seventeen. His red hair was haphazardly chopped short, freckles dotting his nose. Despite the completely unsure look on his face, his blue eyes were bright. Inquisitive.

Frazer's face lit up. "Jack! Hi. Did you get here on the bus okay?"

He turned his gaze on her, still not entering the room. "I used the pass thing you gave me last time I saw you."

"Great. Keep using that. I'll make sure you always have enough to get here and back."

Jack slid a step into the room. Fidgety fingers tugged at the sleeves of his baggy hoody until he crossed his arms, as if unsure of what else to do with his limbs. "Who's that?"

The poor kid looked ready to bolt. Cora stood. "Hey, Jack. It's nice to meet you—I'm Cora."

Something in his shoulders relaxed.

He looked between the two of them.

"Hi."

The Monday after Cora met Jack, Frazer and Cora had an accidental lunch together. After being with a patient that screamed more than any other she'd ever had, Frazer had needed some time outside. Her office was, as Cora had so succinctly put it, boring.

And grey.

Everything felt a little closed. First, she'd tried the canteen, but it was loud and filled with people who were continuously coughing and sneezing. So, with a hastily-made salad roll and a chocolate milk (because yes, sometimes Frazer was five), she walked outside to find a bench in one of the paved smoking areas.

Because at least it wasn't inside.

And, of course, Cora had been on one of the benches. And it wasn't like Frazer could just ignore her and go sit on another.

Accidental lunch was followed that afternoon by an accidental coffee. The next day it was another unplanned lunch.

Sometimes they talked about music. Their top-played, their embarrassing favourites from their teens. They traded jokes in the hallway. Tia eyed them as she walked past, and Frazer forgot to make it look like she wasn't enjoying herself. Between them they planned a training week with some of the social work team and some of midwifery team. They'd have more mentors, more clients.

And around their organising, Frazer learnt that Cora once had a dog that ate only left shoes. That when she was little, her grandmother had taught her to make food that her mother before her had taught her to create. Food that tasted like spice and fish, like the shores of a village that ate their food fresh from the boat. In turn, Frazer told her about her own kitchen, filled with the smell of India.

They spilled a connection between them, let it spread like un upturned glass of milk left unchecked. Frazer tried to tell herself it was all friendship. That there weren't times she wanted to brush her lips against Cora's neck, to go back to that drunken night and do it all again but for longer. With no alcohol—just them and their skin and nothing to smudge the memory of it.

At night, Frazer lay and stared at her ceiling. She'd try to remember everything from that night, the way Cora had rolled her hips, had moaned. The depth of her eyes, the cling of her fingers.

It was blurred at the edges, a flicker of images, sounds, and tastes.

Until, in frustration, her fingers slipped between her legs.

And still, Frazer tried to tell herself it could be friendship.

They never spoke of Alec.

When Frazer sent him an e-mail, she reminded herself again and again that he was Cora's husband. That Frazer had no right to think what she thought. At night, when her hands wandered with those thoughts bright against the back of her eyelids, shame shadowed all of it.

She couldn't even convince herself that there was nothing wrong with being friends anymore.

Cora liked having Frazer around. They talked, they shared inside jokes—being with Frazer was easy and utterly complicated. Cora resisted the urge to tell Frazer that Alec had been angry she'd made spaghetti the night they had their parents for dinner. When the urge rose up to talk to Frazer about therapy, Cora asked Frazer about her day instead. When Frazer brought Cora a coffee, setting it on her desk with a flourish and a grin, Cora tried to stop herself from responding to the natural charisma Frazer exuded. Rather than talking about how Cora dreamt at night of the dining table, of what they'd done on it, Cora brought up the programme. If the urge arose to ask Frazer if their kisses also still burnt *her* lips, Cora mentioned Jack instead.

That night they'd spent together haunted Cora. Ghosted over her skin, between her lips, settled low in her stomach and spread between her thighs.

When she was thinking of that, she wasn't thinking of therapy, of Alec, of anything much. It was distracting and wrong.

Guilt followed Cora like a ghost, always lingering, always there.

What she remembered the most wasn't the kitchen table, though. It was the elevator, the kiss they ignored, the heat of Frazer's tongue against her own, the way her chest heaved under her fingers.

Then Cora was in the elevator again. Going from the eleventh floor where she had been with a patient to get her things from her office. Then she was going to meet Alec for lunch before their session with Doctor Massey. Because, goddamn it, Cora was trying, if nothing else. The wall of the elevator was cool against her back. Why did she go into the slow elevator?

She ignored the voice that said it was to reach Alec later, to spread further and further the time between seeing him.

It stopped after two floors and opened. Frazer stepped in, her eyes glued to her phone. As the doors slid shut, she looked up.

"Hey."

Frazer's smile was the crooked one, the one Cora had realised she did when it was genuine. It was almost lazy, with no force. "Hi."

The elevator started to move again.

And then, there. Cora realised she didn't want it to stop on the ground floor, that she didn't want to get out and meet Alec.

She didn't want to leave Frazer behind.

Don't think. For once.

With sure feet, Cora marched forward and her fingers hit the stop button. At the same moment, her arm pushed Frazer back against the doors. It was more forceful than Cora had intended. The air rushed out of Frazer, and her eyes widened. A moment. A beat. That time in which Cora should have stepped back but instead buried her hands in Frazer's scrub shirt. Gripped it in her fists and yanked. Pressed their lips together and felt the bite of teeth. And Frazer... Frazer pressed back against her. Ran her hands through Cora's hair, tangling her fingers in it as if she wanted to pull Cora even closer.

Cora needed this not to end, but they were in an elevator.

With regret, she pulled back. An inch of space between them. Frazer's eyes were bright. Green. Searching her own.

As seemed to happen when Frazer's lips touched her, Cora's mind was quiet. Quieter than it had been in too long. Cora took a slow step back and leant against the back wall again and just stared at Frazer. Watched her straighten her scrub shirt. The door opened, and when Frazer turned and walked down the hall, Cora followed. Thankfully, Lauren wasn't at her desk. No one was there. It was lunchtime. The door to Cora's office closed easily behind them. The lock turned with no resistance.

Frazer sat against Cora's desk. When Cora pulled her shirt over her head, Frazer did the same with her own. Cora kicked off her shoes; her pants slid easily down her legs. The vibrating from her phone died away once she dropped them with her shirt.

It was easy, in the end, to give in. To step between Frazer's legs. To lean forward, her hands pressed into the desk either side of Frazer's hips and kiss her again.

Under her lips, Frazer's neck felt like silk. Her collarbone tasted like regret should but didn't. Cora's fingers fumbled with Frazer's bra, not used to taking one off at this angle. Frazer didn't even notice as she groaned. Cora's lips wrapped around her nipple.

The thudding of her heart in her ears should have been a distraction. But to Cora, it was like a drum keeping time, a musical score to her infidelity, the rhythm of cheating. Whether with a man or a woman, Cora shouldn't be doing this.

Her fingers tugged easily at the band of Frazer's underwear. Her legs were long, dark, smooth, different.

With her lips under Frazer's navel, Cora paused. Frazer's stomach trembled visibly as her breath washed over the sensitive skin. When she looked up, Frazer's eyes were watching her. Studying her, as if waiting for her to stand and flee.

Like a prayer, Cora asked something she should never ask of Frazer: "Be my distraction?"

Frazer's tongue ran over her bottom lip, warmth spreading in Cora's stomach at the sight. Just once, Frazer nodded.

"And be my friend?" Cora's voice cracked.

Cora didn't know if what she was asking made sense, if it was okay. Was it something she should ask a person, especially

Frazer? How did she ask a question when she wasn't really sure what it meant herself?

Again, Frazer nodded.

And Cora kissed her skin again. Kissed lower until fingers tangled in her hair again and her name was whispered like another type of prayer altogether.

CHAPTER TEN

On the floor of Cora's office, Frazer had found out that Cora was the type for canoodling at work.

Sweaty and dishevelled, Cora had stood and pulled on her pants. Covered her skin with a bra and shirt. Given her a smile. Then slid out of the room. Before the door had closed, she'd turned. "Lunch tomorrow?"

Frazer had nodded, naked and no longer feeling smooth. "Okay."

And now she was lying on her couch at home, wondering what the hell she'd gotten herself into.

"Boys?" Frazer sat up, leaning on her elbows. She peered through the glass of her aquarium at the end of the couch. "Am I an idiot?"

Two of the fish darted behind a piece of coral and didn't reappear.

"I'll take that as a yes."

She dropped back down with a groan. She and Cora. Friends. Who had sex. When one of them was married.

This was not the person Frazer had ever thought she would be. Could she claim she was innocent in this, that the blame lay with Cora? Frazer wasn't the married one, after all.

No.

Frazer knew what she was doing. And it had to end.

It was ludicrous what Cora had asked. Why had Frazer agreed to it? But all Frazer had been aware of in that moment was the pleading in Cora's voice, the lips so close to a place Frazer had felt thrumming with need.

This couldn't continue. Maybe she'd agreed to it when Cora was kneeling in front of her, but she shouldn't have.

Never should Frazer have agreed to that.

She would tell her tomorrow. At lunch, she would tell Cora that this was insane, she had to sort out whatever was going on with her *without* using Frazer.

Though was Frazer really being used? She knew what this was. She knew Cora was married. She was getting sex out of it, and friendship.

It was a terrible thing to do to Alec.

Frazer pulled a cushion over her head and groaned into it loudly.

Tomorrow.

Tomorrow she would tell Cora it couldn't continue.

So it was tomorrow. All morning, Frazer went through prenatal exam after prenatal exam. Her mind was half there and half on what she would say to Cora.

Also, somehow, though it was mathematically impossible, her mind was half on the training program they were starting next week. Soon they'd have more mentors, and that meant more clients. The clients that had a social worker as their mentor would have Frazer as a midwife, and the ones that had a midwife would have Cora as their social worker. Later, that would have to change, but for now, their numbers were small and it would work.

"All is going just fine here, Erin." Frazer snapped her gloves off and dropped them in the bin.

The relief on the face of the woman on the examination table was palpable. "Yeah? Because those pains I was having..."

Three times now, Frazer had reassured her. And she would reassure Erin another ten if she needed to. Frazer wasn't the one carrying a baby around in her uterus. "They were completely normal. Braxton Hicks contractions can be uncomfortable, especially in the first pregnancy. But nothing's wrong." Warm water from the tap washed over Frazer's hands, and she added some soap, looking over her shoulder as she spoke. "Though if you get concerned at all, get yourself into emergency. No need to worry yourself silly."

Erin let out a big breath. "Okay. Thank you. Sam kept saying it was nothing."

"What does he know?" Frazer winked at her.

Grinning, Erin shook her head. "A lot about computers, not a lot about this."

"He would have just been saying it because he *needed* nothing to be wrong."

As Erin slipped her underwear and pants back on behind the screen, Frazer sat down at the computer and quickly updated her file. "Now, this may be the last I see you before you give birth. Unless you're late—though everything is looking good."

"God." Erin rubbed her huge stomach. "My sister was overdue one week and had to be induced." Her face paled. "She said it was more painful than the birth."

"Don't go thinking about that yet, Erin." Frazer leant on her desk. "If it comes to that bridge, we'll cross it. Do you want some more information on it, in case?"

"No." Erin said wryly. "I've read everything you have anyway. And you've answered all these questions a thousand times."

"Well, make an appointment if you need." Frazer grinned. "And hopefully, next time I see you will be to help you get Zack out of there."

Erin wrapped her scarf around her neck and waggled the tassels playfully in Frazer's direction. "It's Blake now."

"Blake then."

"Thanks, Frazer. Bye."

The door to the prenatal room closed behind Erin, and Frazer leant back into her chair. She rubbed her face. There'd been a lot of concerned parents that morning. One guy had almost panicked as he'd told her he'd seen two penises on the ultrasound screen. She'd had to explain with a straight face that one was the umbilical cord.

After he had calmed down, his face had taken on a look of disappointment. "Can't blame me for dreaming," he'd said.

That was when his girlfriend had smacked him upside the head.

Frazer left the prenatal rooms and headed for her office. From there, she'd answer a few e-mails and then send Cora a message.

A message she didn't really want to send. But she had to.

None of this was okay.

"Frazer!"

Oh, God. No.

She looked up at the voice, already knowing who it was. Alec was heading towards her. Jesus, he was actually smiling.

"Hey, Alec." *I had sex with your wife. Again.*

Frazer swallowed hard. Forced herself to curve her lips up in response. "How's your day?"

"Meetings and more meetings. You know how it is."

Actually she didn't. Thankfully. If she ever took a desk job, Frazer would miss the patients too much. The babies. Even the tragic cases—she'd miss helping parents through that. Her job involved a lot of desk time since she'd been promoted, but she liked being on the rotation for exams like today and on the ward for births, even if there was still five days a week of it.

"Yeah. Busy busy." She smiled again. It felt like her face was cracking with the effort.

"I got your e-mail. The first training is next week, yes?"

"Yeah—Monday to Friday, from six to eight."

"Good. And numbers?"

"Still four."

"And Cora is helping out?"

Obviously. What was going on? "Yeah, each night. We have two midwives and two social workers. We're hoping we'll all pool ideas. But it's also a lot of crisis management. What to do if you're concerned, if you need Social Services to step in."

"Good. No lawsuits." He gave a loud laugh that grated.

Was that why this had taken so long to pass through? Wow. Had Frazer been stupid. Of course it was. Why risk being sued when you could leave these parents to fend for themselves?

"Yeah." She gritted her teeth. "We wouldn't want that."

"Exactly." Alec gave her a nod. "Great. Well, good luck next week."

And he disappeared. As she watched him leave, she wondered what Cora was doing with someone like him.

In an effort to avoid the elevator, Frazer took the stairs. Even though she had to go up four flights, she didn't want to be in a room with Cora, especially a room she couldn't escape. All the words Frazer wanted to say would fly out of her head.

Finally arriving in front of her office, breathing harder than she should be considering the amount of swimming she did regularly, Frazer entered.

And froze.

Cora was sitting at the table. Two sandwiches sat on the desk in front of her. She, too, was smiling. "Hey," she said.

As Frazer shut the door behind her, the words she wanted to say started to flit away. "Hey."

When she was pressed against the door with Cora's lips against her neck, Frazer managed to find some. "Cora. Wait."

Her voice wasn't her own, too low, too husky. Throaty.

Lips against Frazer's ear, Cora whispered, "Please?"

Groaning, Frazer's grabbed her and pulled their lips together. Any words she wanted to say flew out of her head completely.

CHAPTER ELEVEN

After a week of sex, Frazer woke up in her bed on Saturday morning alone.

Because she was "the other woman."

She didn't get to wake up with Cora wrapped around her, delicious bare skin pressed against her own.

And that was okay with Frazer. Because she had known what this was going in. Had known Cora was married. Had known it couldn't go anywhere. Had known she was Cora's personal Band-Aid for a marriage that was struggling.

Sighing, she pulled a pillow over her face. Her hair was in her mouth, uncomfortable, and she ignored it. She was too hot, and she ignored that too.

Maybe she could also ignore what she was doing with Cora.

The weekend passed slowly, relaxed. She had lunch with her friends and batted away their enquiries. She drank too many beers and had an afternoon nap. Jemma convinced her to go to a family lunch on Sunday. Her mother asked her when she was going to get married, and Jemma had put a comforting hand on her leg under the table and asked, "Did you know it's one in two marriages that end in divorce now, Mum?"

Really, Frazer did love her little sister.

Sunday night, Frazer got a message from Cora asking if she was free. Instead of saying no, like she should, she said yes.

Cora and Frazer were friends. Frazer really did feel like she could say that now. They ate lunch and had the odd drink and shared messages. Discussed likes and dislikes. Gossiped.

But, when they were alone, which they managed to be every day that week, they had sex.

Really, really good sex.

But it was so compartmentalised. They'd finish, and for one amazingly comfortable minute, they'd lay pressed together, naked and sweaty, if the location allowed such things. Then Cora would stand, slip on her clothes, and slip Frazer a smile and slip out.

She was slippery.

They didn't lay and laugh easily in bed like they did at lunch. They didn't whisper. Didn't stroke at hypersensitive skin in silence while the world went on around them.

And it made it easier, somehow, to look Alec in the eye.

By the time Cora knocked on her door, Frazer had already had a wine.

Would this be being friends today? Or was this sex?

When she opened the door, Cora was on the other side. She had a hooded jumper on and looked like she was settled for an evening at home. As you would be at nine o'clock on a Sunday.

"Hey. Alec was called into work…"

It was for sex.

Frazer wanted to say no. A week had passed since this routine had begun. She wanted to make this the time that she put her foot down.

But the arch of Cora's lips was almost coy. The smell of her perfume drifted in from outside and instead, Frazer stood to the side to let Cora in. Shut the door after her.

She linked their hands and pulled her forward. Kissed her, in a pattern that was becoming disturbing in its comfortable familiarity. Their hands tugged, pulled at clothes. They left them in a trail to Frazer's bedroom.

In the light that washed in from the hall as Cora's lips kissed over her abdomen and her tongue made Frazer roll her hips insistently, Frazer couldn't help but think that Cora had become very, *very* good at this.

Sometimes Frazer wondered if Cora was gay. Or straight. Or bisexual. She wondered what it all meant. Then she realised that it just didn't matter.

Because what she was, was married.

It was hours later that Cora stretched against the mattress with Frazer's eyes tracing her subtle curves, for only a minute.

Her chest still rose and fell as she panted, cheeks flushed and lips curved lazily. This wasn't how Frazer should like her best.

She traced her fingers over Cora's damp skin.

As Cora stood up and dragged her pants on, half asleep, Frazer let her hand fall away.

"What?" Cora caught her eye.

"What, what?"

"You're smiling."

"I just came four times."

With a laugh, Cora dragged on her shirt. "Yes. But you were thinking something."

"You have a nice body."

Head popping through her jumper, Cora flushed. "I'm normal."

"You asked. That was what I was thinking."

For a moment that made Frazer's breath catch, Cora stared at her openly. Frazer had forgotten that she was now the only naked one in the room. "You're not so bad yourself."

As if even that was too much, Cora gave a wave and walked out. The door shutting was louder than normal in Frazer's small house.

Frazer pulled her pillow over her face to cover her grin.

"Are we better?"

Cora looked across at Alec, who stared ahead while asking the question, watching the road as he drove them to work. They'd started driving to work together again. More time together. They were trying.

He'd come in at midnight the night before, no idea she had gone anywhere. Freshly showered, Cora had lain in bed and pretended to be asleep, her heart hammering and trying not to think about whatever that look had been in Frazer's eye right before she'd left. Or about how Alec, so close to her, had no idea what she was doing behind his back. About how Cora couldn't seem to stop.

"I think so."

She didn't think so. On top of that, she didn't think he did either. Whenever they reported back to Doctor Massey, discussed their progress, neither of them were ever happy with what the other had done. It led to heated discussions in their sessions that they later pretended had never happened. He would take steps forward to do what Doctor Massey suggested, then three more backwards.

"Good. I cancelled our appointment this week."

Relief flooded her. It even drowned out the voice in the back of her head that wondered why they hadn't discussed it before now. And if he really thought they'd improved, or if he just didn't agree with the mirror therapy was holding up to him.

"Okay."

"Maybe we could spend the evenings this week having dinner?" he asked.

He was trying. But in ways that suited him. Still, her palms felt sweaty—he was trying more than she was. She, who was having sex with someone else.

Cora cleared her throat, tried to hold her voice steady. "I have the training for the program this week in the evenings."

He knew that. She was sure Frazer had said she'd e-mailed him. Or talked to him. Or something. And Cora had mentioned it, hadn't she? Yes, she had, last week.

"You never told me that."

She was sure she had. "Didn't I mention it last week?"

Alec changed gears smoothly. "You always think you've said things you haven't. You didn't tell me."

She had. She was sure. Or maybe she'd meant to.

Maybe she hadn't. She *had* been distracted. "Well," she said, "sorry."

"Good. It's fine."

He offered the words like a gift, and she took them gratefully. No argument. It was refreshing. She hated feeling stupid for hours at forgetting something or thinking she'd told him something when she hadn't.

"So, dinner?" He pulled smoothly into the hospital car park.

"I can't, Alec. I'm sorry. I have to be there for the training."

His jaw clenched. "Your work takes up so much of your time."

If he hadn't spoken so seriously, she would have laughed. She'd managed to ensure that she always worked the morning shifts, was always at home when he'd wanted her to be. His hours could be absurd. She opened her mouth to point out that he'd had to disappear until midnight on a Sunday, but guilt made her close her mouth. What had she done the second he'd left?

"It's just a week, Alec."

"Fine."

He got out of the car and walked away, leaving her to catch up.

Later, in her office, Cora's hands were shaking, and she couldn't explain why.

She put her bag on the floor and pulled everything out. Dismissively, she dropped her pocketbook, her phone, wallet, keys, everything on the floor. Finally, it was empty. There, at the bottom, squashed, was the pamphlet she'd left untouched for so long.

Emotional abuse? Was that really something?

She didn't *feel* abused by Alec. Sometimes she felt squashed, but wasn't that marriage?

Then why had she taken it? Kept it?

Her hands were still shaking.

She opened the pamphlet. Closed it again. She opened it. Phrases jumped out at her:

Manipulation is an emotional abuser's favourite tool. Does your partner:

Demand all your attention.

Belittle you.

Make you think your time, goals, and dreams are not as important as theirs.

178

Make you question your reality.

She closed it again. Put it back in her bag and covered it in all her belongings.

The room was small. Nausea bubbled in her stomach.

For a minute, Cora almost picked up the phone to make an appointment with Doctor Massey alone.

Instead, she picked up her bag and headed for Frazer's office. They had to make sure everything was ready for the training week. They had to discuss Jack, whom Cora would be seeing again after their first meeting.

And, if she was honest, Cora wanted to be somewhere she felt good.

Maybe all of this was her punishment.

What would Doctor Massey say anyway?

Cora had cheated.

"Great, Jack. Everything looks good."

His cheeks were bright red, and Frazer turned around to let him get dressed. At five and half months along, he was showing now.

"How's the morning sickness?" She asked when they sat down across from each other at the desk.

"The same."

"Did the ginger help?"

He shrugged. "It was okay."

"Good. And dry toast in the morning?"

This time he managed a grin as dry as the recommended toast. "It's been fine—it's all I can afford anyway."

Frazer chuckled. "Well, you have a meeting with Cora after this, don't you?" At his nod, she continued, "That's good. She'll be helping you sort out whatever Centrelink schemes you can qualify for. And she'll also help with finding a way to get you out of that shelter."

With his hands buried in the ends of his hoody, he said, "Sounds good."

There were marks on his arms, ones she had eyed but not mentioned. They'd talked about it before, and he had sworn he'd discuss it with the psychologist Cora had set up. The sight of them made her clench her fists, angry at a world that made someone that unhappy with themselves. "Are you ready to talk about options?"

Jack shrugged again and sighed. It was such a typical teenager motion that Frazer had to bite back a chuckle. "I guess."

"Okay, well. As we talked about, you can keep the baby or give it up for adoption."

He swallowed so heavily, Frazer could see his throat bob. "They're both so final."

When he caught her eye, she was trapped in a well of blue. "They are." Frazer leant on the desk, keeping eye contact. "They are. You have three and a half months to make up your mind. Cora will listen whenever you want to talk. And when I see you for your appointments, I'm happy to talk to you about it as much as you need."

His face was red as he licked his lips, opening his mouth to say something. For a moment that stretched on forever, he hesitated over his words before they burst from him. "How can I pay for a baby? I dropped out of school this year. Any money I earnt working was going to pay for hormones and top surgery— but that was years off, 'cause I couldn't save very fast. I have no cash. I have no way to support a baby. Nowhere to live. How will I raise a kid? I can't even sort my own life out. I don't want the baby to have a, a *mess* for a mo—father."

Desperate to comfort him somehow, Frazer grabbed his hand, now clutching the desk white knuckled. "Breathe, Jack."

He took a deep breath.

Frazer ducked her head and managed to catch his gaze again. With a squeeze of his hand, she said, "You're not a mess. At all. Never say that. Kids need parents who love them. Who support them. We'll take this one step at a time and figure out what is best for *you* and for the baby. Okay?"

Shoulders relaxing a little, he looked up at the ceiling for a minute and swallowed heavily. Finally, he caught Frazer's eye again and said, "Okay."

"And Jack?"

"Yeah?"

"If you give the baby up for adoption, this programme ensures we'll still be in contact with you to make sure *you're* okay. Okay?"

He let a slow breath. "Okay."

This kid was awash in a sea of stuff there was no way Frazer would have been mature enough to handle at seventeen. Hell, her actions lately proved she wasn't mature enough to handle it now. Who let her be in charge of people's wellbeing like this?

Reaching into her drawer, she pulled out a booklet and flicked through it, tearing out a few of the pages. "Take this." She handed them over. "That will get you lunch in the canteen and a drink. What time's your appointment with Cora?"

"In an hour."

"Great. Eat some lunch. Whatever you don't eat, take back with you." Maybe she'd given him enough for four meals. "I'll see you at the next appointment. You have the bus pass?"

"Yeah."

"Good. And remember, you can contact Cora at any time. That's the point."

When he stood up, he hesitated, not moving to leave. Finally Frazer asked, "What's up?"

He ground his toe into the carpet. Watched himself do it. "It hurts too much to bind."

Frazer's heart went out to him. Unsure of what she could say to make that better, she went for something simple. "Sorry, Jack."

"Will it stay that way?"

"Probably, not forever; it depends. But after the birth, it will settle down if you don't want to feed the baby." Frazer was a little out of her depth on how to make him feel better. She didn't want to dismiss it and make him feel like it was a bad thing to worry about, but she didn't want to make it into a big deal either. "Does that make you feel worse?"

He continued to watch his foot. "It all feels pretty bad."

Incredibly grateful she'd got this programme going when she had, Frazer nodded. "I bet it does. But we're all here, okay? And Cora has the name of an awesome psychologist, one who works with LGBT kids all the time."

When he finally looked up, it was with wide eyes. "I can't afford that."

Frazer winked. "Medicare can—and you and Cora are going to sort out your card and get you into the programme that gets it all paid for."

At that, his shoulders relaxed slightly. "Okay."

At the door, he paused. "Thanks, Frazer."

That thank you and the sincerity in his eyes made Frazer think that even if she was making a mess of her private life, at least this was going right.

The prenatal consulting room was silent only for a minute until an odd sensation made Frazer look up from her computer. She started slightly when she saw Cora leaning against the door frame.

"Hey." Frazer breathed out.

"Hi."

When Cora entered the room, she left the door open. At that, Frazer relaxed into her chair. Friend visit. A sandwich was launched towards her, and she just managed to catch it before it hit her in the face.

"Hey!"

Cora sat across from her in the chair Jack had just vacated. "You thought quick enough, calm down."

"Lucky it's my favourite."

Rye with cream cheese, tomato, cucumber, and bacon. Nothing better. Frazer bit in with relish. The bread was fresh. Giving a groan, she settled back to eat. "This is amazing. Thank you."

Cora was looking at her strangely.

"What?"

With a shrug, Cora licked her lip. "You're, ah, rather orgasmic when you eat."

Flicking her eyes to the open door and back to Cora, Frazer grinned. "Well, you'd know."

It worked. She turned bright red. "So my competition is a bacon sandwich?"

"It's bacon-on-*rye*, Cora. There's no competition."

Raising her eyebrows, Cora cocked her head. The heat of her gaze ran slowly down Frazer's body, settling for a split second in her lap before rising again. She simply bit into her sandwich, chewing slowly, the pink of her tongue darting across her bottom lip.

This time, heat spread over Frazer's cheeks. "Maybe there's a little."

The smirk on Cora's lips shouldn't have been so satisfying to see, but it was.

"So, to what do I owe this visit?"

"You just saw Jack, right?" Cora asked.

Frazer nodded.

"Anything I should know?"

"He'll update you."

"Okay."

The programme allowed discussion between those involved in the cases, but nothing had been said that Jack wouldn't build up to telling Cora in his own time. It was better that way, to allow trust between the mentor and the client. It was the entire point.

"How was lunch at your parents yesterday?"

"Didn't want to ask last time you stopped by for a visit?"

Cora chuckled. "I was distracted."

"Clearly." Frazer wasn't complaining. "It was fine. My brother's kids were there, so I spent most of the time with them."

"You like kids?"

"What's not to like? They're loud and sticky and don't really follow social etiquette. It's refreshing."

Cora was staring at her, food halfway to her mouth.

"What?"

"That is the strangest definition of children I've ever heard."

"Well, it's true."

"If there's ever an invasion by aliens, I hope they recruit you to explain society."

Frazer almost choked on her mouthful. "I think I'd confuse them more than help them."

"Actually, I think you'd make it clear. Short, precise definitions. Great."

"Whatever. Anyway—you don't like kids?"

"I do." Cora grabbed a bottle of water from her bag and twisted off the lid. "They're fun."

"Do you want any?" The question slipped out and fell between them. It danced far too close to the area of Cora's life they didn't talk about. Frazer felt like kicking herself.

The sip Cora took was slow, and she took even longer to swallow it as she considered the question. "I did. I think I still do. Maybe. I don't know."

Cora leant back against her chair. She wasn't looking directly at Frazer anymore.

Shit. Frazer shouldn't have asked that.

"I was pregnant." Cora's expression didn't change, but there was a tightness to her voice. "It's why we got married."

And there it was. Truth. Something Cora never offered very willingly.

"Oh."

Oh? Cora opened up and that was all Frazer could say? Oh? She owed Cora more than that.

The air felt heavier in the room, weighed down in meaning. Frazer couldn't stop staring at Cora, waiting for more. Waiting for…something. Yet Cora only stared at her bottle, as if it could suck her in and take her to somewhere she hadn't opened up herself.

Frazer really needed to say something. "What happened?" She had no idea if she was supposed to ask it. But if Cora had opened up to her, Frazer wasn't going to let that opportunity pass.

"I lost her."

It was a term Frazer hated. She hated to use it with parents. Hated the way it used the subject of the person carrying the baby, as if there could be someone to blame.

"Cora." There was really only one thing Frazer could say. Something she'd said far too many times to parents. "I'm so sorry."

Cora shrugged, like people did when they were pretending something didn't matter when it still felt like it had happened yesterday. "It was years ago."

"How far along were you?"

"Twenty weeks. She was stillborn."

When Frazer winced, she was glad Cora was still looking at her bottle. "That would have been really hard."

Straightening, Cora made eye contact, gaze steady. "It was. So I don't know how I feel. It was all too early when it happened, we weren't really ready. Yet, now never seems like the right time, you know?"

Really? It wasn't the right time when you were having an affair with another woman? Strange.

"Yeah. There's never a right time for these things, though."

"Probably not." Cora's voice was even. "Okay, so, I have a meeting with the lovely Jack. I've called some organisations that assist with housing. I'm going to try to get him out of the shelter. See if he has a bank account, work out some government assistance."

Frazer watched Cora stand up. "Great. And thanks for lunch."

And for opening up.

"No problem."

And she left, taking all of her mystery with her.

"You can get me out of the shelter?"

The disbelieving look directed at Cora almost made her smile. "I sure can."

"Why me?"

That wasn't something Cora had been expecting. When she met Jack, she had known he was someone who could surprise her with his depth, with his eyes that darted everywhere and took everything in before commenting. "Well," she said, "why not you?"

"Because there are people in the shelter who need somewhere to go too. Maybe more than me." His eyes dropped to his half-eaten soup, the canteen type that not many people were brave enough to try. "Definitely more than me."

This was the hard part of Cora's job, sorting out what assistance there was to the people she could, knowing that there were always others who needed it, too. How did you explain that to someone that you just had to make the dent that you could?

She cleared her throat. "This programme is for certain people. The money available is only there for those people in the programme." She watched his jaw clench. "However, there are assistance programmes out there too where a referral from this programme gets things moving faster."

Jack still wasn't looking at her. "You mean because I'm pregnant."

"Pregnant," she caught herself with the word "women" just in time, "*people* and people with children often get in first, yes."

There was a heaviness around Jack that was painful to watch. A sign of just how beyond his years he was.

"What if I don't keep the baby?"

"Well, that doesn't matter. Right now, you're pregnant. And when it comes to this programme, it definitely doesn't matter. You stay with me as your mentor whether you keep the baby or not. You would keep your housing whether you keep the baby or not. We're about looking after the parents."

His soup would be cold by now, yet he simply continued to watch it.

"And, Jack..."

His eyes darted up, blue and intelligent.

"If we get you out of the shelter, that just means there's more space there to get someone else off the street. It all works out."

Or they'd try to make it work out.

He gave a nod. "Okay."

"Great. I brought some papers, things to get your Medicare card sorted out, and I wanted to talk to you about something else."

His eyes were back on her. "Yeah?"

"Yeah." She smiled. "I spoke to my colleague down at the LGBT Community Centre, and he had a recommendation for a really great psychologist. I had a chat with him, and he's worked with lots of teens who are trans. He would make space for you if you're interested."

As he stared at her, she hoped he didn't notice that she held her breath. There would be no forcing him to go, but this was something he needed. Neither Frazer nor she were qualified to help Jack with things he had gone through, was going through, and would be going through in the near future.

"I went to a psychologist once."

She didn't say anything, only kept a hand on her water bottle while she watched him.

"She was one my parents found. She talked about phases. About tomboys. About—"

His voice cracked, and Cora wanted to lean forward and squeeze his hand. But she didn't want to cross a line she hadn't been invited over.

With glassy eyes, Jack stared back down at the table, taking deep breaths.

"This psychologist isn't like that." Painfully, Cora watched the flush creep up Jack's neck and over his cheeks. "Not at all like that. We want to find someone who supports *you*. That's all."

Jack took another deep breath. "Okay. I'll try."

Relief flooded Cora's body. "Great. That's great, Jack. And I want you to call me when the first session is finished, if you want.

We'll make sure you're happy with him. If you're not, we find someone else."

"Okay." Jack's teeth worried at his lip, and Cora waited to see if he'd ask her what was clearly on his mind. "Cora..."

"Yeah?"

Jack swallowed heavily. "I just..." His voice dropped low, the sound like gravel. "I just don't know what to do about the baby."

And here was the hard part of what Cora had to do. She couldn't make any decisions for him. She didn't know what the best thing for Jack was. "I know, hon."

"I don't think I have my shit together enough to have a kid." His eyes remained glued on his soup as he moved the spoon around the liquid listlessly.

"There are a lot of resources out there to help you, and I'd be here to help you as much as I can too."

He nodded, but Cora had the feeling he wasn't taking a lot of this in, but rather just trying to get his thoughts *out*. "If I gave the baby *up*," he said, wincing, with his voice cracking over the last word, "well, how would I know that the people who adopt it would be good people? Like, really, I mean."

Cora hesitated. How was she supposed to answer that? "Well, I think you can organise to get some more information from the adoption agency about them. See what kind of feeling you get in your gut."

"I still won't *know*." For a moment, he looked like he was biting back words, chewing on them before they spat themselves out. "What if they're the kind that push their kids into boxes it takes them years to realise they can get out of?"

Cora held her breath for a second and leant forward. How could you know that? "Well..." She bit the inside of her cheek as she thought. "Why don't we think of some questions to ask them, if that's the decision you end up going with?"

"Questions?" Finally, his eyes flicked up to meet hers.

"Yeah. Ones that would help you know what kind of parents they would be. The agency can pass them on, and you can read their answers."

Slowly, he sat up straighter. "Like...if the baby's a boy and wants to dress up as a princess, what would your reaction be?"

"Exactly. Or if your little girl says she's going to be an astronaut, is your reaction to a) tell her she's crazy or b)—"

"Take her outside to learn the stars at night?" Jack was smiling now, so new to Cora's eyes she wanted to capture that look forever. "Okay. Do you have paper?"

The rest was easy. With a notebook Cora gave him, they brainstormed questions Jack would be able to ask. After they thought of more than twenty, he sat tapping his pen against the paper, staring at them. "But, Cora." He looked up, his voice tight. "How will I *know* they would love the baby? Be nice to it? Support it?"

Resting her hand on his arm, she squeezed it gently. "You'll know."

Jack tore the paper out and stuffed it in his pocket. "Thanks."

"Anytime." Cora glanced at her watch. "Now, you have my contact number? And the shelter knows how to help you get in touch?"

"Yeah."

"Great. One last thing: is there anyone else from your family we can contact?"

Jack adamantly shook his head. "No. No one."

"Friends?"

He gave a one-shouldered shrug. "Not from school. But I have a couple of friends from a club. I still see them."

"Good—are you keeping in contact with them okay?"

"One's in a shelter, like me. She's only sixteen. Her parents caught her with her friend after soccer training."

"It must be nice to have someone to look out for you and for you to return the favour."

"It's more nice to have someone I can be myself with."

"That's important too."

At thirty-four, that was something that Cora was really just starting to understand.

CHAPTER TWELVE

It wasn't until three months later that Cora picked up her phone and called Doctor Massey.

Three months of sleeping with Frazer and being married to Alec.

Alec, who liked it less and less if she made other plans on the weekends. Who wanted her at home, waiting for him. Who had gotten a little better after those therapy sessions, but then returned to his normal pre-therapy behaviour. Who had no idea she was sleeping with someone else.

Which she still managed to do. Because somehow, with work and the programme and the times he worked late or went to a conference, it was disturbingly easy to sleep with Frazer.

If it weren't for her friendship with Frazer, Cora worried she would have disappeared into nothingness. Something about being with her made everything else fade away. Since Cora had opened up about her stillbirth, an ease had opened up in turn between them. An ease when they were together, when they spoke. It was nice.

But it was sitting at her desk and looking at her calendar that did it. Her thumb swiped her phone screen easily. Swiped back months. Three, to be exact. And there, on the same date three months ago, were the dates of Alec's conference.

The first night she'd slept with Frazer.

And if she swiped her thumb over it again three times, there was today's date.

Three months.

No one had an affair for three months and a healthy marriage at the same time. No one ignored the signs and warnings she'd read, thanks to her couples therapist. No one stayed with a man because they felt guilty for what they'd done. Or because he implied she'd be useless alone.

Or that he would.

Making the appointment was easier than she'd thought it would be. There'd been a cancellation. One was available in four days, on Friday. When she thanked the receptionist, Cora's hands were shaking. They were still shaking thirty minutes later when she knocked on Frazer's office door and opened it without waiting.

Frazer looked up from her desk, her eyes brightening when she saw Cora. Then they darkened when Cora shut the door behind her, hand falling to the lock. Three months. How had it been three months? It had been so long that Frazer knew what her shutting the door meant.

They had patterns.

Patterns like lunch. Coffee. Conversation. Texts that were never sexual, in case Alec saw; or when they bordered on it, were deleted: the biggest sign of guilt. Flirtations as they made eye contact. Friendship. Sex.

An affair. For three months.

Which had started because Cora needed a distraction from the fact that she'd uttered the word "divorce" to her husband. Because she was unhappy. Because she was selfish.

"Hey."

Frazer leant back in her chair, grinning now. How had Cora found her arrogant? She was cocky, sure. But not arrogant.

"Hi."

"What are you doing?" Cora asked.

"The weekly report on the programme." Cora took a slow, sashaying step forward. Frazer's eyes followed her movements. "You know, statistics, numbers..."

Cora's fingers played at the buttons of her white dress shirt, undoing them one by one. She watched Frazer watch her doing it, something delicious in the way Frazer's pupils blew wide. She'd been looking forward to watching that slow grin curl over Frazer's lips all day.

It was easy, to walk around the desk, to kneel in front of her. To tug at her pants and pull them down and off along with her shoes. Easy to pull her up and turn her, to push her down on her desk. Wrapping her arms around her thighs and pressing her lips against Frazer to drive her crazy was even easier.

Because apparently Cora was the type of person that called a therapist to help sort her head out about her marriage and then went down on a woman thirty minutes later.

It was just nice to feel in control of something.

Frazer's thighs were pressing against her ears, and when Cora opened her eyes and looked up, all she could see was Frazer's arm across her mouth. Her head had dropped back and was hanging over the edge of the desk. For a second, Cora thought Frazer was going to come that quickly.

Until the door opened.

Her heart stopped. Literally, for a moment, it stopped. She'd locked the door; she was sure she had locked the door.

Tia stood in the doorway, her eyes wide. They stared at each other as Cora dropped back on her heels, her hand swiping her mouth. But then Tia wasn't looking at Cora. She was staring at Frazer, who still lay against the desk, tensed and frozen in place.

The door shut with a slam.

"Fuck!" Cora's heart was racing as Frazer stood up and yanked on her pants. "Frazer! Fuck!"

She looked up. Frazer was wide-eyed.

Her lip trembled.

"Fuck." Frazer said.

Cool air had hit Frazer's legs. That was her first warning.

Cool air during sex was never fun.

And then Tia was staring at her upside down and Frazer felt like she'd been caught by her mum. This could not be happening.

It couldn't.

They'd managed not to be caught for three months.

Three months of rendezvous around the hospital, of careful door locking. Of Cora only being in her house on days Alec was away.

Of sex with zero feeling and of friendship with probably too much.

Of avoiding her friends and family as much as possible because she didn't want to see the judgement in their eyes when she shared what she was doing.

And now Tia had caught them. The worst person to catch them second only to Alec himself.

God, would she tell Alec?

She wouldn't, would she?

"Is she going to tell Alec?" Cora asked. She'd not even bothered to stand up but was sitting on the floor next to the chair Frazer now sat in. She looked miserable, and the urge to hold her hand overtook Frazer, a moment's insanity.

"I don't know." Frazer shook her head. "No. She won't. We're friends."

"You are?"

Frazer looked down at Cora, who was terribly pale. Wide-eyed. She looked ready to run away, and Frazer couldn't blame her.

"Yeah. We are." Frazer stood up. "I need to go and speak with her."

Cora scrambled to her feet. "You?"

Blinking at her, Frazer asked, "Well, do *you* want to?"

That was all it took for Cora to go even paler. "No."

That's what Frazer had thought. "Okay. I'll go."

She reached her hand out to squeeze Cora's arm. For reassurance only.

But Cora took a step back, wrapped her arms around herself. Gave a terribly fake smile. "Okay. You go."

It was easy to walk away from that office. From Cora's silent panic. When she walked into the hallway, Frazer expected everything out there to have stopped. For people to be standing about, judgemental looks on their faces. But the other rooms that were in this area were mostly empty; no one was milling in the hallway.

It was almost as if the world hadn't stopped spinning on its axis.

Someone else knew. This thing they were doing was real. It was out there, beyond their reach or control.

It had been easy to bury her head in the sand when no one had known. They left their moments together behind and were friends on the outside. Just last week, Tia had mentioned that it was nice to see Cora laugh with someone.

God.

Hoping she wouldn't see Alec, Frazer walked to his office and saw the desk Tia normally sat at empty.

"Shit," she muttered.

"Looking for me?"

Frazer spun, hand at her chest over her thumping heart.

Staring at her with an unreadable expression was Tia.

"Tia!" Frazer tried a shaky laugh. "You scared me to death."

The laugh died quickly as Tia simply gave a shrug. "Sorry."

They stared at each other. It was absurd, yet Frazer had the urge to fidget under her gaze.

Yep, it was worse than her mother. Frazer liked her friendship with Tia, and Tia was obviously pretty fond of Frazer.

Yet Tia was Alec's receptionist, with what seemed a motherly affection for him.

"Can we talk?" Frazer asked.

For a minute, Frazer thought Tia was going to tell her where to go. She let out the breath she was holding when, instead, she finally got a nod. Wordlessly, Frazer followed her outside and around the back of the main building. Smokers stood around, shivering slightly, with their breath and the smoke mingling to create a strange haze around their faces. Tia walked over to a far corner, away from any listening gossipers, and pulled out a cigarette, at which Frazer raised her eyebrows.

"Are you actually judging *me*?"

Frazer snapped her mouth closed.

Fair point.

Tia took a draw. The smoke billowed out of her mouth in a long stream, and Frazer resisted the urge to wave her hand around to ward it away. She wished she'd worn her jacket. It was cold and foggy. The type of July day in which you woke up to frost over the windshield and had to dig deep into your memory to remember how to deal with it.

How Frazer wished that this was her biggest problem of the day.

Tia was still eyeing her. "So. Frazer." Frazer swallowed and Tia continued. "You're sleeping with your boss' wife."

Not sure what to say to such an obvious statement, Frazer settled with what she hoped was a sheepish, regretful nod.

"When I suggested you approach her, it was because I thought you could pull her out of her shell, not into bed."

God, Frazer was glad this woman wasn't her actual mother. "I—"

"For how long, Frazer?"

She cleared her throat, looked away. "Three months."

When she dared look up again, Tia was staring at her, cigarette smouldering near her open mouth that was circled in shock. Ash eventually fell from the end of her cigarette.

"Around that, anyway." Frazer said, as if that could help.

"So, what, you waited, like, a week to start this up? An entire week into your planning before you seduced the poor, sad woman—"

"Hey!" While she was in no position to be self-righteous, that didn't mean she liked where this was going. "There was no *seducing*."

Tia actually rolled her eyes, the action somehow harsh. Frazer shut her mouth.

"Three *months*, Frazer?"

"I know, Tia."

"Do you?" The words were hard, biting.

"It's not like it's something I'm proud of!" Frazer hissed.

"You didn't look like you were trying to push her off you."

Frazer threw her hands in the air. "Exactly! She was on *me*. It is a...was a—a mutual thing. Something that should have been ended long ago." Only Frazer never had.

"So why didn't you end it?"

Damn it, Tia. Why did she have to ask that? Those cigarettes were looking tempting all of a sudden. "I don't know."

"She's *married*, Frazer. To your *boss*."

"I *know*."

They leant against the wall silently. Watched the people mill amongst the concrete to fill their lungs with air that was very much not fresh then hurry back to busy shifts.

"Do you know?"

Frazer looked at Tia and asked "What?"

"You say you know. But do you really?"

"I know she's married."

"But do you really know what you're playing with? There is another person involved in this. Someone who is unaware of what you two are doing behind his back. Have you talked about this? Is she leaving him? Are they separating? Is she interested in women?"

"We haven't talked about it."

Tia's looked hardened. "So you're not even promised a world of love—you're what, Frazer? Horny?"

"I—" Frazer had nothing to say to that. The point was a good one. She'd been promised nothing. In fact, she'd done the promising. Friendship, while giving Cora...whatever it was they were doing.

"I'm disappointed in you."

Frazer looked up sharply. And wished she hadn't.

Tia dropped the butt to the floor and stamped it out, burying her hands in her pocket as she walked away.

"Tia!"

Without turning, Tia replied, "Don't worry. I won't say anything."

That hadn't even been what Frazer was going to ask. Or had it?

"But you two should."

Teeth worried at her bottom lip as Frazer watched Tia disappear around a corner. Swallowing hard, she kicked the wall. Which only hurt. "Fuck!"

For hours, Cora walked around with a lump in her throat. She got a message from Alec, telling her he would be at work planning a presentation until the early hours, and that he might go out for a drink afterwards to blow off some steam. It was the only moment of the day Cora felt relieved.

Frazer had sent her a text that had simply said that Tia wasn't going to say anything. Which should have helped, but didn't.

With a stab of guilt, she deleted the text. Because that was the person Cora was now, someone who had to delete texts that could be read the wrong—well, the right—way. But that had been okay. Before.

It all felt different now. If she'd had to see Alec, she might have broken down and cried, a confession staining her lips. It had been easy before to walk out and then pretend they'd been doing nothing.

Now someone knew.

She passed Tia in the hallway, who stared her down. Cheeks burning, Cora walked as close to the wall as she could and hurried to find Jack. If there was anyone that could distract her, Jack could.

Since he'd made the decision, it was as if all the tension had left his shoulders. He'd had his meeting with the adoption agency alone but then called Cora the day before and asked to talk.

Taking a steadying breath, one that did nothing to calm her racing heart, Cora opened the door to the office to find Jack already seated. There was no hiding his pregnancy anymore after this long.

"Stay sitting, Jack! Don't be stupid." Cora smiled at him as he struggled to stand up.

Groaning, he dropped back into his seat. "Thanks. I feel like I'm the size of a truck."

"At least you must be warm under all those layers. Must be better than being pregnant in summer." Cora had been, for all of a month.

"That would be hell." He pushed his hair back out of his eyes. "Thanks for meeting me."

"Of course, it's what I'm here for. How's the house that organization found you?"

"It's okay. Kind of a long bus ride to everything, but my housemates are nicer than in the shelter. They're loud sometimes, though."

"Good." What mattered was that he was safe. "And Doctor Freiburg's appointments are still going well?"

This time, a smile played at Jack's lips. "He's good. Much nicer than the psych my parents made me see."

From what Jack had told Cora, that wasn't difficult. "Great. And you've been talking about your options after the baby is born?"

"Yeah." Jack's eyes brightened. "Hormones and things first. I told him I'm okay with taking my time—I'm still not sure about the surgery. About *when* to get it, I mean. I want it, but I don't... I don't *need* it now. Not like I thought I did. I can wait now to get some money together."

"As long as you're comfortable with your choices. It's all that matters."

"I just..."

Cora waited him out. She'd learnt it was what he needed, time to gather courage to say the things he'd never been allowed to before. She watched his fingers play at his bag strap.

"I just, I hear what my parents said, that bisexuality wasn't real. That if I could be with a man, why couldn't I do it as a girl and only be with guys..."

There were many times Cora wanted to slap Jack's parents. And the boy Jack had met at an LGBT meeting who had ignored any means of contact after the word "pregnant."

"I thought I had to get it all done as soon as possible to prove a point." Jack blinked, eyes moist, and looked up at the ceiling. Finally, he caught Cora's eye again. "But whatever I do in the future, I know who I am."

"Good." Doctor Freiburg had been difficult to secure, but she'd managed it with a little begging. And apparently, it was worth it if Jack was feeling secure in himself. It was clear Jack still struggled, but the shadowed look in his eye had softened. "And how was the adoption agency?"

With a one-shouldered shrug, he fiddled with a loose thread from his jacket. "It was okay. I had to find Tom to sign the stupid papers, though."

"Tom?"

"The guy, the father. The other father." Red was tingeing Jack's cheeks. He'd never mentioned the guy's name before.

"Did he sign?" Cora asked.

Jack fell heavily back against his chair. "Once I finally got a hold of him, he couldn't sign fast enough. What the hell should he *have* to sign for? They pretty much said if I couldn't find him, the baby couldn't be adopted."

Red tape: there was always red tape. "I suppose it's to protect everybody, make sure there's no one to challenge the adoption later."

"I guess." Jack mumbled. "Still stupid."

It kind of was, from Jack's perspective. It was his body, and Tom had made it clear he wasn't interested. "How was the rest of the meeting?"

"It was okay... I have a few families to choose from."

Cora ducked her head to try to meet his eye. "Choices can be good. Do you want some help?"

Letting out a breath, he nodded. "Yes, please. I feel a bit..."

"Overwhelmed with the responsibility of choosing a home for the human you're growing inside you?"

He snorted. "That. Yeah."

"Great. I'm happy to help. And after that we could talk about what you want to do? Finish high school? Enrol at TAFE and get an apprenticeship?"

Eyes scanning the wall behind her, he shrugged again. "Okay."

Over the past three months, Cora had spent a lot of time with Jack and with one other client she was now involved with mentoring. It was good to be busy with something that wasn't for work. It was rewarding to get people settled into long-term accommodation, to make sure they had some form of income and access to food—basics most people took for granted—and to give them someone who would listen to them.

And when she was with them, she didn't think about Alec or Frazer, about how she still woke up feeling like she was suffocating, then the next second drowning in the guilt of what she was doing.

In the last few months, she'd barely seen Lisa. Alec got mad when she did and said that this programme was taking up enough of her time.

But now wasn't the time to think about that. She focussed on Jack in front of her. "So, what are your options?"

"There's three I like. One is a single parent; she seems really nice. She's a kindergarten teacher. Another is a family who has two kids already but wants a third. The other two are adopted too—one from Kenya, another from China. I like that." His hands rubbed his belly over his jumper, and Cora wondered if he realised he was doing that.

"And the third?"

"Two dads who are trying to adopt. They've been waiting five years."

Nodding, Cora cocked her head. "Who do you lean to first?"

Jack threw his hands up miserably. "I don't know."

"Hey." When he looked up, Cora asked, "What's going on?"

"I've given over those questions we played with ages ago, but what if, even with the answers, I still can't tell who to pick? I mean, look at how Tom turned out. Maybe I'm a shitty judge of character."

"Jack…"

His brow scrunched together tightly, and he swallowed visibly. "What if you help me? I get the answers soon. Can you meet me afterwards to talk about what they all say? I want to get this right, if nothing else."

If nothing else.

"Of course I'll help."

Being in pyjamas with a glass of wine at seven o'clock in the evening was probably sad to some people. But to Frazer, it was heaven.

All day, she'd skulked around, avoiding her boss and Cora and feeling a renewed guilt that had somehow subsided over three months, settled deep in her belly.

What was she doing?

She'd been so content not dating. Especially at work. And then she fell into bed with her boss's wife and didn't look back. She'd just made some vague attempts in her mind to end it that had failed miserably. If Frazer was honest with herself, she hadn't tried that hard to see those attempts through.

Cora was married. What they were doing was not okay.

The look on Tia's face had driven something home that Frazer had managed to keep at bay for so long: Alec was an innocent bystander in all this. Maybe not innocent in his marriage—Frazer wouldn't know. But he didn't deserve this. No one did.

He was going to get hurt. And Frazer was going to be part of that happening.

She was just taking a sip of her second self-pitying glass of wine when someone knocked at the door. Wine glass still at her lips, she looked at the door for a second. Then decided to ignore it.

So, of course, whoever it was knocked again.

With a sigh, she put the glass down. She'd be mad, but it was seven o'clock. This was still a halfway decent hour. Still, her pyjama pants were covered in images of fish, and she had a sudden feeling she was channelling her grandmother. Not good.

Grumbling to herself, she swung open the door.

"Jemma!"

Arms crossed, her sister stared at her from the doorway. With a scowl. It was like looking at Jemma back when she was fifteen and infuriated that Frazer wouldn't buy her a bottle of vodka.

"Oh, you remember my name?"

Frazer rolled her eyes. "Of course I do. I talked to you yesterday on the phone."

"Yeah—as you got out of having lunch with me. *Again.*"

Frazer clung to the door for support. "I'm sorry." She even attempted a pout.

Jemma looked at her as if she'd farted. "Get that look off your face. I never see you anymore. I miss my sister."

"I really am sorry, Jem. I swear. It's been so hectic at work with the programme."

Jemma opened her mouth to say something else but turned when headlights lit up Frazer's driveway. Her brow furrowed. "You have people coming over? I thought you were busy?"

It was Cora's car. Even as her hands went clammy, Frazer tried to keep her voice normal. "Come on, Jem. Look at my clothes— you really think I was expecting someone?"

With a glance at Frazer's pyjamas, Jemma said carefully, "I guess not."

Cora slid out of the car, hovering for a moment as she stared at Jemma and Frazer in the doorway. Squaring her shoulders, Cora closed the door and walked over to them.

"Hey," she said to Jemma.

"Uh—hi." Jemma gave an awkward wave.

"Jemma, Cora. Cora, Jemma." Frazer's knuckles were white from holding onto the door so hard as she tried not to die right there. Why was Cora here? There was no way Jemma wouldn't ask questions about it.

Everything was crumbling around her. First Tia, now this.

What had she expected?

With her arms crossed, Jemma looked Cora up and down.

Frazer would rather be anywhere else right then.

They nodded at each other, Cora turning to look at Frazer. "Can we talk?"

"Yeah, sure."

Frazer opened the door wider and Cora slipped past. When she looked back at Jemma, it was at a red face and clenched fists. The look verged on murderous. Cora wisely kept moving further into the lounge.

"So she gets invited in?"

"Jem—it's a work thing. I can't say no. We work on the programme together."

"At seven o'clock in the evening at your house with you in your pyjamas?"

All Frazer could do was blink at her.

"Right." Jemma's arms dropped to her sides. "Fine. Call me when you can be bothered."

"Jem!"

Without bothering to turn around on her walk to her car, Jemma just threw her hand up in a wave. This wasn't good. Her sister was never mad at her. Cranky, sure. Annoying, definitely. Never mad.

And why the hell was Cora here? They hadn't made plans. In fact, they hadn't spoken since Frazer had sent her a message that said not to worry about Tia mentioning anything.

When she closed the door, Frazer leant her forehead against it. Took a deep breath. Why hadn't she ended it with Cora months ago? Why had she let it start?

These were questions she didn't want to ask herself.

Finally, she straightened and walked into her lounge room. Cora was standing in the middle, staring at her aquarium. Her hair was in a braid, tendrils around her face. There was still something about Cora, something that remained untouchable to Frazer. They were friends; that was certain. They were friends with benefits. They had good sex. Cora had opened up to her, slowly. They shared more than just coffee chat.

But there were times she was further away. She was married, yes. But Frazer didn't know if it was just that. How could she ever know? They couldn't have a relationship.

And Frazer had no right to feel bitter about that. She'd known what she was getting into.

Or thought she had.

Watching Cora's eyes follow a darting fish, the damn Dory one that always beat up her Nemo, the urge to ask Cora a question that she'd never let herself bubbled up. It traced its way along her throat and almost made it past her tongue: *What do you want, Cora? Are you gay? Are you bi? Are you straight? Do you want to leave your husband?*

But then Cora turned. Caught her eye.

"I thought I'd locked the door."

Frazer nodded. "I know. I thought I saw you do it."

"I mustn't have turned it all the way."

"Probably not."

"What if that had been Alec?" Cora whispered.

That name dropped like a rock between them.

All Frazer could do was stare at her.

"This isn't right, what we're doing, Frazer."

What could Frazer say? It wasn't.

But Cora walked forward, into her space. Almost close enough to touch, but just too far. Cocked her head.

"There's a kid that's just turned eighteen under my care who knows more about doing the right thing than I do."

Confused, Frazer took a moment. She meant Jack. "Sometimes there's more than one right thing." Frazer didn't even know what she was saying. What it meant.

Yet Cora nodded. Held her gaze. She stepped forward again, her fingers trembling slightly, and traced Frazer's cheek. They collided, and Frazer almost fell backwards with the force of her. It took Frazer a moment to catch up, to match the desperation in Cora's kiss. But only a moment.

Their hands tore at each other, nails raking against skin. Somehow, they made it to Frazer's room, their clothes a pile next to the bed, shoes kicked off somewhere on the way. There was naked skin against her, Cora's arms wrapped around her neck. Her legs wrapped around Frazer's waist. Somehow, she fit perfectly between Frazer's legs that were moulded against her.

Cora's hand clung to the back of her neck, her free one grabbing at Frazer's skin. As her fingers ran down and stroked her, their kiss broke, their foreheads still together and their eyes searching for something Frazer couldn't name. Light filtered in from the hallway, enough that Frazer could catch Cora's gaze and wonder at what the depth, the warmth, an iris so dark held. It was easy to cling to Cora's neck in the same way Cora did to her own, to reach down and run her fingers over softness, over wetness. Frazer matched Cora's pace. Their hips demanded more.

When Cora threw her head back, Frazer dragged her teeth over the skin of her neck, across the pulse point that always made Cora groan. Soothed it with her tongue.

Cora was shaking. Her thighs trembled around Frazer. When she came undone, her gaze on Frazer's, it only took a second for Frazer to follow, matching Cora's erratic panting breaths, letting herself fall backwards onto the bed. Cora fell with her and settled between her legs. Her face pressed into Frazer's neck, hot breath washing over flushed skin.

Lazily, Frazer's fingers ran over Cora's skin, over the dampness that had pooled along her spine. All the while, Frazer's heart thudded against her ribs.

The errant thought shot through her mind: *how was this wrong?*

Still breathing too fast, Cora lifted her head, resting it on her hand on a propped-up elbow to look down at Frazer. Her eyes, still so dark, were unreadable. Slowly, Frazer pushed a piece of hair behind Cora's ear and swallowed hard. Cora's eyes were soft. A fathomless, profound soft.

When Cora spoke, the words were a whisper that lingered over Frazer's lips. "That was incredible."

For some reason, Frazer didn't trust herself to speak. She nodded, a smile playing at her lips.

Dipping her head, Cora nuzzled her neck. "*You* were incredible."

Whatever Cora had originally come here to say seemed to have floated away with one desperate kiss.

When Frazer swallowed and finally spoke, her voice was low, hoarse. "You were."

Cora gently kissed her neck. She traced her way along Frazer's jaw and finally settled over Frazer's lips in a kiss. Chaste. As if they had all night. When she pulled back, she was smiling. "We kind of were."

Frazer smiled harder then. Easily. Comfortably. "We were."

That soft look in Cora's eye darkened. She blinked. Sat up.

For the second time that day, cold air washed over Frazer.

She was on the edge of the bed now, staring at the wall.

"Hey." Frazer pushed herself up on her elbows. "Cora?"

Cora didn't look at her. Didn't turn. "I have to go."

And then she was getting dressed. Pulling clothes on haphazardly. Too fast. She stood with her back to Frazer, and when she went to walk out, Frazer called out more desperately than she had intended.

"Cora!"

Cora paused. Hovered in the doorway, a silhouette. Her hand rested on the wooden frame, her head turned slightly.

"I'll see you at work tomorrow."

Frazer was left with the sight of her hallway, the sound of Cora pulling her shoes on.

The sound of the door closing.

Everything had gotten out of hand.

Cora needed a shower. She smelt of Frazer. Of sex.

Of them.

But instead, she was sitting in her car outside Lisa's house, shaking.

She'd gone to Frazer's to end it. To get a clear head so she could go see Doctor Massey. To figure out her marriage. To ask Frazer to just be her friend. Which was what they were. The sex didn't cloud that. They were friends, and Cora needed that.

But then Cora had kissed her instead. Again. Had lain with her afterwards and kissed her neck. Her lips tingled, and Cora pressed her fingers against them.

Cora wasn't even gay. Not that it even mattered. She was married.

206

How was it all such a mess?

She got out of the car. The lights flashed behind her as she pushed the lock button on her car remote and walked up to the front door. She knocked like she used to in university. It was a pattern that came easy—muscle memory.

When the door opened, Lisa looked so happy to see her that Cora burst into tears.

Wide-eyed, Lisa pulled her through the door and into a hug.

With her best friend's arms around her, as her shoulders shuddered in Lisa's embrace, all Cora could think was that she needed a shower.

"Hey." Lisa ran her hands up and down Cora's back. "I hardly hear from you for months and now you're crying? What's going on?"

It just made her cry harder.

"Okay! Sorry!" Lisa squeezed her even more firmly. She swayed back and forth until Cora got herself together and pulled away.

"Wanna sit down?" Lisa asked her.

At Cora's nod, they walked down to the lounge room, Cora dropping onto the beanbag like she always did.

"Wine? Chocolate? Beer?" Lisa cocked her head and looked down at her. Cora was sure she was a mess. Whenever she cried, her eyes swelled up and her face went hideously blotchy. "Vodka?"

"Water."

Lisa's eyebrows raised. "Just water?"

"Yeah."

She appeared a minute later with two large glasses of water and some chocolate tucked under her arm. "Just in case."

When she sat opposite her on the couch, Lisa leant her elbows on her knees. "Cora. What the hell is going on?"

Cora took a huge gulp of her water, cool and soothing. She pulled in a shuddering breath. "I've been having an affair."

She stared at Lisa, absorbed Lisa's shock as her mouth dropped open. Lisa pulled back, away from the words, as if they could physically touch her.

"Please don't hate me."

Lisa shook her head quickly. "God, no, sweetie. I don't hate you. Never hate you. Just give a girl a minute here." She took a sip of her water. Broke off some of the chocolate and ate it quickly. "An affair?"

Cora nodded.

"Like sex?"

Cora nodded again.

"Not with Alec?"

"Not with Alec."

"How long for?"

This time, Cora couldn't look at her when she answered. "Three months."

"Jesus, Cora. Three months?"

Cora winced. "Yeah."

"When I said to get a toy boy, I was joking. Or meant, you know, if you broke it off."

"I know."

"Is that where you disappeared to?"

God, she wished that was where. Sighing, Cora shook her head. "Things with Alec have been...harder."

"He was always too damn controlling."

Cora looked up sharply. "You thought that?"

"I've tried to bring it up a lot of times, Core. You didn't seem to want to hear it."

Sinking into the bean bag as deeply as she could, Cora put her glass of water on the ground. She ran a hand over her eyes. "I didn't."

"What did he say?"

How did she explain it? "He just... He complains I don't make time for him. Since this programme I'm involved in has started up, he's worse, which I hadn't thought was possible. He expects me to be at home waiting for him."

"He always did." At Cora's inquisitive look, Lisa expanded. "At university, it was always on his terms. I heard him once, guilting you into staying with him when we'd planned lunch."

Heat crawled over Cora's face. She bit the inside of her cheek, looking up at the ceiling. "I thought it was normal."

"I know, sweetie... You used to be full of big talk about saving the world. Where was it you were going to volunteer? India?"

A smile twitched on Cora's lips. "Asia." The smile died. Cora hadn't thought of that in years and years. Whatever happened to making her mark on the world in a way that helped people? It had been the entire reason she'd chosen social work.

They sat in silence before Lisa broke it. "I thought you were going to end it months ago. I was proud of you."

"I was. I almost did."

"What happened?"

Cora sighed again. "I slept with someone else. Alec came back from his conference full of manipulation... I felt so guilty, I..."

"You let it work."

Cora waved her hand non-committedly in the air. "Apparently. We went to therapy."

This made Lisa straighten up. "Really? How did that go?"

"It made me really see what was going on. Alec... I don't think he liked it. The therapist was really good, highlighted when he interrupted me, highlighted the things he said. Gave us exercises to do at home that he never did... Alec decided we were better after a few sessions, and we stopped going."

"He decided?"

Cora couldn't look her in the eye at that question, shame biting in her stomach.

"Cora," Lisa said, "how the hell did you manage an affair?"

"We work together."

"You had sex in the hospital?" Lisa's voice was much higher than normal.

"Yeah."

"That's... That's kind of gross, Cora."

Cora gave a sudden laugh. It burst out of her like relief. "Yeah. It kind of is."

And then they caught each other's eye and laughed, Cora's stomach aching with it.

Hours later, they sat on the couch, Cora's head on Lisa's shoulder.

"Do you have feelings for the guy?" Lisa asked.

Cora watched the TV, an old black-and-white movie she hadn't really been following. She shook her head adamantly, not even thinking. "No." Of course she didn't. She couldn't.

"So what were you doing?"

"I don't know. Distracting myself. I'm married. I can't have feelings for someone else."

Lisa just squeezed her hand.

But Cora could still feel the way Frazer's hand had stroked her back. The way she'd looked at her, her entire face softening as they'd whispered to each other.

There was no way Frazer was going to contact Cora.

A message from Jemma, after Cora had walked out, had Frazer burying her face in her pillow.

Nice wedding ring your friend has.

Everything was starting to become far too real.

When she saw Alec at the hospital, all Frazer felt was a swarming hive of guilt in her stomach. Who was she to do something like this to him? At lunch, she rounded a corner and saw him half sitting on Tia's desk, talking animatedly to her. With a shake of her head, Tia shot back some kind of reply. When he laughed again, Tia's look found Frazer standing at the end of the hall and her look had hardened.

Frazer was used to Tia lighting up at the sight of her.

It was only a second before her eyes were on Alec again, but the moment had managed to stir up that hive even more.

Frazer had simply turned on her heel and walked back the other way. The hallways felt narrow. Her breath echoed in her ears.

Poor Alec.

In a staff room, Frazer tried to steady her hand as she poured lukewarm coffee into a cup. She checked her phone again. Nothing from Cora.

She always got up and walked out the second they were finished.

But the other night, they'd lingered.

And then she'd run.

Throughout all of this, their friendship and the sex had been separate. Especially for Cora. She never freaked out—in fact, Cora had always seemed so together during it all. The rules she wanted to follow had been laid out, some unspoken, and since they'd followed them, everything had gone smoothly.

The other night, Cora had definitely freaked out.

After a sip of her coffee, Frazer barely registered the fact that it was far too bitter, even with three sugars.

"You can't even look at him."

Frazer span around. Tia stood in the empty room, her arms crossed. It was all Frazer could do to hold her eye. "I know."

Tia cocked her head. "Then you know you should be ashamed."

Her cheeks warmed. "I am."

"Only because you got caught."

Frazer's mouth dropped open to deny it, then snapped shut. It was true. A simple point, but a telling one. Her cheeks blazed now.

"Frazer." Tia was staring at her. "I never pegged you for the type."

The bench bit into her back. Frazer looked to the ground. "Neither did I."

"Do you know how it feels? To find out the person you trusted most in the world is doing something like that?"

Wordless, Frazer shook her head.

"It feels like shit, Frazer. When my husband did it, the other woman hadn't known he was married, at least." Tia's jaw was clenched, and Frazer still had nothing to say. She'd had no idea.

"You can't say the same. You are knowingly causing someone a lot of pain."

"I'm going to end it." Frazer said. It sounded weak even to her ears.

"Good." Tia straightened. "But I don't believe you."

She walked out and left Frazer to her shitty coffee and even shittier feeling.

Having to find more mentors to train was a pretty excellent feeling. It meant they were expanding, that the programme was working.

It helped ease the tightness in Frazer's chest.

The kinks were being fixed, two babies had been born, and the clients' mentors were checking in with the parents regularly, making sure they were coping. One wasn't, and they'd helped the mother seek out respite for a few hours a week away from the baby. They made sure she'd discussed with a doctor what seemed like a particularly nasty case of postnatal depression. Mostly, they ensured she felt supported.

And now they were ready for another training week, to bring on board some new clients and new mentors.

It was a good feeling.

With Jack due soon, he was now coming in for weekly appointments. Cora had mentioned the last week over coffee that he was choosing parents. That she would be helping.

Because Frazer's patients now had support systems.

It was enough to make Frazer do a happy squirm in her chair.

A new e-mail pinged in her inbox from an A&E nurse who was interested in being a mentor. She had two kids at home and remembered what it was like to have little support and a newborn in your care. The perfect candidate. Frazer sent her an e-mail about the training dates she was setting up over the next few weeks.

If only her personal life was so easy to figure out. If only she made as little mess in her personal life as in her work. Though those two worlds had collided, thanks to Frazer's ridiculously poor decision-making.

A soft knock at the door interrupted her moody musings.

"Come in."

Cora slipped inside and closed the door behind her. Frazer heard the lock turn closed. With her back against the door, hands behind her, Cora didn't move.

Frazer didn't think she was here for the usual reason she locked the door. Frazer walked around her desk and sat at the edge of it, crossed her arms. A few meters separated them, a gulf compared to usual.

Panic played at the back of her mind, and she ignored it. Frazer wasn't allowed to feel panic at Cora's avoidance for the last two days, nor the weird look on Cora's face. They were friends.

"Hey."

"Hi." Cora stared at her. "Sorry for, uh, disappearing."

"That's okay." It wasn't. But it was supposed to be.

"I, I just..." Cora swallowed. Bit her lip. "I think we need to end this. To go back to being...to being friends. Without all the..."

"Sex?" Frazer asked, a smile pulling at her lips before falling.

"Exactly."

Frazer blinked at her. "Oh." Wait. That wasn't a good response. "Oh. Yeah. Of course."

Something flitted across Cora's face before Frazer recognised the relief that settled on her features.

"It's just—I'm married. Married. To a man. And—"

"Cora. You don't need to explain. Really. We shouldn't have let this go on so long."

"No." Cora shook her head. "We shouldn't have."

Her voice was hoarse. Low. And *not sexy*, Frazer reminded herself.

Not at all that.

"Are you okay?" Frazer asked.

Cora nodded. "Yeah, I... I'm okay. I need to figure some stuff out."

"Good. That'll be good, for you."

So what now? Did Cora just walk out and from now on they clicked straight into no sex? That's what Frazer had agreed to. So probably.

Friends. Just like Frazer had told herself since they started to get to know each other.

Frazer had never hinted she wanted more than that. Since it started, she'd known that wasn't an option. Cora wasn't even *gay*. Unless she was bi. Surely she had to be; this couldn't just be experimentation at this point. That wasn't the issue anyway—she was married.

To a man that didn't deserve all of this.

Frazer had been some kind of fun, some kind of distraction, and now that was ending.

Frazer was an idiot.

"Okay." Cora said. "So, I'll see you around?"

Because Frazer was an idiot, she nodded. "Yeah. Of course."

And because she was still an idiot, Frazer stood up and walked forward. Leant her shoulder next to Cora against the door. Looked her in the eye. It was always Cora who instigated. Who sought Frazer out. Who touched first. Who let her know it was okay.

But all Frazer could think was that this was it. There wouldn't be any more.

So this time, she didn't play by unspoken rules. She ran her fingertips against Cora's cheek. Memorised how Cora pushed into the touch. How she turned her cheek slightly, her lips a whisper from Frazer's fingers.

It was easy, to close the gap. To hover her lips over Cora's. Breathe her in, feel the warmth that radiated from her. Watch her eyelids flicker closed.

It was a simple pressing of lips. Of sinking into softness.

It started that way. And then Cora's hands were in her hair, her body flush against Frazer's. Her tongue was demanding, her lips dominating. Nails bit into Frazer's neck, and Frazer pushed back with the same intensity.

Until Cora pulled away. Stepped back. Used a foot of distance as a shield.

Cora's eyes opened lazily. Her eyes traced Frazer's face and then held her gaze for a minute.

Then she unlocked the door and left.

There was no rush of cold air this time. But there might as well have been.

CHAPTER THIRTEEN

"The prodigal sister shows up!"

Frazer instantly thought about turning around and walking out of the restaurant. The leisure centre was just around the corner. She could go back to the pool and keep swimming until all she could do was float. Like she had that morning. And the night before. The smell of chlorine still lingered on her skin.

Soon it would warm up, and she could get back in the ocean. The smell of salt and the warmth of the sun on her back as she swam parallel to the shore all but an enticing memory.

She exhaled deeply. Going back to the pool *or* swimming at the beach was impossible now that her sister had seen her. "Funny," she said and headed to Jemma's table.

"Oh, I'm hilarious. I have a *lot* more jokes like that. We live twenty minutes from each other, yet I've not seen you more than three times in as many months." Jemma put her elbows on the table. "Do you know what that means, big sister?"

"Um... I've been busy?" Frazer reached for the menu.

"No, it means I haven't seen you more than once a month. *Once* a *month*. Me. Your baby sister. The apple of your eye. Your favourite person. The only one in our family who isn't mildly insane."

"Right now I doubt that part."

The joking tone left Jemma's voice and Frazer was left with a sister who was looking at her almost plaintively. "What gives?"

Guilt, an emotion Frazer had hoped she'd be done with now that she was done with whatever was going on with Cora, flipped her stomach. "Jem, honestly, I've been busy. I really am sorry."

Jemma just kept pouting at her.

Frazer rubbed her hand over her eyes. "I've been the worst sister ever. Absolutely shit. You are marvellous, wonderful, *fantastic,* even. You deserve one hundred times better than me. I bask in your glow as a sister."

Jemma jutted her chin out and sniffed. "Good. As long as you're aware." But her lips twitched up. "*Bask*?"

"You seemed to want dramatic."

"Glad you recognised that."

The waiter appeared. With a glance at each other, they ordered two plates they'd end up sharing. As the waiter stuck his pen behind his ear and collected their menus, Jemma nudged her leg under the table.

"How's that programme going?"

Now this was something she could talk about. "Really well. We're starting to set up more mentors. The clients we have now are giving us a lot of feedback. It'll take a few years to really have it settled, and by then, if it's all going well, we should have more funding."

"That's great."

"Yeah, I'm hoping it's something we can see more hospitals set up. To go statewide."

"And," Jemma said, "eventually nationwide?"

"That's the dream."

"Great. So, who was that Cora lady?"

To cover her surprise at the question, Frazer reached for her water and took a sip. "She's working with me on the project."

"Don't bullshit me, big sister. I learnt how to do it from you, so I know all your tricks. Who is she?"

Rolling her eyes, Frazer clenched her fist. "Jemma, that's the truth." Now. "She works with me on the project. And she's a friend."

"Lying."

"I'm not lying!" Frazer's voice rose, and Jemma pursed her lips and leant back in her seat. She even crossed her arms. This was exactly why Frazer had disappeared the last few months. Her sister and her friends could read her like a book.

"Then why so defensive?"

Frazer pursed her lips and looked away. What did it matter if she told Jemma? But what was the point now if it was over? It was why Frazer had gone swimming for a collective six hours in less than twenty-four.

"Frazer." Jemma straightened again, resting her hand over Frazer's, where she gripped a napkin too tightly. "What's going on?"

"Nothing anymore."

Not even blinking, Jemma stared at her. "But there was?"

"It was nothing, Jemma."

"It was something."

Frazer pulled her fingers away, not feeling like she deserved the comfort. "We were... We were sleeping together."

Still Jemma didn't pull away. Didn't flinch. She left her hand where it was, an offering. "And she's married?"

"To my boss."

That got a rapid blink, but nothing else. "How long for?"

"Three months."

Giving a soft whistle, Jemma still didn't move. "Are you in love with her?"

"What? Jesus! No. No. Definitely no." Frazer bit her lip. "It was stupid. Something that should've ended ages ago. But it's ended now anyway." Frazer's heart started to race in her chest.

"Is she splitting up with her husband?"

"I don't know, Jem." Frazer groaned and buried her head in her hands. "They were having problems when it first started, but we don't—didn't, talk about him. We were friends, and sometimes we slept together." More than sometimes. "But we never talked about her marriage."

Frazer finally looked up from her hands, expecting reproach in Jemma's eyes. All she saw was someone clearly listening. "Why aren't you condemning me?"

With a shrug, Jemma answered, "Nothing's black and white. I mean, it's not good. But it's pretty obvious you know that. You don't need me making you feel worse."

For someone reason, that comment did make Frazer feel just that. "It's over now."

Jemma nodded. "Okay. And you have to see each other at work?"

"We really do work on the programme together. So yes. She's a friend…"

"Right. And I'm you're aunty."

"What?"

"Sex is never just sex, Frazer. Especially after three months of it all wrapped up in *friendship*." Her fingers in the air making quotation marks were really unnecessary.

"It can be. It was."

Jemma considered her for a moment. She thanked the waiter as he put down the food but just kept on staring at Frazer. "So you're just going to go back to being friends?"

"Yeah."

"Okay."

"Don't 'okay' me like that." Frazer said. God, Jemma was infuriating.

"Okay."

"Jemma!"

"Frazer!" Jemma mimicked Frazer's tone.

Frazer stabbed at a piece of tomato and shoved it in her mouth.

"Was that supposed to be threatening?"

Sighing, Frazer let the fork clatter to the plate. "Yes."

"Then you're lucky you're a midwife and not an assassin." Jemma's playful look faded a little. "Look. I just think this could get complicated. But if you want to be friends, then go. Try to be friends."

Frazer did want to be friends. Eventually. "Maybe we'll need some space first."

"You think?"

"I really regret my sarcastic influence on you."

"I don't." Jemma ripped apart a piece of bread. "So, when are you going to meet my lecturer?"

Frazer stared at her. "You two have gone public?"

"Not as such. But we've stopped pretending it's a fling. Now that some time has passed, the naughty aspect has disappeared and we've realised we have to actually get to know each other."

It took Jemma a moment to realise Frazer was staring at her. "What?" Jemma asked.

"When did you grow up and become mature?"

"Right around when you were doing the opposite. Oh my God." Jemma gave her the same crooked grin Frazer always had whenever she was being a shithead. "Am *I* the big sister now?"

"You couldn't handle the responsibility."

"Oh, please. Look how I handled your crisis. I'm so the big sister. You've been demoted."

"Oh shush, Miss Sleeps With Her Lecturer."

"Alright, Miss Sleeps With Married Women."

"Wom*an*."

"Like that makes a difference."

There was a loud ticking in Doctor Massey's office. Strangely, it wasn't as loud as Cora's heart, which she could hear thundering in her ears.

They'd redone the paperwork before going over the confidentiality thing again. And now there was silence, which Cora was having a hard time breaking.

"So." Doctor Massey smiled. "What brings you here, Cora?"

Cora swallowed, then took a deep breath. "I think I want to get a divorce."

"You think?" Doctor Massey had a way of keeping her voice completely neutral. No tone inflicted to say what she thought. All she had to do was ask a question, a simple one, and Cora felt tripped up.

"I know. I know I want to get a divorce."

"What's stopping you?"

"Guilt." Cora swallowed again. She looked away and stared at the plant in the corner. It was a large ficus, one of four plants in the office. Frazer's office didn't have anything in it. It was incredibly boring. Maybe she needed a plant.

"Guilt?"

Questions like that, so simple on the outside. Just Cora's own words, again, thrown at her. "For lots of reasons."

"Want to tell me one of those reasons?" Doctor Massey rarely blinked. It was disconcerting. Her eyes only watched Cora, saw through her, and chipped at little parts Cora had kept carefully hidden.

"I tried to tell Alec once before. More than once, really."

"And what did he say?"

Cora tugged at her skirt, smoothing it over her knees. "That I couldn't do that to him. That he'd be a mess. That I would..."

This time Doctor Massey didn't ask anything. She waited for Cora to finish.

"That I'd be nothing without him."

Doctor Massey's face was still so neutral. How did she do that?

"How do you feel about the idea of not being married? Do you feel like you'd be nothing?"

For some reason, tears filled Cora's eyes and she had to swallow past a lump in her throat that felt so big it could choke her.

"I'd feel..."

"What, Cora?"

"Free." She took a deep breath. "I would feel free."

Paperwork was never fun. But at least it was distracting.

Files and folders lined the walls of the patient file room on the maternity ward. At one of the cramped desks, Frazer was glad it was twelve o'clock and all the nurses were off fulfilling general observations and giving medications. It meant she had the room to herself.

The hospital was mostly paperless. This room only held patient histories for more complex notes. To have enough computers free for all the doctors, nurses, midwives, social workers, physiotherapists, and occupational therapists to update patient files every few hours was expensive and kind of insane. The good old patient file wasn't going anywhere in that regards.

There was something soothing about writing out her observations by hand. Filling in comments, signing her name at the end. Being able to read back and see what other professionals had written.

After signing off on her current notes, Frazer searched the files for a particular name, an apparent recovering addict. Never an easy case. One of the nurses had paged her to ask about getting her into Frazer's programme, and she needed to look through her notes.

That was how Cora found her.

One minute, Frazer was alone and elbow deep in the patient's past, and the next, she felt someone's eyes on her. She glanced up from her wheelie chair to see Cora leaning against the door frame, watching her. It was almost creepy.

"Hey." Cora looked strange. Almost nervous. A little jumpy. Maybe too pale, though it was hard to tell in the hyperfluorescent light.

Frazer smiled. Probably awkwardly. "Hi."

Everything felt like it had shifted, only slightly, but enough to the left or right that Frazer felt like she was tripping on her own feet. It all looked the same, but when she placed her foot down, the ground underneath wasn't where she'd thought it would be. Like when you thought there weren't more steps on the staircase and for a split second you thought you were freefalling before you crashed back down, no one else really aware about your inner panic.

"I was wondering if you were free for a coffee." Cora glanced down at her watch, then said, "Or lunch."

Biting her lip, Frazer closed the file and hugged it to her chest. "I've actually got a big patient load this afternoon."

She didn't, but she could make one. She'd avoided Cora for the last few days because it was easier. Their friends with benefits deal had ended, and that usually meant the friends part ended too.

Yet she didn't want that. To not have a friendship with Cora. But when the last thing she remembered about Cora was the taste of her lips, Frazer just needed a bit of time. Some time to step back from that moment and figure out this weird world shift no one else had seemed to notice.

"Oh, okay." Cora nodded.

"Soon, though, yeah?" Frazer asked.

The way Cora's face brightened made something in Frazer's stomach squeeze.

"Yeah, great. How about tomorrow? Lunch in the rain outside?" Cora voice was hopeful and something squeezed again.

Frazer tilted her head, watched her. "Um, I'm really busy tomorrow too."

"Okay. Whcn would suit you?"

Trying to keep her voice light, Frazer gathered what she could of her old self and slid the folder amongst the others. "What about next week?"

Cora's shoulders sagged. "Next week?"

"Yeah." Frazer leant her hip against a desk. "I just think we need, I don't know, a breather." Frazer waggled her hand in the air between them. "From all this."

"I thought we were friends."

"We are. Or we will be—maybe." Frazer had no idea what was coming out of her mouth. Whether to stop it or not, she also had no idea.

Cora was staring at her, definitely pale now. "Maybe?"

Frazer edged past Cora, mindful to not touch her. Cora didn't even turn around, just followed her with her eyes.

"It's complicated, Cora." And before she could see the expression on Cora's face, Frazer smiled. "I have to go. I've got a mountain of paperwork."

She could feel Cora's stare on her back as she walked down the hall.

Complicated?

They were supposed to be friends. That was the deal when they had started, the ground rules they'd put out before themselves. Or rather, Cora had put out—they had sex, but they would stay friends.

It all felt like Cora was standing at the bottom of a pool slowly filling with water. Every time she thought the water had stopped rising, it sloshed into her mouth, leaving her spluttering.

Her session with Doctor Massey had been productive, had helped her put into words all the things she never felt she could with Alec. Words she hadn't managed to say when she and Alec had seen her together. She had another appointment for next week, and Cora wanted it to be sooner. She wanted to spew out everything she'd kept in her chest and not said for years.

At the end, with very little time to spare, Cora had looked Doctor Massey in the eye, relieved about confidentiality agreements, and told her she'd had an affair.

That had at least gotten a blink out of the woman. And one question. *Why?*

Cora had had nothing to say that. Should she make an excuse? Or should she lie? So she simply said, "I don't know."

"I think you do," Doctor Massey had said.

And they'd had to end the session. The next week, she had said, Cora was going to have to answer that question.

So Cora was going to have the session next week and then tell Alec.

It was final. She wanted a divorce. She had wanted one for longer than she would probably ever admit to herself. Today, in the session, Cora had talked about the way their relationship had started, the passion that had made Cora feel safe but had slowly started to feel more like ownership. Alec's constant desire to be with her, to have Cora there when he wanted, had become less like safety and more like isolation.

Sometimes, she'd told Doctor Massey, Alec made Cora second-guess herself so much that Cora had started to take what he said as gospel. There were times Cora had been so sure of something, yet by the time they finished the conversation, she would believe him when he said she was mistaken.

After talking about something that left her feeling scrubbed raw, Cora had wanted to talk to her friend about it, had wanted to talk to Frazer. But Frazer wanted...space.

Outside, the rain came down in buckets, the sound of it filling Cora's car when she parked outside Lisa's house. Her fingers were white knuckled on the steering wheel. Shivering, she pressed her overheated forehead against her cool hands.

Couldn't they just go back to being friends? They had been this whole time, just with the benefit of sex, sex that was admittedly good. Cora had been surprised at how good. She shouldn't have really, because of course lesbians had good sex. Two women could enjoy themselves. Otherwise, they wouldn't be doing it. But she'd never realised it could be *just* as good as sex with a man. Different, yet incredible. Leg-shakingly so.

Cora was going to miss it.

But it had been a diversion. Something to bury herself under while she hid from what was going on with Alec. Maybe she could say that was why, her grand answer to offer up to Doctor Massey, and wait to see if she validated it.

But she would miss her friendship with Frazer more if it disappeared. Three months of friendship was enough to make Cora realise she needed Frazer around.

Cora got out of her car and ran up the path to Lisa's house. The front door was already opening, and Cora dashed inside, dripping a little on the linoleum.

"Hey." Lisa handed her a towel, the door swinging shut and closing out the weather. "Saw you pull up."

"Thanks."

The towel was warm. Cora clung to it when she sat down in the kitchen, watching Lisa get things for tea.

It was nice to have a friend who knew what she wanted.

"Alec still puts sugar in my tea."

"You've never had sugar in your tea." Lisa didn't even bother to look at her while she said it. Cora knew what expression would be on her face anyway.

"I know. He doesn't make one very often."

Lisa slid the steaming mug across the tabletop to her and sat on the other side. As Cora wrapped her hand around it, the warmth seeped into her fingers. "Rain and tea together are a dream."

"I hate the rain." Lisa watched her through the steam over her mug as she took a sip. "Except in summer, I love the—"

"Storms."

They grinned at each other. "How was the session with the head doctor?"

"It was...hard."

There was an understanding in Lisa's eyes. "I bet. Any wisdom?"

"No. She seems to help me find my own wisdom, rather than give me any."

"I like her. Making you realise you have all the tools you need already."

Cora rolled her eyes. "Yeah, yeah."

They sat silently for a moment. Cora blew on her tea and took a sip. It was scalding, almost cleansing. Maybe it could burn all the frustration out from inside of her and leave her with something new to start with.

"Did you tell her about your affair?"

Cora winced at the word. Hearing it said felt like being slapped with a truth about herself. "I chickened out and only mentioned it right at the end."

"Ah, typical Cora. When there was no time to face the repercussions." Lisa's tone softened her hard words.

"Pretty much. She asked me why I did it."

"Good question. Did you answer?"

"That's my homework."

Lisa wrinkled up her nose. "Ew. Homework. And here I thought we'd moved past high school."

"Well, apparently, if you act like a teenager, you have to be treated like one."

Lisa chuckled. "Lucky you."

Cora pulled her feet up on the chair, the towel clamped between her legs and chest. It still held some warmth.

"You okay?"

Cora looked up from her tea. "I don't really know."

"Are you still seeing the guy?"

Cora swallowed. Took in a deep breath. "It was a woman."

Lisa blinked at her, mouth dropping open slightly. Then she closed it again. A disbelieving smile pulled at her lips. "Seriously?"

"Seriously."

"Like *seriously*?"

"Seriously."

Lisa put her mug on the table, staring at her with the same incredulous look. "You know, I told you about my little fling in uni to highlight your need to have some fun. Not so you'd think I was awesome and try to be like me."

Cora snorted. "What can I say? I want to be just like you."

"Are you gay?"

"What?" Cora sat back, shaking her head. "No. Lisa, God. It was... I don't know. A distraction. An accidental one."

"For three months?"

Cora winced, clutching her tea closer. "Yeah."

"Was it good?" Lisa's lips were quickly dragging themselves up into a grin.

"It was—" Amazing. "It's not important."

"And you're not gay?"

"No! I'm married! To a man!"

"So? People discover that stuff late. Or are you bi?"

Cora stared at her. Something weird was happening to her heart. It beat so fast it almost felt like a hum in her chest. "No." She licked her lips. "No. It was—it was stupid. She was a friend, and it got messy because she was, she was *there*."

Lisa winced. "Ow for her."

"I didn't mean it like that, Lise. She's a friend."

"Are you still friends?"

Were they? "I hope so."

"You miss her?"

Cora looked up sharply, brow furrowed. "What?"

"Well, that sounded like you're not seeing as much of her. Do you miss her?"

"I—I miss being friends, yeah."

Lisa looked like she was trying to solve a puzzle, brow furrowed as she pieced things together. "And you were having sex for three months?" At Cora's nod, Lisa asked, "And you don't miss that?"

"I mean, I miss the—I miss parts of it; it was...*nice*. But I just want my friend back."

"So." Lisa was staring at her intently. So intently Cora felt like squirming under her gaze. "You miss her friendship. And the sex was good, but you're not..."

"What?"

Lisa stared at her. But instead of saying anything, she relaxed back into her chair. "Nothing." She shook her head. "Just surprised by this revelation, I suppose."

The feeling that Lisa wanted to say something more sat heavily in the silence that followed, but Cora didn't want to pull at that thread.

"Ah, Cora. You are in a pickle."

Cora groaned, dropped her head back. "I know."

"Do you want to stay with Alec?"

Lisa looked at her openly, taking a sip of her tea. Cora shook her head. "No." Her voice was low, like he would be able to hear if she spoke any louder. "I don't. I want a divorce."

"Oh, honey."

228

Cora looked away from that sympathy. She turned her gaze up, eyes on the ceiling, vision blurring a little. With her lips pressed together, she took in a shaky breath, counted to five in her head, and then looked back to Lisa. "How's your mum?"

Lisa took a second to answer, as if debating whether or not to let the topic change happen. "Worse. She doesn't have many lucid moments anymore."

"I'm sorry, Lisa."

"It's okay. It's almost... This is terrible."

"What?"

"It's almost...easier. She doesn't float in and out and get scared anymore. She's almost...happier in her own world."

"That's not terrible. If she's happier, that's a good thing."

"She's not Mum anymore, though."

Cora couldn't imagine watching her parents lose themselves. They might not all be the closest, but Lisa had been close with her mum.

"She's lucky to have you."

"I was lucky to have her."

"And the immigration authorities, with your dad?"

"Nothing."

The urge to swear at them rose up, but in the end Cora just shook her head. "I'm sorry."

"It's okay." Lisa smirked. "At least I have your gay drama to keep me entertained."

"It's not gay!"

Lisa just sipped her tea.

"You want us to set you up on a date?"

Rob and Andy were staring at Frazer. It felt a little like she was sitting at a table with her parents and had just told them she was moving to another country.

"Yes."

They looked at each other and then back to Frazer.

"Like, with a woman?" Andy asked.

"No, with a man. I've renounced my lesbianism."

Rob snorted. Andy and Frazer both raised their eyebrows at him. "Sorry." He said. "Just imagining you with a man. It was more entertaining than I thought it would be."

"You know." Andy was now staring above Frazer's head. "It really is." She laughed. "It just doesn't work."

Horrified, Frazer looked from one to the other, at their identical smirks. "Please stop imagining me naked with a man."

"But it's funny." Rob grinned at her. "And strange."

"Exactly why Andy's question was ridiculous. Of course with a woman."

"Well, excuse me for being confused." Andy narrowed her eyes at Frazer. "We've barely seen you for months. I thought you'd renounced everything, let alone women and sex."

The image of Cora on Frazer's desk sprung into her mind, and she was glad it was dark so they wouldn't notice the heat in her cheeks.

"What was that?" Rob was eyeing her.

It *was* dark, wasn't it?

"What?" Frazer asked.

Andy nodded. "I saw it, too. She twitched when I said 'sex.'"

"I did not!"

"Oh, honey, yes you did. Has it been that long?"

Frazer let out a breath. "Yes. That must've been it. Help me?" She made pitiful eyes at both of them.

"Frazer." Andy leant forward. "Of course we'll help you. We've been wanting to forever."

As they argued between themselves about who to set her up with, Frazer took a sip of her drink. Maybe if she could get out there, she could wash her mind of Cora. Because Frazer needed to be Cora's friend.

And maybe this would help.

Cora was feeling something akin to panic. Or maybe not akin, but, instead, actual, mind-consuming panic.

Her skin was prickling; everything felt hot and uncomfortable. Was she breathing too quickly? She tried to pay attention to it to but couldn't. Which probably meant she was.

It was rare Alec was home so early. Rare that they were together at this time. It felt like it grated against what was normal.

He sat on one end of the couch, his laptop on. His feet were up on the coffee table. There were times, when they were quiet, she could almost imagine that she could keep doing this. There were times when she wasn't *un*happy.

Was that enough? Was that how she wanted to spend her life, settling on and living for the times she was afloat somewhere between happy and unhappy? Waiting for the next thing to bring her back down? Did she want to always be checking her words, dancing around him to keep him happy?

No.

The television was on, but she was having trouble focussing on it—on anything, really.

When did she tell him she wanted a divorce? How did she choose the right moment? Last time had not gone well. But she needed him to hear her this time. Dr Massey had given her tools she could use to stop his words from changing her mind. But Cora wanted another session with her first. She wanted to feel like she was in charge of her emotions.

It took everything she had not to jump when he dropped his foot over hers on the coffee table. He smiled at her from the other side of the couch.

"It's nice to be home in the evening."

Trying to remember how to breathe normally, Cora nodded. She tried to smile too. "It must be nice, after working so late at work all the time."

His foot ran over hers. "You've no idea how tired I am after work. It's exhausting."

"I imagine."

He used his foot to hook her under her ankle and twisted in his seat, pulling her legs towards the couch. Leaning forward, he pulled her feet onto his lap, reading an e-mail while his fingers ran over her feet, massaging the bottom.

It felt amazing. And that made her want to cry. She resisted the urge to pull her feet away and tuck them up and under her. Instead, she stared at the television and tried to follow the program. Measured her breathing. In and out. Tried to ignore the scratch of panic at the back of her brain.

It was easier when he behaved badly. When he forgot she was a person with thoughts and opinions.

There were times when Alec was the person she fell in love with years and years ago. When he touched her like she could break. Or stroked her skin like now, comfortable in what he was doing. Because why wouldn't he be at home on his couch with his wife of ten years?

Ten years.

And she was going to shatter it.

Shatter his safe bubble.

In bed, hours later, she lay on her side, hoping he'd just sleep. The house settled around them, the odd creak and the groan familiar. With a rustle of the sheets, he rolled over. Her breath caught in her chest as his hand ran up her thigh, over her ribs.

Swallowing, Cora caught his hand in hers.

"I'm tired." She whispered it towards the wall.

Sometimes it worked. For a long time, but especially the last few months, sex between them had been minimal anyway, something Cora had done only if pushed. As it had been the last few years, as she'd felt his grasp around her tighten, she'd not wanted the closeness of him against her, the intimacy it brought. But sometimes, saying no too much led to too much hassle. Questions.

After those few times in the last few months, Cora had always danced away from Frazer at work, lost in feelings of shame, the desire to bury herself in the sensations Frazer gave her, and the desire to erase the memory of Alec left on her skin. In the end she'd cave, falling into Frazer with desperation at her fingers.

But she couldn't do that anymore. Not tonight. Not with what she knew she would be doing in a few more days.

"Cora." He kissed the back of her neck, and it only made her wince. It left a hot spot on the back of her neck that would take hours to dull. "I go away for the weekend tomorrow."

He had another conference. She'd forgotten. At least that made the weekend easier.

"Please?" Another kiss.

"I have my period." She almost choked on the lie.

With a sigh, he rolled over onto his back. He said nothing more, but she could feel him stewing on the other side of the bed.

If Alec was away, maybe she could spend time with Lisa.

Or Frazer.

Maybe Frazer would actually hang out with her. They could go back to being friends.

It was that thought that Cora went to sleep with.

On Sunday, Cora broke.

She'd hoped Frazer would message her over the weekend, maybe to suggest a coffee or lunch or a drink. Maybe Frazer would suggest *something*.

On Saturday, Cora had gone with Lisa to see her mother. The strong woman who Cora remembered was gone. While she'd learnt English over time, the carers said that now she chattered in Vietnamese. Her eyes were brighter than Cora had expected. But at one point, she turned to Lisa and said, in suddenly loud and abrasive English, "Who are you?"

And Lisa had tried to laugh it off, but afterwards they went and had a slightly boozy lunch where Lisa had proceeded to drink a glass of wine like a shot.

Still Cora heard nothing from Frazer.

So Sunday afternoon, she messaged her. A simple:

Want to get a friendly drink?

Thankfully, Frazer only waited twenty minutes to reply.

You don't give up, do you?

A winking emoticon took the bite from the words. And Frazer agreed to a drink. They were going to meet for a beer at that pub on the river again. On a Sunday, it would be crowded. The wind would be cold as it came off the river, but Cora had a faint memory from the last time they'd gone of large heaters outside on the deck.

Cora arrived too early, almost as if she was excited.

Excited to see a friend, she reminded herself.

At the bar, she ordered two bright ales, the one she remembered Frazer had ordered last time. There were two people leaving a table right near the water, and she slipped into their still-warm seats. One of them laughed at how quickly she'd intercepted the table, and Cora grinned at them. Glad a heater was blasting her neck, she took a sip of the beer and enjoyed the feeling of having no obligations.

Alec was away. She was meeting a friend. There was a nice beer in front of her. Even though it was only seven, it was dark, the lights reflecting off the dark water of the river. People chattering and loud laughter surrounded her. These were all simple, easy things. This was something she could do.

It was strange to be remembering things she liked, to have time to do this, to remember who she was before Alec. Or maybe she was finding out who she was after him.

"Hey."

Cora's lips were pulling up before Frazer had completely sat down. "Hey. Thanks for meeting me."

The half smile was on Frazer's face. "Happy to."

The glass cold on her fingers, Cora slid the beer across to Frazer. "You didn't sound that way the other day."

"Well," Frazer pulled the beer close, "I just needed a few days."

"You said maybe." Cora blurted it out. That *maybe* had been the thing that had played over and over in her mind the most the last few days.

Frazer chuckled. "I did. But it's not your...normal situation."

Warmth that wasn't from the heaters spread down Cora's back. "I know. So why did you change your mind?"

"Because." Frazer took a sip. For a moment, it looked like she was considering what to say. Finally, she just said, "Because we're friends."

Relief spread through Cora's chest. "I'm glad."

With hunched shoulders, Frazer looked across the water. "It's chilly tonight."

"Do you want to go inside?"

Frazer shook her head. "God, no. We're inside all day at work. It's so nice out here by the water."

"It really is." But Cora wasn't watching the water. She was watching Frazer watch the water. In the orange light from the heaters, her normally bright green eyes were dark, her dark skin molten.

She caught Cora's gaze on her. "Did you see Jack this week?"

Cora nodded. "Yeah, I'm meeting with him to talk about the parents he has as options. He wants to make a decision the next fortnight."

"It's not an easy one. I'm glad you're mentoring him, though."

"He's a super-nice kid. Once the baby's born and he's feeling up to it, we're going to talk about TAFE."

"He decided against completing high school?"

"Yeah, he said he was always interested in being an electrician. We'll see what we can get set up. He may have to do some bridging courses."

There was an odd look on Frazer's face.

"Are you okay?"

Frazer nodded. "Yeah. I just... Imagine where he'd be if we never got this programme up and running."

"You mean if *you* hadn't."

"No." Frazer shook her head. "I mean we. This was definitely us."

Frazer's eyes were still dark, and they stared at her across the table. The wind blew a strand of hair around her face. Her cheeks were flushed from it. Flushed like they often were in bed.

"Frazer—" Cora stopped speaking as a woman stopped at the table.

"Frazer!"

Looking from Frazer to this woman, Cora watched Frazer stand up, accepting a kiss on the cheek from her.

"Hey, Emma. How's it going?"

The woman's—Emma's—hand lingered on Frazer's arm. "I'm good. Great. Last night was fun."

"It was."

Who was this Emma?

"Cora." Frazer turned to her. "This is Emma. Emma, this is my friend, Cora."

Emma flashed an abnormally pretty grin at her. The blue of her eyes seemed insanely bright. "Hi, Cora. It's nice to meet you."

"Likewise."

Cora swallowed what felt like rocks in her throat and shook the hand Emma held out for her. Of course she had a great handshake.

"Well, I won't intrude." Emma smiled again. Why was she so happy? "Frazer, I hope to hear from you soon."

Frazer smiled back at her. It wasn't crooked, though. "You will. Bye!"

"Bye, Cora."

"Bye, Emma."

Cora watched her walk away. When she turned back to Frazer, she was staring at Cora.

"Sorry about that."

That rock was still in Cora's throat. "It's okay."

When Frazer offered up no more information, instead taking a sip of her beer, Cora couldn't help herself. "Where do you know her from? I don't think I've seen her around the hospital."

236

"We, uh, had a date last night."

Cora made herself smile even as something ugly reared up inside. "Oh. That's nice." What was she supposed to say now? "She had a nice smile."

Staring at her beer, Frazer shrugged. "She does." Then she looked up. "My friends set us up."

"That's nice." No it wasn't. But it should be, this should be something two friends talked about. Cora's heart was hammering strangely; she could practically hear it. The thought that Frazer had stressed that Cora was her friend occurred to her.

"I, uh, have to go." Cora stood up. That panicked feeling was back.

"Cora."

"Sorry, I don't feel well." Grabbing her purse, Cora turned and fled, leaving Frazer calling her name again with two beers she probably didn't even want.

Maybe Frazer could call Emma back over and they could share them.

"She just ran off?"

"Yeah."

Instead of watching Jemma, Frazer watched her fish. The tank was lit with a soft blue light, and she'd cleaned it that day. In her imagination, her little fish world was extremely happy. They were active, darting all over the place, and two of them were hanging near the new plant she'd put in.

She loved her fish. Such a neat, organised little world.

A piece of popcorn hit Frazer in the face. Responding to Jemma with a glare, Frazer picked it off from her chest and ate it. "What was that for?"

On the armchair, Jemma raised her eyebrows. "You don't find that weird?"

"Being hit in the face with popcorn? Yes, yes I do."

"Don't be an arse. Her running away was weird."

"Well." Frazer tucked her hands under her head and went back to staring at her aquarium. "It was less of a run, and more of a storm-off."

Frazer still didn't look away when she heard her sister's sharp sigh. "And *that* is *weird*."

With a shrug that was not comfortable in her position, Frazer opened her mouth and looked pointedly at Jemma, who promptly aimed and threw another piece. It bounced off Frazer's forehead. Three more attempts and one landed, followed by Jemma fist-pumping and Frazer chewing happily.

"Yes, fine, it was weird. It's why I thought the friendship thing should wait... It's all a bit weird."

"Maybe she's in love with you."

Frazer snorted.

"Or you are with her."

Frazer snorted again. "No to both. It's just...complicated."

Complicated like Jemma saying Cora was in love with her setting off a swarm of feelings in Frazer's stomach.

"Sure. Complicated."

Frazer went back to Fish TV. "It is complicated. It should never have gotten to this point..."

"Probably not." For a few minutes, there was only the sound of Jemma crunching on popcorn. Finally, Jemma said, "How *was* your date?"

Frazer watched Nemo nibble at some coral. He was so little. Almost cute. "It was okay."

"Okay?"

"Yes. Okay. She was nice..."

"Nice?"

Frazer looked back at Jemma, who was staring at her expectantly. "Yeah, nice."

"Our *grandmother* is nice, Frazer. Dinner can be *nice*. Your date should be something more than *nice*."

"Our grandmother is nice after three wines, not the same thing." They shared a knowing smirk. "I don't know, Jem. She was nice. I wasn't really feeling it, though."

"Why?"

"She was a bit...boring."

"That's what you said about the last date."

That was true. Maybe Frazer was the problem.

"Maybe, big sister, it's *you* who's boring."

"Hey!" Frazer would have pouted but she didn't want to look five. "Mean."

Even if that was just where Frazer's thought process had been going.

"Just putting it out there. Are you going to go on another date with her?"

God, no. "Probably." Frazer said.

"Great. Give her a second chance."

No. "Good idea."

"You just ran off?"

"I didn't *run*."

Lisa was staring at her. Her eyes were piercing, and it was making Cora feel quite uncomfortable.

"Okay, Cora. You just...*stalked* off? Fled? Stormed? Then came here?"

Cora pulled a cushion against her stomach. "Fine. Yes."

"Smooth."

"I...had somewhere to be."

"Cora, honey. We just established you came straight here. So we both know that's a lie."

"I missed you." Cora smiled at her and batted her eyelashes.

Abruptly, Lisa laughed.

"What?"

"I've missed you is all." Lisa said. "You're a goof."

On the tip of her tongue was the point that Cora hadn't really gone anywhere when it occurred to her that that wasn't what Lisa meant. "I know."

"Good." Lisa was still smiling at her, but gently. Like she would at a child she was cautious to not make cry. "So why did you flee?"

With a loud groan, Cora pulled the pillow against her face. After a second, she let it fall. "I honestly have *no* idea."

"Really?"

Lisa was staring at her again. It really was eerie. "Really. It just felt weird. Which is stupid. Of course she's dating people— she's allowed to." Cora meant it, she really did. "I *want* her to. I was just...surprised."

"Why?"

Cora plucked at a loose string on the cushion. The million-dollar question. Why had Frazer dating taken her by such surprise that she'd needed to escape so she could breathe? Why was it Cora was always feeling suffocated wherever she was? "I don't know... I'm selfish. I'm used to being the only one in her life. I was needy or something." Cora took a deep breath. "I'm telling Alec tomorrow. And I guess I projected that onto her."

"You're telling him tomorrow?"

Relieved to not have to talk about Frazer anymore, Cora nodded. "Yes."

"About the affair?"

"What?" Cora sputtered for a minute. "No! No. No, no. No. About wanting a divorce."

"Really?"

"Yes. Really."

"I..." Lisa considered that for a moment. "What's your plan?"

That was another million-dollar question. "I have half a plan. I'm talking to my psych tomorrow to, just, get some clarity."

"What's your half plan?"

"I'll tell him and go to a hotel. Then I'll rent somewhere."

"*You're* going to move out?"

Core picked at a string on the cushion. "Yeah. I need to feel like this will stick. And if he takes his time to leave or has access to where I am... I don't know; he may make me change my mind." Which was a horrible thing to admit about herself, that someone could twist her thoughts around and around until she thought she wanted something different than what she'd started with.

"Cora... You're really doing this?"

"Yes." Cora really was doing that.

With a nod, Lisa said, "Don't stay in a hotel. Stay here."

"I can't ask that of you."

"I'm serious. And you're not asking anything. I'm insisting."

"Lisa—"

"Would you ever make me stay in a hotel?"

All Cora could do was shake her head.

"Then it's settled." Lisa leant back against the couch. "I have a great guest room. And we can drink wine together. Or tea. There's been a lot of wine lately."

Swallowing past a lump in her throat, Cora stared at her best friend. "Are you sure?"

"If you ask me that again, I'll put my terrible scratchy sheets on your bed."

Cora clutched the cushion closer.

"Thank you, Lisa."

"Shut up. Like you have to say that."

Everything felt like it was simultaneously spinning out of control and falling into place.

CHAPTER FOURTEEN

Monday was D-Day.

Divorce day.

Or more like request-for-divorce day.

And Cora wanted to talk to Frazer about it. She wanted to sit down, now that they'd ended all of the sex, and talk about her marriage. Dissect the thoughts that whirled around Cora's head. Admit that she wanted out and that she really had no idea how that linked to what Frazer and she had been doing. Before, Cora could talk to her and sleep with her. And now they weren't sleeping together and Cora couldn't speak to her.

Cora missed Frazer. But every time she thought of talking to her, something twisted low in her gut. And it was ridiculous. Frazer was allowed to date anyone she wanted.

But weirdly confusing questions kept rolling through Cora's mind: did Frazer kiss that Emma woman? Did they go home together? Did Frazer want to see her again? Of course, it was all simple curiosity. Something inquisitive—the type of questions all friends wanted to know.

Today was the day Cora was telling her husband she was leaving him and she was thinking about *Frazer* and that ugly woman, *Emma,* who wasn't at all ugly, not even a little bit.

"You seem distracted, Cora." Doctor Massey was watching her, seeing everything, as she did.

"Today's a hard day."

"Of course. Do you want to talk about the affair?"

Cora twitched. Even she noticed it. "Um, okay."

"Well, you mentioned it. So I assumed it was something you wanted to talk about."

Damn psychologists—nothing got past them. "I probably do."

"So, back to the original question. Why?"

Cora licked her lips. Her gaze swept over the plants in the room. There was a new one on the desk—small, with red flowers. How did she keep them all alive? A lot of time had to go into them.

It had been too long since the question had been asked, but Doctor Massey was better at waiting than most.

"I... I don't know."

Doctor Massey cocked her head slightly.

Cora sighed inwardly. "Because... It was easier than dealing with what was going on."

She just kept watching Cora.

"And, uh, maybe," Cora really had no idea, "it was a good distraction. Something to think about that wasn't Alec and my problems."

"Distraction is a useful technique. Do you think you were being self-destructive?"

Walking down your own psyche was never fun. "Self-destructive?"

"Well, you told me you've wanted out for a long time now. And you'd tried but retreated. Do you think this was a way of throwing it in, because if you got caught, your marriage would be over without you having to ask for it?"

Cora blinked at her and swallowed heavily. "Maybe."

"Only you know the answer to that."

"I think... I think it was distraction. Definitely. I think... I think it was also a way of knowing that my marriage would end. Like, it secured it. If Alec wouldn't agree to it, I could use it."

"Are you going to use it?"

"No. I just want it to be over. I don't want to use that. I don't want to...to use the other person like that. It stopped being about that anyway."

"It did?"

"Yes."

Doctor Massey regarded her. "What was it about after that, then?"

"It felt good." Cora's voice cracked, and she looked away, anywhere but at the eyes watching her. "It felt good, and I felt like myself... And I didn't want that to end."

Cora had used Frazer. That really wasn't something she was proud of. But at the same time, Cora had enjoyed Frazer's company. And Frazer had enjoyed hers. She just wanted them to be friends again.

"Maybe," Doctor Massey said, "you need to learn to feel that way without relying on another person."

Damn her.

Exhaustion settled over Cora after her session with Doctor Massey.

She was packing two large suitcases on her bed. There was a message on her phone from Frazer, asking if she wanted to grab a coffee and Cora had just ignored it, not wanting to explain her weird walk-off the night before.

It was easier right now to ignore these things.

Most of her clothes fit in the two suitcases. She stepped back into her walk-in wardrobe with a sigh. It was almost completely gutted. The hangers still moved slightly, as if waiting for her to still them and put everything right. It would be easy to stuff it all back inside and close the door, to turn away from it and pretend she hadn't packed to begin with.

Instead, she closed the door to the empty wardrobe and turned her back on it.

Cora's stomach was roiling. Her pulse was hammering. Everything felt surreal, as if she were watching herself from above, collecting her cosmetics and shampoo from the bathroom. Imagining that, she could pretend it wasn't her stuffing them on top of her clothes and zipping the cases shut. Someone else was lugging them down the stairs and hefting them into her car.

None of it was her, and that was easier.

It was all too bizarre. Her marriage was actually ending.

Back inside, her fingers ran along the wall as she walked through to the kitchen, the evenness soothing against her skin. Alec was due home in five minutes.

It felt cruel what she was about to do, dumping bad news then abandoning him. But was there a kind way to do this?

The appointment with her lawyer tomorrow afternoon couldn't come soon enough, although, really, she looked most forward to meeting Jack at a café afterward and talking about what he wanted to do with his future. She'd collected TAFE admission forms and pension scheme forms to assist with the payments.

Perhaps it would give him something to get excited about.

Afterwards, she would go back to Lisa's and drink all the wine she could. And maybe look for an apartment. And then make a resolution to drink less alcohol, because she'd been using it as a bit of a crutch the last few months.

Slowly, Cora could start this life she'd created for herself.

A car pulled into the drive, the tyres crunching on the gravel. A door slammed, then another. Alec collecting his carry-on bag from the back seat. Keys at the door. It opened, then closed. His measured footsteps fell in the passage.

He paused, framed in the doorway as he caught sight of her standing in the kitchen. "Is everything okay?" he asked.

There was an irony in the fact that he chose now to be able to read her mood.

"Alec, we need to talk." It sounded rehearsed because it was.

He stared at her.

"I'm leaving. I think it's best if we get divorced."

Doctor Massey had told her to use the words that clearly said what she wanted, not to soften the blow to save his feelings. If she wanted to feel validated, she had to make sure she actually said what she meant. It had to be clear.

Alec actually laughed. It echoed strangely in the house. "Are you joking?"

She shook her head. "No. I'm serious."

"Well, I'm not going anywhere." His jaw clenched.

"You don't have to. I have my bags in my car, I'm going to stay somewhere else until I can get an apartment or a house sorted."

His eye ticked when she took that measure of control from him. "Cora, this has to be a joke."

"I'm not joking."

His mouth gaped, like a fish, as he tried to pull together the words he needed. "You can't do this to me, Cora."

"I have to do it for me. And for you."

"Don't you tell me what I want!" His hand clenched on the handle of his carry-on. "Please. Stay. I—I thought we were better."

Stay away from blame. Stay away from direct hits at him and only speak of how you feel.

Cora took in a measured breath. "I know you're not happy anymore. I know I'm not either."

"You're going to put me through this? To put my family through this? *Yours*?"

Cora swallowed. Tried to remember she wasn't doing anything *to* him. "I need to leave."

His voice was hard, his eyes like flint. "Your family will be so ashamed of you if you get a divorce."

That may be true. "This isn't about my family."

"If you go, I'll make sure they know it's *you* who left *me*."

One of the stories Cora had read online had said a man methodically ruined his girlfriend's life through social media with lies and threats. "Okay." Cora nodded. "You can say what you want."

His nostrils flared. "Think of your job, Cora."

Cora took a deep breath. She hated underlying threats, the subtlety of the word games Alec played. She always lost them, even as she loathed to play.

"I'll be meeting a lawyer tomorrow, and I assume he will be in contact with yours." She stepped forward, regretting the fact that she was standing in the kitchen. The only way out was past him.

246

He refused to move aside, so she turned sideways to slide past. As she walked down the hallway, he called after her, "You think you can do better than this?"

Cora opened the door and walked out, closing it gently behind her. When she pulled her keys out of her pocket, they jangled in her hand, and she ignored the fact that it was because her hands were shaking. It took her three attempts to get the key in the lock, but finally it slid home. She slid into the car and started it, pulling out onto the road.

Three streets away, she pulled over to the side and turned off the ignition. A gulping sob exploded from her chest.

It was wrenching, how much her chest hurt.

How much everything hurt.

CHAPTER FIFTEEN

Cora was ignoring her.

Which was fine with Frazer.

Except that it wasn't fine; but it needed to be fine.

And what gives, anyway? Cora was so keen to be friends. She'd looked so shattered when Frazer had said "maybe" and walked out. Had asked for a beer on the Sunday.

If she was jealous about a stupid date, that wasn't fair. Cora had set her ground rules. They were friends. The sex was just a…a bonus of that friendship. Now that the bonus was over, they were supposed to still be friends. And Frazer really wanted to be mad about that, about Cora calling all the shots and then walking away when she found out Frazer went on a date. But she couldn't.

Cora was married and was probably a little messed up about all of it. Frazer certainly was. Even now, she never really looked Alec in the eye. Shame filled her stomach when she was near him, and it was too hard to not remember he was a human being she'd happily put in the firing line so she could get her rocks off.

And in the process of getting her rocks off, she had somehow started to toe the line of too attached.

Frazer had no idea how Cora went home to him and sat next to him on their couch or ate dinner with him or slept next to him at night.

Or made love to him. That thought, the one Frazer never let herself imagine, made her bite her lip.

But she didn't care. She wasn't allowed to. Instead, she would focus on work.

Like the new training session that week. The week-long one she and Cora had to get through together. Their planning for it had been completed weeks before, and now they had to pretend to be adults and get through it. Together. Really, they should talk, because Cora hadn't shown up for the first one last night. Which wasn't integral; it was mostly introduction stuff. But it wasn't like her to not show. Frazer had called her about eight times before she gave up.

Walking down a corridor, Frazer saw Tia ahead and called out to her.

Thankfully, Tia stopped.

Frazer gave her a hopeful smile that Tia didn't really return.

"How's your day?"

"Fine, thank you."

"Tia..." Frazer didn't really know what she wanted to say.

"Yes, Frazer?"

Damn it. "I... want you to know your words got through. Cora and I," Frazer glanced around, relieved no one was close by. "We're over. It's finished."

Tia eyed her. "Really?"

"Yeah."

"After three months, just done."

"Yup." Frazer gave her a another smile, this one tight-lipped, and propped her shoulder against the wall. "No more. It should have been finished ages ago anyway."

For some reason, Tia kept eyeing her. Frazer had to resist the urge to fidget under her stare.

"Oh, my poor girl."

That was not what Frazer had expected. "What?"

Tia rubbed Frazer's arm with a gentleness that took Frazer's breath away. "You idiot. You poor idiot."

"Uh...well, I am. But why?"

"And you don't even realise!" Tia gave a laugh. "I'm glad to hear you've seen sense, but the rest of it..."

"Rest of what?" Frazer asked. She honestly didn't think she had ever been more confused.

Tia turned around and walked away, leaving Frazer staring after her. "Rest of what?" There was no response from Tia. "Tia! Rest of what?"

She turned the corner and left Frazer completely confused. What the hell was that about?

Frazer turned around, stepping forward just as someone opened the door that had been behind her, clocking her right in the forehead. She uttered a sharp cry of pain, echoed by a loud, "Shit! I'm sorry!" from whoever it was that opened it.

Clutching her already throbbing head, Frazer wanted to curl inside herself as she recognised the voice.

"Frazer, I'm so sorry. Are you okay?"

How did it always manage to be Cora?

"I'm—I'm fine."

"No you're not."

Arms tugged at her and pulled her into the room Cora had just vacated. It was an empty storage room with a disturbingly bright light in it, which Frazer's head protested to with a throb.

"Cora." Frazer was still holding a hand against her forehead as she looked around the room filled with boxes. One was clearly full of adult nappies. "Why were you in here?"

"The other door leads to my offices. I use it as a shortcut."

Impressed, Frazer looked around. "Smart."

"Let me see your head."

Without a thought, Frazer let her hand drop and watched Cora's face for the first time. She winced when Cora's brow furrowed deeply. "That bad, is it?"

"You have a bruising egg already."

"Awesome."

Gentle and sure, Cora's hands held the sides of her face as she made Frazer angle her head up so she could look at it closely under the light. "I think I just watched it get bigger."

"Even more awesome."

When had Cora stepped closer to her? She looked drawn, with dark circles smudged under her eyes. Had she not slept well? The fact that Frazer meant to ask where she'd been for the training flew out of her head.

Cora looked from Frazer's now apparently oddly shaped head to catch her gaze. Cora gave an awkward smile and let her hands fall away. "Hey."

Frazer chuckled. "Hi."

Maybe it was the hit in the head, but Frazer felt a bit light-headed. Cora smelt nice. Clean and fresh. Without thinking, Frazer moved forward, her gaze going from Cora's eyes to her lips. When Cora swayed forward ever so slightly, Frazer froze, snapping back to reality.

Something dark flitted over Cora's eyes, and she stepped back.

Cora was always stepping back.

"You should get that checked out."

And then she was gone, the door closing with a neat snick, leaving Frazer with a throbbing head and a bad feeling in her gut.

Shit. Fuck.

Rule number one of the lesbian world, especially once outside of high school: never fall for the straight girl. Never.

Okay, now she was mad.

Taking a deep breath, Frazer stormed out of the room with a vicious push of the door. She wove her way through the hallways with her fists clenched at her side. When she reached her destination, her eyes swept the room. It was empty. No one at the receptionist's desk. She quickly turned on her heel. She didn't want to run into Alec.

Especially right now.

Not when she was heavily dealing with high school-type feelings.

The canteen didn't hold the object of her search either.

Frazer burst out of the hospital, shivering as frigid air surrounded her. It cooled her flaming skin but did nothing for the panic rising in her stomach. Turning a few corners, Frazer finally saw her.

Tia didn't even look surprised when Frazer stepped into the courtyard. In fact, she didn't even straighten from where she stood, back against the wall. For too long, Frazer stared at her before walking forward and accepting the packet of cigarettes she held out.

Cigarettes. Something Frazer hated.

But the smoke curled in her lungs and burnt out some of the heavy feelings in her chest. Wrapping an arm around her middle, Frazer stood next to Tia, one foot flat against the wall and brick biting into her back.

"Finally figuring out what I saw?" Tia asked.

Frazer blew out a steady stream of smoke. It was almost blue, rising slowly in front of her to be whipped away in the wind. "I don't know what you're talking about."

"Sure, kid."

Another drag that felt like denial and tasted like an ashy lie.

"I didn't realise you had feelings for her."

Neither had Frazer. "I don't."

"Sure."

There was nothing like an adoption process to distract yourself from your divorce. Or from the woman you couldn't stop kissing.

Who was Frazer to look at Cora like that? Or to just, *be* everywhere, all the time.

Anger had been bubbling in her all afternoon. It had made her meeting with her lawyer easier—she would be making contact with Alec's lawyer this week. The fact that Cora couldn't actually divorce him until they proved they had been separated for twelve months was a headache. One year, and she could actually file. For now, they were separated.

And now Jack was looking at Cora with big eyes, three folders on the table between them. The waiter put down their drinks. The relish in Jack's face was evident as he pulled towards himself the biggest chocolate milkshake Cora had ever seen.

"This is so, so good." He took another sip on the straw, his cheeks drawn in tight. "Though I'm gonna be peeing every five minutes after it."

Her own spearmint milkshake was creamy and delicious, yet Cora couldn't enjoy it. That stupid supply room scene kept playing in her head like a loop. Her guilt at ignoring Frazer's missed calls didn't help. The training week was important; she should have been there. The programme was something she was proud of, something that touched on the volunteering she'd always thought she'd do after university, a little piece of herself she'd rediscovered.

She took a long sip and buried down the feeling. "It's worth it though, right?"

"Totally."

Spreading the folders out over the table, Cora considered them. "So. What are your thoughts?"

Jack sagged a little, his eyes intent on them. "I don't know."

"Any thoughts. Any at all." Cora mixed them up, like a magician moving cups with a ball inside. "Or we can just pull one out and take that one."

"That's tempting."

Choosing one at random, Cora flicked it open. "Okay. Two dads, no kids, one cat. Thoughts. Go! No thinking."

"Uh—um."

"That's thinking."

Eyes brighter now, Jack blurted out, "Um, seem nice. One's an artist, and works from home. The other is some higher-up in a bank. I like that they're kind of, like, a balance. And the one who works from home does a lot of charity work with some refugee centres."

"Great, now—" Cora grabbed the second one and flicked it open, "Single mum. And go!"

"She's, um, a children's book illustrator. She works from home, too. Does contract work with her accounting degree, so has a good income. She lives near the beach. Has a big family, lots of nieces and nephews. That's nice. Cousins for Bug."

"Bug?"

Jack shrugged sheepishly. "I was tired of saying 'it'."

"Okay, and third option for Bug, a mum and dad with two adopted kids."

The chocolate milkshake in front of Jack was now half empty. He swirled his straw around absently. "They're obviously invested in their kids. I like that Bug could have siblings. Bug'd also have experienced parents—that's nice…"

"But?"

Jack was now stabbing his straw into the chocolate mess. "But…I don't know. They have two kids. The other two have been waiting for ages for a kid. I think I'd rather give Bug to a family that had been waiting for ages."

"Okay. That's fine." Cora slipped that folder down next to her on the booth seat. It was a hideous, fluorescent pink. Apparently, they were in a 1950s diner, but Jack had chosen it, and she hadn't wanted to say no. At least the milkshakes were incredible—they tasted like her childhood. "Look at that, progress. Two left."

Jack took a long sip on his straw again. His eyes studied the two folders Cora lined up in front of him. "Can't you choose?" His voice was soft, and he didn't look up.

Swallowing hard, Cora's heart went out to him. "I'm sorry, Jack. This has got to be your decision."

"If Tom wasn't such an asshole, he could help me."

That was true. It was unfair that the one with the uterus got stuck with the responsibility in these situations. "I know. But you'll know what's right."

Jack threw his hands up. "I like both of them. The two Dads would be great, two supportive parents. I know Bug'd at least have open-minded parents. But the woman's involved in PFLAG and is in a great situation. And the questions I sent them through the agency, uh, we sent, they all answered awesomely…" Groaning, Jack slumped across the table, shifting so his belly allowed the movement. He looked at Cora with round eyes, "Do you want a kid? I know you're not crazy."

Cora had to stop herself from snorting. "Trust me, I'm not the best thing for Bug."

"Why? You're married." His eyes dropped to her ring finger. "Though why don't you wear your rings?"

She wasn't married. Or wouldn't be. How did you explain to an eighteen-year-old that being an adult and married really didn't mean you had your life together? "I never got in the habit, the hospital is gross and dirty, and we're always washing our hands. I only wear them sometimes."

"So." Jack wriggled his eyebrows up and down at her. "Baby. Want it?"

Cora laughed, her chest tightening even as she did so. "Not as much as these folder people do."

He slumped back down. "Damn."

"Yeah." She smiled at the top of his head. "Damn. Okay, let's talk about that in a little while. What about after, the next six months?"

He straightened and hugged his milkshake close to himself. "I like the idea of TAFE." He said it slowly, like daring there to be a hole in the plan. As if a future like that wasn't built for him.

"Great, I have a whole bunch of paperwork here." She slid it over, and he picked up one of the TAFE brochures, thumbing through it. "And I've got some paperwork from Centrelink we can get started."

"I can get assistance with TAFE?" His eyes didn't leave the page in front of him.

"You sure can."

Cora might be tearing down her own life with her bare hands, but she could help Jack build a new one.

He nodded, clearly trying to squash down something like glee. "Cool."

"Cool indeed."

The training had gone well.

They had five new mentors, including the nurse from A&E who had soaked up all the information Frazer provided, eyes focussed and interested. They'd all asked a lot of insightful questions, questions that showed they all held compassion and an understanding of what their clients could be going through. All the things Frazer could hope for from potential mentors.

But again, no Cora.

Frazer had messaged her, but had been secretly relieved when she hadn't replied. Her own inner revelation had left her feeling more ill than anything, and she didn't feel like seeing Cora.

But tomorrow night, Cora had to be there; it was the social service side of things. So tomorrow, Frazer would find her and kick her butt into gear. If being near each other was apparently so intolerable, Cora could take tomorrow's session alone.

Frazer had just packed up the room and was switching the lights off when her phone chimed. Expecting it to be a text from Cora, finally, her eyebrows raised when she saw it was her friends.

They wanted drinks. Apparently it was ladies' night at the bar down the road.

The one all her co-workers frequented.

Just as she was about to blow them off, another message came through. This time, it was a photo of Rob and Andy glaring at her. The caption said: *Show or we will come to your house drunk.*

In spite of herself, Frazer grinned. She could use something to keep her mind off everything. Even if that thing was her drunk friends.

There was no point going home and dwelling on Cora. She refused to be that woman. She had thought she could go into this and be just what Cora had wanted: a friend with benefits. Instead, she'd become a gross walking stereotype. All she had to do now was buy two cats and call it quits; though they might eat her fish, and that would be devastating.

Maybe she would just buy a floor-to-ceiling aquarium and become a fish lady instead.

Decision made, she left her car in the work parking lot and walked down to the bar. If the air had been cold before, now it was freezing. Her jacket barely made a difference, and it was with relief that she slipped into the warm bar five minutes later. A cheer from the corner led her to her two friends.

"Yes, yes, I'm here."

"It's a Christmas miracle!" Rob looked like someone who was already a few in.

"It's July, idiot." Andy's cheeks were flushed.

"Guys, it's also Tuesday. And you're drunk."

Andy flashed her teeth. "It's ladies' night!"

"You're straight."

"But you're not." Andy wrapped an arm around her shoulders and held her close, pressing a shot into her hands. "Embrace it."

The dark brown liquid was the same colour as Cora's eyes, and with relish, Frazer shot it back and made it disappear. Like she needed to with these feelings.

Rob whooped and clapped, passing her another. "I do love Cheap Tuesday." He giggled as they all took another shot, then contorted his face as he swallowed the liquid. "Why let the uni students have all the fun?"

Frazer's throat was burning, and her mouth tasted like her first year of university. Even then she hadn't been idiotic enough to fall for the straight girl. "Another?" she asked as if the spirits could make the sick feeling in her stomach disappear.

Andy stared at her, eyes wide. "Rob, quick!" She stage-whispered. "Before she changes her mind and disappears to hang out with her fish!"

Snickering, Rob gestured at the bartender.

"Well," Frazer took the new shot, "we can't have that." It slid down her throat far too easily, with only the smallest of gasps.

They hid in their corner for way too long, Andy chattering about a deal at work. A look of guilt flashed over both their faces, and they asked Frazer how her programme was going. Tempted to bore them with too many details in the same manner they always did with her, Frazer instead kept it short. Their look of relief was satisfying.

"Though I did deliver a baby yesterday that weighed over five kilos. Vaginal birth and all."

Andy blanched so quickly that Frazer thought she was going to pass out. Next to her, Rob's mouth fell open. "Over five kilos?"

"Mhm."

"Isn't, isn't that like, two babies?"

Not really. "Pretty much."

Andy shuddered. "I'm so, so glad I'm never having children. Never. Never ever."

Frazer snorted into her glass of bourbon and coke.

Rob's eyes narrowed. "I *will* talk about trends in the market."

"No!" Frazer held her hands up in surrender. "I'll be good, sorry."

Andy was still oddly ashen for someone with such dark skin. "I hate you, Frazer." Without warning, she perked up, staring past Frazer's shoulder. "Oh! Ten o'clock!"

Looking down at his watch, Rob rolled her eyes. "Honey, it's only eight thirty."

He "oofed" when Andy's hand slapped his chest. His eyes widened. "Oh! Like, there's a hottie at tcn o'clock. Gotchya."

Frazer started to turn to look when Andy grabbed her face, tugging it in her direction. "Be smooth, Frazer! Jeese."

Her friends were far too dramatic for Frazer's taste. As nonchalantly as possible, Frazer sipped her drink and glanced quickly as she turned around. Her eyes widened. Was that really her? She snorted into her drink. Spluttering, she turned back to her friends.

They were staring at her with deeply disappointed looks. Shaking her head, Andy said, "Yeah. That was smooth."

"That's Lauren."

Rob and Andy both swayed opposite ways to look past Frazer. "Who?" Rob asked.

"A receptionist at work."

"Oh." Andy had a wicked smile on her face. "A work affair. That could be hot. And fun."

An affair at work was neither of those things. Well, it had been, and it had been fun. It just hadn't been with Lauren. And it was really only those things if you ignored all the guilt and the confusion that existed now.

"Work affairs *sound* fun," Rob said. "Then they complicate everything."

Frazer pointed her glass at him. "Exactly. Complicated. I don't need that." Because *technically*, she already had it.

Andy all but whined when she said, "But Frazer. She's cute!"

Lauren was cute. And kind of boring. But maybe Frazer needed boring. And what had she realised the other day? That maybe all that thinking that her dates were boring people had actually been Frazer being boring.

She knocked back her entire drink and glanced at her phone. No messages. Nothing.

Not that she expected any.

"Wait!" Rob's eyes, if possible, lit up even more. "The Lauren-you-went-on-a-date-with-Lauren? *That* Lauren?"

Andy *woo'd* far too loudly, and Rob was grinning almost maniacally.

Frazer's glass hit the bar with a thud.

Andy and Rob's faces lit up in matching delight as Frazer stood.

"You're going to talk to her?" Andy asked. Her hand gripped Rob's bicep. She whispered out of the corner of her mouth, "Rob! She's going to talk to her!"

"I know! But sh! We don't want to scare her off." While giving a thumbs-up, he said in a normal voice, "You go, tiger!"

As she turned, Frazer heard Andy say, "Our little girl, all grown up. Or grown up again. Or back in the game. Something."

A glare shot over her shoulder only made them laugh harder.

That giddy feeling that accompanied more than enough alcohol but not yet too much was filling Frazer's head. Maybe Cora had been a step back into the 'game' her friends were always going on about. A step in the right direction, pulling her out of the dating funk she'd been in since she'd been dumped. Though thinking about her messy hospital breakup years ago was not a good idea when about to chat to a date-like female.

"Hey, Lauren."

At the sound of her name, the other woman turned. "Frazer! Hey. Haven't seen you around much lately."

Her voice was warm and playful. Maybe she wasn't as boring as Frazer had thought. Or maybe Jemma was right that Frazer had just wanted everyone to be boring. Not that she'd ever admit to her sister that she'd been right.

"Yeah, my friends dragged me out."

Lauren glanced behind Frazer. "I'm hoping your friends are the ones staring creepily at us and grinning, or I'm going to be a bit concerned."

Frazer turned and confirmed that, yes, her friends were being creeps. Andy even raised a hand and waved at them. Eyes back on Lauren, Frazer shook her head. "Nope, never seen them before in my life."

"Should we grab a bouncer, then?"

Frazer snorted. "I wish. Try and ignore them?"

"The guy is clutching the girl's shoulder and pointing now."

Closing her eyes, Frazer reminded herself to kill them later. "Wanna move?"

Lauren, visibly surprised for a moment, paused, then nodded. "Okay."

It was easy to lead her to the other side of the bar, to a corner they couldn't be stared at. It was near the bathrooms, naturally less crowded. Other drinkers had robbed their tall table of its stools, so they rested their elbows on the wood and stood more intimately than they would have if they were sitting.

The whole situation grated. Lauren didn't laugh right. When she ran a hand down Frazer's arm, there was warmth, but no tingle. No lurch in her lower stomach. That warmth didn't spread...places.

It wasn't unpleasant. It just wasn't *Cora*.

Smiling at something Lauren said, Frazer sucked in a breath. That was the point.

Of course Lauren wasn't Cora. There was no way she could be. That was a good thing. Of course it was different. That was why Frazer had approached her—for something different, for something definitely *not* Cora. Cora was married, straight, and avoiding her and was everything Frazer shouldn't want.

Lauren was queer. Interested. Lauren was pretty. Lauren could be kind of fun. That was nice.

It was easy to brush her hair off her face and lean in. To hover for a second, their breath mingling between them. Kissing her, then, was easier. A natural progression. Lauren pushed back, responded to the kiss, traced her tongue along Frazer's bottom lip and didn't shy from it. In a bar, in the open.

And none of it was Cora.

"Why are we here?"

"Because, Cora, you need to have some fun."

"But why are we *here*?"

This bar was where she'd first drunk with Frazer. Where they'd come to many times afterwards when they could, trying to appear like co-workers having a drink together. This was where they had played footsie under the table when they thought no was looking. They'd drifted into one of the bathrooms once, their hands fast and insistent and grasping.

Lisa looked at her, a glint in her eye Cora didn't often see. "It's *ladies'* night."

Cora stared at her and didn't even attempt to hide her reproach. Ladies' night. "Are you serious?"

Lisa snickered. "Oh, come on, it's funny."

"I'm not gay!"

With a roll of her eyes, Lisa pulled her in and tried to catch the bartender's eye. "I never said you were. Would you relax? But you know, Cora..." Lisa was staring at her too intently.

"What?" Cora asked.

"Nothing." She went back to trying to get the bartender over.

"Lisa, what?"

"Nothing! Really, it was nothing. I'm just worried about you."

Cora started digging through her bag for her purse. "Why?"

When Lisa's gaze caught hers again, her eyebrows were raised. "Seriously?"

"It's not like I've just left my husband after having a crazy affair or anything, Lisa." Cora pressed her lips together in an attempt to smother her smile.

"Yeah, not like that at all."

The bartender finally appeared and took their orders. He poured two white wines for them. "Ladies." He slid them over with a wink and took Cora's twenty. She didn't bother to take the tiny amount of change.

"I spy a table!" Lisa made a beeline for one near the toilets. There were no chairs, so they dumped their coats and scarves on top of their bags on the surface and simply stood next to it. "Here's to you taking some steps you should've taken a while ago."

Cora didn't bother to ask questions about that. More than anyone, Lisa had probably seen what was going on in her marriage. There were odd hazy memories—of flashes of concern in Lisa's eyes during university, of the times where she'd tried to introduce Cora to other men and Cora hadn't really understood why. The confusion she'd felt when Lisa had been frustrated that Cora had cancelled for the fifth time because Alec had wanted Cora to be with him and she had thought that was normal.

They clinked their glasses together, the wine sweet on Cora's tongue as she took a small sip. She'd forgotten how good the wine in this bar was.

Around them, women chattered and laughed, the sounds of clinking glasses and other bar sounds settling over Cora.

"How do you not condemn me?" Cora asked, surprising herself.

All day she'd been melancholy. Avoiding Frazer's texts, guilt gnawing at her for missing the first two days of training. She was going to go tomorrow; or rather, that was how she made herself feel better anyway. The first two days, Frazer could cover alone. But eventually, Cora was going to have to talk to Frazer. But each time she'd tried, she remembered the searching look in Frazer's eye as a bruise was blooming over her skin or the way their breath mingled between them. Cora wanted to blame Frazer for that, but it was *Cora* who had moved forward ever so slightly.

Pushing her glass away, Lisa put her hand over Cora's. "Why would I condemn you?"

"I had an affair, Lisa. That's not... That's not a good thing."

Lisa gave her a gentle squeeze. "No, it wasn't. But it's not black and white. You were..."

"What?"

"It's not my place. I can't know what you were doing."

"It's your place more than most."

"I don't know, Core. You were burying yourself in something else so you didn't have to deal with what was happening with Alec. Was it a good thing? No. Should I condemn you for it? I don't think so. To me, you wanted out either way. And now you're out. The rest is just...semantics."

Cora took a long sip of her wine. She stared at the glass when she put it back down. "Thank you."

Lisa smiled. "Shut up."

A laugh pulled out of her chest, easing some of the constant anxiety and Cora dropped her head in her hand. It was nice to be out, to be distracted. It was strangely freeing. She didn't have to explain herself to Alec. The feeling that she was going home to a fight, or to a guilt trip about why she was spending time with other people, didn't sit in the back of her mind. There was no raging affair to cover up, just her and her best friend.

"So, do you see her?"

Cora straightened and tried to pretend she hadn't been lost in thought. "What?"

"The woman. Do you see her?"

With a groan, Cora slumped back down. "No. Not really. I mean, we work together, so sometimes. I'm avoiding her."

"I thought you wanted to be friends."

"I do." She did. "But it's harder than I thought."

"Still want sexy time?" Lisa asked, a glint in her eye.

"No!" Well, maybe. Which was normal, after having it for so long. "It's just, more complicated than that. I don't need complicated."

There was a look on Lisa's face Cora couldn't place. A question maybe, or some kind of knowledge; it was as if she had a secret and was waiting for Cora to realise she knew it too.

"I have to pee," Cora announced and pushed past Lisa to the toilet.

She didn't, really. But she also didn't want to be confronted by that look anymore. There was no way she wanted to delve into what Lisa was thinking.

Cora pushed the door open and stopped, eyes wide.

Frazer's eyes were blinking at her, and it took Cora a moment to realise they were reflected in the mirror. Frazer was looking at Cora over someone's shoulder, mouth open in shock. Because Frazer was pushed against someone—against *Lauren*, the social worker *secretary*—who was blinking at her over non-reflection Frazer's shoulder.

Frazer's hands were clearly up Lauren's shirt. No, one was. The other was half in her pants.

Everyone just stared at each other for a moment.

Cheeks blazing, Cora turned on her heel and stalked out.

Frazer didn't follow.

Groaning for a third time, Frazer buried her face in her pillow. In a *bathroom*? What was she, eighteen?

In a *bathroom*!

She groaned again, the sensation pulling at her throat, and kicked the blanket off her legs. The sheet was tangled around them and she wound up more wrapped up than she'd started.

Like, really, what had she been thinking?

Waking up in the morning was supposed to feel fresh. A new start. Welcoming a chance to do things anew. Frazer woke up with the slightly sour taste of alcohol and the memory that she made *really* bad decisions, all the time.

Literally all the time.

Ten minutes later, she pulled herself from her bed of self-pity and stepped into the overly hot spray of the shower. Cool water was normally her favourite way to shower, summer or winter. The feeling of overly heated skin always made her feel uncomfortable; it prickled for an hour after.

Today though, she wanted to burn the pathos off her skin.

Instead, she stepped out of the shower, feeling overheated and gross. Her hair clung to the back of her neck, frizzing in the steam. It still felt uncomfortable when she pulled it up and off her face into a ponytail. Her jeans felt too tight when she pulled them on, clean and sucking the life out of her. If she had junk, she'd be worried about blood flow.

She wasn't even hung-over.

Frazer grumbled to herself and flicked the kettle on. It was going to be a long, gross day. Her phone was lit up with messages—her friends, asking why she'd disappeared, Jemma wanting to have lunch if Frazer wasn't too busy seducing married women. A simple click of a button sent Jemma a photo of Frazer pulling a certain finger at the camera. Eyes blurry and fingers clumsy, she dropped her phone in the sink. It clattered, hollow sounding and loud, and made her jump. In a burst of frustration, she left it there.

She dug through her cupboards and remembered she'd run out of real coffee yesterday and had meant to get more.

Before she'd gone to the bar, got drunk, and acted out like a teenager.

Scowling, she pulled out the instant coffee and doled some into a mug. The milk sloshed on the kitchen bench when she poured it into her cup without paying attention, and the steam from the kettle burnt her hand.

In the sink, her phone vibrated against the metal, and she ignored it.

The first sip of coffee should have been glorious, but she'd messed it up, and it was lukewarm. Maybe she liked her shower like that, but coffee either had to be bordering on blistering or filled with ice. In the middle was just blasphemy.

With a clenched jaw, she dumped the contents in the sink. And shrieked when she'd realised her phone was still there.

Frazer had been awake for all of thirty minutes.

This day was already stupid.

She took a deep breath. Then another.

With a huff, she got her things together and got out the door to make her way to work.

Somehow her phone was okay. It smelt vaguely like coffee, but Frazer had apparently grabbed it out fast enough. The skin of her arm stung where the steam had hit it, but she just ignored the pain.

When she got to the hospital intact, the thought that maybe the day had turned around crossed her mind. Until she stepped out of her car, clutching a drive-through coffee to her chest and saw Lauren getting out of her mini just five meters away. The poor woman gave an awkward wave, and in an attempt to make everything less horrible, Frazer quickly waved back. The coffee fell to the ground and sloshed all over her white shoes.

For a second, Frazer closed her eyes and took a deep breath. Tried to remember she wasn't the crying type.

"Shit, Frazer. Was that coffee full?"

Another breath in. Slowly this time. Slowly out. She opened her eyes and stared down. Her shoes were now brown, and she stood in a slowly growing puddle of what had been piping hot coffee. "Yeah, it was."

"Want me to buy you another?" Lauren was staring at her with wide, hopeful eyes.

Because she felt pathetic, Frazer nodded. "Yeah. Okay."

They fell into step.

"So..." Lauren said.

"So." Frazer answered.

"You often leave a girl in the bathroom with her pants half-undone?"

Open-mouthed, Frazer whipped her head around to stare at her.

The thin line of Lauren's lip twitched. And then she laughed. "Sorry, I couldn't resist."

Their pace fell back into step. Lauren was kind of evil. The antiseptic smell of the hospital surrounded them when they entered the building. Frazer bit the bullet and said, "I should say sorry, not you."

Because it was easier than looking at Lauren, Frazer buried her hands in her jacket pockets and kept her eyes on the coffee cart set up just in front of them.

"Well, thanks."

Lauren was apparently a better person than most. Frazer really needed to work on the whole saying sorry thing. Her mother had been saying that since she was a tiny ball of stubborn hands on hips, narrow-eyed little girl.

"Do you have spare shoes at work?" Lauren asked, her lips forming a perfect circle to blow into her fresh cup of coffee.

Leaning against the wall, Frazer nodded. Took a sip and burnt her tongue. She tried not to grimace and show her discomfort. "Yeah, midwifery rule."

"You having one of those mornings?" Lauren looked so comfortable, shoulder pressed to the wall, watching her openly.

"Yeah. How'd you know?"

"The look on your face when you dropped it. Like you expected it."

"I've figured it's karma."

"For last night? I was joking about the up and leaving. It wasn't that big of a deal."

Frazer groaned inwardly as Cora walked through the door Lauren and Frazer had just used and stopped dead at the sight of them. Lauren's eyes, thankfully, stayed on Frazer and didn't notice. Frazer stared back at Cora, though, as the brick against her back bit into her shoulder blade.

Even from this distance, Frazer could see how Cora's face clouded. Her eyes were unreadable, and she turned and hurried to the elevators.

Frazer shook her head. "For that. And other things."

"Cora?"

Frazer's ponytail whipped her in the face again when she turned to stare at her, mouth gaping like a fish. Lauren was almost smirking. "Breathe, Frazer."

"No. Not for Cora."

"You're a terrible liar."

Eyes downcast, Frazer took another scalding sip.

"I won't say anything." Lauren ducked her head to try and catch Frazer's eye. "But you should be careful."

Frazer watched Alec walk through like he owned the place, tablet in hand as he swiped at it without deigning to look where he was going.

"Yeah, I know."

They parted easily, and Frazer made sure to drink the last dregs of her coffee and drop it in the bin rather than attempt to walk with it. It wasn't a day for those kinds of risks, apparently. Taking the stairs, she hoped she didn't fall down them and break her neck. Panting yet unscathed, Frazer dropped all of her things on her desk and flopped into her desk chair.

She was exhausted, only slightly hung-over, and it felt like the day should be finished, though it wasn't even eight thirty.

Digging her phone out and wrinkling her nose at the stale coffee smell, Frazer opened a message from Jemma. A pouting face photo.

Trust her to make Frazer feel bad.

And another from Cora.

Frazer sat straight up in her chair. When her thumb tapped it, the screen was tacky. Nothing happened. She tapped it again, probably a bit too hard, and the message opened.

I'll take training tonight. You take a day off. Have a nice day.

Frazer knew when she was being dismissed.

When her body fell back against her chair, her knee banged against her desk. She let out a yelp.

Maybe she should cocoon herself in bubble wrap before she faced the rest of her day.

Once again, Cora was sitting in an empty house. Lisa was out, and Cora was in her comfortable house clothes, glaring at her computer.

The training had been fine. Avoiding Frazer and Alec had been fine. Not meeting Lauren's eye had been fine. Though Cora was still waiting for Alec to make some kind of play, he had seemed uninclined to do so thus far.

When on earth had house rental prices in Perth become so expensive? Most places were outrageously overpriced, even the hovels in terrible neighbourhoods. She'd never really lived in an apartment, mostly in houses that she'd shared, but maybe now she'd have to. There were a few smaller ones, one with great light that was still stupidly pricey, but less so than most others. It was a fifteen-minute walk to Scarborough Beach too which was nice.

Maybe she'd get a dog. Alec hated dogs. But maybe now, Cora could go to a shelter and get a big, dopey dog that drooled. She had a thing for dogs that liked to lie around with you and take a lazy, twenty-minute walk once a day.

If she was going to do that, she really would need a house. Sighing, she went back to perusing houses, especially ones with big backyards.

There was one not far from Lisa's, and it was only a ten-minute drive to the beach instead. Dogs liked the beach. There was also a viewing in a few days, at a time Cora could probably make. She put the details in her phone.

It was easy to get distracted in a house so quiet and remember how Frazer had stared at Cora's mouth in that storage room. How she had run a tongue over her lip, wetting it slightly. How her eyes had flickered from Cora's mouth and back to her eyes. How dare she?

Breathing hard, Cora tried to tamp down a sudden anger. How dare Frazer? Do *that*. Look at Cora like that, then swan into a bathroom with another woman the next day?

Standing up, with no real thought of what she was doing, Cora pulled a ratty old pair of Volleys on her feet. Grabbing her keys, she stormed out to her car.

The drive was short, and Cora drove the entire way white-knuckled. It was absurd, but Cora had been doing just fine until Frazer. Everything had been okay. Then Frazer had blown into her life with her programmes and long legs and eyes the colour of moss after rain. And now Cora was separated and watching the way Frazer moved in enclosed places. She was feeling jealousy that was ridiculous and made no sense except that she'd seen Frazer's *hands* in someone else's *pants*.

What did *Cora* care if Frazer went on a date? Or where her hands were?

Nothing. She didn't care at all.

Parking half on a footpath, Cora grumbled to herself that it wasn't important. It was only going to take a minute; there wouldn't be any time to get a ticket. Cora was taking control of her life. Because for far too long, she'd had none of that.

270

She marched up to the door and knocked. She only waited all of two seconds, then knocked again.

The door swung open, and Frazer stared at her, wide-eyed. "Cora!"

She was dressed in a skirt that Cora remembered pushing up her legs only weeks ago, and that memory made Cora's fists clench.

"What are you doing here?"

"I need you to stay away from me." Cora's words were measured, hard.

Frazer flushed. "Excuse me?"

"I need you," Cora repeated, slowly, "to stay away from me. I just...this," Cora waved her hand between them "is the last thing I need. I don't need this confusion. I don't need you getting in my head. I need you to stay away from me." Because, for some reason, Cora couldn't stay away from her.

Looking down, Frazer sighed. It sounded exhausted. When she looked back up, she gave a nod. Her eyes were green, so green in the light washing over them from where Frazer stood. "Okay."

"I—" Cora had expected some kind of anger. She had wanted it, even; though why, she had no idea. Cora crossed her arms. "Okay."

They stared at each other for a long moment. Then Cora turned on her heel and turned away. With short, measured steps, Cora started to walk down the path.

Suddenly, fingers wrapped around her wrist and tugged. Cora spun around, and Frazer stood, clutching her wrist more gently than the look on her face indicated she wanted to be.

"Tell me again, Cora." Frazer hissed the words. "Tell me you want it to end, properly. Tell me you want to walk away."

The touch of Frazer's hand was sure, steady. Her thumb swiped along the inside of Cora's wrist, just once, in a motion that was smooth and easy. It sent tingles up her arm that felt like they'd stay for days. Her eyes were bright—challenging her, staring her down as if it were Frazer's place to challenge her.

It was as if they were back in that room, back in that elevator months ago. But this time, Cora stepped back instead of forward.

"I'm straight." Cora said.

"That's not what I asked."

"You're fucking other women in *bathrooms*."

"To forget *you*!"

The words were an explosion that should have blasted them apart, that should have sunk enough into Cora's brain, made an impact. But Cora pushed those words away, far enough away so they couldn't touch her.

Cora took a deep breath and wrenched her hand away. "I mean it."

And to show she did, Cora walked away.

CHAPTER SIXTEEN

"Jemma, why the hell are you smiling?"

It was unsettling. Jemma popped a piece of carrot in her mouth, chewing with the same wide grin. "Oh, please, that woman is *so* into you."

"She's *not*, Jemma."

"Oh, but she is. She really is. It's why she had to demand you stay away from her, because she can't do it herself."

Rather than acknowledge that comment immediately, Frazer sucked Coke through a straw, her brow furrowed. It didn't matter what Cora had meant by it, because Frazer was done. She was done with it all. She'd tried and had become a person she didn't like. She was the lesbian who was into the straight girl, the friend Cora slept with when it was convenient for her. Cora had turned her into someone's secret, a person who felt so dirty that she sometimes showered three times a day. A cliché. Okay, maybe that wasn't completely fair. Frazer had played a hand in turning herself into that, too. But that wasn't the point. That point was, she wasn't that.

Not anymore.

No.

Instead, Frazer went out for dinner with her friends. Saw her sister. She greeted Cora at work and treated her like a co-worker, always asked her how she was, gave her a big smile, and then disappeared. They communicated about the programme via e-mail. They avoided each other or spoke on the phone only if it was *really* necessary.

The world didn't end. The programme was fine. And Frazer was professional and so, *so* done. It was simple, then, to ignore the part of her that missed Cora—not the part that had enjoyed the last several months of sex. Frazer could forget that as needed. It was the part that missed their friendship that was harder.

"Can we talk about something else?" she asked.

"Are you coming to dinner with the fam this weekend?" There was a glint in Jemma's eye.

"Okay, something *else*?"

There must have been a pleading note in Frazer's voice, because Jemma put her elbows on the table and cocked her head. "Fine. How's the programme?"

"Great. Easy—it's slowly setting up. We're still figuring things out, but the feedback from the parents has been great. Some hard stories, though."

"I bet there are." Jemma poked at her chips with her fork and instead stabbed a piece of cucumber. "Is it hard?"

Frazer gave a shrug. "I mean, it's no harder than before. These stories have always existed; at least now we're doing something."

"How's seeing Cora all the time?"

Frazer's fingers gripped tightly around her fork. "I thought we weren't talking about this anymore?"

"As if I was gonna let it go. See how I artfully turned the conversation back to it?"

"Your uni major sucks."

"Don't be silly. I've always been like this."

"True."

Jemma leant forward. "Now—how is it?"

"Ugh. Fine. We don't really see each other."

"But the program?"

"Mostly e-mails now. And when we do see each other, it's professionally." Frazer didn't mention the way she felt Cora's eyes on her. How they seemed to follow Frazer when she was in the room. Which was unfair, because *Cora* had asked *Frazer* to stay away.

"Well, that's good. How's her marriage?"

When Frazer paused, Jemma leant forward. "You know something!"

"I know rumours."

"Rumours are often based on some kind of truth."

"So you really did have a threesome in high school?"

Jemma's eyes went so wide Frazer was worried she'd strain herself. "You heard that?"

"So, it's true, then?"

Pouting, Jemma stabbed at her chips. "It wasn't a, a *threesome*. I fooled around a bit with this guy and girl and, well, that's all."

The mild disappointment Frazer felt at Jemma proving her own theory right was overpowered by the glee Frazer felt at having such juice. "Well, well, little sister. A threesome."

"It was *not* a threesome!"

Her retort was so loud that people looked over, a laugh trickling from somewhere in the café. Red brightened Jemma's cheeks. "Well, it wasn't." She said.

Frazer snorted.

"Please, Frazer, help your mortified sister out. What's the rumour?"

It wasn't important anyway. Frazer wished she hadn't heard anything. "I don't know. Something some board member heard from Alec, who spoke to a surgeon, who told his wife, who told her best friend..."

Jemma waved her fork in the air. "Yeah, yeah. I know how a rumour works. What *was* it?"

"Cora and Alec are getting a divorce. Apparently Cora stole his car and moved all her stuff to a lover's house after torching his clothes."

"Wow. That's a hefty rumour."

"Yeah. Alec has his car, and none of his clothes look burnt. Also, she's not in *my* house."

"Maybe she has another lover?" Jemma was clearly enjoying this far too much.

Frazer tried not to twitch. "Maybe."

"Or maybe the only true part is the divorce."

Frazer shrugged. It wasn't like she cared. "Maybe."

Jemma tilted her head again and stared at her. Really stared at her. "Not that you care," she said slowly.

"Exactly." Frazer didn't trust her sister's tone not to be ironic, but she decided to ignore the insinuation. "Not that I care."

Because she didn't.

Frazer was done.

Cora missed Frazer.

It had taken one morning, a week after telling Frazer to leave her the hell alone, to really get that.

That one morning, she woke up with her heart racing and her hips arching off the bed, heat pooled in her centre and her hand trapped in her underwear.

Cora had never had a sex dream. Not one so vivid, so concurrent, so obviously about *sex*. She had never woken up in that position, a groan tearing from her throat and the memory of eyes staring up at her. One that left her mouth dry and other parts of her definitely *not* so.

It was really hard after that to convince herself that she simply missed the friendship parts of Frazer. But she did genuinely crave those parts too: the coffee, the lunches, the easy silence between them as they worked on the programme. The way her smile was all crooked and appealing. She missed how she could say something that dragged out a bark of laughter, as if she were managing to take the woman by surprise. Frazer was a bundle of cockiness layered over someone always looking to improve. Cora missed Frazer's urge to brainstorm, her willingness to adapt her ideas to ones Cora suggested.

The night before, though, as sleep had started to wash over Cora, she'd instead thought of how Frazer had the softest eyes. The green of her irises would almost dampen when she looked at Cora. Her senses still remembered the wet press of Frazer's lips against her own, the heat between her neck and her shoulder. Caught on the cusp of awake and dreaming, she'd barely questioned the shift in her thoughts.

Cora yanked her hand away. Kicking the sheets off, she stumbled through Lisa's hallway and slipped into the bathroom. The stream of water from the shower started steaming quickly when she turned it on and slipped in, leaving her clothes in a messy pile on the floor. Her feet tingled from the heat of the water after the touch of cold tile.

She sighed, wishing the memory of ghosting fingers along her skin would wash off her and down the drain. She missed Frazer. A lot. Yet the other woman seemed fine, almost happy. It made Cora feel...disgruntled. If they saw each other, Frazer greeted her cheerfully and asked how she was, like she would any other colleague. Kind of like she had before Frazer had approached Cora to help with the programme. Back in the easy days when Cora had assumed she was an obnoxious idiot. Cora almost preferred when Frazer had avoided her.

She didn't want to miss Frazer.

And today she had to speak with Alec.

That thought was like a bucket of cold water, even in the heat of the shower, and Frazer slipped to the back of Cora's mind.

It had been almost two weeks, and he had literally ignored her at work, which was actually quite a nice thing. But her lawyer had suggested trying to have words with him. They would spend twelve months separated before they could petition for divorce. They should go over that, so that maybe once twelve months passed, he would sign the document with her. Neither would have to attend the hearing if that happened, and a month and a half later, they would both receive divorce papers in the mail. Done. Easy.

Even if he said he wouldn't now, hopefully in twelve months he would have changed his mind. Cora could dream.

When she wandered into the kitchen, Lisa was sitting at the table with her legs pulled up under her. A half-eaten bowl of cereal sat in front of her.

"Morning." Lisa was looking at her strangely.

"Good morning."

"You, ah…sleep well?" Lisa was now smiling up at her.

"Yeah, I did actually."

"Really well?" Still with the smile.

Cora paused with the kettle in her hand, the water sloshing up the sides of her carry mug. Heat started to work its way up her neck. "Why do you ask?"

Lisa's smile grew into a grin that could only be described as shit eating. "Heard some interesting noises coming out of your bedroom when I walked past this morning."

It wasn't heat anymore. Her cheeks were a furnace.

"Good dream?" Lisa took a mouthful of her cereal with utter relish.

Slamming the cap on her mug, Cora started to walk out with it. "I have no idea what you're talking about."

"Cora! Stop! I'm sorry." The laughter bubbling through Lisa's words was evidence to the contrary, but Cora turned around in the doorway. She raised her eyebrows. "Really? You're sorry?"

"Kind of. Who on earth were you dreaming of?"

"No one important."

Lisa looked like she wanted to push it further, but instead asked, "Did you hear back about the viewing?"

Grateful the conversation topic had changed, Cora nodded. "I got the house ten minutes from here."

"Hey! That's great. When can you move in? Not that I want you to leave. I've liked having you here."

"I've liked being here." Cora really had. It had given her a safety net as she sorted out her head. "I can move in over the weekend. I sign and get the keys on Friday."

"That's great. And today you're talking to…"

Cora hummed. "Yeah, talking to Alec today." A fortifying sip of coffee didn't help, so she took another. "Wish me luck."

"Good luck." Lisa gave her a thumbs-up. "You'll be great."

"Thanks." Sighing, Cora straightened. "I should go. I'll see you tonight?"

"Yup. Celebratory dinner and wine for your new place?"

"Always."

In the hallway, Lisa's voice called out, "Try not to think about that dream while you're driving! Don't want to crash and have to explain to some pretty ambulance driver you were sex daydreaming."

"I hate you!" Cora yelled back with a chipper note, the door closing behind her on Lisa's snickering.

The drive to work was accomplished without drifting into inappropriate thoughts. When she walked into her office area, Lauren wasn't in, and Cora breathed a silent sigh of relief. Whenever she saw the other woman now, Cora bounced between being overly friendly and almost tripping over her own legs to avoid eye contact. It was unprofessional and a little bit stupid, but she couldn't stop. Lauren made her feel nervous and a twist of something that felt like jealousy but that Cora wanted to pretend was dislike. Because she didn't want to be jealous. Jealousy meant things Cora didn't want to feel.

Why had she thought an affair had been a good idea?

Her bag dropped on her desk. Cora flicked her computer on, eventually scrolling through e-mails. How did she get twenty e-mails in twelve hours? An update from Frazer about the programme had her clicking it open faster than was probably normal. She scanned it, her teeth grinding at the overly professional tone. As if Cora wasn't someone Frazer had spent a lot of time with finding different ways to make her—

"Cora?"

Her cheeks were hot for the third time that day, and it was only eight thirty. Cora tried to look friendly. Another woman Cora was currently terrible at looking in the eye. "Hey, Tia."

"I just wanted to let you know that Alec confirmed he could talk at eight forty-five. I just thought I'd let you know."

"Thanks." Cora's voice squeaked a little. "I'll be there in fifteen minutes, then."

Cora did not want to have this conversation at work. It felt unbalanced and inappropriate. But Alec had bounced all of her calls and refused to accept any time outside of work to meet in a café Cora suggested. She had the uncomfortable feeling that he wanted to have the meeting where he sat in a position of power.

Instead of leaving like Cora had figured she would, Tia eyed her. It felt like her mother was staring at her. "How are you going?"

That tone was too soft and too caring. Sometimes, when Cora thought she was fine, all it took was someone asking that question with that look and with that intonation to make Cora realise that no, no she wasn't fine. A lump formed in her throat, and even with eyes that were suddenly prickling for no reason, she smiled. "Yeah. I'm fine."

Tia crossed her arms. Looked down at her with raised eyebrows that weren't about motherly recrimination but concern. "Once more, with feeling."

Swallowing heavily, Cora looked to her screen for a respite before looking back at Tia. "I'm fine, really."

"Okay. But just know, honey," Tia straightened, ready to walk away, "you don't have to be."

She left Cora with the lingering feeling of wanting a hug.

The wood was hard under Cora's knuckles, biting at them as she knocked.

"Come in."

Slipping into Alec's office, she closed the door behind herself and sat in the chair across from him.

"Hi, Alec."

He sat stiffly in his chair. His suit was crisp, his hair neat and styled perfectly. But his face was drawn, with blotches of darkness under his eyes. "Good morning."

For a moment, they simply watched each other. There was something uncomfortable about it, uneasy. It was like they were waiting for the other to start something.

Finally, Cora said, "I spoke with a lawyer."

The sigh Alec gave was exhaustive. Long. "Why?"

"About the divorce, Alec."

"We aren't getting one."

So this was how it was going to go. "We will be."

A muscle ticked in his jaw. "You can't leave me, Cora. It's not fair. I didn't *do* anything. You can't prove grounds for a divorce."

Getting into the reasons of their divorce wasn't something Cora really felt like doing. It was a dance they'd done for too long, and Alec had a defence, an excuse, a blame for everything Cora said. "I don't need to prove grounds for a divorce, Alec. Not in Australia."

He leant back in his chair and watched her. "I'm not signing anything."

Why couldn't he just make this easy? Why did he want to be married to someone that didn't want to be married to him? "Well, for now you don't have to. We have to be separated for twelve months, then I can petition the court alone, though I'd prefer if we co-signed, because the process will be a lot smoother."

"I won't sign anything that says we were separated."

Sighing, Cora crossed her legs and tried not to sound defensive. "Alec, you can't keep me married to you."

He stared her down, or tried. But when she didn't look away, it was him that broke eye contact. "I can if I don't sign."

"I'll have a rental contract as proof. Bills in my name." The lawyer and she had gone over all of this.

"Why, Cora?" He was looking at her now as if he really had no idea.

"We weren't happy."

"Don't tell me what I was!"

She took a deep breath. "Okay. I wasn't happy."

"I can change. Be different."

Maybe, once, he could have been. But looking at him now, the way he bounced from argument to argument, the man he was, she didn't want him to. Not for her. "It's too late, Alec."

When he swallowed, she could see his Adam's apple bob. His eyes looked glassy. "You can't do this to me."

"I'm not doing anything *to* you, Alec."

Something hardened. "I will make your life here hell."

Somehow, Cora had expected that. "That will make more problems for you."

"I don't want you working here, Cora. I want you out. Your job here is, is nothing."

He'd always thought that his job was more important. He'd always thought all of his plans were more important. Sometimes, Cora wondered if she'd just been a plot point in his plans, the wife to tick off the list. He'd actually laughed when she'd mentioned that she wanted to go to different countries to help with aid programmes. "Don't start that, Alec. I have unions, Human Resources."

"Get out."

That muscle in his jaw ticked again, and she stood. "Okay."

"Cora," he said when she was at the door. She turned. "You'll regret this."

As she walked out, she didn't know if that had been a threat or merely an observation.

"How are you?"

Tia had appeared in Frazer's office, and Frazer jumped so hard that the papers in her hands went flying. "Jesus, Tia!"

"No, just Tia." She winked. "My other identity is a secret."

Frazer gathered her papers with her eyes down and her heart pounding. She gave Tia a snort to cover over her embarrassment. "You're hilarious. Very witty."

When she straightened, Tia had moved from the doorway to the chair across from her and Frazer jumped again, less dramatically this time.

"See?" Tia said, "I'm fast like he is too."

"And more blasphemous."

"True."

Frazer put the papers back on the table, straightening them into neat piles. "Any reason you wanted to give me a heart attack?"

"Just wanted to see how you are. After all the...drama."

"There was no drama."

Tia pressed her lips in a straight, judgemental line. "No, there wasn't, really. You just...ended it? That easily?"

Easy was not the adjective Frazer would use. "Yes."

Tia blinked at her, and Frazer sighed.

"Really, Tia. I'd known how wrong it all was. And the, the rest of it, it doesn't mean anything."

"Then why have you avoided me at any opportunity?"

Frazer cleared her throat. "Have not."

"Have too. Since we had our nice shared cigarette, you avoid me at all costs." Tia picked a piece of lint off of her pants. "It's obvious."

Frazer also avoided Cora. Unless she had no option. Then she smiled as widely as she could and said hello and tried to ignore the way Cora's eyes tracked her around the room. It was irritating. She'd told Frazer to leave her alone, so that's what Frazer was doing. Stop staring. It was just rude.

"I've been busy."

"No busier than before."

That was true. "Sorry."

"I don't want an apology, I need to know you're okay."

Frazer smiled. It felt too big, so she dialled it back a little. "I'm fine."

Tia heaved a sigh that sounded like she carried the burden of suffering all the idiots in the world. "Sure. Okay."

She stood up and walked out. Frazer heard her say, clearly loud enough to make sure Frazer heard it, "That was as convincing as when Cora said it."

"What did you say?" she said just as loudly.

The damn woman kept walking.

About to get up and give chase, mostly to vent her frustration, Frazer slumped back in her chair when her mobile rang. "What?" she snapped as she answered after seeing her sister's name on the screen.

"Well, aren't you a bucket of sunshine this morning?"

"What do you want, Jem?" It took a lot of effort to dampen the anger that bit into her tone.

"Seriously, who peed in your cereal?"

"I hate cereal." Frazer used her toes to push herself back and forth on her chair.

"Okay, your coffee?"

"No one. I have a busy day and I'm tired."

"Tired of hiding from Cora's *I love you* eyes?"

She grit her teeth. "Did you call for a reason?"

"Nope!" Her voice was far too chipper for Frazer. "Pretty much to ask if she'd confessed undying love yet? Or if you got caught in compromising situations again as you try to bury your obvious feeli—"

Frazer hung up. The phone rang again immediately. It rang for almost a minute before she caved and answered.

"Feelings you're holding for your now *not* married lover. Any gossip like th—"

Frazer hung up again and turned her phone on silent. Probably snickering to herself, Jemma wouldn't try to call back again after that anyway.

Everybody was stupid, and Frazer felt like she was coiled tightly, ready to snap at the closest person. At her hip, her pager trilled, and Frazer stared at it happily. The ward had a patient who was at ten centimetres.

At least something nice was going to happen that day.

It was that stupid dream.

It was like a phantom, the way it trailed over her mind, touching its fingers to parts of her that needed to be left alone. The conversation with Alec wasn't enough to ruin it, and neither was trying to remember why Cora had walked away that night. Why she had felt the need to make a point of walking away?

A point to Frazer or to herself? Cora wasn't sure anymore.

In the cafeteria, Cora was pointedly *not* watching Frazer laugh at something Lauren said at another table, at the way she threw her head back in mirth, her throat exposed. She pushed away the memory, or the dream memory—or something—of her lips on Frazer's soft skin, the sigh in her ear as she sucked slightly.

It was like a rush and a slowing all at the same time. As if all the air had been sucked out of the room, yet all of it had blown into her lungs and overinflated her.

It was as if Frazer had taken everything in stride and Cora was the one left floundering.

Across the room, Frazer was settling her chin in her palm. She beamed. Positively beamed.

And Cora was sitting there, aggressively chewing a carrot and staring.

Telling Frazer to leave her alone was supposed to make everything easier. After so long, it was supposed to be a step back while everything else fell into place or fell apart so Cora could figure her life out. Instead, she missed Frazer with an ache that wasn't about missing friendship.

Carrot grated down her throat.

Cora wanted Frazer to be looking at *her* like that. She wanted to be the one that made Frazer laugh so hard that she flushed.

Cora wasn't straight.

Cora didn't know what she was. But somehow she had fallen for obnoxious, cocky Frazer and hadn't even noticed until she was laying in dirt she'd tripped herself up in.

Frazer looked up and caught her eye. Her eyebrows furrowed as she looked away and back at Lauren.

At an age she had thought she was past such things, Cora had a revelation. One that had her scraping her chair backwards and walking blindly out of the room and through the closest door she could disappear into.

It was a treatment room, thankfully empty of nurses who were off doing more important things.

Her hands were shaking. Her mouth was dry.

Had this really taken her almost four months to realise? Really? Was she so blind to her own emotions?

Though, in reality, hadn't she been that way for years?

Miserable in a marriage and never crawling to get out.

Her fingers fumbled with the phone in her pocket.

"Lisa?"

"Cora, hey! Want to have lunch?"

Looking blindly around the room, Cora couldn't think of anything she wanted to do more. But she was stuck at work. "I just ate."

"Damn, I'm craving a burger. You sound weird. What's up?"

"I think I like women."

A pause.

Then Lisa said, "Like, how?"

"The same way I like guys. Apparently."

"Well, no shit."

Cora squeezed her eyes shut, her lips tugging up as she suddenly felt like she could breathe properly. "You knew?"

"Well, yeah."

"Why didn't you tell me?"

A sigh echoed in Cora's ear. "I don't know. I thought about it, but I tried to nudge you there and you shut down. I guessed you just needed to figure it out on your own."

"I kind of just realised."

"What, like, now?"

"Yeah." Cora felt giddy. Like things had clicked into place she'd never known *weren't* in place. "Literally."

"And you called me?"

"Yeah—why?"

"Nothing, that's just...sweet."

"You're my best friend."

A chuckle from Lisa was soft in her ear. "So, what now?"

Cora licked her lips and stared at the wall. What now? She had no idea. Right now she felt a little high. The fact that her marriage was ending in a divorce—a fact that she hadn't yet mentioned to her parents—was barely on her mind. It barely registered that, really, Frazer should be the last thing on her mind.

"Cora?"

"I'm here. Just processing."

"As flattered as I am that your first thought was to call me, I thought you'd be dragging a certain woman into a room somewhere in that hospital..." A pause. "Unless you don't want to?"

"I, uh, kind of angrily told her to leave me alone last week."

"Oh."

"Really angrily."

"Good one," Lisa said.

"I thought so."

"Your level of denial is amazing, Core."

Cora sighed. "Yeah, I know."

"I thought you wanted to be friends?"

"Uh, well, I saw her with another woman and yelled at her."

"Very friendly."

"Apparently. So I freaked out that I was jealous and told her to go away."

"Did you pull her pigtails?"

"You," Cora said, "are hilarious."

"I know. So, what are you going to do?"

"I have no idea?"

The door behind her opened, and Cora turned to apologise to whichever nurse was entering and found herself face-to-face with Frazer. A very red-faced, opposite-of-calm-looking Frazer. If Cora didn't know her better, she'd imagine Frazer looked ready to punch her.

"Lisa, I'll call you back."

Ending the call on Lisa's loud protest, Cora dropped the phone in her pocket.

"Hi." Cora said. Or squeaked, actually. Frazer looked really angry, and Cora had no idea how to talk to this version of her. After a week of calm smiles from Frazer, it was almost scary.

"Hi?" Frazer asked. "Hi!"

Cora cleared her throat. "Frazer—"

Frazer crossed her arms and *glared* at Cora.

"No." Frazer said. "You need to stop. You need to stop this now."

"I—"

"I don't care, Cora, okay?" Frazer's eyes were a blazing green, the flush of her cheeks setting off her anger. "I don't *care*. You need to stop. I did everything you asked of me, all the time. Every time. We were friends. We had sex. When you wanted, in the circumstances that suited you. Then you wanted it to stop, and it did. And *then* you got pissed I was with someone else and asked me to stay away from you, and that's what I've been doing. But I can't keep doing that if you keep *watching* me all the time."

"Frazer—"

"I have been *polite*. I have been your *colleague*. Did you stop to think of *me* in all of this?"

Heat flushed Cora's face, because no, no she hadn't.

"And," Frazer said, jaw clenching as she took a breath, "it doesn't matter anyway. I need you to stop. To stop this and let me be. You have to stop looking at me like *that*."

Cora tilted her head. She shouldn't be smiling right now, but the grin on her face hadn't wiped itself off since she announced to Lisa that she liked women. And Frazer was so *angry*, and she looked really hot like that. Her eyes were almost glittering.

"Like what, Frazer?"

"No! No acting like you have no idea what I'm talking about. You can't glare at any woman I speak to like you want to slaughter her or at me like you want to strip me naked right there. You can't want sex, then just friendship, then for me to disappear, then follow me with your eyes like that. It's not *fair*." Her nostrils flared. "You need to leave me alone."

Everything in her body language told Cora she needed to back away. Instead, she took a step closer. Her eyes flicked to Frazer's lips, and somehow that made Frazer even madder.

"I need you, Cora, to leave me—"

It was the worst thing she could do in that moment. Cora knew that. But she needed Frazer to *get* it. She closed the gap, pressing

Frazer against the door, their lips crashing together. Frazer's hands gripped her shirt, and in that second, Cora realised how much she missed *this* part of Frazer. How her body responded, how Cora wanted to sink into her and never crawl out.

But then those hands that had gripped her pushed her away, and Cora stumbled backwards.

Frazer shook her head at her, jaw set.

For more than a second, Frazer had responded to her. She'd kissed Cora back.

"You don't get to just kiss me whenever you feel like it, Cora. You don't get to tell me to leave you alone, then kiss me."

And then Frazer whirled and yanked the door open, slamming it behind her.

Frazer was mad.

And Cora was *really* into women. One woman in particular.

A woman who was really, really mad at her.

CHAPTER SEVENTEEN

Frazer was beyond angry.

She was furious.

She had spent a good week being *Zen* and being *calm* and being okay with Cora telling her to, basically, get lost.

For a week, she had ignored the weird eyes Cora had sent her. Had spoken with Lauren, and discovered they got along quite well. Friendships were good. Real ones, where she didn't spend her time wondering when they'd next stumble into an office, kicking shoes off and fumbling with zippers. Frazer spent time with her annoying sister and had dinner with her friends. She threw herself into her programme, taking on another client to mentor. With two for herself, she was regularly making contact and being free for them to contact her. Plus, she'd opened up times in the evening to do information sessions and organise a Parenting Skills night, where anyone could come for free to get basics and ask questions that seemed stupid but really, really weren't.

There had been fifteen people, more than she had thought there would be, most of them in their teens. There were a few older ones as well, women in shelters without much support, one woman a recovered narcotic addict who was getting back on her feet but looked so knocked down.

Keeping herself busy had been easy. Her friends were happy to have her back, and Jemma often just lay on Frazer's couch with her and poked her in the leg. She made sure Frazer was distracted.

It had been nice.

So how *dare* Cora?

And kiss her? Like Frazer would be happy to go back to being her sex buddy now that she was getting a rumoured divorce.

At the cafeteria table, Lauren had snorted and said, "She's looking at you like she wants to eat you."

Frazer had turned around to see Cora's gaze on her, open and hungry.

How *dare* she.

But now, Frazer needed to calm down. She had a weekly check-up with Jack and needed to get through that, then go the hell home. Or to a bar. Or somewhere. Not a bar, because alcohol and her needed to stop being a thing. Whatever she did, Frazer needed to forget the burn of Cora's lips and the gaze that followed her everywhere.

"Hey, Jack!" Frazer turned on her professional self, because her real self was close to cracking down the centre.

"Hey, Frazer." He followed her into the exam room, round and very pregnant. "How are you?"

"Good! How are you?"

His hands fisted the cuffs of his oversized hoody that couldn't hide his belly anymore. He lived in that thing. "You don't look okay."

Frazer sat down at her desk, trying to look happy but probably looking like she was about to puke. "Really? Strange. I'm great."

He sank into his chair, his gaze never leaving her. "You look like you're about to cry. Or hit someone. Either one."

If Jemma had asked her that, Frazer would probably have gone on an extensive rant. But this was a patient, so Frazer relaxed her laser beam smile. "Sorry, I'm tired. I've been doing too much lately. How are *you*?"

He shrugged. "Peeing constantly. My chest hurts. I feel like it would be easier to roll everywhere."

Frazer uttered a genuine chuckle. "So, as expected?"

"Yeah. Will Bug be out soon? I...I want..." Eyes on his lap, he shrugged awkwardly.

"You want your life back?"

The follow-up shrug was even more uncomfortable. "That's a really bad thing to say." His voice was barely above a whisper.

Something tugged in Frazer's chest and she tried to catch his eye. "No it's not. You're doing an awesome job, and it's normal you'd want this part to be done so you can have your life back to being *your* life. That's not selfish."

He mumbled something, and when she clearly hadn't understood, he repeated himself. "I feel selfish not keeping Bug 'cause I want a life." Redness was crawling up his neck, and he shifted uncomfortably.

Standing up, Frazer walked around and knelt next to his chair until he had to look at her. "You are *anything* but selfish, Jack. What makes you think that?"

"I'm thinking about myself."

"Sometimes you have to... Want to know what I think?"

He stared at her openly, still young enough to think that people in authority had a better understanding of the world. Little did Jack know her life was like a soap opera.

"I think," she said, keeping her voice even, "I think it would be *more* selfish to keep a baby when you didn't want to because you were worried about guilt. You're doing something incredible by giving this baby to someone who desperately wants it—for it and for the family and for yourself."

Glazed eyes stared at her like chips of marble. "You think?"

She nodded. "If you wanted Bug, wanted to be a parent, then that's okay too. If you want to change your mind."

He shook his head. "I don't... I just..."

She squeezed his hand, and he clutched tightly enough that Frazer's fingers ached. And she let him. He cleared his throat. "I, uh... My uncle tracked me down."

"Really?"

A small smile played at his lips. "Yeah. He, uh, got hold of my e-mail through my cousin's friend."

Frazer nudged his hand. "And?"

"We had lunch at the start of the week."

"And?"

He was grinning now. "It was nice."

Warmth spread in Frazer's chest. "Jack, that's great."

"It's okay."

The look on his face betrayed that it was a lot more than okay. Maybe he was waiting for the other shoe to drop, and that thought made Frazer ache for him. She waited for him to elaborate.

He took a deep breath. "He's not talking to my parents since he heard they kicked me out. He wants to help me. He had a lot of questions about transitioning...but not like my parents. Genuine questions. He wanted to know. I told him about pronouns and my name, and he just said okay. He asked about Bug and what I was doing and said he'd help me out, whatever I was doing."

"I'm so glad for you, Jack."

"I thought my family had just forgotten me." His voice croaked, and Frazer felt her heart clench.

"Obviously not." Frazer considered her next question carefully before asking, "Were the two of you close?"

"Kind of. He got divorced years ago and has two kids."

"You have cousins." Frazer cocked her head. "That must be nice?"

Jack straightened up. "It was... It is. We were pretty close. I thought—I don't know—that we wouldn't be friends anymore."

"Sounds like you will be. What does your uncle do?"

"He used to be a principal for a high school years ago. Then, one day, he quit, said he was sick of the system that did nothing to help kids. Now he works for a social media company."

"It sounds like he could be understanding of what's going on?"

Jack met her eyes. "I told him most of it all, and he just asked what help he could give me."

If Frazer was into that kind of thing, she would kiss the man. "That's great."

"It is, isn't it?" And Jack looked younger than normal in his obvious happiness. "He was really interested in your programme and said he'd like to talk to you about making contacts with high schools to find referrals."

And the man got better and better. After the conversation wound down, Frazer did a simple exam of Jack's stomach, noting that the baby was still in the correct position.

"It'll be soon, Jack. You have a way to get to the hospital, still?"

He nodded. "It used to be an ambulance or Cora, but my uncle's bought me a mobile and a SIM card. He wants me to call him."

Seriously, this man was dangerously close to getting bear hugged. "Good. That's good. And everything is sorted for the adoption?"

Wrapped in his hoody again, he crossed his arms, almost hugging himself. "Yeah—I chose a family?" He smiled, looking more assured. "Did Cora tell you?"

Of course she hadn't. All Cora did was tell her to go away and stare at her with weird sex eyes and kiss her when it was the last thing Frazer felt like at that moment.

"No! I haven't managed to hand over with her about clients. Who did you go for?"

"I chose the two dads. I was leaning towards the single mum, but then I read that statistics showed gay male couples are the least likely to get a baby. Even more than single parents. So..."

Frazer smiled at him. "Good choice."

"I should go..."

"Do you have enough coupons for the bus?"

"My uncle is waiting in the car park."

That did it. If she ever met him, she was going to embarrass herself. "Great. Be safe, and we'll see you soon, okay?"

"Yeah, okay."

"Oh, and Jack."

"Yeah?"

"Did you think about during the birth? Drugs, no drugs?

"Oh." He rummaged in his pocket and pulled out a piece of paper, wrinkled and a bit tatty. "I wrote up a kind of plan. Like you said. Basically, I want all the drugs. Google told me the baby may be sleepy when it comes out, but besides that, it has no effect."

What would they do without the internet? "Sounds like a plan. Okay, mate. Bye."

He waved and waddled out, the stoop of his shoulders too much for his age.

Frazer let out a long breath and collapsed into her chair.

Without Jack there, her pleasure at his happiness started ebbing away and Frazer felt herself getting angry again. Her phone vibrated in her pocket—a message from her sister that she didn't bother reading, opting instead to call her.

"Frazer! So, you want to come?"

"Come where?"

"Did you not read my message?"

"I missed you so dearly that I called instead."

"Liar. Dinner tonight? Meeting the lecturer..."

Frazer straightened. Now there was a distraction. "I'm so, so in. I can't wait to glare at the man corrupting my tiny sister."

"We both know I've always been corrupted. So, seven? The good Indian place in Cottesloe? The only one that Awa says she'll set foot in?"

She chuckled. No food was as good as their grandmother's. "Sounds good. See you then."

They hung up, and Frazer looked forward to a swim in a couple of hours. She could go channel her anger into the pool and then glare at the man she'd heard a lot about for too long.

And pretend Cora hadn't kissed her.

The first thing Cora did when she got back to Lisa's was Google lesbianism. Then bisexuality. Then pansexuality.

She wasn't clear on the difference, and six websites later, she felt pretty confident she was one of them.

Then, just to see, she put *how to get a woman back after you told her you were straight then told her to leave you alone then realised you were bisexual or something and now want her back but she's mad.* Unsurprisingly, she didn't find a lot.

When Cora heard Lisa's key in the door, she shut her laptop with a snap, feeling like she'd been caught looking up porn.

"Hey!"

Lisa walked in and dropped her bag, proudly holding a box out in front of her.

"Hey, what's this?"

"Open it."

For a moment, Cora was almost nervous. What on earth would Lisa buy her that fit in a box that size? It looked like a cake box. She laughed loudly when she saw it.

"Lisa, is that a rainbow cake? With rainbow icing?"

"Yup! Happy you-discovered-you're-gay-or-queer-or-bi-or-pan-or—" At Cora's raised eyebrows, she shrugged. "I looked stuff up and wasn't sure where you'd sit on the whole spectrum thing. I wanted to be inclusive."

Cora wasn't about to admit that she, too, had no idea and had resorted to the internet.

Instead, she peered down at the cake. It was the most *rainbowy* cake she'd ever seen. Something safe that Cora hadn't realised she'd been missing settled in her chest. She swiped at her eye and then stood into a hug she wrapped around a surprised Lisa.

"Thank you." She squeezed Lisa tightly.

Lisa squeezed her back. "No problem."

"Oh God." Cora pulled back, eyes wide.

"What?" Lisa asked.

"Do you think my parents will buy me a cake?"

Lisa paled a little, giving her a nervous smile. "Um, maybe?"

No, they wouldn't.

"Well, let's look on the bright side." Lisa clasped her by the shoulders. "They're only gonna take one of the two bombs in: the divorce or the whole lady-loving *thing*. So *I* say, drop both, then run and see which one they cling to."

"Do you think I can just, you know...*not* tell them?"

"You could always take an Alec cardboard cut-out with you to family events."

296

Through her panic, Cora actually laughed. "Yeah, just carry him around and see if they notice. Maybe they'll be too worried I've lost my mind and they won't care when I also mention I'm divorced and trying to get a lady back into my bed."

"We can always dream."

Cora blinked at the wall, the extremely elated feeling she'd had since her sexuality epiphany seeping away. Her parents were going to be angry about the divorce—especially her mother. She had no idea how they'd greet Frazer, if that ever happened.

"Maybe." Lisa squeezed her shoulders again. "Maybe you can just stick with the divorce news and announce the other one when you feel you need to."

Nodding enthusiastically, Cora let out a breath. "Yeah. Good. I like that plan."

"You manage to talk to Frazer?"

"Uh..."

"Did you just kiss her and hope she'd get it?"

"Um...*no*." Cora busied herself by finding a knife to cut the cake.

"Cora! That was a joke. You so did, didn't you?"

Cora waved the knife in her hand around. "She was ranting and angry—"

"With pretty good reason..."

"Yeah, okay. With good reason. But I couldn't get a word in edgewise, and I thought she'd just, you know, *get* it once I kissed her."

"How'd that go?"

Cora sighed and walked back over to cut cake. Changing her mind, she went back to the drawer and just held up two forks.

Lisa smirked. "That well, huh?"

"She told me to stay away from her and stormed out."

"Cora..."

Stabbing her fork into the cake, Cora looked at her hopefully. "Yeah?"

"You're an idiot."

She sighed. "I know."

Lisa sat opposite her and starting attacking the cake as Cora chewed on her bite. "Did you get your keys to the new place?"

"Yup. Want to come to Ikea with me? It only occurred to me an hour ago that all my furniture is at the old house."

Lisa's eyes lit up. "Can we have lunch there?"

"Of course."

"I can buy plants."

"You have a thousand plants."

"And I need more."

Cora scoffed. "Yeah, okay."

"So. What's your plan?"

Groaning, Cora dropped her head on the table. "I had an epiphany today. Can't that be enough?"

Lisa's hand patted her head.

"Yeah. It can be."

The smell of chlorine still clung to Frazer, and she was starting to regret showering at the gym rather than at home. Sometimes she wondered if they sourced the shower water from the pool. Glaring at some guy sleeping with her sister as they carried on an inappropriate affair—not that Frazer was one to talk—would pack less punch if she smelt like a swimming pool.

Parking her car on a residential street that would probably get her a fine, Frazer walked to the restaurant. The swim had left her with aching muscles and an ache in her stomach. The pounding of her arms through the water and the silence only swimming brought still hadn't been enough to defuse the choking anger at Cora.

Or the situation in general.

The breeze from the ocean washed over her. As she often did, she wished she lived closer to the beach. She was only a thirty-minute drive away, yet it would be so nice to be a walk away, to drive past it every day to and from work and remember that she wasn't surrounded by people but really by a huge stretch of water. The salty air was intoxicating.

With regret, she pushed the door open to the restaurant and left the smell of ocean behind her. That regret quickly left her as the scent of spices replaced it.

It smelt like family lunches at her grandmother's house, ones that hadn't made her feel awkward. Like the skin of her grandmother and the heady spices clinging to her clothes. Like Sunday spent learning to make food. The scent made Frazer long for Sundays at her Awa's side as she had taught Frazer how to make idli-sambar, paalpradaman, kappa and kheer. Her stomach growled just at the thought.

Spotting her sister at a corner table, Frazer weaved her way through. A woman sat next to her, and Frazer threw a questioning look at her sister. Where was the lecturer? The woman had sleek-looking black hair cut into an angled bob and looked nervous for someone who appeared so put together. She couldn't be much older than Frazer.

Jemma gave a nervous wave and stood up. "Hey, Frazer!"

They hugged, and then Frazer turned to the woman at the table. "Hi, I'm Frazer. And you are...?"

The woman gave her a grin that was far too dazzling and held her hand out, shaking it firmly. "I'm Meg."

Why did Meg have such lovely, piercing blue eyes?

"Nice to meet you."

Frazer looked back to her sister, who had two bright spots of colour on her cheeks. Frazer said, "I thought—"

"Meg is my lecturer." Frazer barely caught Meg's wince as Jemma rushed to finish. "Well, *was*. I mean, she's my girlfriend."

Meg with the amazing eyes was Jemma's girlfriend? Jemma had a *girlfriend*?

Frazer looked to Meg, then stared back at Jemma. "You're *gay*?"

"You're one to talk."

"Not what I mean, Jem." The words hissed out between Frazer's teeth.

Between them, Meg had closed her eyes as if to gather strength.

"I'm not gay. I'm... I'm queer."

Frazer stared at her. "What's the difference?"

Another shrug. "I don't really have a label. I didn't think you'd care."

Meg raised her hand, and they both looked at her. "In my defence, I thought you knew."

"In *my* defence," Jemma said, "I didn't think it mattered."

That gave Frazer pause. Wasn't that what she'd been campaigning for her entire life? This sort of thing not mattering? She took in a deep breath before speaking again. "A little heads-up would have been nice is all I'm saying. I referred to Meg as a guy and you never corrected me."

Jemma leant forward, eyes intent. "Why should I? Why can't I just introduce you to the *person* I'm dating."

Frazer shut her mouth. This was ridiculous. Of course she didn't care that Meg was a *girl*. In fact, those words were ones Frazer had muttered over a hundred times. "Okay, it doesn't matter. I'm just surprised." Frazer's eyes widened. "Oh, shit. Mum's going to blame *me*."

Jemma rolled her eyes. "Probably. At least there's two of us?" She winked at Frazer and between them, Meg chuckled.

Frazer turned to stare at her, and the woman smiled.

"Sorry," Meg said hurriedly, "it's just, my brother came out at the dinner table, and I just followed by saying that since it was a theme, so was I. My dad dropped his water."

"Awkward family dinner." Frazer said.

Meg passed her a menu. "Yeah it was. But they got over it."

Frazer took it. "Good to hear. It really is nice to meet you... Sorry."

"No worries."

Jemma puffed her chest out. "I knew you two would get along."

Only by a tiny bit, Frazer managed to resist hitting her.

They ordered plates to share, enough to leave leftovers to take home. It was strange to sit with her little sister and a girlfriend. Her sister had never really dated, had never really brought anyone around for Frazer to meet. She'd wondered if her sister was just picky...or slow. Or preferred casual to serious. Or just wasn't interested.

And here was a woman just over ten years older than her baby sister. A woman who had been an authority figure. Should she be worried? Okay, so her sister wasn't a fifteen-year-old minor but twenty-five. And the age gap really wasn't a big deal at their age. But...it was her baby sister. So what if Meg seemed absolutely lovely?

Frazer gave her a long look. She really was incredibly nice.

Frazer hated that.

Over korma and naan bread that practically melted in Frazer's mouth, Jemma looked across at her and asked, "So how's Cora?"

Frazer almost dropped her fork. Her eyes flickered to Meg, who chewed slowly and conveniently stared at her plate. Frazer did not want to talk about *Cora*. Or even *think* about Cora, with her stupid pretty eyes and skin that was smoother than anything.

Who was infuriating and had told Frazer to leave her alone.

"Um, fine."

"Yeah, but have you spoken to her?" Jemma just kept on going. Why couldn't her parents have just bought Frazer and her brother a puppy like they'd asked all those years ago? She kind of hoped now that Meg was terrible in bed.

"No, not really."

As if Frazer felt like opening up about her poor choices and her love life drama to apparently newly-gay Jemma's perfect girlfriend.

"Meg knows everything anyway, Frazer."

This time Frazer did drop her fork on her plate. Most likely without luck, she tried to *not* glare. Meg was now staring between the two of them openly. "Jemma!" Frazer hissed.

301

"It's not like she knows them." Jemma was gazing at her as if she really had no idea what the big problem was.

Anger threatened to boil over in Frazer's stomach and she took a gulp of her beer to try and smother it and not misdirect it at her sister. Even though she deserved it. "Not the point."

Meg was looking back down at her plate. She stalled with a large sip of wine.

"What if I'd told Rob or Andy all about your affair with your lecturer?"

Jemma shovelled a forkful of food into her mouth. "It's not like they would tell on me; they're cool."

Clearly, her sister and she were very different people.

There was an urge to defend herself, which Frazer knew was stupid, but she turned to Meg anyway and said, "Try not to judge me too harshly on crappy choices."

Meg shrugged. "Slept with a student. Still hoping the faculty don't find out. No judging."

"Good to hear." Frazer fiddled with the label on the bottle. "I left Cora alone like she asked. She watched me all over the hospital, I yelled at her about it—"

"You yelled at her for looking at you?" Jemma's eyebrows raised.

"She wasn't just *looking*...but, like, *watching*."

The incredulous expression didn't leave Jemma's face. "Okay. But, like, what kind of watching?"

"I don't know."

Meg asked, "The kind with longing glances...her eyes following you all around the rooms?"

"Maybe."

Meg smirked. She and Jemma clearly belonged together. "Girl wants you," she said.

Jemma nudged Meg with her shoulder, eyes wide. Her glee was infuriating. "Right? She so does."

Frazer ripped apart some bread. Shredded it, really.

"Put down your phone."

Wide-eyed at Lisa, Cora did just that, all but dropping it on the sofa in a poor effort to look innocent.

"We agreed." Lisa crossed her arms. "No messaging Frazer. Give her a few days to calm down."

"But, she doesn't know—"

"It doesn't matter. She needs a few days."

Cora sighed. "Why are you always right?"

"Because I have no relationship of my own, so I invest in others." Lisa plopped down across from her on the floor. "That's why we got you your keys early. To give you the distraction of a new house."

"Yes, yes, I know. The Ikea delivery is late, though."

"Probably takes a while to get most of their store into one truck."

Cora chuckled. "It's not my fault I needed everything."

They sat on the couch Lisa had bought her as a surprise gift, the only thing in the house right now besides Cora's two huge suitcases in the corner.

"The place is nice," Lisa said, her gaze wandering over the feature wall behind Cora.

"Yeah, I like it."

She really did. The 1950s duplex held an inexplicable charm for Cora, even with the old lady next door who had smelt strongly of cats when she'd said hello. The backyard wasn't huge, but existed. It had two bedrooms and one bathroom, and best of all, Cora could smell the ocean.

"Has it had renovations?" Lisa asked.

"Yeah, just last year. All the rooms."

"I love the floorboards."

Cora hummed her agreement. "I want to get a dog."

"Seriously?"

"Yeah, why?"

"They need so much...time."

"I know... I want to adopt an older one. I read the other day that any dog over ten rarely gets adopted."

"You're too nice."

"Am not. I want company here." Cora shrugged.

"What if you want to travel?"

"I don't really have any plans for that right now." It was enough just trying to sort her life out.

"But..."

"What?"

"Well, I thought now you might look at getting involved in some of those overseas organisations you talked about so much at uni."

Cora stared at her. "I hadn't really thought about it."

Which was the truth. The fact that her whole life had just started to open up before her again hadn't completely registered. But surely she couldn't. Cora had her job at the hospital, and the programme...

The sound of a large vehicle filtered through the lounge room window.

Lisa bounced. "Things are coming!"

It took them hours. Cora had paid extra to have people help them assemble everything, something she'd hesitated on but was grateful for when she watched boxes of her bed, a book shelf, side tables, dining table, and more get carried through. Lisa had insisted part of the fun was assembling the furniture, but Cora had strong memories of wanting to set fire to her bed at university as she'd struggled to follow the directions.

There was so much stuff, and it took Cora's breath away.

Long after the helpers left, Lisa and Cora stayed up putting the new sheets on the bed, filling the kitchen drawers with new equipment and generally trying to make everything look a bit cosier.

They sat back on the kitchen floor with their beers and looked around.

"I'm exhausted." Cora groaned.

"I know... And you still have to get things like a TV. And I need to buy you some rugs and paintings. It still looks..."

"Sparse."

"Yeah." Lisa held her bottle out. "We'll make you a home, don't worry."

Cora clinked her bottle against Lisa's.

Cora had a house. A house that was going to be filled with *her* things. One to echo memories and thoughts and times that she'd built, not that felt built around her. "I need to arrange with Alec to get some of my things."

Her photographs. The thermo mix her mother had bought her as a wedding gift. Knickknacks, mugs she'd bought as souvenirs on the odd trip. Things that made a house a home.

"Want me to come with you?"

Cora let out a breath. "Yes, please."

A home. That was hers.

Maybe a dog.

You weren't supposed to run in hospitals. Everyone knew that.

There were fragile, old people and sick, young people and every mix of those two things walking the hallways. You were more than likely to fall over a basket of bed sheets or slip on a recently mopped floor or take out a co-worker—one who really didn't deserve it. They had information sessions about how even if there was an emergency, you did not run.

Instead, everybody speed-walked.

And after years of practice, Frazer, like most of the staff, could move through hospital corridors almost as fast as if she ran.

Which was exactly what Frazer was doing now.

She weaved between some nurses and doctors chatting in a hallway, none of whom batted an eyelash, reading her body language and stepping forward or back to make room. They didn't even miss a beat of their discussion. Rounding a corner widely to avoid collisions, Frazer hopped in a circle to wheel around a sheet basket. Someone yanked a medicine trolley out of her way, and she waved her thanks.

She was slightly red-faced yet *not* breathing hard when she burst through the double doors to the maternity ward, thanks to all her excessive, angry swimming. She was burning so many calories lately that all she did these days was eat just to keep up.

All the swimming did nothing to burn away her anger at Cora, though.

"Frazer! Where's the fire?"

Her favourite nurse, Gavin, was raising his eyebrows at her like he was concerned for her sanity. She flashed him a grin.

"I was paged for an emergency."

His eyebrows raised even higher. "There isn't any emergency."

Okay. Maybe it hadn't been an emergency. "Well, okay, I was paged for a birth."

"Okay, midwife of ten years, since when does a normal birth constitute an emergency?"

Sagging dramatically across the nurses' station desk, Frazer pouted up at him. "It's my first patient from the program..."

Gavin's eyes lit up. "Oh! You mean—"

"Jack in room three."

Gavin looked up with a scrunched expression at the bed list on the white board.

"We don't have a Jack, wc have—"

"*Jack*. We have Jack in room three." Frazer straightened so she looked less like a sulking fifteen-year-old. "Jack is transgender."

"Oh." Gavin's face went from confused to more confused to relaxed. "Oh! I get it now. Okay." He walked around the desk and swiped out the name written on the board, the dead name that legalities would have forced Jack to check in with, and replaced it with *Jack*. "I didn't know."

Frazer had half run there because the last thing Jack needed was to be dead-named while pushing out something the size of a small watermelon. Even if the admission team had used Jack as his name, the computer system would have automatically sent the old information to the ward.

"Thanks, Gavin."

"So...that's a complicated situation. How old is the kid? I haven't seen h-him, yet."

"Just gone eighteen two months ago. He hasn't had the money yet to make the name change legally." Frazer turned on a charming smile and batted her lashes at him, asking, "Can you make sure the rest of the staff is informed and that the name above his bed is changed?"

He crossed his arms. "And?"

Gavin always knew when there was more. "And make sure Trish the night nurse isn't working his end of the ward tonight."

The woman was notoriously conservative.

He huffed a laugh. "That's a given. No problem. So you're doing the delivery?"

"I've been with him for the last four months; he's comfortable with me. I'm not going home until the bub is born. And I have to make the call to the adoption agency after the birth."

"Ah..." Gavin bent over the computer, checking boxes and typing a note. "Just making sure everything's checked so all the right people know it's an adoption case."

"You're the best, Gav."

"I know, lovely. This ward would be a mess without me."

That was entirely too true. "That's why I head-hunted you for maternity."

He rolled his eyes. "That and you tried my cupcakes at a work Christmas party and wanted them for yourself."

Also entirely too true.

"Don't know what you're talking about, Gavin. Are Deidre and Sam here?"

He winked. "You mean the two lovelies that are the exact opposite of Trish?"

"That'd be them." She looked around to see if anyone was close by, then lowered her voice to add, "I've been making sure they're always rostered on in case I wasn't around for Jack's birth."

He gave a nod. "Got it. Deidre's in a birth in room six and Sam is with a couple that are having some complications in room ten."

"She okay?"

"The obstetrician has been called. Probably going to be a caesarean."

"Which couple?"

"Ashley and Daniel Simmerman?"

Frazer sighed. "Ah, I saw them for a prenatal exam a few months back. She's tiny."

Gavin held his hands apart a foot. "Tiny, tiny. I have no idea how you women do what you do."

"Eight years on this ward and you have no idea?"

He waved his hand at her. "Smartass, you know what I mean."

With a chuckle, she walked towards Jack's room, leaving Gavin behind to run the ward.

In room three, Jack sat on the bed, flushed but looking otherwise okay.

"Well." Frazer smiled. "A week early? In a hurry?"

He gave a shrug, clearly uncomfortable in the hospital gown. "Apparently."

His fingers looked small pressed against the huge swell of his abdomen.

"How you feeling?" Frazer grabbed his chart from the end of his bed and looked over it quickly. Nothing of importance jumped out.

"It hurts. I don't love it."

Frazer tried to resist quirking her lips but wasn't sure she managed to. "I'm yet to hear someone tell me how much they adore childbirth."

"I'm not surprised. It feels like an elephant is sitting on my stomach."

He managed a small grin, a sheepish one that made Frazer feel a bit better for him. This wasn't an easy thing for Jack, and she was incredibly glad Cora had found him therapy that had helped him prepare for this.

The thought of Cora made Frazer's stomach flip with anger.

Frazer winced in sympathy. "That sounds horrendous?"

His eyebrows shot up. "Isn't this, like, your job? Every day?"

"Yeah, but it doesn't mean I'm not aware that it hurts like crazy."

"Do you have kids?" He stared up at her.

"Would you still trust my skills if I said no?"

The rapid nod of his head made her smile.

"No, I don't. I think if I decided to have kids, I'd adopt, actually."

He cocked his head and stared at her. "Really?"

"Yeah."

"Watching babies come out put you off?"

She chuckled. "You could say that." And also, Frazer had seen far too many parents, like Jack, who had babies to give. Or, perhaps *should* give.

"Righto, Jack. Sorry, but I need to do a quick internal exam. I have to check how far you're dilated."

His cheeks flushed more, but he shuffled on the bed. "I'm so glad this will be over soon." His voice was low, like he was offering secrets he wasn't used to sharing.

It was a matter of minutes before Frazer was washing her hands and Jack was wriggling back up the bed.

"How far apart have your contractions been?"

"The emergency nurse said seven minutes. That hasn't really changed."

"Okay. Well, I've been in here," Frazer glanced at the clock above the bed, "for about six. So get ready."

He started breathing, hard, eyebrows scrunching up and fingers digging into the material over his stomach. "God, it's that exact?"

Frazer rubbed his knee. "It can be. Squeeze my hand if you need."

He did just that, and Frazer was thankful she'd had siblings to toughen her up. It was not a light grip. "Breathe slowly, that's it... Five, four, three, two...one."

The grip loosened and he looked at her with slightly glassy eyes. "Am I at ten yet?"

Frazer wished for his sake he was. "Sorry, you're at four."

"Four? Four! This has been hours and I'm at *four?*"

His eyes were so wide, Frazer almost grimaced. She'd put that look on his face.

"That's two-fifths of the way there?" She went for a helpful tone, and he simply narrowed his eyes at her.

"Drugs. I want all the drugs."

The house was quiet, and it didn't bother Cora.

Lisa had gone home hours ago, but that wasn't important. Because Cora was settling into her own space, finding places for her own things. Learning how she fit into this strange, new freedom. Tomorrow she would talk to Alec about collecting her more personal belongings.

She could face him.

Hopefully.

Then she could have her books. Two bookshelves were set up, ready to be filled. The vase, another thing from her great grandmother—one of the first things she bought herself in Australia after she'd come from Thailand—could go in the centre of a middle shelf. She needed to find the book her maternal grandmother had given her too, completely in Korean, with illustrations that took her breath away. She'd buy a rug soon too, a neutral colour, one that complemented the dark wood of her bookshelves. Maybe she'd buy sheet sets, brand new, good quality. Something nice to lay between and feel warm and secure. The ones she'd bought from Ikea were fine, but maybe it would be nice to spoil herself a little.

Cool white wine, the first sip of the evening, went down very well.

A flush coursed over her cheeks at the memory that so did Frazer. Frazer, who wouldn't speak to her or look at her. Cora really needed a plan.

It was ridiculous. Stupid, even. There was no way she was in a good place for a relationship. The old one was barely over. Yes, there had been overlap, but what she had been doing with Frazer had not been emotional, right?

Cora wanted to slap herself.

How had she been so oblivious to the fact that she hadn't just been having a physical affair but an emotional one? Getting up and never letting them bask in the aftermath, keeping talk and sex separate. That had been her smart idea, her proof to herself that the affair meant nothing.

Never mind that Cora had sought Frazer out every day and Frazer her as well. And not just for fast, hot sex in an inappropriate place, but for comfort, for an ear, for a joke that she knew Frazer would appreciate. For the balm of her smile, so easily given. She had fallen into the well of Frazer's eyes, the scent of her skin, the curve of her neck until the heady aftermath she'd always stayed away from, as if it absolved her from true wrongdoing, became part of her too.

God, she missed Frazer.

A laugh bubbled out from her lips, and she shook her head at herself.

She'd really thought she was straight. That it hadn't meant anything. Cora could be really, really stupid sometimes.

The sound of clacking computer keys filled the house, echoing off the walls. She looked things up on the internet for an hour. Sexuality. Pansexuality. Bisexuality. It was endless and fascinating, and there was a whole world that Cora now felt personally involved in.

Cora, who had always known where she fit: daughter, student, girlfriend, wife, straight. Always assumed, and not thought about too deeply.

She liked the term *queer*. That it was all encompassing. But still, it didn't sit right with her.

Cora liked specifics. She liked to know where she was, *who* she was. As she fell down a rabbit hole of terms and identities, her eyes grew wider and wider.

It was slowly dawning on Cora that, at thirty-four, she had actually never known who she was but had just slipped onto others' ideas of who she was supposed to be like an old hand-me-down coat. Comfortable, soft, expected.

But not original. Not what she would have picked out for herself.

Twelve tabs sat open on her browser. It was all a little overwhelming. Should she say she was bisexual? Of all the things she had read, this one felt most comfortable.

Bisexual. She said the word out loud, to see how it fit. "Bisexual."

It rolled off her tongue.

Another laugh dribbled past her lips. She'd barely drunk any of her wine, so enthralled with what she read. With what she had discovered.

She'd fallen for Frazer without even realising it. And Cora was supposed to be smart.

She jumped when her phone vibrated on the wood tabletop. It was just after nine, and she hoped it wasn't her parents. They still didn't know about the divorce, and with the good mood she was in, she didn't particularly want to talk to them about it right then.

Three seconds after opening the message, Cora was pulling on her jacket, keys jangling in her hand, and running out the door.

It was Jack.

It seemed like hours, but was really only twenty minutes later that involved some broken speed limits Cora wasn't very proud of, until she was walking onto the maternity ward. A quick sweep of her gaze across the patient board behind the nurses' station located Jack's name—something Cora and Frazer had discussed but that Cora had been worried about—and room number.

The fact that the correct name was being used made Cora nervous. So Frazer had been here, making sure it all went smoothly. Had she been on call?

There was a time when Cora would have known that. They would have commiserated over coffee about their timetables— about anything, really. Then they would have shared a look, and Cora would have tried to stay late in the hospital when she knew Frazer would be there. And even after that, they would have disappeared somewhere not entirely appropriate and walked away not too long after, sated and flushed.

Room three loomed ahead of Cora, and she stood outside it, teeth worrying her lip and rocking on her heels. Frazer was on the other side of the door; she had to be. When Cora entered, Frazer's eyes would probably flash with an anger that froze Cora's insides.

She knocked and slipped in when she heard Jack's voice call out to her.

Jack was standing opposite the bed, leaning over its edge, his elbows digging into the mattress. He faced the door as he took deep breaths, his eyes now on her, glassy and a little distant. He swayed back and forth, even as a dazed smile graced his lips. "Hey."

Cora smiled back at him. "Hi."

Behind him, her hands massaging the small of his back, Frazer didn't look up. "Hi, Cora."

"Hi."

Their greetings were neutral, bordering on friendly. Jack, his gaze now back on the bed, was probably none the wiser to the lack of eye contact and the flush creeping up Frazer's neck.

For a moment, Cora willed Frazer to look up. Even if the look was cold, it would be better than nothing.

Frazer's eyes stayed fixed, intent on her hands. No hope, Cora thought. Not the time for that.

There was a chair near the bed, and Cora placed it on the side opposite Jack. She gripped his hands at the centre of the bed sheets, and he looked up, their heads barely a foot apart.

"Thanks for coming." He swallowed hard, his throat moving.

The mentors weren't expected to be this involved, unless the parent had no other support. But there wasn't much that would stop Cora being there for Jack, seeing as he had no one else.

"I had nothing better to do." She kept her gaze on him, trying to block out Frazer's presence behind him, and he huffed a laugh at her words. "Didn't you want an epidural?"

His hands didn't stop gripping hers tightly. "I did. But then Frazer said I wouldn't be able to stand up or walk, so I want to wait until I'm more, uh, dilated." He stared at her. "I don't like the idea of not being able to move much off the bed."

"That would suck."

"Totally."

"How dilated are you?"

He blinked heavily. "I don't remember. Frazer?"

When Cora looked from Jack to Frazer, everything stilled. Frazer stared straight at her, eyes green as ever and filled with intensity. In that moment, it was as if Frazer had forgotten the question.

Her eyes flew back down. Her hands moved in slow circles along Jack's spine. "You're eight centimetres."

Whimpering, Jack dropped his head on the bed between his arms. "Birth is shit."

Cora chuckled. "Yeah, I imagine so."

"I want the epidural now." His voice was muffled with his head still buried.

"Okay. I'll go page the anaesthetist." Frazer disappeared easily.

Quiet settled around them but for Jack's panting. He moaned softly, swaying again, and Cora sat and let him grip her hands.

The next thirty minutes were a flurry of activity. Jack ended up back on the bed, blood pressure cuff and pulse oximeter on. An anaesthetist swept in and then swept back out, the epidural placed. The glassy look on Jack's face intensified, but the pain that scrunched his face up, making him look much older than his eighteen years, smoothed away.

It was only a few more hours. A few more hours of coaching Jack, of avoiding Frazer's eyes. A few more hours until Frazer was between his legs and Cora was sitting behind him, his head thrown back, his weight pushing back on her front as she gripped his forearms so he could bear down with a grunt tearing from his lips. Between Frazer and Cora, the first client of their programme, their joint venture, trembled with the pain and effort of bringing forth a new life.

With Jack's final push, Frazer smiled and held up the newborn baby, a wail turning it from a mottled blue to the bright, safe red of life. Thrashing, screaming life, too small and yet so large in the sterile room. Cora, eyes wide, watched Frazer cut the cord and wrap the baby in a blanket. Against her chest, she felt the sobs Jack lashed out.

"I want to hold Bug." His voice cracked, but his arms were already reaching out.

The baby, when Frazer placed him in his arms, blinked blurrily up at Jack, a fist curled next to its cheek. Cora didn't move. Frazer didn't move. And between them, Jack continued to sob while the baby sucked its fist. Cora stared at Frazer, who stared at the baby who had brought them all together.

CHAPTER EIGHTEEN

"You look exhausted."

Frazer jumped, her feet dropping off her desk as she straightened in her seat. Maybe she'd been falling asleep. Just possibly. Her office was warm and comfortable, and she was so sleep deprived after been up all night with Jack and then thinking her office was a good place to crash afterwards.

Sitting across from her at her desk, her arms crossed and her lips pursed as if trying to smother a smirk, Tia was watching Frazer like she'd been there for ages.

Frazer rubbed her eyes, feeling like a child. "Aw, thanks, Tia."

Tia raised her eyebrows. "Well, you do."

Frazer slumped back into her chair. "What do you want?"

"How was your on call last night?"

Frazer swallowed. That was the question of the day. A birth hadn't affected her like that since the first one she'd done without a supervisor, the life in her hands flailing and screaming with lungs powerful enough to knock over her new parents. "Fine."

Fine did not cover it, but not much else could.

"Good to hear. Did you get much sleep?"

Frazer shrugged. "I got a few hours in an on call room."

Lies. It had been at this very desk.

Really, it had been a few hours of staring at the wall, remembering the depth of Cora's eyes as they'd stared at her. Instead of anger, a feeling of nothingness had settled over her. Frazer was too tired, too numb, to take any of it in.

After a long moment that would be etched in her mind for the rest of her life, Jack had handed the baby over to Frazer, who had handed it over to the adoption representative.

Afterwards, Cora and Frazer had sat with Jack until he fell asleep, the bruises under his eyes overshadowed by the grief that shimmered in them. At the first sign that Jack was completely out, Frazer had slipped out of the room and left Cora whispering her name behind her.

Frazer didn't have it in her.

"A few hours isn't enough. Shouldn't you be going home?"

Frazer didn't want to go home. She didn't want to be thinking. She wanted to be buried in work. Or sleeping in her office and pretending to be buried by work. "I'll go home early?"

Tia raised her eyebrows at her.

"I will!"

"Sure you will."

Sighing, Frazer asked, "Did you come here just to mother me?"

The answer of silence had Frazer looking up at sharply. Tia was watching her, a look on her face Frazer couldn't decipher. "Tia?"

A purse of the lips. A quirk of the eyebrows. "Cora has been watching you."

God, was that all? Frazer rolled her eyes. "I know. I told her to stop."

"She hasn't."

Frazer really didn't need this right now. "Tia, what do you want from me? We ended it. She told me to leave her alone, I told her to stop watching me all the damn time. I'm staying away from her."

Tia's arms dropped to her sides. "Okay. But maybe you shouldn't?"

Maybe she shouldn't? This was Tia who had been so mad it had been going on. Frazer's affair with Cora had been stupid and selfish and *wrong*. And now Tia was saying— "What?"

Tia's lips pursed again as she stared at Frazer, as if assessing her. "Do you want to be with her?"

All the air rushed out of Frazer's chest. That was never a question she'd let herself think about. One that she wouldn't let whisper at her in the back of her mind. And one she'd found herself shying away from more and more.

Suddenly, it felt like she couldn't breathe. Her brain made a humming noise. Useful. "No," she said.

Tia just gave her a doubtful look. "Right."

Frazer squeezed her eyes shut. Opened them again. Stared at Tia, who just shook her head, threw up her arms, and walked out.

Which was infuriating, because Frazer actually meant it.

No good relationship could be built on the foundation they'd set up. It was a mess. Cora was a mess, and barely separated, if the rumours were true.

Today sucked.

"Alec, I need my things."

He stared at her from across his desk. Blinked. Tapped his pen against the papers in front of him. Blinked again.

Once more, she'd had to approach him at work because he avoided any of her attempts to organise a better place.

"Your things?" He asked.

Cora sighed internally. "Yeah, my things. I need to come around and collect some stuff."

Alec dropped the pen and sat back in his chair, holding his hands up in supplication. "Cora, it's *our* house. You can come home whenever you want."

The chair she was in was one she'd sat in many times over the last couple of years. They used to have lunch across from each other, sometimes in silence, sometimes fluffed up with idle chatter. Now the chair felt foreign beneath her, as did the man across from her; he had for a long time. Maybe, really, he always had.

"I don't want to come home, Alec. I just want to get some of my things."

He puffed air out of his nose. "Why? Why are you doing this, Cora? Come home. We can sort this out—we can go back to Doctor Massey. Why throw away everything we have?"

Cora was already back with Doctor Massey, focussing on her own needs.

Her throat was tight, the pleading note in his voice threading around her heart and constricting. "It's too late for that, Alec."

"It's never too late."

But it was. He wasn't going to change, Cora could see that now, so clearly it was almost blinding. He'd been this way, this controlling, from the beginning, but then, it had been layered in charm, in softness, in the security of feeling like he wanted her around so much for *her* sake. Not because he needed to know where she was all the time. Not because he needed to feel like he owned her. Not because he felt like she was *his*.

"Alec, I'm sorry. It *is*." They stared at each other, before Cora pushed on. "I'll come around this evening when you're still at work."

She didn't mention that Lisa would be going with her as insurance, as a shield. In case he tried to be there to stop her, to cling to her things and keep them from her.

That muscle ticked in his jaw. "You can't just go around when you feel like it."

So much for it was "their" house. Cora took a calming breath, one that felt shaky. "I know. It's why I'm here talking to you about it."

"Are you fucking someone else?"

"What?" Cora actually spluttered the word. She hadn't known people did that in real life. Heat flamed her cheeks. "No, of, of course not."

He was staring at her, his eyes cold. It took everything in her to meet his look. Because, she told herself, she wasn't.

Not anymore.

And somehow that got her through his interrogative stare.

"Take all of your stuff, Cora. There is no way you're going to get the house in the divorce. You'll get nothing."

It didn't seem wise in that moment to say that she didn't want the house. She didn't want anything. She'd rather start fresh, start new. To sort out the money side of the mortgage and move on. Because mostly, all she could think about was Frazer's eyes, the green that followed her, and the words Cora wanted to say but wasn't sure of.

With a nod, Cora stood and fled the room and the man that she didn't recognise. Her fingers were shaking, and for the first time since all this had started, Cora wondered how she was supposed to keep working with her soon-to-be ex-husband.

And her ex-lover.

On her way out, she gave Tia a smile where she sat at her desk. It felt thin, like it stretched her cheeks. Tia just watched her, unblinking.

With a straightening of her spine, Cora went to see how Jack was doing.

The canteen smelt like fried food, and Frazer's stomach grumbled so loudly that the man in the line ahead of her turned around to stare at her with raised eyebrows. She just stared back at him blankly. When it grumbled again, he gave a snort, and she gave in with a wry grin.

Her tray ladened with everything fried from the menu, she scanned the room for somewhere to sit and wrinkled her nose at the sight in front of her. Every table looked full, the room flooding over with the sick, their visitors, and the hospital staff alike. If the rain would stop lashing down outside, she'd go find a cement wall to stare at that was at least in cleaner air than here. Clutching her tray closer, she spotted a free table at the back, near one of the doors that led out of the canteen.

She kicked herself into gear and made a beeline for the table, eyes focussed. Luck was on her side for once. She put the tray down with a clatter, a handful of chips already on its way to her mouth as she sunk into the terrible plastic chair.

Salt and grease covered her tastebuds in a wonderful explosion of calories and amazingness.

She shoved a few more into her mouth and chewed sloppily as she unwrapped her burger. It had probably been sitting there for hours, but at this point she didn't care. If people weren't sitting all around her, she'd give a happy wriggle. Food was bliss.

It was bliss because yes, she was starving and had been up all night. And also maybe because she was eating her feelings. But that was a perfectly normal thing to do. Every woman's magazine around agreed that everyone did it sometimes.

And Frazer had a lot of feelings.

But none that were probably healthy.

Though her plan could be considered healthy.

When her phone vibrated, she swiped a message open without paying much attention to it, a handful of chips on their trip to her mouth, followed by another one.

Cora was looking for her. To talk about Jack.

That just made Frazer want to completely separate herself from Cora.

It didn't matter if Frazer had feelings for her. Even if most of them were glazed with anger at the present time. It didn't matter that Cora had stared at her all through the birth of Jack's baby with a look that Frazer recognised from the night Cora had turned and ran. After what could have definitely been considered more than just mindless sex.

She punched the message closed. She would swing by Jack's room and make sure nothing was going on after lunch, but she wouldn't see Cora to do so.

Because whatever was going on between them was unhealthy. And it wasn't something that could continue. Even if Cora was getting a divorce, she was still entangled with her husband. Still straight, probably. As far as Frazer knew, anyway.

Frazer licked tomato sauce off her thumb and didn't even care that she looked completely unprofessional. Because she was being professional enough in her private life.

She was going to give up on Cora all together, even as a friend.

"Hey, Frazer."

Of course it was *her*. Frazer's head jolted up. "Cora. Hi."

This was going to be truly fucking difficult when they ran a programme together. And when Cora looked stunning and tired, and all Frazer wanted to do was ask how she was.

"You, uh, have something...here." Cora slid into the seat opposite Frazer and gestured to the general area of her own chin.

"Oh. Thanks." Well, that was embarrassing. A swipe with her napkin revealed a bright streak of sauce. Frazer was the epitome of smooth.

But Cora didn't seem to mind. She was staring at Frazer openly, a furrow between her eyebrows. Frazer had just wanted a break from that stare and that look she didn't understand. "Have you seen Jack today?"

Frazer put the last bite of her burger down on the tray, her appetite gone. Why couldn't Cora have left her alone? Had she seriously made a point of hunting her down here in the canteen? Just because she hadn't answered her text yet?

Granted, Frazer hadn't exactly answered any of the communications she'd received lately.

Why couldn't she have ignored the attraction she'd felt to Cora months ago and simply used the woman for her social work connections and got her programme off the ground, sans raunchy affair?

"I did. He seems okay. We can discharge him tomorrow."

"He just said he was looking forward to getting out of the hospital, so that's good. He's...fragile, for now. But I think he feels he did the right thing." Cora said, still staring at Frazer.

Trying to break that intense look, Frazer took a sip of her water, considering her words. "Well, you helped him a lot. And he'll have support over the next six months at least, as much of it as he'll need."

"First success of the programme."

Frazer nodded and stared at Cora, giving up on the hope that she would stop. The bustle of the canteen carried on around them, background noise to a look far too intense.

This was exactly what Frazer couldn't do anymore. She'd done her gross, very public work breakup years ago. She didn't need anything like that again.

And neither did Cora.

Cora had enough to deal with.

"Cora—"

"Frazer—"

They both gave a soft chuckle, and Frazer watched Cora bite her bottom lip, eyes still intent on Frazer's.

"I'm sorry for the other day, kissing you."

Frazer had known she would be. "It's okay."

"No, it isn't." Cora tilted her head, watching her. "It wasn't how I should have done it."

Those words, loaded with meaning, did not go with Frazer's plan. The plan in which they would move on, separately. Her heart sped up in her chest as that look in Cora's eyes started to make sense. The way she'd stared with concern when Frazer had been hit in the head, her fingers soft on Frazer's skin. The incredulous, oddly joyful look on Cora's face as Frazer had ranted at her to stop watching her.

The same look on her face now.

Not *how* Cora should have done it. Why couldn't she have just said she shouldn't have done it at all?

But not *how*.

This was a terrible idea, one that couldn't go anywhere good. Exhaustion settled over Frazer, layered and heavy.

Standing, Frazer looked down at Cora, who stared up at her, eyes widened with what looked like surprise.

"I have to go, Cora."

"Frazer—"

Frazer pursed her lips, swallowing back the tide of emotion that swelled in her throat. Never had her name left Cora's lips like that, tied to a note of pleading. Almost desperation. How ironic that Frazer was about to walk away from it after hoping to hear it. Even if that hope had been subconscious.

"Please don't." Frazer said.

When Frazer took a deliberate step back, Cora's arm darted out, her fingers wrapped around Frazer's hands and gripped them like a vice. They felt hot, burning with Cora's intention.

This was not the place for this and was exactly the type of thing Frazer wanted to avoid. They shouldn't be seen doing this. Because even if Cora was getting a divorce, it was too new. Alec couldn't know. Cora was still entangled.

It was all too much of a mess and not one that was good for either of them.

Cora stared up at her, and Frazer shook her head. She didn't trust herself or the words that she would say. There was a sting in the back of Frazer's eyes that she didn't expect.

And somehow, thankfully, Cora got that. Because ever so slowly, she let her hand fall from Frazer's, fingertips skimming Frazer's own.

Before she changed her mind, Frazer grabbed her tray and walked away, Cora's look piercing into her back. She dropped her food into a bin, her tray thumping on top of a pile of others. Frazer pushed her hands deep into her pockets and exited the way she had come.

When she saw Alec standing in the doorway, staring at her with a look she couldn't read but unfortunately could make guesses about, it felt for a minute like she couldn't breathe.

It took everything she had to force a smile onto her face. To grin at him. "Hey, Alec."

To keep her voice even and walk past him like she didn't want to study his face to figure out if he knew.

There wasn't anything to know anymore.

The key slipped into the lock with ease.

With Lisa's hand a comforting caress on the small of her back, Cora took a step inside.

The smell of the house washed over her: the heady wood scent that she only ever noticed if she'd been away from home for a few days, the scent of the detergent they used on their clothes. A stab of nostalgia, deep in her gut, took her by surprise, carved through her. All Cora wanted to do was curl into a ball on her new couch next to Lisa and cry.

Since Frazer had walked away that afternoon, Cora had been in a daze. Everything all day had felt sliced open, raw. The air grated against her exposed nerve endings. Patients skimmed over the edges of her consciousness, when she should have been focussed on them.

Something had passed between Cora and Frazer over that table, barely with any words, but Cora had seen the look on Frazer's face, the glittering in her eyes, and realised: it was over. Frazer had walked away, and this time it was with both of them understanding the other, without the need to say it.

It had left her feeling as if she'd been flayed raw, with everything settling against her to scrape at what was left. Maybe, in a few days, Cora would be able to approach Frazer to ask why, to ask what, to ask when. But not yet; not when everything felt like it did.

Cora needed a break, even if that just meant avoiding confrontation for a while.

A break would be amazing.

In the meantime, her old life was clouding around her, and Cora gathered what strength she had left to walk down the hallway. Her eyes didn't scan the photographs on the wall, and she tried to ignore the simple familiarity, a comfort despite everything, of walking down a hallway she knew, the floor beneath her feet ghosted with thousands of her past steps. Dull, early-evening light filled the kitchen when she and Lisa walked in. It was not so dark that they needed to switch on the lights, yet not so bright that it avoided creating the hush that gloom often did.

Cora placed down the large cardboard box she'd been carrying, a huge suitcase next to it. Lisa immediately took her own case down into the living room. Before leaving, they'd decided Lisa would pack the books while Cora collected other things.

It didn't take long, which was both a relief and a surprise.

Kitchen items, gifts specifically for Cora, ended up in the box—items from her grandparents, some photo albums, her mug collection.

All of it.

"I'm just going to get the last of my clothes."

Lisa straightened. "Want me to come?"

With a shake of her head, Cora said, "No, it's okay. It won't take long. Just the clothes, more bathroom stuff, and the painting in the guest bedroom."

She already had half of the books piled in. "Okay." She pulled another book off the shelf, opening it to check for Cora's name before adding it to the case.

Cora had always loved writing her name in her books, a stamp of ownership, something that was hers. All those words, a map of a story, and she got to claim it. So many words, all at her fingertips. She used to think it was silly, claiming ownership like that. But now, her eyes trained on Lisa packing them away, Cora saw it for what it was.

"Thanks for coming." Cora's voice was quieter than she had intended, but she meant it. She hadn't been sure if Alec would try to do something, to ignore her wish for him to not be in the house. Knowing Lisa would be there had made coming that much easier. Especially after the day Cora had had.

Lisa didn't even turn around, but she didn't need to.

"Anytime, sunshine."

Cora dragged the suitcase upstairs. It was so strange to think that this could be the last time she would be inside here.

First, she got the painting from the spare room, a sweeping seascape from Rottnest Island, the one she'd bought from a man selling his artwork on the street, her eyes roaming his creations until they'd settled on this one. After leaving it resting against the banister next to the stairs, she paused outside the bedroom door. With the suitcase handle biting into her hand, she pushed the door open and stepped inside.

The second she did, she froze, grip tightening even further as sweat broke out over her body.

Alec sat on the edge of the bed, waiting for her. "Hi, Cora."

Cora's mouth was suddenly dry. Her tongue traced her bottom lip, as if that could help. "Alec. Why are you here?"

Why couldn't he have done this one thing?

"We need to talk." His voice was oddly calm, in a way that made her feel anything but.

"We have talked." Cora really didn't have this in her. Not after the day, not after everything. What more was there to say?

"I think I get it now."

That comment intrigued her. He understood her motives for the divorce now? Was he going to apologise, to start a dialogue? Did he want to talk it out, to get some closure?

When she didn't say anything, and just watched him with a careful eye, he continued. "You're fucking Frazer from Midwifery."

Everything stopped around her. His expression hadn't changed. He simply watched her, impassive. There was a ringing in her ears, the feeling of the world tilting on its axis.

She cleared her throat. "Why would you think that?"

"Don't patronise me. It's not what I think, it's what I know. I saw you in the canteen." His eyes hardened ever so slightly.

The canteen? Cora cast her mind back, thinking as fast as she could. Nothing had really happened for him to see. Cora had been hyperaware of where they were, of the fact that they could be noticed.

Despite the panic crawling up her throat as Alec watched her, studied her for a reaction, something occurred to Cora. What kind of relationship would that have been for Frazer? The hidden type, the type with a woman trying to crawl out of an unhappy marriage? Was that why she'd walked away?

But nothing had happened in the canteen. All Cora had done was grab Frazer's hands as she'd gone to leave. That was all. It was nothing, nothing compared to what he could have seen other times, in other rooms of that building.

"What do you mean, you saw me in the canteen?" She asked. All she could hope was that her expression showed confusion, not rising stress.

When his eyes narrowed, Cora knew she'd failed. "Don't play stupid, Cora. You're not smart enough to fake it." Cora said nothing to that, so he carried on. "It was all over your face." Now his expression was twisting, something like disgust painted over his countenance. "I could see it."

Could Cora deny it? Should she? "It was nothing, Alec."

Lies wrapped you up in more lies. And it had never been in Cora's nature. She couldn't look him in the eye now and completely deny it.

His bark of laughter was harsh, jarring. "What, do you think you're gay now?"

"It wasn't like that, Alec. It was over before it began." Her heart was thumping in her chest, the force of it making her dizzy. She couldn't tell him the whole truth, she just couldn't.

He watched her for a moment, his brow furrowed. "So come back to me, then."

What? How could he ask her that? Unless, he thought that the divorce had been about that. "Alec..."

"You... You were confused, I get it. But you just said it was over before it began. So come back."

"I'm not leaving because of that, Alec."

There it was again, that hardening of his features. "It has to be for that."

"I've told you, it's not because of that. I filed for the divorce because *I* wasn't happy. For a long time."

"We went to therapy."

"And nothing changed!" In spite of herself, anger burst out into her voice.

"You can't blame me for this, not when you're making those kinds of eyes at a woman like a damn lesbian."

Cora needed to leave. She needed out of this. There was no way this could go anywhere good. A deep breath was no help. "I'm not blaming anyone. But it's over, Alec."

"It's only just started, Cora. You think I'll let the two of you carry on at work? You think you can just divorce me and start an affair with some lesbian and there won't be repercussions? For her either?"

God. He was going to threaten her job and Frazer's. What about the programme? Cora bit the bullet, knew what to say, twisted the truth even tighter. "There's nothing going on with Frazer." There wasn't, not anymore. And there was no way she'd let her stupid decisions ruin Frazer's career. "Nothing."

"But you want there to be."

The bitterness that clouded his voice was so strong, Cora could almost taste it in the air. She shook her head, but knew her denial was weak, the words catching in her throat. There was no way she could force a lie of that magnitude out of her mouth. Let him think it had been a crush on her part, because the hint at threatening Frazer's and her job was enough to make her hold the secret of the affair close, hidden from his sight.

"Get out, Cora. This isn't your house anymore."

She'd known that for a while, and here was Alec, finally catching up.

"I need my things."

His eyes flashed. His lips pressed into a thin line. "You have ten minutes. I'll be downstairs. Lisa needs to get out too."

When he walked out, it was with his head held high. She sidestepped to let him pass her and walk through the doorway. Away.

But he paused next to her, their shoulders almost brushing.

Cora had to physically stop herself from stepping away from the heat of him, the touch of him. She could hear his breathing, laboured, like it always was when he was angry.

"You *will* regret this, Cora." The hissing anger there left no room for doubt that this time, he was using those words as a threat. Yet still, he didn't raise his voice. "Your family will be ashamed. *You* will be ashamed. You'll end up sad and alone. What do you think you can really be without me?"

For a second, he lingered, watching her face, she knew, for any kind of reaction. She gave him nothing.

Finally, he walked away.

Trembling, Cora grabbed the last of her clothes. She took photos in frames that were hers, that were of her family, her friends. She raided their bathroom, cramming everything in and half sitting on the case to zip it closed. It thumped on each step as she dragged it down the stairs. A wide-eyed Lisa was waiting in the hallway. She saw Alec only from the corner of her eye in the kitchen.

"Got everything?" Lisa asked.

Cora nodded.

"Are you sure? Take a minute." Lisa squeezed her arm, and Cora resisted the urge to melt into the touch, to any gesture of comfort.

"I have everything I need."

And without a word from Alec, or to him, they walked out of the house.

That night, lit only by the glow of her aquarium, Frazer researched.

She brought up every government page she could think of related to health. She checked the paperwork for the programme budget the hospital had provided her to see if the grant that funded them was hospital based, privately based, or from the government.

Over the course of hours, she sent out countless e-mails and applications. It was easy to put into motion something she'd always considered doing but had wanted to start with the safety net of her full-time job underneath her. Her last breakup had left her a mess on the floor, and the stability of her job had been a big part of what had dragged her off it.

And her aquarium.

At that thought, Frazer lifted her glass of Coke towards her fish and drank to them. They really were gorgeous. And Frazer really needed to clean the tank. Not her favourite job.

This time, she wasn't going to lose herself in it. Not that it had been a breakup. They hadn't even been together, after all. But Frazer was going to do something good with this weird energy she had swirling around in her.

Her phone vibrated on the couch next to her knee, and Frazer grabbed for it, holding it up to her ear. "Hey, Jem."

"Frazer! What's the emergency?"

Taking a deep breath, Frazer said the words she'd barely let herself think. "I'm quitting my job."

CHAPTER NINETEEN

Cora kept a careful eye out for Frazer the next day at work, but to no avail. Cora didn't see her anywhere at all.

Part of the reason Cora wanted to find her was that she felt almost brave enough now to ask the why, the how, to find out why they couldn't even be friends. The questions itched in her throat and she had nowhere to point them. She wanted to make sure what she had really seen on Frazer's face.

A ping from her e-mail late in the morning perked her up, but her shoulders sagged as she read it. Frazer simply said not to worry, as she was going to cover the programme details for a while. Apparently, Cora only needed to focus on any mentoring duties.

Despite this, she still looked out for Frazer anyway. She also really wanted to talk to her about the vague threats Alec had made and make sure he hadn't done anything to Frazer. She wanted to reassure her that Cora was fairly certain he thought the entire thing a one-sided crush.

Yet Frazer wasn't anywhere.

So Cora sent a reply to the e-mail, brimming with questions, but it went unanswered.

Later that afternoon, Cora had slipped into Jack's room. He was due to be discharged that afternoon—there had been no complications. When she entered, he was back in his street clothes, flinching as he shifted feet, zipping up his bag that rested on the bed.

"Hi." she said.

"Hey." He managed a smile at her, though he was pale. It didn't quite reach his eyes.

"How are you feeling?"

"Like I was hit by a truck and repeatedly run over."

Cora's lip quirked. "So, great, then?"

"Fantastic." This time, the smile did reach his eyes.

"I'm sure Frazer already sorted it out for you, but do you need help getting anywhere?" She hated herself for her not-so-subtle question about whether or not he'd seen Frazer.

"Nah, my uncle is picking me up. He wants me to stay with him for a few days until I feel better."

Someone wanting to look after Jack forced an inexplicable lump into Cora's throat. It wasn't everything, and it might not be enough, but it really was something. "That's great. Did you take him up on his offer?"

His shaggy hair, in need of a cut, swayed as he nodded. "I did. There's an Xbox."

Cora laughed—one of the first things he'd told her was that he wished he'd thought to grab his Xbox when he left his parents' house. "Well, an Xbox. There's not much more you can ask for."

This time, the grin lit up his face. "Exactly."

"Are we still on for next Wednesday?"

"Definitely. Big life decisions to discuss and all that." His hands sat heavily against the bed.

"Or, you know, we can just catch up and save the big decisions for a few weeks or however long away. You've already made one of those this week."

"Would we call giving a baby up for adoption a big decision?"

Cora shrugged. "Oh, fine, a small one."

He fiddled with the zip a minute, and Cora couldn't resist the urge to repeat things she already knew he was aware of. "Jack." She waited patiently until his eyes met hers. "You still have us around. It's the point. Not just to kick your ass into employment and study. Call me if you need to talk before we have dates set up, okay?"

His shoulders relaxed. For a moment, his teeth worried at his lip before he asked, "Even though I didn't keep the baby?"

"Like we've always said, this programme focusses on the parents. We want to make sure *you* have support after all this."

Eyes back on his bag, his voice was small as he said, "Okay."

Cora walked towards him and wrapped him up in a hug. For a moment, his entire body froze, before he melted against her. The grip of his fingers was tight against her back, and she didn't let go until he did.

"Thanks, Cora." He held her gaze. "Like I told Frazer this morning, I really don't know where I'd be without this programme..."

So Frazer had seen him. Why hadn't Cora been able to find her all day, then? "And you'll never need to know," she said.

Cora left him then, when his uncle had messaged him to say he was on his way.

The next day, Cora sent Frazer another e-mail with more questions, pretending she wanted clarification about the programme.

No answer.

The third day, she did the same.

Nothing.

And now, four days on, and Cora still hadn't seen Frazer anywhere. Nor had she been able to bring herself to ask about her.

Finally, though, she snapped and found herself edging towards Alec's office, heading upstairs and trying not to let her heart beat out of her chest. The thought of seeing him made her feel nauseous, but Cora couldn't think of anyone else to ask. Unless she could run into Tia, but even the thought of seeing Tia after everything made her hands go clammy.

But with everything going on in her life, Cora missed Frazer, and somehow, that burnt harsher than anything else. She had never been like this before, and she didn't know how to deal with it.

Trying to look inconspicuous, and probably not managing it, Cora looked around the corner and saw the object of her search. Tia sat at her desk, tapping away at her computer with a bored expression. With all of her powers of avoidance, Cora had managed not to run into Tia too much since the day Tia had walked in on her and Frazer. Just the memory of it had heat crawling up her cheeks. It would have been less embarrassing to get caught by her mother.

She choked back a horrified noise. No. That definitely wasn't true; if that had happened, Cora would have crawled into a ball and died right there. When Tia had walked in, it had simply *felt* like she'd died the death of a thousand humiliations.

Finally, Tia looked up and caught Cora staring at her. She raised her eyebrows, probably wondering why just Cora's head was floating around the corner, staring at her strangely with bright red cheeks. "He's not here."

With a sigh of relief, Cora walked around the corner and stood in front of the desk. It felt a little like she was standing in front of the principal at school. She had to resist the urge to fidget. "Hi, Tia."

"Hey, hun."

Tia was softer than she had been the last time Cora had talked to her, softer even than when she'd told Cora it was okay to not be okay. Tension left Cora's body at the smile on Tia's face.

"How are you?" Cora asked.

"I'm good. It's a busy time of year. We have to organise a lot of budget reports and other boring things."

"Sounds thrilling."

"Oh, it's so exciting I barely want to leave at night."

That made Cora chuckle. "At least it'll settle down in a week."

Tia gave a hum of agreement. Her eyes searched Cora, and it felt as if the woman was seeing straight through her. "Can't find Frazer?"

Apparently Tia really could.

Cora gave a nod that left shame in her stomach. But she needed to know.

"Honey, didn't you know—Frazer quit."

Suddenly, all the air had left the room. She swore the colour was draining from her cheeks. "But she'd—she'd have to give two weeks' notice, at least?"

"She did."

Cora turned around at the sound of Alec's voice, seeing the slightest widening of Tia's eyes in the single moment before. At the sight of him, Cora tried to offer a professional greeting. "A—afternoon, Alec."

He was dressed as impeccably, as always, and Cora wondered how he held himself together so well. Without a glance at her, he walked past them and into his office. All he said was, "Come in."

And she followed, because Cora really didn't know what else to do. Cora looked at Tia, who gave her what Cora guessed was supposed to be an encouraging smile. She returned it weakly.

Frazer had quit? Had left?

Cora really didn't want to talk to Alec. After their confrontation in the house the other day, she just wanted to stay as far away from him as life would allow. That day, she'd gone home exhausted and had ended up exactly where she had wanted to be: sobbing on her couch against Lisa, unable to really say what had caused the tears to start.

She'd really started to understand why Frazer had walked away. How could they build anything on such a soggy foundation? But Cora had still wanted to get some closure about it all, to talk it out, calmly. To warn Frazer about Alec.

But now Frazer had quit. What about the programme?

Not wanting to give him the upper hand for once, Cora slid into the seat opposite his desk before he'd even gone around it. No invitation, no more waiting for him to indicate what to do.

Habits were hard to break, but she was working on opening cracks in the hopes that one day they'd shatter with the smallest of force.

His only reaction was to raise his eyebrows ever so slightly before he sat down. And to stare at her.

It took everything not to shift uncomfortably under his gaze. She squared her shoulders and looked right back. "Frazer quit?"

"Why do you care? Because of some strange crush?" He cocked his head, waiting her out for some kind of tell.

"I care about the programme."

"Ah. Of course." The tone of his voice made it clear he in no way believed her. "Well, she's taking it with her."

That answered some questions and brought up more. How could she do that? What about the funding? Where would Frazer take it? But there was no way she'd ask Alec all of that. He wanted her to, though, Cora could tell. He liked that he knew something she didn't, that he held information that she wanted. So instead, Cora went down a different route. "How could she leave without two weeks' notice?"

His lips quirked, in something that only faintly resembled pleasant. "She gave them. After she e-mailed her resignation to HR, I called her in here and then waived the two weeks. I told her to leave that day, as is my right."

So Alec had used what power he could. Charming.

It was amazing how much of him she now saw clearly. Parts of it had been seeping into her point of view for years, things that made her uncomfortable, things she excused because she was wrapped up in her image of him, the one he'd presented to her when they first met and that she'd clung to like mist.

Now, removed from him for even a short time, she didn't see anything she liked anymore.

"Okay. I'll expect an e-mail from her about the programme, then." Cora stood to go. There wasn't any need to mention she had already received one. "Thank you."

"Cora."

She paused and turned. "Yes?"

"You should be careful about your reputation."

She felt herself go cold. "Excuse me?"

"A security guard I spoke with could just *swear* he saw you kissing someone who fits Frazer's complexion completely."

Cora felt her expression shifting into shock that would give her away completely, and she mentally grasped at herself, trying her best to shift her features into a picture of calm. She said nothing.

"Months ago, actually." His voice was calm, almost jovial. His eyes were hard, cold.

Had he always been such a contradiction?

Still, Cora said nothing. Silence had often felt safer.

"So be careful of that reputation, that kind of thing in a professional environment...when married."

His eyes glinted, with what, she didn't know. She hadn't known eyes could really do that, the intent behind words slicing through a look like that.

With her heart racing in her chest, Cora walked out. She tried to ignore Tia's sympathetic look, who, with the office door wide open, had heard everything.

Would Alec call her family?

Would he get the word out all around the hospital?

Had she really thought she could stay and work here?

"Have you even gotten out of your pyjamas once, Frazer?"

Looking down at her beloved fish print pyjamas, Frazer shrugged at Jemma, who was standing in Frazer's doorway with a look that bordered on judgemental. "I take them off when I shower."

Jemma's face wrinkled up. "That's disgusting."

"I also washed them and wore a different pair one day."

Jemma's face wrinkled even more. Green eyes, the same as Frazer's, down to the freckle in them, bore down on her. "Have you left the house in five days?"

"Yes!"

"Not including the day you went to work to hand in your resignation?"

Frazer pursed her lips. She had nothing.

Her triumphant chortle carried Jemma past Frazer and into the house. As she usually did, she flopped down on the couch as if she lived there. It was infuriating.

"Please, make yourself at home." Frazer closed the door and stood over her sister with her arms on her hips.

"Already done, big sis. Got any beer?"

Frazer huffed, then went and got her one, taking a juice for herself.

Once they were both settled, Jemma looked at her seriously. "Do I need to be worried?"

"Jemma, you've known me your entire life. You know I'm useless at sitting around doing nothing."

"But that's what you've been doing."

"I've been working from home."

"You don't have a job."

"Don't I?"

Pushing herself up on her elbows, beer hanging precariously from one hand, Jemma stared at her. "You do?"

"I do."

"Don't be a butthead. That's your cue to start explaining."

"I know." Irritating Jemma wasn't just fun, it was revenge for all the sleepless nights when she had been a tiny ball of rage her parents insisted on bringing home from the hospital.

"Frazer." The whine was strong in this one.

"I'm opening a clinic."

Jemma sat up completely. "For real? What type?"

"That's the exciting part—two types, actually."

The expectant look on Jemma's face meant she was waiting for Frazer to elaborate.

She didn't.

"Damn it Frazer!"

Frazer chuckled. "Fine. Half the time I'll be a child health nurse, after a six-month online course, and a private midwife. The other half of the time, the programme will operate out of the same location."

Joyous disbelief was starting to paint Jemma's face. "Seriously? But, wasn't the programme based in your hospital?"

"Well, that's what I've been checking and sorting out. Turns out the grant the hospital chose to direct to me is government based, which means the hospital doesn't control it. That money comes to me. And I applied to a couple more grants that exist for people setting things up independently for the community. I had a call yesterday from someone saying my application looked really promising and that they loved the idea."

Jemma looked ready to burst with excitement. "Really?"

"Really." Frazer's cheeks were hurting from trying to repress her grin. Moments like this were when she really loved her sister.

"Well, why didn't you do that before?"

"I liked my job at the hospital. Plus, it was security. I always had the vague idea I'd take it to a bigger scale one day, but I wanted the safety of a full-time job. Plus, the resources there made it a lot easier."

"What's a child health nurse do, anyway?"

"They work with kids in the community, from birth to four years. The idea is I'll be tying all of this with the programme. Some patients will be normal paying patients, subject to the private billing rates, while the others will be paid for by the programme. With working as a private midwife, I can ensure some extra money in my pockets."

"So you haven't just been sitting in your pyjamas staring at your fish?"

"Really not." Frazer loved proving her sister wrong, although for once, Jemma didn't sound all that disappointed. "There's so much paperwork to clear, licenses to apply for. I have to prove my qualifications. Now that I know I have enough money, I've been looking at locations."

Cross-legged on the couch, Jemma shook her head in disbelief. "You're awesome, you know that?"

Fraser didn't quite feel that way. "Why? I quit my job after having an affair and realising working with both the woman and the husband was a stupid idea."

With a theatrical wince, Jemma said, "Okay, that wasn't so awesome. But this whole programme thing is going to be."

"I hope so."

It was actually mildly terrifying. Sink or swim. And Frazer had been doing a lot of sinking lately.

"Frazer?"

"Yeah?"

"How do you know that it couldn't go anywhere with Cora? I mean, you know she's interested now... She told you as much. And you walked away?"

Flicking her nails against her glass, Frazer sighed. "How could we actually have a relationship—in that hospital, working with her husband?"

"She's getting divorced."

"Yeah, and they've been separated for all of a couple of weeks... It wouldn't be healthy."

Jemma was watching her carefully. Too carefully. "Okay. I get it."

The words had been prepared on her tongue to defend herself, and Frazer had to swallow them back. "Really?"

"Yup, really. You're completely right. She's in a mess right now, you're in a bit of one, and what *could* end up great will probably only end terribly." Jemma rolled her eyes. "What can I say? You're *way* more mature than me."

Frazer snorted. "Yeah, my decisions have been *so* mature lately."

"Shut up, big sis. Everyone makes mistakes."

Frazer's eyes trained onto her aquarium, as they always did when she was thinking. "I know."

"Good."

The aquarium was so clean it was almost as if the glass was non-existent. An entire world she could control, could keep safe. Life never really changed in that little world.

"Are you excited?" Jemma asked her.

That question was easy to answer. "I really am."

Cora had never worked anywhere but the hospital.

Of course, she had a typical teenage job history: babysitting and some retail. But as soon as she'd finished university, Cora had taken the Social Work position at the hospital and had stayed there. Now, in her new living room, surrounded by her books and with a new soft rug under her feet, the cursor of her laptop was staring at her.

Writing her resignation had been easy, far easier than she had imagined. It was staying that would be a nightmare, to continue working in close proximity to Alec. Why do that to herself? With Frazer gone, Cora had no reason to stay. Maybe if she'd had more friends, a circle of people she was close to, she would have considered staying. But there wasn't one person she would truly miss there, no support network. This was something, she now knew, that had been Alec's doing. He'd always kept her close, as if scared she'd disappear, instead of trusting her to stay. It had been smothering—and isolating.

She liked her job, but there were so many different jobs out there, finding a new one wouldn't be difficult. Until she did, she had some savings. Luckily, she'd always kept a separate bank account—Alec had convinced her it was better for tax purposes.

Maybe she would go on a holiday abroad. See something new, get a new experience to enhance her life. She could go alone, be alone for the first time since far too long. Or she could do something she had always wanted to do. She'd overheard a conversation just the other day, and the idea had been prickling in the back of her mind since then.

The idea should have terrified her, but instead, Cora felt excitement bubbling under her skin. With a smile that was almost guilty, Cora sent the resignation to HR and bounced her leg up and down, staring around the spartan room.

Opportunity spread out before her, and Cora was almost breathless with it.

Since leaving Alec's office that afternoon, this plan had taken form in her head. Using the hospital's intranet, Cora found the number she needed. It was only a moment's work to tap it into her mobile and bring the phone up to her ear. "Hey, Simon, it's Cora, from Social Work. Sorry to call you after-hours."

"Uh, hey, Cora, no worries. Everything okay?" He obviously had no idea why someone from a different department would call him at eight o'clock. Cora had never exactly spoken much to him either.

"Yeah, everything's great. Look, I remember you talking the other day about that volunteer programme you help with and how someone had to go home due to an emergency. You're down a person for the final six weeks?"

"Yeah." His voice streaked with obvious surprise. "I was going to go cover it myself, but there was no way to organise the leave in time."

"Do they need someone else?" she asked.

"Well, the orphanages there always do. Why, do you have someone in mind?"

"Actually, I think I do."

"They'd have to have all their clearances, immunisations and such, done."

"That won't be a problem."

"Great, who is it?"

Frazer,

Sorry to inform you that I will be unable to assist with the programme for the next month, possibly more. I have arranged to carry on as mentor for Jack through Skype, and he knows he can contact you for further immediate support. The other client I have passed on to one of the other mentors. I supervised an introduction with them yesterday. It's Jill from A and E. They hit it off and will be fine, I'm sure. However, the client knows she can also contact me through Skype if she ever needs to.

As for the social work side of things, as per your e-mail, I assume my services are unneeded there as you only requested I continue as mentor for my current clients.

If you have any queries, please e-mail me, which I will be sure to answer, unlike you have done with the several I have sent you.

All the best,

Cora.

Frazer grimaced and read the e-mail again. And then a third time. She made a mental note to check in with Jack and the other client as soon as possible.

She also tried to ignore the very obvious dig.

It had just been...easier not to reply.

The urge to ask Cora why she couldn't be a mentor for the next month overtook her, but she made herself shove her phone into her pocket instead. It was none of her business.

And really, what did Frazer expect? She'd cut Cora out of the programme. It hadn't been intentional, even if it had been a little unfair, but she had needed to make sure she could do what she had been thinking of doing.

Okay, it had been more than a little unfair. It had been completely unfair. But talking to Cora just clouded her mind. It clouded everything about Frazer's judgement.

It was why she'd walked away.

"So, what do you think?" Rob's hands were casually in his pockets as he watched Frazer take everything in.

He stood in the middle of the open area, in what had been a reception area. The space was large and full of light. It was slightly out of the centre of town, making it affordable, and close to both a bus and train line so it was fairly easy to get to. There were six rooms that went off from what could be made into a waiting area. If Frazer got desperate, she could rent one room out to someone who worked privately.

Rob cocked his head at her, waiting for an answer. Frazer bounced on her toes.

"I love it."

CHAPTER TWENTY

The sun was setting through the tiny plane window, and Cora watched it with a kind of awe. Sunsets always amazed her, even after these last five weeks, when she'd seen many of them—incredible ones that stretched over the horizon, painting the coast an orange that shouldn't have been natural. The ocean would be so tinted with the colour that it was difficult to tell where sky ended and water began. Some of the kids from the orphanage would watch the sunsets with her, and she'd quiz them on what colours they saw in English.

In turn, they taught her the words in Indonesian. *Mereh* for red. *Jeruk* for orange. *Biru* for blue, her favourite word, for how it felt when it left her lips. Her favourite sound, though, had been their laughter whenever she pronounced everything terribly.

It had taken Cora a week to organise everything she needed to leave, but it had been more than worth it. Alec had pulled the same thing with her that he had with Frazer and had refused her two weeks' notice. He hadn't seemed to care about what he would be putting the respective departments through to find replacements as he had informed her of this with clear relish.

Little did he know, she'd been hoping he would do exactly that. The excitement of what was ahead of her had been growing even as he had sat at his desk and exerted his final bit of power over her. Her enthusiasm had been hard to contain. And suddenly, she'd been on a plane flying to Indonesia.

She missed nothing about home, really. Everything in Indonesia had been busy, hectic. There was always something to do in the orphanage, even if all that needed doing was playing with kids that clung to any adult near them. She organised aid, distributed it among the four sister orphanages where it was needed. She liaised with people who distributed financial grants and organised the people who came in carrying bags and bags of donated items that the orphanages could never have enough of. They always needed more formula, more nappies.

It had kept Cora deliciously occupied and focussed, and she'd felt the band that had been strapped around her chest for years loosen. She could breathe, she could laugh. Guilt played no part in anything she did, and Cora realised she had found something she wanted to do time and time again. Something that was hers to enjoy, to make a difference, to raise awareness. The programme she had started with Frazer, without her realising it, had opened up in her that need to do more. That need she'd once had but lost.

Having something she was doing for her own happiness made Cora feel as if she'd grown a few inches.

She hadn't walked as if on eggshells for so long now.

The familiar dip of the plane descending barely registered. Her eyes were still on the sun now almost completely gone, to be watched by someone else.

Even though she'd barely missed anything from home, she had missed Frazer.

Cora had Lisa, a friend she was so grateful to have. Yet always, like an undercurrent below everything, she missed Frazer. It had only been a matter of months, but the shock of her had resonated through everything Cora had thought she'd known about herself.

Yet there'd been nothing from Frazer, no e-mail, no anything. So Cora didn't try to contact her, trying to respect what Frazer clearly wanted.

And all of that was okay, because Cora had realised that she was very much okay, comfortable in her own skin, and living her own life.

There was a smile on her lips as the wheels touched the tarmac with a jolt.

"Jemma, I don't have time for this."

"Frazer?"

But it was Tia's voice on the line, and Frazer winced. She really needed to look at her caller ID before answering. "Tia! I'm so sorry. I thought it was my sister."

The chuckle down the line warmed her even more. "I figured as much. How is your delightful younger twin?"

"We're nothing alike."

"Right. And I'm not fabulous, nor the best secretary anyone could ever hope for."

Grinning, Frazer answered, "Well, now you've made it impossible for me to argue that." She sat in her parked car, not wanting to get out until she was off the phone. The weather might be warming up, but her car was still comfy.

"Exactly."

"Can I help, Oh Modest One?"

"Yes, you can. I've found you a social worker."

The words caused a clench in Frazer's stomach. She had to remind herself that this was a good thing—they needed a social worker. The first one that Frazer had found had left after the first week of the clinic's opening, when he was offered a job at a hospital that guaranteed better hours for almost double pay.

It hadn't been long after that she'd found out the man had taken Cora's old position at their old hospital. Frazer couldn't even blame him. She had, however, been left with the unsettling feeling that Alec knew *something* about her situation. It was the same feeling she'd had when he'd called her to his office purely to tell her to vacate the premises immediately.

Another reason Frazer was oh so happy she'd left. And that she'd walked away from Cora—it could never have worked under those circumstances.

Though not long passed before she began to wonder where Cora had gone and what she was doing. Tia had told her that Cora had quit. But even she didn't know where she was. What Cora was doing.

Thankfully, the new business kept Frazer distracted. Thankfully, Tia had also come on board as her receptionist. Frazer soon realised that she'd be lost without the woman.

"That's, uh, great. I was starting to get desperate." Frazer said, noticing that she'd been quiet on her end for far too long.

"I have it on the best authority that this one is good. Probably the best for this position."

"Wow. That's high praise coming from you." Frazer couldn't let a conversation with Tia go by without at least one ribbing.

"Yes, well, then you know it's true. She can meet for an interview tomorrow."

"So fast? Great. What time and where?"

"Café on the corner of Banksia and West at three o'clock."

If they could get a social worker, that meant they would be fully staffed. Frazer had considered not using one, but after having Cora on from the beginning, she'd realised how invaluable her knowledge of the workings of the government, her connections, and her ability with people had been. If the programme was going to do what Frazer wanted, she needed one.

And maybe she'd left it so long because, in reality, Frazer felt like the position belonged to someone else. Which was Frazer's fault, since she'd iced Cora out.

But it really was time to let go of that.

"Great, thanks, Tia. I'll see you tomorrow at nine."

"It's your turn for the coffee."

"As if I'd forget."

Frazer ended the call and then jumped as it started vibrating immediately. This time, a quick glance at the screen cued her to the appropriate response.

"Jemma, I really don't have time for this."

"Oh really? And what are you doing?"

That caught Frazer off guard. She looked up at the McDonald's she'd been about to enter. "Uh—"

"You're about to go to Hungry Jack's and ruin everything you did during your swim."

Frazer jutted her chin out. "Nope!"

"McDonald's?" Her silence prompted a snort from Jemma. "You are so, so predictable."

"I earnt it."

"Yes you did, big sister. *But* Meg and I are at that Japanese place you love, and we ran into Andy and Rob, who I still swear are married, even if Rob has a boyfriend—who's glaring at me as I say this. Anyway, they said they've been trying to get you all day, so we voted, and you have to come join us for dinner."

Looking longingly at the McDonald's, the smell of grease and fat already permeating her car, Frazer considered sushi. And noodles.

And her friends. Friends she actually hadn't been blowing off, but whom she had genuinely not had time to answer today. What with opening the doors to her private midwifery practice, and her online course, then starting another training week for new mentors—not to mention keeping up ongoing training for current mentors and finding new clients, Frazer's life had been dominated by work. And she loved it.

It would take a long time for it all to come together, but it would. And that was amazing.

"I'm on my way."

The restaurant was bustling, but it was easy enough to spot the table filled with the five people she was looking for. Mostly because they all caught sight of her and waved madly.

Their idiocy amused her today, she decided.

She made her way over and worked her way around the table for one-armed hugs. Meg and Jemma's shoulders got extra tight ones.

Meg had grown on her. Her job had been on thin ice since the university had discovered she was dating a student. However, Meg and Jemma's plan to keep it all under wraps until Jemma wasn't in Meg's class had worked. As Meg wasn't technically Jemma's teacher anymore, it was just frowned upon. Well, Meg had described it as more like *glared* upon.

"Hi! I'm sorry. I swear I wasn't ignoring you. I really was busy."

Andy poked Frazer in the side as Frazer sat down next to her. "Sure."

"It's true. Promise." Frazer slashed her hand in a cross over her chest. "Cross my heart and all that."

"Well!" Rob clapped his hands together almost gleefully before he casually dropped his arm over his partner Daniel's chair. "Now that Frazer is here, shall you do the honours?" he asked him.

Always a little on the quiet side compared to the rest of their loud group, Daniel gave a little shrug, the pink in his cheeks obvious even against his dark skin. When he'd won a West Australian Indigenous Art award a few years ago, he'd been the same shade of embarrassment. He hated being the centre of attention.

Reaching a hand across the table for the bottle of champagne, he held it up, a grin stretching across his face. "We're, uh, getting married."

Andy squealed, Frazer clapped a hand over her mouth, and Jemma applauded. Meg, having only just met them not long ago, said a happy, "Congrats!"

It took a few minutes for Jemma, Andy, and Frazer to stop hugging them both and sit back down. And then the questions started flowing.

"How?" Frazer asked.

"When?" Jemma squealed.

"Who asked who?" Andy yelled over all of them.

Rob looked happier than Frazer had ever seen him. The two of them were such opposites. Even their jobs as artist and as "finance something"—Frazer really did have to learn what Rob actually *did*—showed that. But they worked.

"Uh, Daniel asked me," Rob said. "When is next year. And as for Frazer, ever the hardest questioner," Rob winked at her, "the how is we're getting married in Ireland. You are, of course, all invited."

"And," Daniel spoke up, "When Australia gets its shit together, you're obviously all expected to come to the wedding we'll have here. So, you know, if Ireland is too far, or too expensive, there'll be that option."

"Screw that!" Andy was practically glowing. "Who knows when that'll happen. I'm coming to Ireland!"

"Same." Frazer wouldn't miss that for anything. Plus, she had only been overseas the once. What better reason to force herself onto a plane again?

Jemma turned to Meg, who looked mildly overwhelmed. "Too soon for us to make an arrangement a year in advance?"

Meg shrugged. "Not at all. I've never been to Ireland, I'd go without you if I had to."

"Well," Rob said, "If you guys broke up, we'd probably invite you over Jemma anyway."

He ducked the balled-up napkin Jemma sent his way.

The glasses of champagne all soon went up after that, meeting in the middle accompanied by a lot of raucous laughter.

It had been amazing to sleep in her own bed again. Because Cora hadn't realised that she'd not only missed Frazer but also her own mattress. It was as if her brain had refused to acknowledge the loss because maybe she would have left Indonesia after two days of that uncomfortable, lumpy bunk.

And she'd barely gotten to use her bed before she'd left. Everything in her house was new. Nevertheless, Cora had really, really missed it.

When she woke up the morning after her arrival, it was to a voicemail from Tia.

Still free for coffee? Great you're back.

Strangely, Cora and Tia had exchanged a few e-mails while she'd been away. It had felt nice, as if someone motherly was checking up on her. Her own mother was still not speaking to her after Cora had told her about the divorce, then left to go to Indonesia for over a month.

She was exaggerating slightly. Her mother had checked on her, had sent e-mails and called her a few times. But the conversation always circled back to Cora's divorce and pleas for Cora and Alec to try to work it out, which had meant that Cora was occasionally screening her calls and messages. It was easier that way.

Unsurprisingly, her father had been the understanding one. He'd just sighed.

"Cora, I can't tell you how to live your life," he said. "My mother wanted me to marry her best friend's daughter, but instead I married your mum, whose parents were from the *wrong* part of Asia. My dad talked her down. Your mum'll get over it."

If her father could be that understanding about her divorce, Cora could only hope he could tolerate other things, too.

Cora's sexual identity had been settling over her. It was like a birthmark she'd always had but not realised: it was meant to be there, something she'd just not noticed. Her comfort level with it rose faster than she could have imagined. When Cora's need to come out to her parents arose, which it would one day whether there was a woman in her life or not, hopefully her father could apply that story to this situation, too.

She kicked the covers off and padded through to her kitchen. It was nice to be back in the house she had yet to have a chance to make into a home. She made a quick tea and opened her back door to sit on the stoop. It was a bright day, winter definitely on its way out. The colder season always disappeared quickly in Perth; soon they'd be complaining about the heat. A deep breath left the taste of salt in the back of her throat, and Cora was relieved her place was so close to the beach.

Eventually, she got herself moving, looking over the job applications she'd sent off the last week before she'd flown out of Indonesia. By that point, she had the steaming heat of another tea warming her hand, and she noted with pleasure a reply from one job requesting an interview the following week. After sending a confirmation, Cora shut her laptop. It wasn't the job she was hoping to get, but it was one with decent hours with Child Protection. The one she actually wanted was with the organisation she'd just spent five weeks volunteering for. Simon was going to give her a hand if he could.

She whiled away the rest of the morning with cleaning her house. Thankfully, it didn't take too long as Lisa had dropped by to run the vacuum over the floor and stay a couple of nights to deter break-ins. She met Lisa for lunch at a simple sandwich bar.

"So, are you going to get a dog?" Lisa asked when they were sitting down with their food.

"Probably not now. If I want to keep volunteering, it wouldn't really be fair. And I imagine my psychologist would recommend against it during these volatile times."

"One—why? And two—you're still seeing that psych?"

"Yeah, I am. Alec, I don't know, messed with my head. I feel better—" At Lisa's raised eyebrows, Cora rolled her eyes. "I really, really do. But I just want to, I don't know, make sure I stay that way."

Lisa rested her hand on her forearm. "I think that's a great idea." She squeezed. "But seriously, no dog?"

"Not for now."

Lisa's shoulders slumped. "Oh."

"So disappointed?"

"I was excited for you to get a puppy. Then it could be mine by extension."

"I definitely wouldn't have time for a puppy, Lise."

"All dogs are puppies, Cora. Until the day they die."

"Okay, fine. But still, I don't think I can. Why don't you get one?"

"My mum's allergic."

Her mother who was in a home in twenty-four-hour care. "Were you thinking of having her come to stay with you?"

Lisa picked at the bread of her roll. "I don't know. I feel bad, putting her in a home. It's so against her culture."

"She seemed happy when we went." And Cora didn't know how she felt about her friend becoming her mother's full-time carer. The sacrifice that would require on Lisa's part, as she had no money to employ someone to help out and her siblings were no longer in Perth to give a hand. It was different than taking in someone who was still partially independent. Lisa's mother required full-time, around-the-clock care.

"She *is* happy now. She's in her own world. I suppose I'm thinking more of myself."

Cora gave a disbelieving laugh. "Yes. You're so selfish, thinking of taking your mum in full-time."

Lisa gave her a sheepish smile. "Yeah, yeah. She is happy there. Maybe I should get a dog—a tiny one."

"Gross."

"They're the best kind."

"If you say so." Cora bit into her roll, chewing and swallowing before she continued. "But I'm all for the dog. Then *I* get a dog by extension."

"I see what you did there."

"I'm crafty."

"Are you going to call Frazer?"

Cora almost choked on her next bite. She coughed loudly until Lisa passed her a glass of water with a bemused look on her face. Through watering eyes, Cora asked, "Why would I do that?"

"Because, I don't know, you *like* her. And if not that, why can't you be friends now?"

Cora wiped at her mouth with her napkin as she tried to figure out how to explain it. "It feels done, somehow. Like, she clearly wanted out, and I can't blame her, and now it's been over a month since we even talked. There are some things better left alone."

"But—"

"So, will you adopt from a shelter? 'Cause pet shops are kind of evil."

With only a subtle roll of her eyes, Lisa let her change the topic.

Coins jangled as Frazer shoved them into the parking machine and tapped her foot as she waited for it to print out a ticket. She checked her watch again. Okay, she wasn't late. But technically, for an interview, she should be there early. Not walking in right on the dot.

Or maybe that's exactly what she was meant to do as the employer.

Frazer blew a piece of hair out of her eyes, marvelling at what she was now. An employer. She was better cut out for working *with* someone, not having them work *for* her. But she could do this.

The machine finally spat out a ticket, and Frazer threw it on her dash. Trying to appear calm and collected, like an employer probably should, Frazer entered the café with her shoulders straight.

Because surely that would make her look confident.

When she pushed open the door, she scanned the room for someone who looked like they were waiting for her.

Frazer wasn't entirely sure how that would look, but she tried anyway.

Her gaze stuttered, then paused completely at a corner table where Cora was sitting, blinking at her as if in as much shock as Frazer felt to see her.

For a second, Frazer considered fleeing. Then she remembered she was an adult. Also, Cora had already seen her, which meant fleeing wouldn't work. So she squared her shoulders, which had dropped quite drastically from their previously confident position, and forced a smile as she walked over. It was possible that it looked insane, and she tried to tone it down. Smiling winningly at Cora had been easy once.

Why did Cora have to be there?

But really, it was okay. They could say hi, be nice, and Frazer could go and do the interview while not focussing on just how incredible Cora looked. She was almost glowing, her skin healthy and a shade darker than when Frazer had last seen her. Her eyes were bright, even while widened in surprise.

Why did Cora have to be there, looking amazing?

"Cora! Hey!" That was far too over the top. Frazer cleared her throat and made herself calm down. "How are you?"

"I... I'm good. How are you going?"

Frazer went to bury her hands in her pockets, her balled-up fists skimming her sides awkwardly, because it turned out she was wearing pants that didn't have any. How awkward. "I'm great—fantastic. I'm here to do an interview."

Cora's tongue swiped her lower lip, and Frazer hated herself for watching it. The point of not seeing Cora was that Frazer had hoped all of *those* thoughts and feelings would go away.

"That's nice. I'm just here to meet Tia."

Frazer's mouth dropped open. Her brain clicked over, and she had to shut her eyes for a few seconds to gather her strength.

"Uh...Frazer? You okay?"

Blowing out a slow breath, Frazer finally asked, "Are you by any chance looking for a job?"

Cora's eyes widened. "*No.* She wouldn't."

Pulling her phone out of her bag, Frazer raised her eyebrows as she dropped into a chair next to Cora. "Wouldn't she?"

Apparently, Cora couldn't say anything to that. In less than thirty seconds, Frazer had Tia on the phone, the device held between them, the speaker on so they could both hear.

"Frazer! So nice to hear from you, how—"

"Tia, cut the crap." Frazer was glaring at her phone.

"I'm guessing you're not about to join me for that coffee, Tia." Cora said dryly, leaning closer to the phone.

Her hair fell forward and brushed Frazer's hand. It smelt different, nicer. Fruitier. Not that Frazer was smelling Cora's hair. That would be creepy.

"Oh, you know what? Something's come up?" Tia's mirth was practically palpable. "Though, you know, I think Frazer's there to do an interview and I heard you were looking for a job?"

Before either of them could say anything, the call disconnected and they were left staring disbelievingly at the phone.

"She's an evil genius." Cora said.

"I genuinely feel bad for her husband." Frazer jammed her phone away and sighed. "Sorry to waste your time."

She started to stand up, but was pulled back down with a thump by Cora's hand. "Aren't you here to do an interview?"

"Are you really looking for a job?"

Cora's fingers left Frazer's hand, and Frazer had to resist the urge to rub at the sensation she left behind.

"I am," Cora said. "And you came to do an interview…"

This was her opportunity to leave. Frazer could stand up and go again. It would be so easy. Throw herself into her friends, her sister, her clinic, swimming.

And go home alone to her aquarium.

But Cora had really been incredible with the programme.

They'd made a great team.

Frazer crossed her legs, leaned back into her chair, and examined Cora, who stared right back at her, gaze unwavering. It made Frazer ache inside. "Alright." Frazer said. "Where have you been the last five weeks?"

"Indonesia."

Not what she'd been expecting. "A five-week holiday?"

"A volunteer programme." Cora countered.

"Oh."

And Frazer went silent, because nothing in her repertoire could prepare her for this situation.

"So," Cora prompted, "tell me about the position."

No. She didn't deserve to know. Which was catty and unfair and a stupid thought. "I need a social worker."

"I happen to know one of those."

Frazer chuckled, despite herself. "Are they good?"

"The best."

The confident grin Cora gave her floored Frazer. She'd seen hints of it, but this was new. A little exhilarating. "Good to hear."

"What do you need a social worker for?"

"You really don't know?" Frazer asked.

"I could guess."

"I've taken the programme out of the hospital system and have installed it in its own clinic. I'm working out of there privately as a midwife and soon as a child health nurse three half days a week to keep myself afloat for cash. But to really keep it going, I've discovered a social worker is invaluable."

Cora's smile turned shyer. "Invaluable, huh?"

Frazer simply nodded. The waitress interrupted whatever thought she was forming to reply with. They both ordered a flat white and waited for her to leave.

"How are you funding it, Frazer?"

"Grants, government funding, paying myself minimally. Eventually, I want to make it completely government funded, to have it work with Medicare."

"Is that possible?"

"Here's hoping."

Cora gave a laugh that sounded half-hysterical. "Frazer. That's amazing."

And Frazer let herself grin. "Yeah, it kind of is."

And suddenly, talking became easier.

Frazer barely noticed the waitress bringing their coffees and then taking their empty cups away. Cora wanted to know everything about the clinic, seeming to hum with ideas and plans of her own. It was as if it hadn't even occurred to Cora that Frazer hadn't offered her the job, and it had barely occurred to Frazer anyway.

"I saw Jack last week," Frazer said at one point, their second coffee empty in front of them.

"I Skyped him a few days ago—how was he when you saw him?"

"Good. I won't be seeing him again. If you're staying as mentor for him—"

"I am."

That was a relief. "Good. Then it will be all you now. It's just support, helping him get back on his feet. He, uh, mentioned you'd got him into TAFE?"

"Yeah, I'm meeting him in a few days to go with him to enrol and actually catch up in person." Cora studied the mug in front of her, fingertip tracing the handle. "He seems to be coping well, all things considered."

Jack really did. The psychologist really seemed to be helping, even with only one visit per month now, and Jack seemed so keen to get his apprenticeship started.

"He does." Frazer said. "He told me his uncle won't lay off him, but you know, it was with that frustrated teenager roll of the eyes—the one that shows he really appreciates the concern. I think he feels he did the right thing."

"Then that means he did."

Another thirty minutes had passed when Frazer realised the time. "Shit! I have to go."

The glimmer of disappointment in Cora's eye didn't go unnoticed. "No problem."

They stared at each other a moment, Frazer hovering on her seat.

"So... You, uh, want the job?"

"Yes."

No hesitation. "I'll e-mail you some of the info and the address. See you tomorrow at nine?"

"It's a da—plan." Cora bit her lip. "This was, actually, really nice."

"It was." She widened her eyes. "Do *not* tell Tia that!"

"No, never. She'd be insufferable."

They shared a knowing smile, and Frazer tore herself from her seat. "I'll see you tomorrow."

"Tomorrow."

A thought occurred to Frazer, something that struck her as important, considering who Cora was, considering the roots of the programme. Considering who Frazer was. "Cora?"

The look Cora gave her seemed filled with hope. It made Frazer pause. Licking her lips, she pushed on, ignoring what that meant.

"I don't really want someone who works *for* me. If you come back on board, are you interested in doing it as partners? Equal say, just as with the hospital programme?"

For a moment, Cora stared at her, brow furrowed. Slowly, she smiled. "Yes, I am."

"Great." Something was expanding in Frazer's chest, leaving her a little breathless. "Okay."

Because who knew the programme better, really?

Then Frazer was walking backwards, and soon she was going to make an idiot out of herself by running into something. Wrenching her eyes off Cora, she turned and walked out.

The smile didn't leave her face even as she pulled a fine out from under her windscreen wiper. The overinflated cost barely made a dent in her cloud nine.

Damn Tia.

CHAPTER TWENTY-ONE

"So clearly, working at the clinic is going well?"

Cora nodded at Doctor Massey. "It really is." And it wasn't a lie. "I feel like I've been there since it opened."

"Didn't you say two weeks ago it was going to be part-time?"

Cora smiled for no reason she could really think of. "The hours were supposed to be part-time, but with the mentoring and hours put in training new mentors, I'm bordering on full-time anyway."

Never mind all the hours she sat across from Frazer, heads bent over spreadsheets and documents spread between them, almost meeting in the middle, heat bouncing between them. They could spend hours brainstorming like that. Disappointment, low in Cora's belly, always tugged when those evenings came to an end. Frazer always walked away after saying goodnight, a look in her eye Cora didn't know how to read.

"It's just so amazing in there. They've set it up to be so welcoming. Tia is perfect for the front desk, and they've covered a couple of walls with posters and pamphlets. It's so gratifying to see people being welcomed into a space with zero judgement."

Doctor Massey was nodding, so Cora just kept going.

"Frazer's in talks with a few doctors who are going to volunteer once a month each, which means we'll have a doctor in every week." The idea was growing, taking hold, and the community was going to be better for it.

It was so much bigger, so much better, than what they could have built with the hospital breathing down their necks, demanding statistics and budget reports and constant updates. What they'd dreamed up huddled together over desks was exactly this, what it was becoming.

Cora loved it.

And being around Frazer every day was a bonus; she couldn't deny it.

Doctor Massey was looking at her strangely. And then, Cora realised.

She was trying to bury a smile.

Unable to control the one that tugged at her own lips, Cora gave a laugh. "What?"

Leaning back in her chair, Doctor Massey clasped her hands over her clipboard in her lap. "This is the first session we've had in which you've talked like this—this passionate."

That made Cora pause.

It was true.

When she was with Doctor Massey, Cora had been allowing herself to talk. Talk and talk and talk. She let out all the things that she had bitten back for years. Some of them were things she didn't even think anymore, but discharging them felt like freeing herself. It was as if with each intense, angry, frustrated, hurt emotion she let out, Cora started to let it go too. She was being given the tools to build her life back up, and she built with vigour.

And yet, in today's session, Cora hadn't felt that need. Words had tumbled unfettered from her mouth, focussed on the clinic and everything they were doing. The smile on her face tugged harder at her cheeks, and Doctor Massey gave her a nod.

"Cora, how would you feel about going from seeing each other once a week to once a month?"

"That would feel great."

With nothing left wrapped around her chest, breathing freely, Cora left her appointment.

In her car, she pulled out her phone. A message from Frazer lit up the screen, asking if they were still on to have a quick meeting that afternoon. Cora sent back a quick affirmation and started her car.

She felt light, even if she couldn't get a feel for what Frazer was thinking.

It was like the days before they'd slept together. Or during, but without the sex. They flirted, or at least Cora definitely did, and she thought Frazer was doing so too. Cora brought Frazer coffee all the time, and when Frazer disappeared for something to eat, she always dropped something on Cora's desk that she'd picked up for her.

But she did for Tia too.

At a traffic light, Cora fiddled with the radio. It was a strange day, overcast yet muggy, the air sitting heavily and tugging at her clothes. It needed to rain. She tapped her fingers on the steering wheel, waiting for the light to turn green.

Yet, what Tia didn't get was the same lingering look. The same husky laugh. The gentle touch of fingers at her wrist. The feeling that stayed in her chest, like butterflies, was another thing Cora didn't imagine Tia was getting.

Cora felt ridiculous, like a teenager. But she couldn't forget that Frazer had walked away, and that stopped Cora from feeling like she could walk forward.

Yet still, Cora watched Frazer.

The light finally turned, and Cora pressed her foot down slowly, heat stinging her cheeks. It was almost embarrassing how much she watched Frazer.

Just that morning, Cora had been photocopying some pension application forms for a client. She was crammed into a tiny side room that probably should have been a cleaning product storage room, but they used it to store the photocopier. Subtly, or so she had told herself, she had looked over her shoulder so she could watch Frazer talking to Tia. She had been leant over the reception desk, sprawled really. Frazer was always so comfortable in her own skin.

When she'd walked into that café that day, it had been one of the only times Cora had seen Frazer so out of her comfort zone, unease playing at her edges. And then, at one point, the smile she'd given Cora had been quirked up further on one side, so real, so Frazer, that Cora's breath had caught in her chest. Frazer was giving that smile right then to Tia, who looked up just in time to catch Cora staring.

Really, it was embarrassing.

Whatever was going on with Frazer, it was nice to have her friend back.

"So, you guys are, like, working together?"

Jemma was staring at Frazer, lips pursed in a straight line as if trying to hold something in.

Frazer nodded. "Yeah, why?"

"Interesting." Jemma's face was red with the effort of whatever she was doing.

Frazer had been chatting perfectly comfortably with Jemma and Meg in her living room, no one bothering to get up and switch on the lights as afternoon had turned into evening. Now they were washed in the blue light of the aquarium, something Frazer normally loved. Yet, now she was regretting having told her sister all about Cora's return a few weeks ago.

"What's that supposed to mean?"

Jemma simply shook her head.

"Jemma?" Frazer knew she wanted to say something. Jemma always wanted to bloody say something.

Meg, cross-legged on the couch next to Jemma, rested her hand on Jemma's knee. "I think," she said, "what Jemma wants to say is...it's, uh...a little strange."

"What? Why?"

Okay, Frazer knew it was. But she wasn't going to admit to it easily. In so many ways, it made so much sense. No one knew as much as Frazer about the programme except Cora. She was perfect for it, and passionate about it. And she was someone who could share it with Frazer rather than just work for her. It made sense.

"Well..." Meg was clearly speaking for Jemma, who was biting her lip and watching Frazer's fish swim lazy circles. "You guys were sleeping together."

"So?"

"And then Cora practically told you she wanted more, and you walked away." When Frazer opened her mouth, a defence on her tongue, Meg hurried on. "Which makes perfect sense! She was in no place for a relationship, and you worked together, and it was a terrible idea."

"Exactly."

"But, well..." Meg didn't seem to be able to continue.

"What?" Frazer asked.

"Oh, come on, Frazer!" Jemma burst out, throwing her hands up. Meg looked at Frazer as if to say, *well, I tried to help you.* "As if all of that's just gone away! It was, like, two months ago, and I know for a fact that she messed with your head and you fell pretty hard."

"I... I did *not* fall pretty hard." Even Frazer knew that was a lie.

Jemma and Meg stared at her, eyebrows raised like they were already starting to merge.

"Stop that, you two. It's too soon for you to become one person."

Meg stage-whispered to Jemma, "Oh, look, sweetie, she thinks she can deflect."

Jemma shook her head. "You fell hard."

Flopping back against her seat, Frazer shrugged. "Okay. Fine. Yes. I liked her. But look, now we're, you know, being friends."

Which was easier and what worked.

Meg and Jemma spoke at the same time. "Friends?"

"Yes."

"Like the first time?" Jemma asked.

"And the second?" Meg chimed in.

Frazer glared daggers at them.

Meg snapped her fingers. "Oh! I know. Like the third."

Clearly Frazer needed to be more intimidating. This woman had gotten far too comfortable with her. "You guys are hilarious."

"Oh, we know." Jemma grinned. "But really, Sis. She's been working there for a couple of weeks now—you feel nothing?"

Pressing her lips together, Frazer gave a one-shouldered shrug. That's not what Frazer had said. But Frazer just didn't have the energy to put herself out there. She felt happy, good, even, with her clinic and her life. "I feel hungry." She stood up, walking into the kitchen and calling out behind her, "You guys want some dinner?"

Meg's voice, clear as a bell, came through. She clearly didn't even try to keep it down. "See? Deflecting."

"So, you're officially enrolled in TAFE, Jack."

Jack swished his straw around in the milkshake they'd bought in the same diner as months ago. It was still bright pink and very fifties and still had the best milkshakes Cora had ever tasted.

"Thanks to you. And Frazer." He was still wearing the huge hoody, now not clinging to him so much. A little of the weight he'd gained had started to go.

"We only helped. You got yourself here."

He gave the awkward shrug she'd started to realise was pure Jack. "Still..."

"And you're happy with what you chose?"

"Yeah, I always liked pulling apart appliances when I was a kid. May as well learn how to put things back together."

"Being an electrician's a great job—and you'll get paid for your apprenticeship in a few years."

He stabbed his straw in his drink again, nodding. "My, uh, my uncle asked me to move in with him."

Cora grinned. "Really? That could be great."

"I said no."

Cora's grin fell. "Really, why?"

"I don't know. I like it now, living alone. And I appreciate all of his help, but he has two kids. I like my cousins but..."

"You want to do it alone."

He nodded. "Yeah. It... I didn't like that my parents had that control, you know? To make me feel like they did, to kick me out when they wanted. Now, I'm kind of in control. And I like that."

At Cora's face, he quickly spoke again. "I don't think my uncle would lord any of that over me, but it's just...nice to be in control of what I'm doing."

"I get it."

Jack smiled at her. "Good. But he said he wanted to help, later, when I start hormones. With the money. To help me by paying half. And I didn't want to tell you until I knew for sure—I got a job."

This time, Cora's grin didn't fall. "No! Really? Where? Doing what?"

"Nothing fancy, but it's part-time, stacking shelves for a supermarket after hours and mostly on weekends. It means it won't interfere with studying, and once I start doing practical work, it won't get in the way then either."

"Jack. That's fantastic."

His cheeks were tinged pink. "Thanks."

"And you're okay to do that kind of lifting?"

"I start in two weeks and I asked Frazer." he said, watching her carefully. "She said I'll be fine by then."

"That's great."

Taking a long sip of his milkshake, Jack cocked his head. "Why do you go red whenever I mention Frazer?"

"What? I don't go red."

A grin was taking over his face. "Yeah, ya do. Always."

"I don't."

"You're bright red."

Cora was; she could feel it. "It's because you talked about me being red, it's psychosomatic."

"You like her, don't you?"

"Of course I do. We work together." Cora had no idea how to stop this conversation.

"No." He made a kissy face, puckering his lips. "You *like* her."

"Don't be absurd."

"It's all right." He fiddled with his straw. "She likes you too."

"Drink your milkshake, teenager."

The grin on his face was huge.

They drank in silence for a few minutes, the heat slowly fading from Cora's cheeks. How did he know? And was he right? Did Frazer like her, too? Cora was going to go insane with all of these questions.

"Cora?"

Looking up from her almost-finished milkshake, Cora was met by Jack's intense blue-eyed gaze. "Yeah?"

"Do you think Bug is okay?"

Cora couldn't stop herself from leaning forward and wrapping her fingers around his wrist. "Yeah, I think Bug's more than okay."

"Good." And then he smiled again, driving the grown-up from his eyes until just Jack was looking back at her. "So, you going to ask her out?"

Cora groaned.

"Drink, ladies?" Tia was pulling on her jacket. She gave Frazer and Cora an expectant look.

Even though Frazer didn't need to be anywhere else, she checked her watch. "Yeah, I suppose I could have one." Because, you know, her fish were waiting at home for her.

Cora nodded, "Okay, yeah, I'm in."

"Great!"

As Frazer switched off some lights in the back, she heard Cora ask, "As much as I'm all for this programme, Tia, why did you leave a full-time job with great pay?"

Grinning to herself as she turned off the photocopier, Frazer listened to Tia's answer. Frazer had been just as surprised when Tia had called *her* to ask for the job. Something, though, had stopped Frazer from prying too much, the topic of Alec one between them that still felt untenable.

"Honey, I'm near retirement. I don't need a full-time job; my husband's got that covered. This way, I get to work *and* feel like I'm contributing to something."

"I thought you and Alec were friends."

Frazer froze. Cora hadn't mentioned Alec since she'd started.

"We were. But, you know, I wasn't deaf all these years." Tia's voice dipped low for a moment as she said something Frazer couldn't catch. The next moment, she was speaking normally again. "After the threats I heard him say to you and Frazer, I knew it was time for me to move on. And, I did mean it: he needs someone full-time, and I've been wanting to go part-time for the last year leading up to retiring; I need that."

"Don't be silly. You're never allowed to retire." Frazer walked up to them.

The smile Tia tossed her was one that always struck Frazer as affectionate mixed with exasperation.

"Talk to me when you're my age."

"Don't be silly. I'll never be your age."

Cora laughed, and Frazer felt a glow in her chest at the sound. Tia simply snorted.

Frazer followed behind Cora and Tia, keys in hand. Cora was wearing a pair of black skinny jeans that hugged everything nicely. As she always did, she looked put together, beautiful, a fact that had definitely left annoying months ago and had wound up all the way at enthralling.

Damn Jemma and Meg for getting inside her head.

As Frazer locked up the front shutter, Cora asked Tia, "Point Bar, down the road?"

"Sure." Tia answered. "Frazer?"

As always, she had to jiggle the key to get it out of the lock. "Sounds good."

She and Cora stepped left, while Tia started walking right.

"Uh—Tia! Bar's this way." Frazer pointed, just to make sure she got it.

Tia turned, cocking her head to watch them. "I know."

"Didn't you want to go for a drink?" Frazer asked.

"I never said that. I have a hubby waiting for me at home. Figure out your stuff!" Tia gave them a cheerful wave and walked off.

Cora turned to Frazer, brow furrowed. "Did we just get played by Tia? Again?"

That woman was a genius. "We really did."

They stood for a moment, watching each other as evening traffic passed them just meters away.

"Did you want to get a drink?" Frazer asked.

Cora nodded. "Yeah, sure." Frazer made to keep walking, but stopped when Cora added, "As what, Frazer?"

"What do you mean?"

Frazer knew what she meant. But she didn't want a conversation which could be misinterpreted. She didn't want to go home wondering what Cora had really wanted to say. She didn't want to kick herself for saying the wrong thing. Frazer was tired of swimming herself into a stupor, going home, and then still playing over their last conversation in the canteen—or, lately, their conversations at the clinic, which felt lingering and too fast all at the same time.

"Are we going as friends?"

Ever so slightly, Frazer felt her shoulders sag. If that was what Cora wanted, she could go along with that. She had been for months. She'd been kidding herself when Cora took the position that they were just friends again. But Frazer was happy, and the clinic and her friends could be enough. "Yeah. Friends."

"I don't want to be friends, Frazer."

For a moment, it felt as if Cora had slapped her. But then her tone sank in, the soft look in her eye. Everything slowed around her and Frazer, tired of always waiting, took a step towards her.

That was all they needed. Cora was stepping into Frazer's space, taking up all of her air and running soft fingertips down her cheek. Her eyes were deep, watching Frazer's every movement. There was no hesitation in Cora's movements, no trepidation.

When Cora kissed her, there, on the street for everyone to see, it didn't feel like explosions and fireworks, but instead, Frazer felt a settling. Like all her little pieces were coming back together.

EPILOGUE

"Have I mentioned I really don't like flying?"

Cora's hair whipped around and flicked her in the eye. "What?"

Swallowing, Frazer gave her a sheepish wince. "I absolutely hate it."

"And you waited until we are on a twenty-hour flight to Ireland for your best friend's wedding to tell me this?"

"Maybe."

"But you told me you've flown before."

Fingers clutching the arm rest, Frazer shrugged. "Once. To Japan. It was horrible."

"Do you hate it like a hyperventilating mess, or do you just need distraction?"

"Distraction."

Frazer wiggled her eyebrows and Cora raised her own.

"No. We're on a dirty plane. Not happening."

Nerves had her stomach twisted up and not much could put Frazer in the mood for *that* right then, anyway. Still, she pretended to look crestfallen. "No urge to join the mile-high club? Even after being on a plane three times—"

"Four."

"Four times to your volunteer places the last year?"

Cora shook her head, grabbing Frazer's white-knuckled hand and pulling it onto her lap to link their fingers. "None."

With a sigh, Frazer said, "Fine. Distract me with words, then."

Frazer thought she was going to talk about Daniel and Rob's upcoming wedding, but Cora just cocked her head and stared at her. It was unnerving, and the vibration of the plane's engine truly starting up was making Frazer's stomach revolt.

"Did you mean it?" Cora finally asked.

A year together, and Frazer still couldn't always follow Cora's thought processes. "That I don't like flying?" The engines beneath them rumbled as the plane started to reverse and Frazer felt as if her stomach had dropped out of her body. She nodded rapidly. "Yup. Definitely meant it."

"No." Cora's thumb rubbed soft circles on the back of Frazer's hand as she spoke. It was gentle and soothing, and Frazer felt her stomach partly crawl back where it belonged. "I meant what you said when you came into my bed drunk last week after Rob's stag party."

Even in her mildly terrified state, Frazer felt heat creep up her previously—or so she had assumed them to be—wan cheeks. That night had been filled with a lot more alcohol than was healthy. There had been some kind of shot someone had lit on fire, as if that was ever a good idea, and later a blue cocktail that looked radioactive. "Which part?"

"The part where you asked me to move in with you, after serenading me by singing how we're better when we're together."

That night had not been Frazer's best. And the taxi driver had had Jack Johnson playing. She swallowed, ignoring the twist of nerves. "Well, yeah. I meant it."

A smile was tugging at Cora's lips.

Frazer clutched her hand tighter while the engines powered up and the flight attendants made weird motions with their arms and explained emergency procedures. One shot them a dirty look, ostensibly because they were clearly not paying an iota of attention.

Cora's eyes shone with amusement. "You had a drunken realisation that you wanted to make banana pancakes? Sleep late without an alarm?"

Frazer grinned. "Did my singing proposition work?"

Cora returned the smile. "I was sad for my neighbour. She's so deaf, she missed out."

"Well, I'm nothing if not romantic. Are you saying yes?"

Cora nodded. "If it wasn't just drunk Frazer suggesting it."

"Nope, I've been thinking it over the last few days. I definitely meant that part where I said I wanted to have the same key."

Really, she hadn't intended to ask such a big question while intoxicated. But she'd come in humming silly romantic songs and Cora had been sprawled out in her bed, her hair a cloud and her hand stretched over the pillow Frazer normally used, as if reaching for her.

Twisting in her seat, Cora tugged Frazer toward her so they collided in an awkward kiss. "You really want to do it?"

"Yeah." Especially if it got her kissed in such a distracting way. Cora's lips were soft, and the pressure made her stop thinking about the fact that they were about to be in a metal tomb in the *air*.

That hideous pressure that indicated they were about to start going way too fast down the take-off strip moved them apart but didn't stop Cora smiling.

"Did you want to stay at your place? Or mine? I mean, mine is kind of small. But the location is pretty decent."

Yeah, they were definitely taking off now. Frazer leant back in her seat and squeezed her eyes shut as the plane taxied down, clutching Cora's hand in a manner that was probably far too hard. Her heart thundered in her chest, and she just made out Cora's voice.

"Try to answer, Frazer. It'll help."

Her eyes were still closed as the plane tilted and truly started to leave contact with the ground, in a way no person was supposed to. Frazer gave a sharp nod. "Uh, new place?"

"Great, that's what I was hoping you'd say. Near the centre? The beach? A suburb?"

Frazer made a face and heard Cora's soft chuckle.

"Okay." Cora said. "Not the suburbs."

"The beach?"

The noise of the wheels retracting made Frazer jump, and the plane started to level out, Frazer's grip loosening as it did so. She finally opened her eyes to see Cora still twisted around to watch her with a gentle look on her face, as if to make sure that the minute Frazer opened her eyes she would know Cora was there.

Cora nodded as if Frazer hadn't just panicked in a way she'd never seen. "Excellent. The beach. Clearly that means we need to go south of the river."

Frazer widened her eyes and stared at her. "*South?*"

Cora blinked. "Yeah. South. Why would we want to stay *north* of the river?"

"Oh my God." Frazer stared at her. "I'm in love with one of those people that think the *south* of the river is better."

"Because it is."

"But you live north."

Cora snorted, something she rarely did. Frazer normally found it endearing. Not right now, however. Right now, she felt scared. Okay, *scared* was exaggerating, but she did need the distraction.

"Give me one reason it's better," Cora said.

Her eyebrows were raised like they always were when she was waiting for an answer she knew would be unsatisfactory.

"Okay, it's close to the city." Frazer said, patting herself on the back.

"Oh, please. With traffic, it takes just as long." Cora settled back against the seat, arms crossed.

"Scarborough Beach."

"Leighton Beach."

Damn. "Uh—there's better nightlife in the north."

"When do we *ever* go out anymore?"

She had Frazer there. They had the odd drink out with friends, but there were great bars for that everywhere. "Oh!" she tried. "I meant restaurants."

"You did not, you just thought of that. But," Cora held up a hand to ward of Frazer's defence, "I concede a point."

Jutting her chin out, Frazer grinned. "As you should."

"But I'll win."

Frazer rolled her eyes. "Will not."

"Fremantle."

Damn again.

"Fine. True. Ten points, you win." Frazer sighed heavily. "But it'll be a much longer drive to work."

"But so pretty..." Cora was grinning triumphantly.

"True."

Their hands interlocked. Cora's smile softened. "We're going to do this?"

"Looks like."

"Do what?"

Frazer jumped, turning in her seat to glare at Jemma, who was hanging off the back of the, thankfully empty, chair next to Frazer. She flashed a grin. "Bit jumpy there, Sis."

Frazer narrowed her eyes. "I'm in a plane thousands of metres in the air. It's not normal to *not* be jumpy. Go put your seatbelt back on."

Cora snorted again, and Frazer ignored her.

"Whatever. Meg sent me over to remind you, once more, that you have to collect your luggage at the stopover because something happened and it won't get transferred to the next flight and... What are you going to do?"

Taking a second to follow Jemma's thought process, Frazer felt her chest puff out a little. "We're moving in together."

Jemma's entire face lit up. "Guys! That's amazing. Really?"

"To the south of the river." Cora chimed in.

Frazer resisted the urge to pinch her leg.

The look on Jemma's face turned to one of horror. Her eyes went from Cora to Frazer. "No? The *south*? Sister, I thought better of you."

And with that, she straightened and walked down the aisle to her seat at the back of the plane next to Meg.

Frazer rolled her eyes. "Thanks for that."

Cora smirked. "Anytime."

"Now she'll tell Tony, and we'll have to listen to a lecture about the housing market."

"Will your brother really do that?"

"He will. And I'll send him a text that says how excited you are to get information on price differences in rentals and for future investments."

Cora gasped theatrically. "You wouldn't."

Of course Frazer wouldn't. That would be far too cruel. "Would too."

"What if I said that I'm sorry?"

At Cora's slight pout, Frazer melted. A little. "Maybe I won't seat you next to him."

"You're the best." Cora fluttered her eyelashes at her and quickly dropped a kiss on Frazer's nose. "So, what film should we watch?"

"We're not going to do that gross couple thing where we start the movie at the same time even though we have separate headphones, are we?"

Cora was leaning forward, already tapping through the entertainment system on the back of the chair in front of her. "Of course we are."

Grinning, Frazer watched her flick through comedies. "Are we that gross couple?"

"Sh, Jemma will hear you."

Frazer settled back into her chair with a laugh and waited for Cora to choose something. She was off to see two of her best friends get married. With Cora next to her. She barely felt the gnawing fear that the plane might plummet to the ground at any moment.

Cora turned to her with a wink. "Stop looking so smitten."

"Never."

About G Benson

Benson spent her childhood wrapped up in any book she could get her hands on and—as her mother likes to tell people at parties—even found a way to read in the shower. Moving on from writing bad poetry (thankfully) she started to write stories. About anything and everything. Tearing her from her laptop is a fairly difficult feat, though if you come bearing coffee you have a good chance.

When not writing or reading, she's got her butt firmly on a train or plane to see the big wide world. Originally from Australia, she currently lives in Spain, speaking terrible Spanish and going on as many trips to new places as she can, budget permitting. This means she mostly walks around the city she lives in.

CONNECT WITH G BENSON:

Website: www.g-bcnson.com
E-Mail: gbensonauthor@gmail.com

Other Books from Ylva Publishing

www.ylva-publishing.com

All the Little Moments

G Benson

ISBN: 978-3-95533-341-6

Length: 350 pages (132,000 words)

Anna is focused on her career as an anaesthetist. When a tragic accident leaves her responsible for her young niece and nephew, her life changes abruptly. Completely overwhelmed, Anna barely has time to brush her teeth in the morning let alone date a woman. But then she collides with a long-legged stranger.

Wounded Souls

(L.A. Metro Series – Book #3)

RJ Nolan

ISBN: 978-3-95533-585-4

Length: 307 pages (87,000 words)

Dr. Ashlee Logan has spent the last two years on the road with only her Great Dane as a companion, trying to escape her past. While serving her country, former Navy doctor Dale Parker had her life shattered in a single moment. LA Metropolitan Hospital brings the two women together. Can they overcome their pasts and find happiness together, or are they forever destined to be... Wounded Souls?

Crossing Lines

(Cops and Docs Series – Book #2)

KD Williamson

ISBN: 978-3-95533-589-2
Length: 215 pages (74,000 words)

Despite all the upheaval around them, Nora Whitmore and Kelli McCabe found their way...together. Unfortunately, little by little, things fall apart around them. Can they navigate through seemingly impassable obstacles? Or will the lines they cross keep them part?

Fragile

Eve Francis

ISBN: 978-3-95533-482-6
Length: 300 pages (103,000 words)

College graduate Carly Rogers is forced to live back at home with her mother and sister until she finds a real job. Life isn't shaping up as expected, but meeting Ashley begins to change that. After many late night talks and the start of a book club, the two women begin a romance. When a past medical condition threatens Ashley, Carly wonders if their future together will always be this fragile.

Coming from Ylva Publishing

www.ylva-publishing.com

Not-So-Straight Sue

(Girl Meets Girl Series – Book #2)

Cheyenne Blue

Lawyer Sue Brent buried her queerness deep within, until a disastrous date forces her to confront the truth. She returns to her native Australia and an outback law practice. When Sue's friend, Moni, arrives to work as an outback doctor, Sue sees a new path to happiness with her. But Sue's first love, Denise, appears begging a favor, and Sue and Moni's burgeoning relationship is put to the test.

Heart Trouble

Jae

Dr. Hope Finlay learned early in life not to get attached to anyone because it never lasts.

Laleh Samadi, who comes from a big, boisterous family, is the exact opposite.

When Laleh ends up in the ER with heart trouble, Hope saves her life. Afterwards, strange things begin to occur until they can no longer deny the mysterious connection between them.

Are they losing their minds...or their hearts?

Flinging It
© 2016 by G Benson

ISBN: 978-3-95533-682-0

Also available as e-book.

Published by Ylva Publishing, legal entity of Ylva Verlag, e.Kfr.

Ylva Verlag, e.Kfr.
Owner: Astrid Ohletz
Am Kirschgarten 2
65830 Kriftel
Germany

www.ylva-publishing.com

First edition: 2016

Credits
Edited by Astrid Ohletz and Michelle Aguilar
Cover Design by Streetlight Graphics

Manufactured by Amazon.ca
Bolton, ON